Sandstorm

JUNE KNOX-MAWER

Sandstorm

WEIDENFELD AND NICOLSON · LONDON

First published in 1991 by George Weidenfeld &
Nicolson Ltd
91 Clapham High Street, London, SW4 7TA

British Library Cataloguing in Publication Data
applied for

ISBN 0 297 84044 4

Typeset by Deltatype Ltd, Ellesmere Port
Printed in Great Britain by Butler & Tanner Ltd,
Frome & London

Ah, Love! Could thou and I with Fate conspire,
To grasp this sorry scheme of Things entire,
Would we not shatter it to bits, and then, –
Remould it nearer to the Heart's Desire! . . .

THE RUBAIYAT OF OMAR KHAYYAM

PART ONE

Rose

1

ROSE knew her mother was going to cry. It was the way she was fiddling with the clasp of her handbag, as she sat tense and upright beside her on the station bench.

Rose looked away at the long curve of the railway track, glinting in the morning sun, and the line of blue hills beyond. Sure enough, when she looked round again, her mother was unfolding a lace-edged handkerchief embroidered with her initials, and applying it to the crepey skin under her eyes. So far the tears remained unshed, brimming around the pale grey, rather bulbous stare she knew so well.

'Please don't cry, mother.'

She willed herself to reach over and take the plump hand in the cream suede glove. Other people's hands she held easily, but not her mother's. She could not explain why this was. Friends were constantly engaged in demonstrations of daughterly affection. It was not that her mother was aloof; rather the opposite. But there was something in her nature, a pliant, spongy, self-effacing quality, which had always made Rose so impatient that any kind of closeness seemed impossible. Even now, she found it difficult to keep a note of irritation out of her voice.

'There's no *need* to cry, mother. I'll be back in less than a year. The wives always come home for the hot season.'

'But Arabia's so far away.' Her mother's voice quavered. 'And you're still only eighteen.'

The inconsequence of this made Rose laugh. 'Mother! I'm not a schoolgirl, you know. I've been a sober married lady for almost three months. Don't you trust Geoffrey to look after me?'

A watery smile broke through on her mother's face. Rose took her by the arm.

'Come on. Let's go and see what the two of them are doing.'

They were halfway down the platform when Geoffrey and her father emerged from the stationmaster's office at the far end. A wave of secret pleasure swept over her at the sight of the tall figure in Army uniform. She still enjoyed the novelty of admiring her husband from a distance, and thinking that he now belonged to her. Yet just last year he had simply been one of a circle of young officers, stepping forward to be introduced to her at the Wynnstay Hunt Ball.

Hurrying ahead of her mother, she wanted to put her hand on his arm, to feel quite sure again that everything was going to be all right. The mixed fragrance of toilet water – essence of lime – and polished leather that she caught when she was standing close to him, was a reassurance in itself.

'The train will be here in five minutes,' he told her. He gave his brisk smile, twitching his moustache in the way she teased him about. 'They've apologized for the delay. A cow got on the line higher up the valley by the Fron.'

'The Vron,' she said, correcting his English pronunciation. She was not Welsh-speaking, but being born in Wales, like her parents, she was used to hearing the place-names given their native inflection.

A small crease appeared between his eyebrows and he moved slightly away. Behind him, her father was consulting the heavy silver watch hanging from his waistcoat pocket.

'The *Zulu*'s not what it used to be,' he pronounced. The *Zulu* was the famous GWR engine that drew the train on the Paddington run once a day. As a child, Rose thought it the perfect name for the shiny dark green monster that let out its whistle-stop war cry as it came pounding round the bend, past the trees at the end of Glyn Hall gardens. Smoking train and red-brick house seemed to belong together, products of the same Victorian energy that had impelled her grandfather to found the local colliery and the slate quarries in the 1850s.

'Well!' said her father, almost sharply. He was a twentieth-century version of his ancestor, a red-faced burly man who never showed his feelings. At any hint of emotion, his authoritarian manner became positively formidable. 'Checked your luggage, have you?'

'All present and correct, sir,' Geoffrey said in a tone of surprising meekness. Obviously he regarded her father as some kind of off-duty commanding officer, Rose thought. 'I've tipped the porter to get everything on board.'

The imposing assortment of cases and boxes was stacked in a pyramid higher up the platform, where the luggage van would stop. People nearby eyed them curiously. The yellow labels on the brass-studded cabin trunks and the brightly-coloured cane baskets, brought back by Geoffrey from India, looked exotically out of place against the grey stone of the station.

Rose herself felt just as conspicuous, standing there in the turquoise linen coat and skirt she had worn to go on her honeymoon, the wide-brimmed hat with a matching scarf tied under her chin. The departure to the Near East on a diplomatic appointment of Captain Geoffrey

Chetwynd and his new bride, the former Miss Rose Maddocks, had been a prominent item in the North Wales papers only last week. Now here they were, the happy pair posed for the fond farewells, before a small but attentive audience comprising the two porters and the stationmaster, Mrs Morgan at the paper-shop counter, Mr Isaac Jones from the Post Office, and a couple of family groups on a cheap summer outing to London.

The five minutes seemed to last for ever. Through the railings she could see Bob the coachman waiting by the wagonette that had brought them down, the old black mare already twitching impatiently to be off back home again. And there, pressed against the gate, was Betty, who had been told not to come as there was so much to do in the house with the Church Mission tea party that afternoon, but who had come nevertheless, on Rose's old bicycle no doubt, and was now waving to attract her attention.

Rose hurried across.

'Sorry, Miss Rose, I knew I shouldn't. But I forgot to give you this.' Her small white face with its chickenpox scars was split in a grin as she pushed a package through the railings. Rose could not resist a quick look inside there and then.

'Oh, Betty! You're so sweet!'

The beaded pincushion, complete with pins, had obviously been made for the occasion. It was a private joke between them. The secret shortening of Rose's hemlines to ankle-length, with Betty on her knees in front of the long bedroom mirror, her mouth full of pins, took place whenever a new dress arrived. The two of them were almost the same age. Ever since Betty came into service at the hall four years ago there had been a closeness between them, with Rose paying regular calls on her family at the terrace house in Colliery Row.

Now the girl flushed at Rose's pleasure. Then quickly she reached through the rails.

'Hang on, Miss! There's a bit coming loose at the back.' Deftly she tucked up a strand of hair that had fallen from under the hat.

'Promise not to let the sun get at it,' she said. Betty was proud of Rose's hair which was a soft copper blonde, just a shade or two paler than her own, and wavy rather than curled. 'You know how it turns it red, and you don't want to end up looking like me.'

Rose snatched at Betty's hand and squeezed it hard. For the first time that morning, she felt tears coming.

'Don't forget to bring me back one of them old sheikhs.' Betty was trying to laugh.

In the distance there was the wail of the *Zulu*'s whistle coming down the valley, and her mother's voice behind her.

5

'Darling – the train!'

Rose was only grateful that suddenly everything was happening so fast. In a flurry she found her father bearing down on her. There was the familiar rub of his beard as he kissed her by the ear.

'Keep the old flag flying out there, dear girl.' His voice was raised against the grinding of brakes and the rush of steam. To her surprise, he seemed to be trembling as he held her tight by the arms. Then he clapped his bowler on his head again and stepped back for her mother. She was crying in earnest now, a wet cheek pressed against Rose's, her handkerchief forgotten.

'Don't forget to telegraph, darling. From London.'

The stationmaster was holding open the door of a compartment with a reserved label on the glass. He was someone Rose had known since childhood, a small wrinkled man with badly-fitting teeth and a strong Welsh accent. As he helped her up the step, he gave her an enormous wink. At the same moment, he plucked from his lapel the pink rose he always wore in the summer and handed it to her with a bow.

'Best of luck Miss – Mrs Chetwynd. Come home safe.'

Once again Rose felt that treacherous snatch in her throat. But now Geoffrey was letting down the window strap, leaning out to check the loading of the luggage.

'There'll be a letter every week,' she managed to say to her parents. They nodded like obedient children. 'And there'll be lots of time to write on the ship.'

Out of the corner of her eye she saw the green flag raised. As if in answer to her prayers, the whistle sounded. There was a shuddering underfoot, and then with slow laborious thrusts the train moved away.

The two of them stood together at the window, Rose leaning out to wave, Geoffrey behind her. The small figures on the platform disappeared behind the bend. She was overcome by a huge sense of relief and a longing to collapse into her seat. But Geoffrey stood where he was, pressed up against her. With a sudden dart, he snatched off her hat and threw it on to the rack.

'Geoffrey!' she protested. 'My best hat!'

His arms tightened around her waist, so as to pin her more closely to him. He laughed softly in her ear, with that little gulp at the end she had come to know.

'Geoffrey darling! Please let me go.'

'But sweetheart, why? This is so nice, isn't it – close together like this?'

He laid the side of his face against hers and touched her ear with his tongue. She felt his whole body swaying against her, a slow insistent movement in time with the rhythm of the train. Instinctively, she stiffened.

The implication of it, and the strain of the last half-hour, seemed to drain all strength out of her. To her shame, she felt her legs trembling.

She leaned her forehead against the glass, closing her eyes to the spinning fields and the trackside houses.

'Anyone might see us.'

He did not reply but gave a low groan of pleasure and moved his grip to her hips.

'Someone might even come in.' Still holding the pink rose, she tugged ineffectively at his hands. He sprang back wincing.

'Damn!' He sucked his thumb furiously.

'Sorry, darling!' She reached out to take his hand. But he was already winding his freshly-laundered handkerchief around the small bead of blood where a thorn had caught his flesh. Slumped back in the corner seat, he scowled up at her.

'It was only a joke, for heaven's sake. Why do you have to be so damned stiff and starchy?'

'I – I don't know.'

Feeling wretched, she sat down opposite him. Why did these horrid moments have to spoil things between them? There had been more than one over the past few months, though she had tried her best to be 'understanding', as her mother put it.

'Don't you realize how a chap feels, after weeks on end of being on his best behaviour with your parents? We've hardly been on our own since our honeymoon.'

It was true that after their week's holiday on the Norfolk Broads – rather rainy, but good sailing for Geoffrey – they had been on the move almost continuously, staying with family and friends. With Geoffrey's posting coming up so soon, there had been no question of making a home in England, or even settling into rented accommodation for such a short period. Almost the worst time had been the fortnight spent with his mother in that icy Northumbrian manor house where the talk was all of the family regiment and how proud his father would have been at this new turn in Geoffrey's career. According to Lady Chetwynd, an appointment as Political Advisor to the British Resident at Aden promised a glowing future in the service of Empire. And what social splendours lay ahead for Rose! Though with her extreme youth, she would have a great deal to learn, of course.

Rose sighed. Tentatively, she leaned across and put her hand on Geoffrey's knee. But her touch was ignored. Crossing his legs, he unfolded *The Times* with a slap and frowned down at the columns of the front page.

'He is rather spoilt, I'm afraid,' his mother had said with a complacent smile, pouring tea with a sweep of her chiffon sleeve. 'The only child, after all. And all those servants in India.'

From Rose's point of view, it had been easier to give in to him, right from the start. After all, he was ten years older than she was, a much-travelled, worldly-wise bachelor, who had only come her way through a chance introduction by mutual friends.

'I may not be going back to India,' he had told her, dancing close to her at another party. His courtship of her had been as open as it was rapid. 'It looks as though I may be posted to Arabia instead. How would you like that, Miss Maddocks?'

At that stage, she had only laughed, though her heart was pounding in just the way described in the romantic novels. He was undoubtedly the most handsome man in the room. His eyes were a brilliant light blue, but it was hard somehow to get behind them and find out what he was thinking privately. Not that there were any complications. His proposal, when it came, seemed part of the same enchanting play that had replaced ordinary life ever since their first meeting. Up till then, that way of life had been extremely ordinary. The daily routine of Penrhos College for Young Ladies had given way, almost imperceptibly, to the rituals of Coming Out, which seemed to be simply a matter of putting up one's hair and accompanying her mother to endless tea parties and bazaars, with the occasional tennis party for the 'Young People'. Even her beloved riding had been taken over by regulation attendance at the local hunt meetings. These at least had led to the grand climax of the Hunt Ball, her first formal dance and her first taste of the strange sensation of falling in love.

Soon after, Geoffrey's appointment was confirmed and their engage-ment was announced. From then onwards, Rose's mind had been full of images of sun-bleached deserts and the black tents of the Bedouin, camel journeys by moonlight, and the minarets and bazaars of an Oriental city. Instead of the poetry and fiction she usually devoured, she sought out in second-hand bookshops the accounts of the nineteenth-century travel-lers and archaeologists in Arabia.

'I don't know why you're bothering with that old stuff,' Geoffrey said one day. In his crisp military way, he told her that Aden, where they were posted, was very much a British settlement, a garrison port run on Indian Army lines. Its social life was famous – golf, tennis, dinner parties and so on. Conditions were still fairly rugged but piped water and even electricity were promised soon. Being right on the southernmost tip of the peninsula, there was little contact with the Arabian tribes, no need in fact to travel outside the town at all.

Rose had to confess to a tinge of disappointment. There had been times too in their private life together when she had wished for a more romantic approach. Did all men make love so violently, she wondered, so strangely even?

'You make me feel like an animal,' she said in a moment of humiliation on their wedding night.

'Isn't that what we are?' he had replied.

Now there was this silly incident of just a few minutes ago. Why was it that he seemed to find it so difficult to approach her with tenderness?

When they were in company together, he treated her with an elaborate gallantry that friends found charming. But when they were alone everything was different. Rose began to feel that their lives were divided into two separate compartments, the private and the public, with no kind of communication from one to the other.

There were odd moments when she sensed that he was repelled by their love-making. In the aftermath, for instance, it was as if it was something he had been compelled to do which produced a release from tension, but no glow of pleasure, or even that gratitude vaguely hinted at in feminine conversations or the more daring women's novels.

On the whole, it was best not to dwell on such things, Rose decided. It only made one more self-conscious. After all, they were only at the start of their lives together and she was still inexperienced in the ways of the opposite sex.

With one of those switches of mood at which she was adept, she turned her gaze out of the window. The train was rolling out of the border countryside now, making for the Midlands. The smell of the sun on the plush seats of their compartment took her back to family holidays, travelling by train in the opposite direction to the coast of North Wales. Now some huge, unending, grown-up holiday lay ahead of her. First London, with the elegant-sounding hotel and the shops where she still had so much to buy, all the introductions and engagements that had been arranged through Geoffrey's colleagues at the India Office. Then there was the actual voyage out, more than a month aboard the *Medina*, the P&O liner King George and Queen Mary had sailed on to India two years ago.

She let her mind range ahead, sitting quite still, trying not to let Geoffrey's restless turning of the pages impinge on her daydreams. After a few minutes, he flung down the paper.

'Seems as if there might be a war after all. And I shall miss out on the whole jolly stunt.'

'A war?' she repeated, startled. Even the word sounded queer. 'Where?' No doubt he was talking about somewhere like the Balkans or South Africa.

'In Europe, of course. There's every sign. The Germans won't be

9

happy until they've had a go at being top dog. According to the paper, the German Navy's building up as fast as they can turn out the ships.'

'But the Kaiser is a relation of the King's,' Rose protested.

Geoffrey snorted. 'Means nothing. They're out to smash the Austro-Hungarian lot. France won't stand for that, and we'll come in with them. Little do the Germans know that, of course.'

Rose looked out again at the peaceful countryside. It all seemed unbelievable. 'They won't come here – the Germans?'

'Good God, no. Won't get further than the French frontier. It'll all be over in a couple of ticks.'

'And what about us? What about Arabia?'

Geoffrey brought out his pipe, something which made him seem not exactly old, but totally reliable in Rose's eyes.

'Turks might be a problem. They're bound to side with Germany. And the Germans would love them to have a go at the Empire. Aden, though.' He shook his head. 'It would be pretty much of a sideshow out there, I'm afraid, whatever happens.'

He had changed his mind about the pipe, stuffing it back in his pocket. He seemed on edge, his mind somewhere else.

'Come on. Time we got some lunch.'

The restaurant car was still almost empty, starched white tablecloths gleaming in the sun. Clattering sounds and smells of cooking came from the kitchen. Rose felt suddenly hungry.

'I was just coming along to take your booking, sir.' The elderly waiter was standing in the doorway, smiling and flustered. 'Luncheon is served in ten minutes.'

'That's no good to me. I want my table now.' Geoffrey's manner with servants was imperious and Rose flinched as she saw the man's expression change.

'Very good, sir.'

'And send the wine chap along, will you?'

The wine at least came promptly, a Chablis that Rose was praying would be sufficiently chilled. Sipping it and judging that it was, in fact, just cold enough, did something to take the edge off Geoffrey's impatience. How immaculately he kept his hands, Rose thought, watching his short blunt fingers playing with the stem of the glass. Covertly she glanced down at her own, folded in her lap, and wished they could acquire the ivory smoothness described in her mother's magazines. But gloves were such a nuisance in hot weather and once the sun had browned them, what was the point? There were scratches too from all the riding and picnicking of the last few months.

'Rose.' He had been looking at her out of the corner of his eye. But now he faced her, with a new tone of voice. She had begun to eat the grapefruit that had been put in front of her.

'Yes, dearest?'

'It's still not too late, you know.'

'Too late for what?' The grapefruit tasted metallic. She laid down her spoon, tensing herself for something she knew was going to upset her.

'For you to change your mind about coming out with me.'

At first his words refused to make sense. 'What do you mean?' She took a larger gulp of wine than she had intended and felt the fumes swim to her head.

'Oh, I don't mean not come out at all, darling.' He leaned across and patted her hand. 'Just to hang on in England for a few months so that I can get myself settled into the job. Perhaps you could stay in London with those cousins of yours for a holiday. After all, the whole business will be completely new to me, going over to the administrative side and all that. And I'm quite sure your parents would like to have you for a bit longer.'

There seemed to be a sense of things collapsing around her, as if she had lost her footing on a familiar staircase.

'What a strange time to mention it,' she said, with an attempt at dignity. 'After all the preparations I've been making.'

'If you recall, the subject has come up in the past. But you simply turned it aside.'

This was true. She had never imagined he was serious though, rather that he was offering her the alternative out of politeness, as a way of softening the break with her family. There was silence for a moment.

'I don't understand,' she managed to say. 'You know how much I've been looking forward to it. Travelling out with you, and all that. Besides,' she went on feebly, 'how would you manage on your own, organizing the house for a start?'

'My dear girl, as far as I know we don't even have a house to move into yet. It may have to be garrison quarters, and you'd hate that.'

'But what about the war?'

He shrugged his shoulders. 'Even more reason for you to stay put for a bit. Things will look a lot clearer in a few months' time.' He turned to the waiter. 'Yes, we ordered lamb curry for both.'

Ever afterwards, the smell of curry brought back to Rose a feeling of nausea, compounded of the rolling of the carriage and the shock of dismay at Geoffrey's suggestion. Silent with misery, she watched him mix up the rice and the meat with the chutney and side dishes, in the Indian style, and then attack it with a spoon. His face twisted in a grimace as he tasted it.

'Call this a vindaloo! More like nursery pap!'

He plucked the waiter's sleeve as he passed.

11

'Chilli sauce – if you have such a thing, which I doubt.'

'Sorry, sir.'

'Oh – never mind!'

Rose could not bring herself to take more than a mouthful. It was all she could do to control her face. If her chin began to tremble, even slightly, she knew she would burst into tears.

Geoffrey glanced up at her as she stood up quickly, almost knocking over the bottle of wine.

'The glare in here,' she murmured. 'It's giving me such a headache. I need to take a nap before we get into London. Sorry.'

She hurried away between the tables and into the corridor. To be alone was what she craved at that moment, more than anything else in the world.

The jolting of the train threw her from one side to the other. Just as she put her foot on the little hooded section that linked one carriage to the next – something she had always hated as long as she could remember – they plunged into a tunnel. In the blackness, she forced herself to stand still and hang on to the handrail. Everything seemed to be disintegrating around her. The flooring beneath her swayed and shook. Nothing was safe any more, and the dark would go on for ever. Even when they came out into the light again, the roaring in her ears went on. Unless she could find some fresh air, she thought she might faint.

The faces of strangers inside the compartments looked up at her through the glass with what seemed expressions of disdain. Whatever happened, she must not be sick. The lavatory door said engaged. But there, just ahead, was an open window. Gratefully she leaned out and took a deep breath. The sour smell of soot flew back in the wind, another childhood memory. She felt something catch in her eye.

'Never turn your face to the engine,' was the familiar warning from the grown-ups. Now she was trying to rub away the piece of grit with her handkerchief, making it even more painful. It really was too aggravating – as if things were not bad enough already.

Back in the compartment, she scrutinized the eye in the small oval mirror that was flanked by sepia-coloured views of the Lleyn Peninsula. A wan face peered back at her. There was a smear of soot down the side of her nose, and her eyelids were puffy and pink. Even her mouth was different, turned down at the corners with an expression that made her quite plain. Yet only a few hours ago, as she set out from home, Betty had said she looked as pretty as one of those ladies in the soap advertisements.

A movement at the door made her look up. But it was only a young couple she had noticed earlier, making their way further up the corridor. They were obviously newly married, laughing and holding each other's hands when they thought no one was looking. Rose felt a fresh pang of misery.

She sat down in the far corner and leaned her head against the window. Perhaps if she closed her eyes, the pain would go away. When she opened them again, the outskirts of Paddington were sliding past and Geoffrey was standing in the doorway.

'Thought it best to check through the luggage van.' He glanced sideways at her. 'What have you done to your eye?'

'It's nothing. Just a piece of grit.'

They were slowing alongside the platform. Helping her down, he said, 'You wait here while I find a porter.'

The noise of the place was deafening. Doors clanged, people pushed and shouted, while the hubbub of rolling wagons and shunting engines rose up in clouds of steam beneath the great glass roof. Even when they were outside waiting for a taxi, she found her head was swirling with the chaos of it all.

When the cab appeared, the loading-up was done with surprising speed. Sitting inside, Rose watched in disbelief as Geoffrey closed the door behind her. The next minute, his face appeared at the window.

'Will you be all right on your own?'

In her confusion, she thought he was leaving her there and then, making his way to Tilbury for the first possible ship.

'I'm late already for my appointment at the India Office. I've given the driver instructions and paid him. Here's something for the porters at the hotel. Can you manage to get settled in?'

She nodded.

'I may be late. I shall be expected to dine with Sir Graham. Don't wait up if you're tired.'

Through the back window, she saw him jump into the nearest hansom. For that instant he was simply a figure in the crowd, a fair, good-looking man in army uniform with an urgent appointment to keep. And Rose? Who was she now, she asked herself in a moment of panic, and where was she going? Somehow or other she had committed herself to someone who seemed as remote from her as a perfect stranger.

As she sat there holding her travel bag tightly on her knees, looking out at the swirling, chattering streets, she realized she was experiencing a sensation she had never known before. For the first time in her life, she felt completely alone.

✤ 2 ✤

Looking back years later on that journey to London, it seemed to Rose that in more ways than one she had crossed the frontier into another country. A different turn in the conversation, a moment of weakness, and the frontier might have been closed to her for ever. Destiny was not in the habit of handing out second chances. But some instinct had made her keep her emotions under control until she had decided how best to handle the situation.

As it was, Rose's mind was clear from the moment she woke up the next morning. Also, the nagging irritation in her eye was no longer there. She blinked experimentally. The piece of grit had vanished of its own accord, and with it the overpowering sense of misery that had still been with her as she fell asleep.

Turning over, she saw Geoffrey sprawled under the covers, breathing heavily. The hotel had evidently just been modernized and smart twin beds were part of the new decor. So when he had come in last night, she had barely stirred, exhausted by the events of the day. She had just been aware of his movements as he pulled off his clothes without putting on the light, and fell into bed.

Even now there was a faint smell of whisky in the room. She would have to watch his drinking, she thought, especially in the tropics. But no doubt every man had a weakness of one kind or another. It was the duty of a wife to try and cure him of it, or at least to ensure that it did not affect his career.

Quickly she slipped out of bed, brushed her hair and put on her dressing gown. As an afterthought she added a generous splash of her lily-of-the-valley cologne.

She was still standing in front of the mirror when there was a tap at the door. In the confusion of her arrival, she had quite forgotten she had ordered breakfast in the room.

It was the same elderly maid who had brought up her supper yesterday evening. Conspiratorially, Rose put her finger to her lips.

'My husband's still asleep, I'm afraid.' She saw the maid glance around in some dismay as she put down the tray. 'Sorry about the mess,' Rose whispered. 'We're packing to go abroad.'

14

'That's all right, madam.' The thin grey-haired woman spoke under her breath. Then she actually smiled. 'What excitement! Wish I was coming with you.' She made a move to the window. 'Shall I draw back the curtains, madam?'

'Better not.'

'Very well, madam.'

Rose watched her tiptoe out on creaking black shoes. Turning to the tray, she discovered how hungry she was and quickly sampled a few forkfuls of kedgeree. What a lark it was, having breakfast in bed, something that was only permitted at home if you had a really bad cold. Tomorrow she would order hot chocolate, another forbidden luxury.

Meanwhile there was tea, China tea. As she sipped, she studied her husband's sleeping form, lying turned away from her, with one arm flung out over the sheets. Even now she could not quite explain to herself why it was so important to her to travel out with him. She had been hurt, of course, badly hurt, to think that he could dispense with her company so casually, even for a few months. Something told her that, at this stage, their marriage was highly vulnerable. A separation of any kind could only weaken their relationship dangerously.

I might lose Geoffrey altogether, she said to herself.

I would lose Arabia too, another voice added unexpectedly. That I could not bear. Ever since she was child, Rose had particularly hated the idea of cancellations and changes of plan. But this was different. Right from the start, she had felt the strangest pull towards this unknown country, half fascinated and half fearful of what it might hold for her. The idea of the place hung in her mind like a key that must not be mislaid. She had said nothing of this to others, of course. It sounded so absurd.

From the bed there was a light snore which meant he was about to wake up. Pushing aside the tray, she got up and went across to him. For a moment she bent over him, suddenly aware of this mysterious male existence of his – the fair stubble along his jaw, engraved cufflinks and watch-chain thrown in a jumble on the table at his side, leather boots fallen under the bed. Very gently she touched his shoulder. She was not really sure how next to proceed. She only knew this was the way women could win an argument without any more of those awful confrontations.

'Geoffrey,' she said in a whisper.

With a start, he flung himself round. He was staring up at her with a look that was almost fearful.

'What is it? What's wrong?'

'Nothing, dearest. I just wanted to say good morning.'

He blinked up at her, still startled. Then with a groan he reached out for the glass of salts standing half-empty and took a long gulp.

'What's the time?'

'It's not late. Wait.' With a start, she flew to the door to fasten the lock. It was exciting to think that at any moment someone might knock to come in for the tray. Then kneeling beside him, she pressed her mouth down on his, opening it slightly in the way he had shown her.

'So I'm always stiff and starchy, am I?' she teased.

'Darling – I didn't mean . . .'

'Well I certainly would be, if you left me behind to be a spinster again.' She put her hand inside his pyjama jacket and stroked his chest. 'Besides, what would people say at the idea of the new bridegroom, arriving without his bride? Just imagine the gossip, the scandal!'

For a moment she felt him on guard.

Ever so slightly, he drew away, frowning. Then he closed his eyes and pulled her into bed beside him.

'So we'll be together, right from the start, the two of us, just as we planned?' she murmured. 'And I promise I'll be good. Learn to be a proper memsahib, and look after you.'

'Naughty girl. Spoilt little girl,' he said in a low voice. 'Disobeying my wishes already.' He pushed her down into the pillows. 'I think she deserves to be punished.'

He made love rapidly and methodically. Occasionally, just for a moment, Rose felt it was almost something she could grow to enjoy. Perhaps it was like swimming or bicycling, simply a matter of confidence. If only it wasn't all over so quickly. Just as you were beginning to give yourself up to these strange sensations, everything seemed to get out of control. The violence of it both frightened and excluded you.

Afterwards, all Geoffrey said was, 'Well, if you're sailing with me on Saturday, you'd better get dressed. There's a lot to do.'

Soaping herself in her bath, Rose reflected, not for the first time, how odd it was that a perfectly ordinary thing like the female body could be such an instrument of power. You paid for that power, of course. At this very moment I could be pregnant, she thought, suddenly solemn. It was yet another reason for going out to Aden with Geoffrey. If such a discovery was made while she was waiting in England, the journey out would have to be postponed until after the baby was born. Everybody would insist on it. Rose shivered as she dried herself. However primitive medical conditions were in Aden, anything was preferable to the prospect of bringing a baby into the world at her parents' home, with Geoffrey seven thousand miles away.

But now here he was, calmly whistling through his teeth in a way that showed he was cheerful and at peace with the world, with no sign at all of his strange mood of yesterday. Still in his shirt-sleeves, he devoured three pieces of toast and marmalade from the breakfast tray in quick succession, washing them down with a cup of cold tea. By the time he had finished, Rose was ready in her navy blue muslin with the white spots and the navy straw boater to match. Everyone said how dirty London was. The soot and the dust meant you must never wear light colours, even in the summer, if you wanted your outfit to last without having it washed and ironed every other day.

Walking towards Wigmore Street on Geoffrey's arm half an hour later, she could see for herself that she looked smart. Here and there in a plate-glass window she caught a glimpse of herself, and thought it was worth the feeling of tightness around her waist to produce that fashionable fullness of the bodice, and the swirl of accordion pleats below. Some of the female figures she passed seemed to be positive miracles of constriction, counterbalanced by the most enormous hats she had ever seen.

They were on their way to the Army and Navy Stores. There was such an imperial ring to the famous name, she was disappointed as she followed Geoffrey down into the cavernous basement smelling of mothballs.

'It's the Tropical section,' Geoffrey said. 'You can get anything and everything here.'

Over the doorway was a large brass clock – inscribed 'The Times of Empire'. Stopping to study the different hands, Rose discovered it was midnight in Australia and mid-afternoon in Bombay. There was no mention of Aden, she noted. Inside, a sleek-haired young man in a black jacket was beckoning them towards one of the curtained alcoves.

'They've had my measurements,' Geoffrey told her, taking off his jacket. 'Now we have to see the results.'

'If madam would like to look around the department for a moment,' the gentleman in black suggested.

The curtain was twitched across. Rose wanted to giggle. It was rather like Christmas charades. She wandered along the different aisles with their red baize carpets and felt she was already in some far-flung corner of Empire. One set of shelves was lined with white helmets of different shapes and sizes. 'The Metropolis', 'The Cawnpore Tent Club' read the labels. Further along, there was a towering stack of something called Pukka Luggage, giant cases bound in brass and covered in brown canvas. A picture of a half-naked black man striding through the jungle with the Pukka Wardrobe Trunk on his head demonstrated the convenience of the product. Then there was a whole corner devoted to safari equipment, where Rose almost bumped into a dummy sahib, dressed in khaki riding-clothes, whip and binoculars in hand.

At the counter a middle-aged flesh-and-blood couple were inspecting

17

what looked to Rose like lengths of white veiling. Perhaps they were preparing for a daughter's wedding.

'We'll need enough for a double bed,' she was startled to hear the lady say, in one of those piercing 'abroad' voices.

Another assistant leaned over to Rose. 'Were you looking for a made-to-mesure net, Miss? Or are you buying it by the yard?'

'Net?' Rose took off her left glove to establish her married status.

'Mosquito net,' the assistant replied with a touch of impatience.

Rose paused. Then gratefully, she saw the sleek young man beckoning her back to the cubicle at the other end of the room. Here at least her status as 'madam' was established. A chair was brought for her and Geoffrey appeared in all the glory of official full dress, looking like the hero of a Beau Geste novel. The gold of the epaulettes against the starched white uniform, the polished sword hanging from its embroidered sash, brought an air of romance into the musty little room. Geoffrey twitched his moustache as he viewed himself sideways in the mirror.

'Pretty good, eh?'

'Headgear, sir?' The assistant was holding out two of those white helmets. 'Pith or topee? Topee's smarter even though it's heavier, being solid cork – as you'll know, of course,' he added hastily.

It certainly was smart, Rose thought, with the green flash of the Regiment giving the military touch. A memory stirred of newspaper pictures of the Royal Durbar. 'Doesn't it have a plume on top?' she cried, clasping her hands in her enthusiasm.

'Rose! Political Advisor is hardly the Viceroy.' His tone was rebuking, but from under the helmet he bestowed on her one of his charming smiles. What would he do if she rushed into his arms at that very moment, she wondered?

'It is India though, sir?'

'Arabia,' Geoffrey replied curtly, unbuckling his sword. 'Aden.' He was suddenly bored. Irritation would follow, as Rose well knew. But the assistant was opening another box.

'Spine-pad, sir? Cholera belt? I believe the heat's worse than India.'

These sinister objects of padded red flannel looked to Rose like some kind of hospital dressing. She was glad to hear Geoffrey say he already had these items in his Indian equipment.

'I hope I shan't be needing anything like that,' Rose said with some trepidation, when Geoffrey had disappeared to change.

'I imagine madam will not be venturing into Aden's sun,' replied the young man smoothly.

'I might need a topee though – for riding perhaps?'

18

'In the ladies' department. Perhaps madam noticed it over on the other side?'

Rose had indeed noticed it. The skirts and jackets of stout brown holland on display had reminded her of the lady hikers who came mountain-climbing to Wales. Seeing her expression, the assistant took pity.

'I believe there is a custom that new travellers purchase their topees on the voyage out, at Simon Artz, Port Said. That's where the East begins, they say.'

Where the East begins . . . Dreamily Rose repeated the phrase to herself, as she made her way through the crowded pavements back to the hotel. Geoffrey was having lunch at his club and she was savouring the sensation of walking alone through London. Crossing into the green of Hyde Park, she saw instead in her mind's eye the bleached dunes of the desert and the glitter of minarets on the horizon. Then both images were blotted out by the sight of a strange procession coming towards her across the grass. Hundreds of women were marching in a long orderly phalanx, banners flying, watched by crowds on either side. As they marched, they chanted together, quavering high-pitched chants, but Rose was unable to catch the words.

'What is it?' she asked someone nearby.

'Votes for women,' the lady said nervously. 'These awful suffragettes.'

Rose was intrigued. She had never seen a suffragette demonstration before, although ever since that poor woman had thrown herself in front of the King's horse at the Derby the newspapers had been full of such things. But this solid, well-organized body of marching women made a different kind of impact. Rose was struck particularly by the expressions on their faces, all so serious under their feminine hats, and the courage it must take to walk past men who jeered openly at them. One working man took out his pipe and spat in their path. Rose felt a wave of sisterly indignation.

'Don't you speak to them, they're mad,' squealed the nervous lady, tugging at her arm. The procession had come to a halt in front of them and the women were moving around, distributing leaflets. 'Smashing stuff at the British Museum, setting fire to postboxes! You should hear what my husband says about them.'

But Rose was being approached by an elderly marcher in bonnet and spectacles, who looked just like one of her chapel-going aunts, in spite of the sash across her bodice proclaiming 'Equality or Die'. 'And what are you doing to help the cause?' this personage demanded.

'I'm going abroad, to live in the Colonies,' she found herself explaining. 'So there's not much I can do to help, I'm afraid.'

'Spread the word as you travel!' the aunt-like lady urged her. 'Let the world know that we are at last on the move in England!'

'Not the kind of thing that would concern the memsahibs, I shouldn't think,' a woman in gown and mortarboard put in sourly. 'Too busy keeping the natives in chains to worry about their own enslavement.'

Rose couldn't help smiling. It was something that came back to her that evening as she walked in the wake of her husband up the steps of the Colonial Institute to attend one of their regular soirées. Inside, the foyer was swarming with memsahibs, all with the kind of voices, Rose thought, that were meant to pierce through language barriers from one end of the globe to the other. For a moment it occurred to Rose that if she had chosen, she would rather be with the marching women any day. Would she have the courage to go against convention like that, though? As a small mark of feminine independence, she had at least chosen to wear the new pink dress with its slightly raised hemline, in spite of Geoffrey's disapproval. As introductions took place, she wondered if it had been the wrong choice after all. A certain Lady Marford, widow of a famous Governor, who was holding court at the centre of the throng, studied her with a particular curiosity.

'Goodness, what a child!' she declared. She extended her hand with a gracious dip of the bosom which reminded Rose of pictures of Queen Mary. 'You must have barely come out.'

'I'm afraid so.'

When Rose smiled, Lady Marford like most people was at once won over.

'But you'll do very well, my dear, I'm sure you will.' She lowered herself into one of the basket-chairs set among potted palms and beckoned Rose to sit beside her. 'You look fit anyway. Doesn't she, Maud?'

The lady standing behind her, a Miss Campbell, nodded stiffly. She seemed to be acting as a kind of female ADC and was as gaunt as Lady Marford was voluminous. From what Rose could gather, she was something to do with the Church of England in Bombay. The third person in the group was a Mrs Fortescue from Karachi, referred to as the Collector's Wife. Rose did not like to ask what a Collector was. Certainly he would be rather a different figure from old Mr Hughes, who collected her father's rents. Mrs Fortescue was a pretty woman, though it was hard to guess her exact age. Her complexion had that crumpled-tissue look about it that seemed peculiar to travelling memsahibs. Together, the three of them began patting Rose's future back and forth like a tennis ball.

'Good servants are the secret. Indians, of course. You could never trust an Arab in the house.'

'Make sure they wash the vegetables in potassium permanganate,' snapped the Church of England lady. 'And don't forget to mark the level in the whisky decanter.'

'The Aden heat will be appalling,' sighed Mrs Fortescue. 'The greatest care must be taken not to let the sun get on your skin at all.'

'And remember, the natives are always watching you.' Miss Campbell looked grim. 'Among Muslims, the female arms and shoulders must *never* be revealed under any circumstances.'

'Not that you will find yourself among Muslims very often,' Lady Marford added reassuringly, 'apart from the occasional official reception.' A new and more exciting thought suddenly struck her.

'Of course, there might be the chance that your husband will be Acting from time to time.'

'Acting?' Rose was puzzled. 'He has done a little in the way of amateur theatricals, Gilbert and Sullivan and so on. But he's not very good.'

There was a ripple of laughter. Lady Marford was positively gasping, fanning herself with her gloves. She took a restorative sip of claret cup.

'Acting in the Colonies means standing in for one's seniors, dear girl! It occurred to me that if Harry Rawlinson goes on leave, your Geoffrey might be Acting Resident, which would make you First Lady, hostess at the Residency and so on.'

'Lady Marford knows all about that.' Miss Campbell nodded meaningfully. 'After ten years as burra mem of Bengal.'

'Don't worry. You can't go wrong with the Blue Book,' Mrs Fortescue reassured her. 'Absolutely invaluable when it comes to placing people. At dinner parties, that is.'

'We had a Green Book at Ootacamund,' said Miss Campbell.

'Well, whatever the colour,' Mrs Fortescue rejoined, 'it's called the Civil List and it has a Warrant of Precedence that settles all problems, once and for all.'

Feeling distinctly out of her depth, Rose looked around for Geoffrey.

'Your husband's over there.' Lady Marford nodded her feather-decked coiffure in the direction of the staircase. Leaning against the balustrade, Geoffrey was deep in conversation with two young men in military full dress, one with a monocle, the other wearing a long ginger moustache. Neither of them appealed to Rose. 'You newlyweds,' teased Lady Marford. 'You can't bear to let him out of your sight, can you?'

'I – I was going to let him go off to Arabia without me,' Rose replied on an impulse. 'Let him settle down first and then join him later.'

For a moment, there was a startled silence.

'Dear me, no. That would have been very unwise.' Lady Marford's voice was sharp.

'Besides, you'd have missed all the fun of the journey out together,' said Mrs Fortescue. Rose had the feeling she was trying to be tactful.

'It was Geoffrey's idea, actually,' Rose went on. 'He seemed to think he ought to have a few months on his own there.'

Was it her imagination, or did she catch the tail end of a warning glance pass between the three women?

'But I persuaded him against it,' she added.

'Quite right, my dear,' declared Lady Marford briskly. 'Geoffrey has had quite enough of the bachelor life in India.'

There was a pause that was not entirely comfortable.

'After all, it's not a good idea for a young man to be deprived of feminine company in, shall we say, outlandish situations.' She patted Rose's hand. 'We don't want any scandals, do we?' She lowered her voice so that only Rose might hear. 'If anyone should pass on any tittle-tattle about the past, my dear, about India . . .' But the other ladies drew in more closely and she broke off.

'Of course, Aden is not the *ideal* place for a wife.' Lady Marford resumed her usual booming tone as she gazed towards invisible horizons of heat and dust. 'There will be hardships, and few modern amenities, I fear. Though being a port, there will be certainly be a – a cosmopolitan side to the social life.'

'Used to be a punishment station, didn't it?' Miss Campbell laughed harshly, until quelled by a look from Mrs Fortescue.

'Have you ever lived there, Lady Marford?' Rose asked.

'I have stayed there – passing through, that is. Eleanor Rawlinson, the Resident's wife, is a great dear, quite an unusual person. She paints, you know. But there are lots of unusual people in Aden – characters, you might say.'

'Do you have any hobbies, Mrs Chetwynd?' asked Mrs Fortescue.

'I love riding. I was hoping I might get a horse there.'

'Riding,' mused Lady Marford. 'I can't think where you would actually ride *to* in Aden. It is rather a confined sort of place, you know.'

'But if there were beaches . . .' Rose faltered a little, then gathered confidence. 'To ride in the desert is a dream of mine.'

'Well, you know, the desert is not really Our Territory,' Lady Marford said with a touch of majesty. 'I believe you have to obtain a pass to go beyond the frontier into the hinterland. Your husband would have to, that is.'

'I see.' Rose tried again. 'I'm fond of reading, of course, and I'm not too bad at languages. I'd very much like to learn Arabic.'

'Dear me! There's no need for that. Any Arabs you may meet officially will all be able to speak English. Remember that funny little sultan, Maud?'

Maud rolled her eyes towards the ceiling.

'I forget his name now – Mohammed or Ali it would have to be. He came to London for the Coronation and we were asked to keep an eye on him, along with the Indian princes. He *was* so funny in those ridiculous suits he used to wear. He spent all his time in Waring and Gillows buying the most hideous furniture for his palace in Aden. And when we asked him what he liked best about England, he said he couldn't decide between the lifts and the escalators.' She heaved a sigh and rearranged her pearls. 'Such a pity when they become Westernized, I always think.'

'I couldn't agree with you more, Lady Marford.'

Geoffrey was leaning over the back of her chair, nodding in a pleased way at Rose. With him was a tall white-haired man in his seventies.

'Rose, this is Sir David Trevelyan – well known to the rest of you ladies, of course. Sir David is one of our most distinguished Orientalists.'

'Retired Orientalist, a mere curator in fact,' said Sir David with a wry smile. 'A corner of Arabia in Kensington called Leighton House – perhaps you can pay us a visit? But you must be busy getting ready for your departure. Saturday, isn't it?'

'Saturday,' agreed Rose. She was grateful for the revitalizing effect Sir David seemed to have on the little group, just when conversation was becoming something of an effort. 'And I'm only just getting used to London. After Wales, everything seems rather overpowering.'

'Sir David!' Lady Marford tapped him on the arm with her fan. 'You must take Mrs Chetwynd in to supper. The new bride has precedence, remember. And we mustn't be late for the speeches.'

'If only we could be,' murmured Sir David, offering his arm to Rose. He flashed her a conspiratorial smile, his brown wrinkled face suddenly young again. 'Perhaps we can plan an escape, though.'

They were making their way up the stairs past rows of sepia photographs of Englishmen in plumed helmets, set amidst palm trees and camels and white colonnades.

'Is your picture there, Sir David?' Rose asked, rather daringly.

'Good heavens, no! I'm afraid I blotted my copybook too often. Started off in the Diplomatic in Baghdad and ended up as a wandering archaeologist in Aden country, actually. No, not Governor material at all.'

He paused to catch his breath for a moment, quickly wiping his forehead. Rose noticed that his hand was trembling and the red silk bandanna handkerchief was rather frayed at the edges.

In the supper room the others caught up with them but Sir David did not relinquish his place at her side, urging her to consume unladylike quantities of salmon and strawberries, and providing a sotto voce commentary on the other guests. Rose had a hundred things to ask him, but he interrupted her.

'Speeches now,' he told her in a whisper. He gave a warning nod towards the top table.

'Imperial Policy Today' was the theme of the evening, it seemed. Rose was irresistibly reminded of a Chapel preacher at home as Lord Crawshaw of the Indian Civil Service braced himself for his opening peroration, eyes glittering, bald head shining in the lamplight.

'A true imperialist,' he declaimed to the rapt faces before him, 'is one who with all humility believes that divine providence has bestowed unequalled advantages on the British race, in order that it may prove itself worthy of an exalted mission among mankind.'

Rose moved further behind the large arrangement of delphiniums, so as to avoid Lord Crawshaw's gaze. How on earth could she be worthy of such a mission? And what exactly was that mission anyway?

Somewhat to Rose's surprise, he was followed by a female speaker, a Mrs French Sheldon, who described herself as a 'rough and ready explorer'. She certainly looked rather rough, Rose thought, with her large red face and odd assortment of fringed and embroidered garments from other lands. She was prepared to be impressed, but in spite of herself she began to feel sleepy as Mrs Sheldon spoke at length in a slow deep voice of her journeys through Africa. Law and order, it seemed, were in their infancy in the Dark Continent. According to Mrs Sheldon, it was a wondrous thing that so few white men had been able to hold subject so many millions of blacks at all.

'As for myself,' the redoubtable lady declared, 'I always travelled alone.'

'I don't wonder,' came a whisper from Sir David.

'My caravanserai was gathered from cannibal tribes,' she continued. 'But I slept in my tent at night with more sense of security than I could find in any house in London.'

Rose heard a low groan at her side.

'I really think I shall not survive much more of this without a glass of champagne. Shall we slip out for a moment?'

Under cover of the applause, Rose followed her companion through a side door nearby. The voice of the next speaker came faintly after them.

'Looking at the map of Empire, I confess to feeling a glow of rapture,' the President of the Institute was declaring. Sir David handed her a glass of champagne as they moved out of earshot.

'All this talk about missions and raptures. The whole idea of Empire has become a sort of religion with these people.'

24

They were sitting down now, on one of the small gilt sofas by an open window. He turned and looked quickly at her.

'How does it feel to be always the most beautiful woman in the room, I wonder?' he mused, half to himself.

Rose was silent, blushing violently. No one had said such a thing to her before. Could he be flirting, a man old enough to be her grandfather? And yet his voice was quite dispassionate.

'Never mind, you're too young to know yet. Sorry.' He chuckled abruptly and looked away.

There was silence for a minute.

'Dear Mrs Chetwynd.' His voice had lost its bantering tone. 'Or may I call you Rose? Not just because it suits you so well. But, for some strange reason, I feel we've known each other a great deal longer than a mere hour or so.'

'Please do.' She said it without hesitation.

'I expect the memsahibs have been going on to you about India. Gave you the impression Aden was some rotten little branch office of the great Raj, no doubt?'

She nodded, smiling. Sir David grunted.

'Well, it's not. Aden township maybe. But, Arabia itself – Arabia Felix as the Romans called it, Arabia the Fortunate – that never has been a British possession, never will be.'

'I didn't realize . . .' Rose began.

'And yet, you see,' he went on impatiently, 'we're bound together with the Arabs more closely than with any other people in the world. Sometimes they hate us. Sometimes they love us. But they understand us and we understand them. There's a kind of rapport between the two races – well, I believe so anyway.'

He closed his eyes and laid his hands across them. Rose was silent and intent, watching his face with its fine features and deep-drawn lines.

'Some Englishmen give their hearts to the desert, English women too,' he said in a low voice. 'And what they are given in return is beyond treasure. They have found their destiny. Do you know a poet called Walter de la Mare? There's a line in one of his poems, "Crazed with the spell of far Arabia." That is how I have been all my life.'

'I envy you,' Rose said quietly.

'I became a convert to Islam, you know, when I was still quite young. That was what put paid to my diplomatic career.' He stared down with his hawk-like look at the chattering crowd in the gallery below. 'Put paid to my marriage too.' He turned to Rose, his face no longer tired but alight again. 'That is what Arabia can do for you, Rose. It can tear you apart, painfully sometimes, burn you out even. But what is left is your real self, a self you perhaps never even knew existed. Freedom, escape, call it what you like – out there it's in the air you breathe. It's the spark that flies from the people themselves.'

'Will it be like that for me? What do I look for?'

'You won't even have to look. Just be yourself. Go everywhere you can. Meet people. Be bold.'

At the far end of the room, the string quartet came to the end of their Strauss selection. People began to move away but Sir David said, 'Do you like music? Shall we see what's coming next? Otherwise we'll have to go back and hear more about imperial policy.'

Rose smiled and nodded. She leaned back against the sofa. Through the windows the scent of plane trees drifted in on the warm air. The clatter of the traffic had died away. Now the music began again softly and slowly, a piece she had never heard before, and yet she felt she had known it all her life. She closed her eyes, letting it flow over her. There was a melancholy cadence to the theme, a sense of yearning that stirred her deeply. As the last notes died away, she sat up straight and brushed her face with the back of her hand.

Without looking at her, Sir David placed his red silk handkerchief on her lap. 'Have you not heard it before?'

She shook her head, dabbing surreptitiously at her cheeks.

'Rimsky-Korsakov. *Scheherazade*. The Arabian Nights and all that – or the European idea of it, at least.'

She looked at him with a smile as she returned the handkerchief. 'Do you believe in such romances?'

'I believe in *Kismet*,' he murmured. 'Destiny, my dear, destiny.'

❧ 3 ❧

'MIGHT I suggest a little beef tea, madam? A P&O speciality.'

The elderly steward bent over her solicitously with his tray of steaming cups. As he spoke, the ship began another slow heave to starboard, like a giant whale rolling its way from one wave to the next. With a practised hand he braced himself against the rail, still holding the tray aloft. Rose wondered how he could even stand on his two feet.

'No, nothing, thank you,' she managed to whisper. She was lying prone on a long deck chair, wrapped in her travel rug. To the right and left of her, there was a line of similar reclining figures. It was well-known that this was the best way to cross the Bay of Biscay, and although it was chilly in the wind, anything was better than the fug of the cabin. Rose's stomach lurched just at the thought of it.

The steward tried again. 'I remember one lady who always swore by champagne. A bottle of Moët and Chandon and a hammock on deck and she could get through a typhoon, she always said. Reckon we could fix you up if you'd like to try, madam.'

Rose shook her head, managing a smile. Then with an effort she reached out to the tray. 'Perhaps I will try a little then.'

The hot salty liquid was curiously comforting, as long as you sipped it slowly. It had an old-fashioned nursery taste taking you back to days in bed as a child with bronchitis. There was the same sense of being not just looked after, but thoroughly spoilt and cossetted, about the whole shipboard routine. Not that there had been much chance to enjoy it so far, with such bad weather.

She wished she could remember the embarcation at Tilbury more clearly, but in the excitement of the day everything blurred together. At the dockside, there was the anxiety first of checking one's luggage through the customs sheds while the ship itself towered above them like a fortress, the famous blue and white flags fluttering in the sun above the tall raked funnels. Following Geoffrey up the gangway was like crossing the drawbridge, escaping from the crowds into a private world of security and comfort.

There had been a slight hitch over the cabin. While Rose was exclaiming over the flowers, a huge vase of roses and lilacs sent by her parents, Geoffrey had turned on the unfortunate steward who had carried in their baggage.

'But this is starboard. And I distinctly booked port.'

'Does it really matter, Geoffrey? Oh look, and the sweetest card from Betty – kittens and forget-me-nots. Must have cost her far more than she could afford.'

'So damn well look sharp – and get us transferred right away.'

'I'll see the purser, sir.'

'Never mind. I'll see him. Wait here, Rose.'

It was fifteen minutes before he returned. There was no point in unpacking, so Rose amused herself examining the elegant furnishings, the bunk beds under pale blue quilting, the blue-painted cane armchairs, the bow-fronted dressing table with its neat little stool screwed down to the floor. She hoped the cabins on the other side were just the same – and why was one side different from the other anyway? She stood on tiptoe to peer through the porthole at a telescopic view of the estuary, cranes and gulls, tugs and mud flats all gleaming in the yellow afternoon light. The strangeness of it all was thrilling, and she felt impatient now to be on the move.

Out in the corridor there was no sign of Geoffrey. Standing there, she was startled to hear the sound of someone crying in the cabin opposite. The door was open and at that moment a youngish girl with pale blonde hair came to close it, a handkerchief pressed to her face. Above it, her eyes met Rose's.

'Is anything wrong?' Rose asked.

The woman removed the handkerchief and shook her head. 'Sorry.' Then the door was closed.

Rose felt a lump in her own throat. Perhaps you were supposed to cry as you sailed away from home. For a moment she thought of her parents sitting down to tea on the terrace, of dear Betty looking at the clock in the kitchen and thinking of her.

Then Geoffrey was back again, whisking her through a maze of red-carpeted corridors, and finally into an identical cabin on the other side of the ship.

'If you go starboard out you get the very worst of the sun all the way. It's port out, starboard home, everyone knows that,' he told her.

It seemed that the purser was an old friend, someone Geoffrey knew from P&O journeys to India. Not only had he 'sorted out' the cabin problem, but he had rearranged the seating in the dining room so that Rose and Geoffrey would be at his table.

'That's pretty good on a ship like this,' Geoffrey explained. 'Obviously the Captain's table is for all the old nobs, Governors and judges and such like. And then the Chief Officer usually has the ICS hands.' He saw her look of doubt. 'The Indian Civil Service, the Heaven-Born, my father's lot. You must have heard that a dozen times, Rose.'

'Sorry. I still get muddled with all these initials. Is everyone aboard going to India then?' she asked, thinking of Sir David.

'Most. Let's hope we've got a decent crowd at our table anyway. They try to keep the army people together as a rule, so we're not jumbled up with the planters and the box-wallahs – the business boys – and the rest of the hoi-polloi.'

To Geoffrey's evident relief, placed next to them that very first evening was a bluff, red-faced major from one of the Gurkha regiments.

'Did you ever serve on the North-West Frontier?' was his opening gambit. After this one battle saga followed another, a monologue strewn with references to Lewis guns and Verey lights and the virtues of the Pathan as a fighting man. Next to Rose was a police commandant from Bangalore, a silent man with watchful eyes whose wife was as fat as he was thin and more interested in working her way through the menu than making conversation. The couple opposite – Director of Forests from Borneo – seemed rather nice, Rose thought, a good-looking pair in their thirties. But the purser himself, a Mr James Spalding, she had disliked from the moment she saw him.

'Prerogative of the bride,' he had greeted her, as she and Geoffrey had arrived in the dining room a few minutes after the gongs had sounded. There was a soft clammy touch to his handshake, and the smile he flashed at her disappeared quickly again between ginger beard and moustache. 'To keep the rest of us waiting, that is.'

Everyone laughed politely. Rose was about to explain how she had been delayed by having to change out of one of her evening frocks for something less formal, on being told by Geoffrey that you never 'dressed' the first night on board. But just in time she saw his warning frown.

'What a lovely room.' She gazed round the elaborate gilt and mahogany panelling, the deft waiters threading their way through the pink-shaded tables and the chattering diners. 'It's just like an enormous hotel.'

'Good old P&O,' murmured the forestry man. 'Never quite knows whether to be French Empire or Scottish Baronial.'

'Did the King and Queen actually have their meals in here?' the fat lady asked eagerly.

'The *Medina* has its own state suite, so naturally their Majesties dined in private for most of the voyage.' Spalding paused impressively. 'The King, of course, enjoyed his strolls on deck and his visits to the bridge too, being a naval man. Queen Mary was very gracious too, when she was in company. I was fortunate enough to be presented to her at the Deck

29

Sports, on the way home from the Durbar. Her Majesty, I remember, actually joined in the thread-the-needle race. As for their retinue, Lord Fitzmaurice and Lord Shaftesbury were especially jolly. There was a pillow-fight contest half-way across the slippery pole, and you should have seen them!'

Spalding's accounts of the royal voyage passed the time until dinner was over and they all rose for the royal toast. Spalding looked at his watch. 'I'd better be back to my duties. We'll be casting off in fifteen minutes.'

Rose turned to Geoffrey excitedly. 'We must go up on deck.'

But Geoffrey was deep in conversation with the Major. 'You go if you want to. I've seen it a dozen times.'

Everyone seemed to be moving in the same direction, surging along the stairways and the corridors. The scents of the women reminded Rose of a crowded department store, until the cool breeze of an English dusk met them on deck. You could almost feel the ship leaning to port as people pressed to the rails.

'Let's not go under before we've started,' a man joked from behind. There was a nervous laugh or two. The *Titanic* was still a name in everyone's mind. Remembering the pictures and the headlines of last year, Rose felt a sudden chill. Great ships could sink even in these modern times. She heard the woman next to her catch her breath.

'Are you thinking what I'm thinking?'

Rose nodded. Then in the glare of the deck lights, she recognized the pale face and the blonde hair.

'You're the lady who was crying. Are you all right now?'

'Not too bad, thank you. It will take a little time . . .'

'What happened?'

'I've just left my little boy at boarding school – the first time. He's only eight. I shan't see him for another two years.' Her chin began to tremble. 'My parents will be good to him, I know, but . . .'

The rest of her words were swept away in the blast of the ship's siren. There was the rattle of anchor chains and Rose could feel the whole ship throbbing and stirring under her feet. As they began to glide slowly away from the wharf, there were shouts of farewell, a few faint cheers amidst the chatter. Further along the rail, a girl of about Rose's age leaned forward.

'It's a marvellous moment, isn't it?' she said to Rose. Her round pretty face shone with excitement. 'Ever done it before?'

'No, never.'

'Forgive me,' the blonde lady broke in. 'I'm Mrs Dudley, Marion Dudley. And this is Miss Grant who's sharing my cabin.'

'Cynthia,' said the girl, putting her hand out to Rose. 'Are you one of

30

the fishing fleet too, then?' Then her gaze fell on to the new wedding and engagement rings, glinting in the light. 'Oh, sorry! You're obviously not.' She laughed at Rose's bewildered expression. 'That's what they call us, you see. Unattached young ladies who go out to India to stay with relations are all supposed to be fishing for husbands. And those who come back single . . .' She paused, still laughing.

'They're the Returned Empties!' Mrs Dudley completed the sentence, suddenly looking more cheerful. 'I should know because I've been one myself. Then I met my husband in Bombay and two months later we were married. He's a sessions judge now, in Cawnpore,' she added, with a touch of pride in her voice. 'And where's yours?'

'Down in the dining room, still finishing his brandy.'

'Oh, you're *à deux*. What a shame!' Cynthia Grant's eyes sparkled under her curly black fringe. 'I thought the three of us might have some fun together, like the Three Musketeers.'

'No, I meant, where is he posted?' Mrs Dudley went on. 'And what does he do?'

'He's a soldier really. But he's to be Political Advisor to the Resident at Aden.'

'Aden, goodness!' There was a pause as they all looked back at the lights of the docks, fading away in the distance.

'I had an uncle who was stationed there – he died of heat-stroke, or something.' Cynthia was obviously one of those girls who spoke first and thought later.

'The shopping in the Crater bazaar is supposed to be marvellous,' Mrs Dudley chimed in hastily at the same moment.

They all laughed, as they began to move away from the rails.

'I hope we shall see something of each other, in spite of my husband,' said Rose.

'We shall, we shall,' Miss Grant called over her shoulder.

That was only the day before yesterday. And now here was Cynthia in the chair alongside, her eyes half-closed, her boater tilted over her nose, seeming to Rose like someone she had known for years. She had liked her at first meeting. Since then they had promenaded the decks together and scrutinized the notice-boards for news of the shipboard entertainments to come – quoits contests, dance marathons and other mysteries. Geoffrey had decreed that the only thing to do the first few days was to sleep. But Rose found it impossible to stay in the shuttered cabin with so much to explore. Cynthia meanwhile displayed all the expertise of a second-time traveller.

'Wait till we're in the Med,' she kept saying. 'It's heaven. You'll see.'

Of course if you were rich, she explained, you could avoid the dreaded

31

Bay altogether. You simply took the Blue Train through France and caught the steamer at Marseilles. But somehow even the rough seas were all part of the P&O spirit of adventure.

Soothed by the influence of the beef tea, Rose watched two of the Lascar crew-hands squatting nearby, polishing the brass fittings with dark intent faces. They were the first coloured people she had ever seen. She enjoyed the contrast of their flashing smiles under their scarlet turbans, the sound of their soft, sibilant chatter, and the touch of the Orient that they brought to the grey, wind-swept decks.

In the chair next to her, Cynthia opened her eyes.

'Sorry about what I said about Aden – the uncle who died of heat-stroke. It was back in the 1890s and he was the most terrible drinker.' She looked round at Rose with a grin. 'I wouldn't want to depress you about the place.'

'Well, people don't seem enthusiastic about our prospects, and I gather we're the only people getting off there, which isn't exactly encouraging. Then at breakfast this morning the police wife – that's the fat one – said, "Oh, but it's just a coaling station, isn't it?" '

Rose's imitation made them both burst out laughing.

'But there was a letter for us at Tilbury that cheered me up,' Rose went on, 'from the Rawlinsons. He's the Resident at Aden and Lady Rawlinson had enclosed an awfully nice note to me, saying how much she was looking forward to my coming, and I wasn't to worry about anything as she'd be showing me the ropes.'

'That's marvellous. Some of these burra mems can be absolute dragons, but she sounds a real friend. Does she say where you'll be living?'

Rose pulled a much-folded letter out of her cardigan and consulted it. 'She says that one of the big Arab houses on the isthmus is being done up for us. But they're expecting us to stay at the Residency for the first few days. There's to be a party for us to meet people the evening after we arrive . . . There are plenty of tailors in the bazaar who can copy any dress you give them . . . And I'm not to believe half of what people say about Aden being the last place on earth, kind of thing. "If it was good enough for the Queen of Sheba it's good enough for us," ' Rose quoted. 'Not quite sure what that means.'

'She's supposed to have built some old stone water-tanks there,' Cynthia said vaguely. 'People off the ships always get taken to see them.'

'Then she says she's sure I shall enjoy the social life. Apparently the European community is very gay – rather like being on board ship. And Geoffrey's pleased because he's heard that his old bearer from India will be with us. He's just arrived with one of the regiments.'

Rose thought Cynthia looked doubtful for a moment. 'Hm! You may have to tread carefully there. If he's used to looking after a bachelor, he may not take too kindly to the memsahib's ways.' Then she smiled. 'I'm sure you'll be the perfect soul of tact, though. That reminds me, I really must write a letter or two myself.'

She scrabbled in her travel bag for writing pad and pen, while Rose leaned back and closed her eyes. The sea seemed to be calmer now. She would write some letters that very afternoon, first to Mother and Father, and Betty, then Sir David as she'd promised, thanking him for her visit to Leighton House. It was odd how that particular memory of London dominated every other. Walking into the place had been rather like hearing the *Scheherazade* music, as if something had claimed possession of her, drawing her towards another world that was at the same time both strange and familiar.

'You are not who you think you are,' a voice seemed to say, as she stood at the entrance of that exotic inner room. 'This is where you really belong.'

There was a dreamlike quality about the whole experience. Outside was the busy London street and the red-brick façade of a Victorian house like hundreds of others. Inside, you walked through gold and ebony doors into an Arabian court. There was the cool sound of splashing water that came from a fountain in the centre, carved out of solid black marble, and on every side tall pillars inlaid with Arabesque designs in turquoise and gold and tiled mosaics in deepest lapis lazuli, glinting in the sunlight which flooded in from the great glass dome overhead.

Sir David seemed part of it all, with his thin dark face and loping traveller's stride, as he led her on through the upper rooms. Leighton's paintings of turbanned sheikhs and veiled slave girls lined the walls, alongside mementoes of Sir Richard Burton and other travellers.

'Of course, it isn't exactly the real thing,' Sir David said, as they stood together in one of the galleries. Latticed screens from Cairo enclosed the velvet divans and dusty tasselled cushions of a harem that never was. 'And yet in a way it's the essence of Arabia, seen through rose-coloured glasses. An idealized memory, you might say. I love it because it's such a perfect example of the English passion for the East, a sort of shrine to the great days of the Anglo-Arabian love affair.'

As she left, he had given her a present, 'for good luck'. Unwrapping the tissue paper, she had been moved to find a miniature edition of the *Rubaiyat of Omar Khayyam*, bound in a velvety suede, the colour of grapes.

'Remember, Arabia's not all poetry,' were his last words. 'There's the flies and the smells as well. But you can't have one without the other, not in real life anyway.'

Leighton House was not real life either. But the memory of it was powerful and disturbing. It hung in her mind like an icon, more vivid somehow than any of the shipboard scenes that now surrounded her.

The Mediterranean was all that Cynthia had promised. The sun shone out of a blue sky. The sea glittered. The decks, which were sanded down daily by the Lascars, had the feel of an endless marine promenade. Women put up their parasols and looked for seats in the shade of the awnings to watch the cheerful, pointless team sports, egg-and-spoon races, quoits and deck tennis.

Rose discovered how much she loved the sun, basking on cushions to read her books despite the remonstrances of the older ladies. Geoffrey preferred the indoor life, playing his way through a complex bridge tournament. He would stand around the salon tables for hours on end watching the games of chance. More than once she came upon him sitting in a corner of the bar with the purser, Jim Spalding, over their rum punches. Joining them, she was always made to feel she had just interrupted an important conversation which could only be resumed when she had left. Spalding was in his tropical whites now, but they only seemed to emphasize the pudgy pallor of his features and his bright red hair. Rose thought it odd, this friendship. The officers on the whole lived a life apart, and social mingling was not encouraged, apart from mealtimes.

'It's different with the ship's doctor, of course,' Mrs Dudley said teasingly to Cynthia one evening. The three women were sitting out after dinner around the open-air dance floor. Chinese lanterns bobbed and glowed in the shadows, and on the dais in the corner the ship's orchestra was playing a selection from the Lilac Domino. Through the crowded tables the young Irish surgeon was to be seen, making his way towards them.

'Well, he is very charming,' Cynthia admitted in a low voice, fluttering her eyelashes in the approved fashion. She took a sip of her crème-de-menthe frappé. 'I mean, whatever's waiting for us at the other end, this is where we have fun, even flirt a little. Of course, it's different for you,' she added hastily to Rose. 'Being a brand-new wife and having such a handsome husband with you. But Marion now.' She giggled. 'You have your admirers, admit it.'

'Admirers?' Marion's eyes rounded.

'That funny old tea-planter from Ceylon. You know, he's always hovering round you . . . ' she broke off. The young Irishman was at her side, bowing politely to the three of them, but with eyes only for Cynthia as he requested the next dance.

Watching them glide away together, Marion said, 'I have a feeling that this is not so much a flirtation as the real thing. It's not unheard of, you

34

know, for matches to be made on one of these journeys out. Only the last time, I remember there was a young governess who announced her engagement at Bombay to someone she'd only met a day out of Tilbury. He was a Heaven-Born, so the senior ladies were of the opinion she'd done very well for herself.'

Rose picked up her bag. She was tired of being a wallflower. Besides, she had the feeling that at any minute she would be approached by one of the noisy young men who had been casting glances at her from the next table, and that would be even worse.

'I promised to meet Geoffrey in the casino. Why don't you come too?'

But on their way down Marion encountered the tea-planter and a couple from Rangoon who reminded her that she had promised them a game of whist. So Rose went on alone, making her way through the crush of the drawing rooms, and the salons. It was true what they said about shipboard romances, she thought. Half the passengers seemed to be involved in some kind of flirtation or other. You could feel it almost like a physical change of temperature, a recklessness in the air, compounded of the seductive beat of the music and the soft throbbing motion of the ship, the secret exchange of glances, chance encounters in shadowy corners. Rose felt it herself, searching for her husband's face as she brushed through the onlookers in the casino. So that when at last she closed the cabin door behind her, she would have liked him to make love to her there and then. He was lying on his bunk, naked except for a sheet. She took off her clothes and knelt beside him. But he only half-embraced her, drawing away to prop himself up on the pillows and pour out another whisky from the bottle at his side.

'You're getting fat.'

He was watching her idly as she slipped on her kimono. Rose, who was proud of her curves, knew it was untrue. Perhaps it was said as a tease. But there was a cold edge to his voice that cut like a knife.

'Anyway, it's far too hot,' he said, turning over. 'Thank God I'll be able to sleep on deck after Port Said.'

❧ 4 ❧

A<small>FTER</small> Port Said . . . It was a phrase Rose had already come to know well. People told her that Port Said was the turning-point of the voyage out. Port Said was the gateway to the Orient, the first taste of the East. At Port Said, you went ashore and bought souvenirs from the Simon Artz store. But first the touts and the traders came on board, and the gully-gully man who was a kind of Arabian Nights magician fallen on hard times.

'But why is he called the gully-gully man?' Rose asked the others. They were standing in a circle to watch the antics of the little man in the ragged cloak and turban. 'What does it mean?'

No one could tell her, unless it was part of his abracadabra patter as he went through his trick of producing chickens out of nowhere. His pidgin English was laced with references to famous figures and events.

'What is Lillie Langtry doing with chicken?' he cried, putting his hand on Rose's sleeve and bringing out yet another cheeping bundle of feathers. Everyone laughed and clapped, though Rose found herself blushing at being referred to as the middle-aged mistress of the late King, beauty though she was.

'Bit out of date, isn't he?' joked the red-faced Major next to her. 'I'll guarantee she couldn't hold a candle to you anyway.'

She was glad to escape to Geoffrey, who was standing at the rails. Down below was a swarm of little boats piled with oranges, figs and apricots.

'Like some?' he asked with his old sunny smile, putting his arm around her shoulders. He slipped some money into a basket fixed to a rope. The next minute the basket came up again, loaded with fruit.

'Magic,' said Rose. She was trying to take it all in, this jumbled scene of movement and colour that had sprung out of nowhere, as if the curtain had gone up on a theatre set. Naked boys were diving for pennies. A strange language, sounding both violent and enjoyable, went rattling back and forth between the men on the wharf in their long white robes. You had to screw up your eyes against the fierce dazzle of the seafront buildings, bleached ochre and washed lime under a dark blue sky. Behind them was the constant commotion of shipping coming and going in the canal basin. There was no glamour about it all. The effect was shabby, commercial, seedy-looking. And yet there was the tang of another world opening up. You could sense the dryness of the desert, spreading out unseen on either side of the water. Nor was the smell like anything Rose had known before.

'Unemptied chamberpots,' Geoffrey said. 'That's the smell of the East.' But she could see the expression of pleasure on his face.

'You're glad to be back, then?'

'I think I am.' He looked down at her, his eyes very blue under the shadow of his panama. 'Especially with Mrs Chetwynd at my side.'

Standing close to him, the sun on her shoulders, Rose wondered why it could not always be like this between them. She took a bite out of one of the tiny nectarines and licked the juice from her fingers.

'When can we go ashore?'

'Later, when it's cooler.' He hesitated. 'And Rose, I wonder if you'd mind. Jim Spalding's arranged a dinner for some of the officers at a place he knows. Men only, I'm afraid. He's keen I should go, you see.'

'Well, yes. Of course.'

'I'll go and tell him then.'

She stood alone for a little while leaning against the rails, trying not to feel disappointed. The new passengers were filing up the gangway just below, about a dozen of them. To Rose they looked very much like the people already on board – military men in khaki, harassed wives with children, a couple of nannies. At the foot of the steps, waiting for the family groups to go up first, was a young man who was not English. He was smiling politely, yet he seemed aloof, with his smooth coffee-coloured features and cream silk suit, obviously expensive. This must be the Mr Karim whose name she had noticed among the others on the passenger list.

Because she was still revolving Geoffrey's words in her mind, Rose was unaware that she was staring at the young man. As he reached the top of the gangway, he glanced up at her in the way people do when they realize someone's gaze is upon them. What extraordinary eyes, thought Rose. For a second, she felt she must know him. An odd flash of something like recognition passed between them, as they stood just a few feet apart. But it was impossible. Embarrassed, Rose turned away.

'Thought the Gyppos went second class,' drawled a man's voice next to her, while the newcomer was still within earshot.

'Not with the kind of money they're making these days, my dear,' a woman replied. 'Still, as long as he's not at our table.'

For some reason this exchange stayed in Rose's mind for the rest of the day, causing her intense irritation.

'Don't you think it bad for English people to refer to Egyptians as

Gyppos?' she asked Cynthia later that evening. 'Especially in their own country. And why should they want to avoid them?'

'It's called the colour bar, dear girl. You'll come across it all the time, don't worry.'

They were sitting on the terrace of the Metropole Hotel drinking coffee, served strong and gritty in tiny blue cups. With them was the charming Irish doctor, Francis Nunan, or 'Cynthia's young man', as he had come to be known. Earlier, with Geoffrey, they had all been shopping at Simon Artz, a rambling emporium further along the seafront. Rose had chosen a topee and Dr Nunan had bought Cynthia an amber bracelet which Rose had secretly coveted but did not like to mention to Geoffrey. Now Geoffrey had left them, driving off in a broken-down carriage with Jim Spalding and four other officers for their dinner engagement in the native quarter.

'Just a bit of a lark,' the purser had explained. 'It's a P&O tradition. Aren't you coming, Doc?'

But Francis Nunan had remained firm in his refusal.

'We three could take a tour,' he musingly said now to Rose and Cynthia. 'But it's the Bajiram festival – the streets will be packed. Besides, I have to get back on board. Someone looks like developing appendicitis and we may have to get him off to a hospital. Are you coming with me, or do you want to stay a little longer?'

They would stay, they announced. Just for a while, as it was so hot on board. Besides, they had ordered the Metropole's speciality, rose-flavoured Turkish delight with pistachios.

'And a hubble-bubble to follow,' teased Cynthia. Then, seeing his look of hesitation, 'Dear Doctor Nunan, we're hardly likely to be abducted by white slavers with all our fellow-passengers to defend us.'

It was true that most of the familiar faces from the dining room seemed to be gathered at the tables around them. After they had finished their dessert, Cynthia looked round restively.

'We could do a trip on our own – just a quick trot there and back. See the sights. There's no shortage of transport.'

'Shall we?' Rose was immediately infected by the spirit of adventure. Faintly, the noise of merrymaking reached them above the English conversations: drums beating, snatches of chanting, the shriek of tin whistles. 'I'd love to see this festival they have – Bajiram?'

'It's the end of Ramadan, the big religious fast. I should think they feel like celebrating after four weeks of that.'

The next minute the two of them were climbing into one of the kerbside victorias that had long ago lost its springs, and Cynthia was explaining to the driver that they would like a short excursion round the Arab quarter.

He was a merry toothless character who set off with a jolt.

'*Tamam! Tamam!* Good, good!' he cried.

Ahead of them an extraordinary tram was making its slow way along the Quai du Nord, pulled by a mare and a donkey. Under the driver's whip, their own steed outstripped this vehicle at a canter. But soon the road gave way to a series of narrow lanes and they were leaving the European-style buildings behind, slowing down to thread their way through brightly-dressed throngs of natives. There were children trailing strips of tinsel and coloured ribbon, women with veiled faces carrying piles of saffron cakes on their heads, peddlers with handbarrows and brass urns selling sherbet and lemonade, and all pursued by the banging of drums and any kind of tin utensil available. Paraffin flares threw down a patchwork of light over the jostling figures. Flags hung everywhere, and hands reached out to the carriage as they rattled by.

'Don't start,' Cynthia warned, as Rose reached for her purse. 'Otherwise they'll never leave us alone.'

A beggar covered with sores clung to the door until the driver pushed him away with the end of his whip. Rose shrank back. His nose seemed to have been actually eaten away.

'You'll see plenty of those,' Cynthia said quietly.

Somehow, after that, everything seemed to change. They were no longer among the cheerful crowds, but hemmed in by a tangle of alleyways. There were wooden huts like bathing cabins on either side, lit by strings of lurid bulbs. In the open doorways women were sitting unveiled, all seemingly stout and ugly and daubed with paint. As they sat, they sewed busily, looking up to call out to the occasional passer-by. Chalked up on the doorposts were various figures that looked like prices.

'They are sewing for money then?' Rose asked uncertainly.

Cynthia laughed. 'Try not to be shocked, Rose, but the prices are not for their needlework.'

Rose was aware of a wave of revulsion, stronger even than the shock she had experienced at the sight of the beggar. One of the women called out to them as they passed, laughing and gesticulating. A group of Frenchmen standing on the corner came swaying and shouting towards them. The smells of cheap scent and frying food made her feel suddenly sick.

'We have come too far,' Cynthia called sharply to the driver. 'Back! We go back now!'

It was while the driver was struggling with the reins, trying to turn into the next street, that Rose thought she saw Geoffrey. It was just a fractional glimpse of two Englishmen in evening dress – what looked like Geoffrey's fair head and the red beard of Mr Spalding. They were emerging from one of the larger houses, a horrible, run-down place with peeling plaster and the name Maison Dorée picked out in red across the front. A motor taxi was waiting nearby and before she could call out, the two men were driven away.

Rose had the distinct feeling that they had seen her. She was about to tell Cynthia but something stopped her. At the same time, the gharry had come to a halt. Cursing and expostulating, the driver jumped to the ground and bent to examine the undercarriage. From his gesticulations it seemed that one of the shafts had broken. They could go no further.

'*Khalas!* Finish!'

The cry was taken up by the circle of bystanders.

Rose felt a prickle of panic across her shoulders. More than anything else she longed to get away from this awful place.

'Perhaps we could walk back?'

'For heaven's sake, don't get out,' Cynthia whispered. 'Just sit tight until we see another cab.'

A group of giggling young Arabs had emerged from the house where Rose thought she had seen Geoffrey. Two of them were no more than boys, holding hands as they encircled the carriage with insolent dancing steps and mocking cries. In the harsh yellow light, Rose could see that their eyes were painted like dolls' and their cheeks daubed with pink. From the open windows above came the sound of a gramophone playing a much-worn record of an English music-hall song. A large Negress in a bedraggled green evening dress pushed her way through. 'Come in, why not? Come inside and wait!' She stood in front of them, swaying and holding out a bottle of wine. 'You thirst? You drink?'

'Thank you very much,' Rose said, trying to control the tremor in her voice. 'We have to go back to the ship.'

With a shrug, the woman spat on the ground, then turned away.

Meanwhile the horse stood patiently between the shafts, drooping his head. The driver had abandoned his efforts at repairs and had disappeared in search of a cab. The young men pressed in closer around the carriage, no longer smiling. Hands began to tug at the carriage door as the chant went up: '*Inglizee! Nasrani!*' Somewhere behind them there was the crash of glass. Rose jumped. Cynthia squeezed her hand.

'Won't be long.' She looked round. 'See, something's coming.'

The trap bowling along the lane towards them looked reassuringly spick and span. Sitting in the back was a young man in a white dinner jacket. As he came closer, the lamplight picked out his dark features and black cropped head.

'Oh Lord!' Cynthia exclaimed. 'I thought it might be an Englishman.'

'It's Mr Karim,' said Rose.

'Who?'

'One of the new passengers. I saw him coming on board this morning.'

The trap stopped alongside. The young man jumped out and bowed decorously. But his expression was tense.

'You are in trouble. You must come with me, quickly.'

Cynthia's face already expressed relief.

'We would be very grateful.'

Neatly he handed them both inside. Almost before they realized it, he had paid off their driver, ignoring Cynthia's protest with a quick shake of his head. Sitting opposite him as the trap moved off, Rose realized how young he was, probably little more than her own age. It was a face of striking beauty, if you could use that expression about a man, full at the mouth and broad at the cheekbones, with the strange slanted eyes she had noticed before. He looked from one to the other with a concerned frown.

'This is a bad place for young English ladies to visit. It could be dangerous.'

'We only meant to take a drive round.' Cynthia mustered her dignity. 'We had no intention of stopping. I am Miss Grant, by the way. This is my friend Mrs Chetwynd.'

'I am Hassan Karim.' He was looking at Rose now.

'I saw you coming aboard this morning,' she said. 'Are you going to Bombay?'

'No. To Aden.'

Rose was startled. She had by now assumed that no one was going to Aden, that no one ever did. 'So am I – my husband and I.'

'What will he do there?'

'He is to be Political Advisor to the Resident.' Now it was her turn to be curious. 'Do you live there, then?'

There was a fractional pause. Hassan Karim leaned back, resting an elegant silk ankle across his knee. 'I have been studying at Cairo University. I am visiting family.' Then the subject was changed. 'Your husband will be alarmed to hear of your mishap with the carriage.'

Rose and Cynthia exchanged glances. They were nearing the Quai du Nord again.

'I think it might be best if we didn't tell anyone about our – rather foolish expedition,' Cynthia said in a low voice. 'We might both be in trouble.' She looked up at Hassan Karim from under her fringe, appealingly.

For quite another reason, Rose added, 'It would be best kept to ourselves, perhaps.'

Mr Karim smiled, a quick shy smile, just a hint of collusion in it. 'If it is of assistance to you, I shall be totally discreet.' He leaned forward and spoke to the driver. 'In which case,' he went on, 'we should get out and walk the rest of the way to the ship. It's only a hundred yards, and you will cause less attention that way.'

'I think we should go back to the hotel,' Cynthia whispered to Rose, as Karim was paying the driver. 'Then we could go back on board with the other passengers. It would seem more natural.'

'Is there something strange then about walking up with an Egyptian gentleman, rather than an Englishman?' Rose was surprised to hear herself sound almost severe.

'A little.' Cynthia laughed.

Their companion had now turned to wait for them. His face was impassive but Rose felt certain that he knew what they were saying.

'You've been very kind, Mr Karim,' she said as they moved on together, Cynthia trailing a pace or two behind. Again Rose was struck by that odd sense of affinity she had felt that morning on first seeing him. She felt at ease with him and at the same time absurdly self-conscious. She was aware of him adjusting his pace to hers in a graceful un-English way as he walked softly at her side. Ahead of them loomed the *Medina*, glittering with lights like a palace.

'They are taking on coal. Have you seen that before?'

He pointed to the lines of coolies, bent beneath their loads, as they streamed up and down the gangplanks that bridged the barges and the hold.

'They are the ants, human ants that make the wheels go round. A terrible life, but mercifully a short one.'

He glanced at her sideways as if to judge her expression. She looked quickly away, concentrating on the scene before them, but carrying in her mind's eye a picture of his face, burnished by the light of the flares. Highly picturesque, she told herself, putting the memory firmly in its place among her travel impressions.

'We'd better go on board,' he said, 'or your clothes will be spoiled. The coal-dust gets everywhere.'

At the top of the steps, groups of passengers leaned over the rails to watch the various comings and goings. This time Rose heard none of the remarks that had been exchanged that morning as she walked behind them with Mr Karim. Cynthia made her farewells to go in search of Francis Nunan.

'Your husband will be looking for you, Mrs Chetwynd,' he said as they stopped at the stairway leading down to the cabins.

'Not yet, I don't imagine.'

There was a pause.

'May I offer you a drink then?'

She shook her head. 'I don't think so, thank you.'

42

'I hope you don't imagine that I was visiting those bad places myself,' he said suddenly. 'I had been out to dinner with friends in the suburbs, you see.'

'Of course.'

Why was it so hard to carry on a natural conversation? Nervousness was actually making her tremble now. Reaction, she said to herself. She had been through a most disturbing experience. The memory of Geoffrey's face outside the painted house flashed through her mind and she felt a choking in her throat. Suddenly all she wanted to do was lock herself in her cabin and lie down in the darkness. Geoffrey was sleeping out on the upper deck. She could hear the voices of stewards supervising the arrangement of mattresses and passengers moving about overhead. The heat seemed to muffle all her reactions but she forced herself to be polite.

'No doubt we shall meet again. Or at Aden, of course, going ashore.'

Again she saw that look of hesitation. He seemed to withdraw a little.

'That may be difficult. So many people coming and going,' he added quickly. 'Meantime, only five days till journey's end. You must enjoy them to the full.'

'And you?'

'Alas, I have work. And people I must meet with are travelling on another part of the ship.'

It seemed imperative that they should shake hands. It was as if they would not be meeting again. He was not very tall and their eyes were almost level as he took her hand in his. For some reason she was acutely aware of the dark skin, and the pale pink palm against hers.

On the lower deck, the band was playing a final selection.

'And I cannot even ask you to dance. My religion forbids.'

They both smiled. A group of people were coming towards them, talking noisily.

'I really must go now,' Rose said. 'I am very tired.'

He made a formal bow and they parted. But when she looked back from the bottom of the stairs, she saw he was still standing where she had left him, watching until she disappeared.

5

IN the days that followed Rose found herself looking out for Mr Karim in the dining salon and along the promenade decks, but there was no sign of him. At times, Rose found herself wondering if she had imagined the entire episode at Port Said, until Cynthia mentioned the strange vanishing trick Mr Karim seemed to have performed.

'He did say he had work to do,' Rose replied, almost defensively. 'And there were people he had to meet who were travelling second-class.'

'Oh, they always find their own level, you know,' said the police commissioner, who happened to be sitting with them on deck. 'They're happier that way, d'you see.'

The subject was not mentioned again. Deep inside herself, Rose felt the swell of anger that she had experienced before at the patronizing British tone. But she said nothing.

Later on, there was a moment when she caught a brief glimpse of Hassan Karim at the fancy-dress dance, the night before the *Medina* was due in at Aden. It seemed to be the custom among P&O passengers to make their appearance on this occasion in the native dress of the people they ruled. The stout Major made a particularly unlikely *fakir* or holy man, with a string of prayer beads in one podgy hand and a large whisky in the other. Among the red English faces, framed in Indian turbans and tasselled fezzes and the headshawls of desert sheikhs, Mr Karim's appearance was curiously austere. Rose noticed him at once, with his close-cut dark head and white dinner jacket, standing motionless and alone behind the swirling crowd of merrymakers. Rose saw him glance quickly around the dance floor. Then his eyes met hers, where she sat at one of the larger tables with a noisy circle of young people. He gave a quick smile and gravely dipped his head. The next minute he had moved back into the shadows again. A match flared. There was the glow of a cigarette, and he was gone.

Rose felt her cheeks burning. A sudden secret elation made her spring out of her chair and catch Doctor Nunan by the hand. The beat of the dance tune and the lilt of the silly words sung by the orchestra leader – moon and June and lagoon – seemed to match this sweet sense of intoxication that had no rational explanation.

'You seem in a jolly mood, Rose.' Francis Nunan was not the best of dancers, but he was trying hard to keep up with her.

'Well, it is all rather fun, isn't it?' Rose flung back a strand of hair that had escaped from her Spanish-style mantilla, a last-minute loan from Marion Dudley. 'I mean, life can be exciting, can't it?'

'At times very exciting.'

Something in his voice alerted her. 'At times?'

He lowered his face close to hers and said in her ear, 'We're not supposed to announce it until midnight. But Cynthia would want you to be the first to know. We're engaged – going to be married quite soon in India.'

At these words, Rose's high spirits were strangely dampened. Of course she was thrilled for Cynthia, who had become such a friend, thrilled for both of them. But as she tried to explain to her the following morning, it was almost a pang of envy that she had felt. Their relationship seemed so ideal, in contrast with the uncertainties of her own situation. The news had also brought her up sharp against the realities of life. Marriage was the inescapable world that you inhabited for ever. The voyage was an interlude that had come to an end, its fragmentary hints and signals of other lives to be put behind one. Ahead lay duties and difficulties that seemed to quite overshadow the enticing Arabian horizons promised by Sir David in London.

'It's not that I don't love Geoffrey,' she said to Cynthia. It was one of these last-minute confidences as they stood together once more at the ship's rail. 'It's just that sometimes he seems impossible to get close to, almost as if he wishes I weren't there at all.'

'He is a rather private kind of person,' Cynthia said awkwardly.

Then with her old impulsiveness, she seized Rose's hand. 'You will tell me if you ever need someone. I mean, we shall always be friends, shan't we, see each other whenever we can? Even if you can't come to the wedding, we mustn't drift apart, must we?'

'We shan't,' Rose told her.

'And you promise you'll always turn to me? If things go wrong . . .'

'I promise.'

The *Medina* had left the Canal behind and was making speed through the southern half of the Red Sea. With Sunday School memories in mind of the miraculous crossing by the Jews, Rose had spoken to an elderly Anglican minister on the promenade deck. She was eager to know the exact locality of the parting of the waves. As the reverend gentleman was deep in his Bible, it seemed an appropriate question.

'Sorry. I'm afraid I have absolutely no idea at all.' With a startled look, he slammed his Bible shut. 'If you'll excuse me, I'm due for a round of deck tennis.'

'It's always the same, isn't it?' Rose sighed as she and Cynthia looked down together at the glittering water. 'No one seems to be able to answer the really interesting questions.'

They were rounding the coastline now towards the gulf of Aden and the lighthouse island of Perim. At that magical point where Africa and Asia almost touched, the ship swung close to shore. Rose could see tiny figures standing on the eastern sandbank, gazing out at the floating wonder of the *Medina*.

'I envy them, somehow. Their lives must be so uncomplicated.'

Cynthia looked amused. 'Well, they undoubtedly envy us. So who is right?'

Rose was silent, concentrating on her first glimpse of Arabia. The desert was a tawny haze, quivering in the heat of the morning. The mountains behind floated by like a succession of ruined castles, Gothic crags and spires that were gold in the sun and an extraordinary violet colour where the deep shadows lay. Rose felt an absurd longing to be on that shore, alone and free to wander as she wished, encountering whoever might cross her path.

'The Arabs call this strait Bab-el-Mandeb,' Cynthia said. 'It means the Gate of Tears. Or is it Afflictions?'

'Not much difference, I shouldn't wonder.' Geoffrey's voice broke in from behind. He had come upon them silently in a way he often did. He turned to Rose with a frown, his mouth working at the corners. 'But there'll certainly be tears and afflictions if my wife doesn't get down below and finish her packing.' It should have been a joke, but Geoffrey was not smiling. 'They're already waiting to take the luggage on to the disembarcation deck.'

'I was just on my way down. It won't take me ten minutes.'

She turned to Cynthia and kissed her. 'It's not really goodbye. But just in case we miss each other when we dock.'

'Remember your promise,' Cynthia murmured.

Rose turned away quickly to conceal tears and vanished through the swing doors down to the cabins. In fact, the little room was almost cleared. The heat inside was unbearable and she was thankful when she had finally snapped shut the locks on her trunk. She took a last look in the mirror as she pinned on her hat. Her gloves she would carry. To struggle into them, finger by finger, was an unendurable thought. The awful stickiness of silk stockings and button shoes was bad enough.

The old Lascar porter was hovering in the doorway. 'Good fortunes, lady.' He grinned. 'Aden lucky place.'

On an impulse, Rose gave him her last English shilling. The little man's cheerfulness made up for all the dire warnings of the English about her home-to-be.

Even so, she had to admit to a slight sinking of the heart as she went up on deck again to find Geoffrey. There was bustle everywhere, but the ship itself was startlingly silent. The ceaseless low vibration of the engines had died away, the anchors had gone down, and the *Medina* had come to rest a hundred yards offshore. Rose paused in the shade of the doorway and looked across at the cruel glare of the sun on sprawling rooftops and fortifications. The Union Jack was hanging limply from the barrack-like buildings alongside the jetty. The gold and indigo peaks of early morning had turned into a huge volcanic ash-heap that seemed to radiate an invisible barrier of heat.

'The famous barren rocks of Aden,' drawled the Major from a nearby deckchair. 'They've even named a march after them – you'll soon get to know it.' He gave his barking laugh. 'What did Kipling call the place? A burned-out barrack stove, was it?'

'I say, don't depress the young lady too much,' intervened the purser, who had been taking his farewells of Geoffrey. 'She has got to live there, after all.'

With his usual sneering smile, Spalding was about to shake hands with her but Rose moved across to take a closer look from the rails. Apart from the ugliness of the town, its dullness was what impressed her most, after the lively seafront of Port Said. No cries of traders here, no gully-gully men, no hint of secret attractions down dirty side streets. There was an air of regimented tedium about the place that said in so many words, 'This is a British imperial possession, make no mistake about it.'

From under the awning on the embarcation desk, Geoffrey was beckoning her over to where a group of officials had set themselves up at a long table.

'The harbour authorities need your signature.'

Two Englishmen in crumpled white stood up to greet her, the older one mopping the perspiration from under his topee.

'Welcome to Aden, Mrs Chetwynd. I'm St John Davies, doctor at the quarantine station. This is the deputy police commissioner, Richard Matthews. Just the usual papers to be gone through, I'm afraid.'

It was Rose's first taste of the colonial manner, the casual half-humorous tones of officialdom addressing fellow-officialdom, paid-up members of the same club as it were, with a set of rules that set them entirely apart from the outside world. She was amused to notice that each Englishman had three minions at his side to wield the more menial instruments of authority – ink-pad, rubber stamp, and leather-bound register respectively. She was also aware of Mr Matthews's quick glances up at her through his glasses as he copied out her date of birth.

47

Geoffrey dashed off his signature with an impatient flourish, carefully readjusting his cuffs.

'Isn't there anyone from the Residency to meet us?'

As he spoke, one of the Arab clerks stood with a salute and pointed towards the waterfront. Out of the flotilla of passenger boats a smartly painted launch was speeding towards them, brass glinting in the sun, the British ensign fluttering at the stern. As it slowed down at the steps below, Rose saw a tall woman in dark blue emerge from beneath the fringed canopy to be handed aboard by one of the sailors. She knew at once it was Lady Rawlinson. Indeed, the face that came smiling up the gangway to greet them was exactly the one that Rose had imagined, not pretty but highly attractive in its sharp-boned way under the brim of a plain blue hat. It seemed that she too immediately recognized Rose.

'Mrs Chetwynd? I'm Eleanor Rawlinson.'

She put out her hand. To Rose's relief it was ungloved, like her own, and damp with perspiration. How perfectly right Mrs Rawlinson looked in her informal linen dress, though. It made one feel immediately over-elaborate in the tight-fitting suit and starched blouse which the London shop had assured her would be a model of perfect coolness in the tropics. Her boater would also have been more appropriate, rather than the formal red straw.

For a brief moment, exchanging greetings, they were outside the shade of the awning. Rose felt the sun strike down on her back like a sword. To her horror, her head began to swim. There was a buzzing in her ears and a speckled darkness seemed to descend on her. Geoffrey was standing behind her and in desperation she leaned back against him to steady herself.

'What is it?' she heard him ask, as if far away, with unmistakeable irritation in his voice. His hands gripped her shoulder, shaking it slightly as if to correct her in some way.

Lady Rawlinson answered for her. 'It's nothing. Just the heat. She needs to get out of the sun.' Her voice was gently reassuring as Rose felt an arm slipped round her waist.

'Does she need a doctor? The medical officer's just over there.'

'We need to get her home, that's all. Don't worry, Mrs Chetwynd.'

The word home seemed to pull Rose together for a minute. 'Please,' she managed to say, and then, 'I'm sorry, so silly . . .'

But even the effort of speaking was too much. She concentrated on managing the steps down supported on each side, and let herself be lifted on to the launch. More than anything she wanted to lie back against the cushions, but Lady Rawlinson made her sit with her head between her knees. She only prayed that she would not be sick.

It was like being in a bad dream. Everything was fragmented and distorted. She was in some sort of motorcar with the hood up, the roar of the engine merging into the noise in her ears. Then everything was silent, and she felt as if she were being sucked underwater. She must have fainted away, because now here she was, propped up on pillows, lying in a darkened room. She seemed to be wearing someone's nightgown and as she tried to sit up she felt a low dragging pain that was vaguely familiar, except for its severity. Instinctively, she clenched her muscles against it, fighting panic.

As she moved, she discovered that someone had wrapped a towel between her legs. There seemed to be quite a lot of blood, perhaps because last month nothing had happened at all.

It was a nightmare, Rose decided, willing herself to remain absolutely still. How could this be actually happening on the long-awaited, all-important day of arrival in an unknown country? Even lying motionless, she was drenched in perspiration. The heat around her was different now, a breathless hothouse pressure that was new to her. The air was stirring, though, with a slow movement like the beating of a giant wing. A faint regular creak made her look up to the ceiling where a long flap of canvas was being drawn backwards and forwards on a length of cord that disappeared behind a shutter in the wall. The next minute the shutter opened a crack and Rose glimpsed, low down, a bright eye in a dark face. Then the crack widened to reveal a small boy crouched outside. The length of cord came to an end looped around the heel of his right foot which he was still wagging automatically to and fro to keep the canvas moving.

Seeing Rose, he let out a hiss of surprise. Then with a quick movement like a cat he turned away and called to someone in a low voice.

From further along the verandah a light appeared, and with it a tall black woman with a white shawl tied back from her face, handsome and impassive as an ebony statue in the glow of the lamp as she moved towards the bed. For a moment she paused and studied the young Englishwoman, smiling now, and making low clucking noises at the back of her throat. She said something Rose did not understand and turned to put the lamp down on the chest of drawers. In her other hand she carried a large copper bowl. Water and sponge were inside and a clean white cloth hung over her arm. Deftly, without another word, she began attending to Rose's needs.

At first, weak with embarrassment, Rose said, 'But you mustn't . . .' And then she simply lay back. 'Thank you,' she said finally. 'You're very kind.'

The woman wiped her hands which were small and supple like a dancer's, jingling the silver bracelets on her wrist. A musky fragrance came from her, spiked with garlic. Smiling again, she put her finger to her lips.

'Rest now. Memsahib coming.'

I should be worried about myself, Rose thought, when she had gone, leaving the lamp on the dresser. Something is obviously wrong, for I am never ill in this way. Yet she lay there quite calmly until Lady Rawlinson came hurrying in.

'Poor girl. What a thing to happen – giving us such a fright.' The kindness of her voice and face was too much for Rose and to her surprise she burst into tears.

'Go on. Have a good cry.'

Lady Rawlinson, sitting on the bed, leaned forward to put her hand on Rose's forehead. There was a fragrance about her too, Chanel No. 5, with the faintest whiff of gin. It was nice to be told to cry instead of urged not to, 'for heaven's sake', as Geoffrey would have done.

'Didn't you realize you were pregnant, my dear?' she went on in her clipped husky voice.

'Pregnant?'

'Well, not very. About six or seven weeks, the doctor said.'

'And am I . . .'

'Alas no. I'm afraid you lost it.'

Even in that moment of shock Rose, wildly, wanted to laugh. It sounded like a parcel she had mislaid, a parcel she didn't even know she was carrying.

'Hardly surprising, really,' Lady Rawlinson went on soothingly. 'All the excitement of the voyage, the change of climate, so much to adapt to.' She took Rose's hand in hers and smoothed it, as if she were comforting a small animal. 'I am so sorry, though.' There was a tactful pause. 'Had you been planning to start a family?'

'Heavens, no!' Rose said, without pausing for thought. She was beginning to feel an odd sensation of relief at being delivered from such an ill-timed prospect. After all, you could hardly feel sad about something that could certainly not be called a baby.

'Then that's all right. With such an early miscarriage, you haven't even had time to get used to the idea. I've had two or three, you know. Women do in the tropics.'

'You have children, though?'

'Oh goodness, yes. Two boys. Both at school in England, sadly.' She got up and straightened her dress at the mirror.

'You'll have plenty of babies, don't you worry.' She glanced round with a faint smile. 'Or maybe you're not keen on the idea just yet?'

50

'Well, not just yet perhaps.' Rose hesitated. 'Did I faint right off, by the way? What happened?'

'Doctor Jack gave you something to keep you under a bit. He looked after everything. And Amina of course, my darling ayah.'

Rose felt herself blushing. 'How embarrassing.'

'Not really. Things out here are not like England, you know. Much more down-to-earth, for all our colonial airs and graces. It's still a pioneering life in a lot of ways, in a place like this.'

She was standing close to the lamp and Rose saw for the first time the network of lines around her lively blue eyes, the rough skin, reddened along the cheekbones. She was tugging at some kind of fastening on the wall. The next minute the bed and Rose were enshrouded in a canopy of white netting.

'The mosquitos get in so quickly once it's dark. And there's nothing the little beasts like better than fresh blood from England.' She tucked the netting under the end of the mattress. 'At least it's a bit cooler. You won't need the punkah now.'

'Oh, the punkah.' Rose saw that the canvas flap on the ceiling was motionless. She smiled shyly at Lady Rawlinson. She now felt she had known her for years.

'You're so kind. I'm only sorry to be such a nuisance. Surely I can get up soon?'

'Not for a couple of days. You'll be right as rain then, according to the doc.'

'But there must be all kinds of things I should be doing.'

'Nothing that can't wait. Nobody hurries with anything in this climate, you'll see.' Absent-mindedly she straightened a framed watercolour of palm trees and a camel hanging over the chest. 'I mean, it took me all of three months to finish this, for instance.'

'I like it,' Rose said politely, though privately she thought it rather a picture-postcard composition. 'Someone in London told me you painted. Lady Marford.'

'Oh, Lord. That old battleaxe!' They both laughed. 'Anyway, we must be sure you're back on form again for Friday. The cream of Aden society are coming to dinner to meet you. Then there's the King's Birthday Parade. And after that we can get you settled into your house. Your husband's already getting things organized. Which reminds me, I'll tell him he can come up to see you now, bearing a cool drink perhaps? Fresh lime, a dash of gin? There's ice off the ship today, special treat.'

'Just the lime juice, please.'

When it came, brought by Geoffrey, Rose drained the glass greedily.

'Aden thirst,' Geoffrey said.

51

He let the net drop again, so that when Rose looked up at him, he seemed to be standing at a distance, his face blurred by the gauzy barrier between them. Communication was more difficult than usual.

'I'm so sorry,' Rose murmured.

'Can't be helped,' he replied stiffly. 'All the same . . . Had you no idea at all of your condition?'

'I'm afraid not.' The coldness of his tone appalled her. She wanted to say, 'What about you – had you no idea what had happened?' But she could not. What did women say at such times?

'It could hardly be a worse beginning,' he went on. 'I'm afraid you really must try to be a little more responsible about yourself.'

She was silent. A sense of feebleness swept over her again, and an awful weariness of spirit.

'Is it that you are actually ignorant about certain processes and functions?'

She shook her head, fighting tears.

He sighed and turned away. 'Well, everyone's been very understanding about it. But we certainly can't afford to let it happen again. It may be there is a weakness in your system that doesn't stand up to this climate. Not that we wanted a child at this stage, of course.'

Again, Rose could not bring herself to speak. Geoffrey was adjusting his cummerbund, smoothing his hair at the mirror.

'I must go down now. Dinner here's on the dot, and I'm not too sure about the Resident. Seems an odd sort of chap, mad about the natives.' He paused, looking down at her. 'I have the room next to you if you need anything – rather than disturb our hosts any further.'

Rose turned away.

Later, when the bearer came in with her dinner, she pretended she was asleep. Through half-closed eyes she had a glimpse of a ramrod figure in starched white suit and a scarlet turban, as he padded out again. A faint spicy smell reminded her that he had left the tray behind on a low table at the foot of the bed. Moving cautiously, she drew it inside the net and discovered she was ravenously hungry, though what she ate was unimportant – stew of some kind or other.

When she had finished, Rose sat carefully on the edge of the bed. The tiled floor was cool underfoot, a comforting touch that encouraged her to stand up and walk very slowly around the room.

Pausing at the window, she pushed open the shutters. There was a hint of a breeze on her face. Leaning out into the warm darkness, she smelled spices again, and wood-smoke, and some kind of animal dung. The air had the salt dampness of sea in it too. You could see the lights of the harbour and in the distance the sparkle of a great ship moving across the water.

It must be the *Medina* leaving for India. Ten o'clock was sailing time, she remembered, and then she recognized the long double hoot of farewell from the ship's sirens, a melancholy sound like the call of an owl, fading into the night. Rose thought of Cynthia and Francis Nunan, standing close together at the rail perhaps, looking back at Aden and thinking of her. Dear Marion Dudley, the odious Spalding, and that strange Mr Karim. All the enclosed little world of the past six weeks evaporated now like a puff of smoke from the *Medina*'s funnels. For a wild moment she wished herself back on board again, for ever voyaging, for ever safe . . .

Movements below the window drew her back. Her room was on the far side of the Residency, overlooking the compound. Under the trees there was a fire burning, the flicker of paraffin lamps as figures moved to and fro. Behind a trellised partition, the mysterious secret life of the servants was going on, untouched and unobserved by the foreigners. Rose heard the clash of pans, someone laughing, sounds you could understand amid the background chatter of a language that had the strange, harsh incoherence of an orchestra tuning up.

She moved on to the verandah at the front of the house. Here the counterpoint of English voices drifted up, cheerful farewells as the dinner guests made their departure. Two women in silk shawls moved out towards the carriage waiting at the steps, and the Arab groom handed them up inside. The stiff shirts of the men gleamed in the moonlight. A cigar glowed and went out.

'Good night, everybody,' a deep voice called out. 'Drive safely.'

Rose imagined the stocky figure of the Resident in the doorway, with Eleanor Rawlinson behind him. She had yet to meet him but from the photographs he was decidedly not good-looking. At this moment, she felt a sudden satisfaction at her detachment from everything, secure in her vantage point in the shadows, a mere observer of these strange overlapping worlds – the shipping in the harbour, the Arabs in their quarters, the English below. Far away, on the eastern horizon, invisible as yet, the desert that contained them all was a presence you merely sensed, like a huge animal lying asleep.

Returning to bed, Rose was aware of curiosity stirring in her, something of her old capacity for hope and surprise. The last thing she heard was a bugle blowing faintly from the barracks, a sound that would punctuate so many of the days that lay ahead. It was a moment she would always remember. Turning over to sleep beneath the damp cotton sheet, she felt for the first time that her body belonged to her once more. Never again, she vowed, would she allow it to let her down in such a stupid fashion. From now on she needed every ounce of strength she could find, in order to cope with a much worse sickness, a sickness that lay at the root of her heart. How else could she bear the awful bewilderment of being subjected daily to demonstrations of Geoffrey's indifference to her? What had happened to them? Why?

She questioned herself over and over in this way, but one thing she knew for certain was that she had been cheated. Love had seemed so simple and so sure. Now it was hard to believe it had ever existed.

❧ 6 ❧

'You must forgive me, Mrs Chetwynd. I've been an appallingly bad host, I'm afraid.'

Descending to the dinner party at precisely two minutes to eight on her gold watch – an eighteenth birthday present – Rose paused on the stairs. A short, broad-shouldered man had emerged from the balcony halfway down and was waiting to greet her on the landing. It was Rose's first glimpse of the Resident. He was definitely better-looking than his photograph, she decided. The white dinner jacket set off his grey hair and his brown face, and the King Edward beard he had grown suited him well.

'I expect Eleanor told you I've been travelling up-country for the past three days,' he went on, taking her hand with a smile that made her feel at once at ease.

'Up-country.' She repeated the phrase because she liked it. It opened up hidden vistas that lay beyond the garrison buildings and the fringe of dusty gold-mohr trees around the parade-ground.

'A place called Dhala, up in the mountains. A bit of a trouble-spot, I'm afraid.' He must have seen her glancing at the scar that ran along his jaw, only partly covered by the beard, for he touched it with his thumb. 'One of the sheikhs went for me with his dagger – chap who's known to be something of a fanatic. That was years ago. I was trying to sort out a blood feud between the two tribes up there and he thought it was nothing to do with an interfering Christian. Probably right too.' He laughed. 'After all, laying siege to each other's been a national sport with the Bedouin long before we arrived on the scene.'

He paused to pluck the extinct cheroot from its amber holder, tossing it over the balcony. Then with a light touch he took her by the arm and led her downstairs.

'But how are you? That's what I should be asking. Completely recovered, I trust.' Shyly he added, 'Rotten luck. I'm sorry.'

As they reached the doorway of the reception room Geoffrey came down the stairs behind them, a little breathless, and with an anxious look on his face that was new to Rose.

'Sorry to cut it fine, sir. The polo went on rather late.'

'That's all right, Chetwynd.' Rawlinson's tone was casual, but his glance was sharp. Standing in the full glare of the paraffin lamps suspended from the rafters on chains, Rose noticed a curious quality about his eyes. The right iris was a very much lighter grey, with a fixity about it, almost as if it was sightless. It gave a vulnerability to his expression that Rose found oddly touching. 'I was taking your place, I'm afraid,' he went on. 'Escorting down the beautiful Mrs Chetwynd.'

He paused, then stepped ahead of them into the room.

'Ah. I see our guests have already arrived.'

This remark, as Rose was to learn, was always delivered in the same tone of faint surprise. In fact, it was a well-known Rawlinson ritual to allow his visitors to assemble before going in to greet them. Unkind critics said it was because he had heard that this was how things were done by the King at Windsor, a procedure that was therefore appropriate for the viceregal representative in far-flung Arabia. In fact it was a tactful way of allowing latecomers an extra margin of safety. It was universally considered the worst of crimes to be more than three minutes after the hour for a dinner appointment at the Residency and Rawlinson, who was a kind man, preferred to ignore the fact.

Whether it was because she had not yet fully recovered her energy, or because she was more than a little nervous, Rose's impressions of the evening were strangely blurred. The other guests seemed to her like characters in a rather outlandish comedy-drama, the kind described in the theatre pages of her mother's favourite magazine, *Ladies' Realm*. Colonel Beattie, for example, Commander-in-Chief of the garrison regiment, was the perfect stage officer with his bristling black moustache and shiny black mosquito boots. Major Wilson, his second in command, was almost a replica of his superior, except that he was fair instead of dark. Their wives seemed to Rose to be interchangeable too, with their weary manner and ankle-length dresses of drooping voile. A young subaltern, very tall and thin called something like Warrington-Boon but referred to as Algie, completed the military entourage. He was the ADC.

While the introductions took place, Rose felt as if she were on parade for inspection. Geoffrey's role was easily accepted. His Indian background, his rank and his savoir-faire were immediately reassuring. But Rose they could not place. She could read on their faces, the women especially, that wary, slightly baffled look of the English seeking to find a social label.

'From Wales, eh?' boomed Colonel Beattie. 'Speak the lingo, do you?'

'A little. We're on the borders really, Denbighshire. It's fairly Anglicized.'

'Used to be a fine shoot up on the moors there. Birds flew high, straight off the mountains. Watkin-Williams land. D'ye know it?'

'We used to go there for picnics,' Rose replied. To fortify herself, she took rather too large a sip of sherry. She realized that this was the wrong answer, and her lack of landowning connections, or a sporting back-ground at least, had been marked up against her.

'I trust you're not a supporter of your fellow-countryman, Lloyd George.' This was the Major's idea of changing the subject. 'The wretched fellow sounds more like an anarchist than a Liberal to me.'

Rose was rescued from this particular impasse by the intervention of Eleanor Rawlinson, who beckoned her over to where she was talking to a roguish-looking man in a monocle. Bowing low, he took her hand, kissed it and returned it to her all in one elegant gesture.

'Nicko Athenas at your service. Actually, being Greek, the name is rather longer than that, but the English would never manage it.' His wildly-inflected pattern of speech swept her along so that all she had to do was smile and nod. 'You're not English though, I gather. So with Lady Rawlinson's permission, may I introduce you to some other dangerous foreigners who've infiltrated this imperial outpost? Why should the military monopolize the delightful newcomer?'

Joining the group next to them, Rose felt at once a loosening of tension. The circle of faces was lively and welcoming, though she was quite at a loss as to who exactly everyone was or what they did, as they all seemed to be talking at once. The only woman in the group was a large weather-beaten person who told Rose in broken English that she was the head of the Danish Mission, working in the native township for the furtherance of education for Muslim girls. Then there was an exceedingly handsome Frenchman called Pierre, whom Athenas described as 'our merchant prince – hides and skins and all the perfumes of Arabia', and a swarthy Italian count who was planning to look for buried treasure in the interior. In the meantime he was dealing in scrap iron.

'Scrap iron? In Arabia?' Rose could hardly believe her ears.

'Old rail-tracks, broken-down hulks in the harbour,' the Count said mysteriously. He tapped his large nose. 'They will be the armaments of the coming war. All the countries of Europe are buying.'

Athenas held up a warning finger. 'No talk of war this evening, please. We have a German cruiser in the harbour, remember. And I hear that the Captain has been invited to dinner by the Resident.'

'Talk of the devil,' murmured the Frenchman, as all eyes turned to the door. A stoutish, balding figure in a dark blue uniform ablaze with gold braid advanced towards Sir Harry, a junior officer at his heels.

'Ah! Good evening,' drawled Rawlinson. 'Korveten-Kapitan Grashof

57

of SMS *Geier*,' he announced to the room with a commendable German accent. 'Please don't apologize, Herr Grashof. I had your message that you might be held up a little.'

The tableaux of greeting marked the end of the first act, Rose thought. Now the dinner-party drama was moving on to a different scene. At her side was the ADC holding out what Rose thought for a moment was a programme of some kind.

'You've seen the placement?'

He pointed to her name at the centre of the table plan. Mrs Geoffrey Chetwynd, in neatly printed italics, seemed suddenly a total stranger, a self-possessed woman of fifty perhaps, someone she wouldn't even like.

'Next to His Excellency,' he added, sotto voce, as if he was in church. 'New bride and all that – H.E. will be taking you in, of course.'

As if by clockwork, the Resident appeared at her elbow.

'Shall we?'

With Sir Harry at her side, Rose found herself at the head of a stately crocodile that wended its way through the arched entrance at the far end of the room. The Residency was a great dark barn of a place, originally the nineteenth-century headquarters of the first British agent, but it had been transformed by Eleanor Rawlinson's gift for colour. Sea-blue walls set off the stone floors, and the regulation furniture of heavy teak was interspersed with hanging rugs and gilt-framed English paintings, small pieces of bronze and alabaster collected in their early days in Beirut and Baghdad. In the dining room, the glow of candles set off bowls of pink oleander. Heavy crystal and silver with the royal crest adorned the long mahogany table.

'Perk from the Government of India,' Sir Harry murmured as she took the seat next to him.

Behind each chair stood a bearer in white, the brass badge of the Residency gleaming in the scarlet turbans and cummerbunds.

Rose was amazed at the elaborate formality of it all. Behind the scenes, as she had already come to know, the regime at the Residency was a spartan one, with its makeshift plumbing and cockroach-infested kitchens. An official dinner party was a charade, she thought, a dream picture of gracious colonial living as it ought to be. In reality everyone knew that the five-course menu of mulligatawny soup, Red Sea salmon, tough chicken, caramel cream and devils-on-horseback was only edible at all because of Lady Rawlinson's supervision of the aged Somali cook, and his equally ancient charcoal range, in temperatures like a ship's boiler-room. But no one would dream of mentioning the fact. It was on a par with their own perspiring efforts with shirt-studs and long gloves underneath bedroom punkahs, part of the price of running an Empire.

It seemed to Rose that, once seated round the viceregal table, guests abandoned any attempt at spontaneous human communication. Everyone had a part to play and lines to remember – Rose's role was the ingénue newcomer, anxious to please and eager to learn. You cut up your conversation neatly, like your food, turning first to the right and then to the left, while discussing in strict rotation the vagaries of the climate, news of mutual acquaintances in other parts of the Empire (name-dabbling as much as possible) and the current state of polo, sailing and golf.

'I wondered if there was any chance of doing some riding?' Rose ventured of the Colonel, who was on her right. 'Is it difficult to keep a horse?'

'Keep a horse?' the Colonel bayed. His gaze worked its way upwards from her low-cut neckline to the spray of jasmine she had tucked above her fringe. 'We don't want you galloping off into the desert with the Bedouin now, do we?'

'Well actually, that's something I'd rather like to do.'

Everyone laughed, and Rose felt herself blushing.

'Riding into the desert, I mean.'

At least she had broken the cocoon of unreality, just as she felt she might start to suffocate. Somewhere out there, beyond the Residency gates, was a strange harsh country with a history that went back to the days when the British were still painting themselves with woad. Yet these people seemed to be doing all they could to ignore it. Even at the other end of the table, the Count was holding his audience spellbound with his magazine-style stories of big-game hunting in Africa, jungle trips in South America, and the gambling tables of Monte Carlo – anything but the country in which they all now found themselves.

But suddenly there was a change. It was as if her words had released a spring of tension around the table. Everyone began talking at once about the Arabs and Arabia. Nicko the Greek had only last year made an extraordinary trek up to the Yemen border, visiting the trading posts of the old incense road. The Major described the fine bloodstock mare he had been able to buy from the Imam's stables at the Sheikh Othman oasis. Even the Colonel remarked that shooting for sand-grouse with the old Sultan of Jehal had been the best sport he had had for years.

'If you really would like to make an expedition out to the Protectorate borders, I could certainly arrange it,' the Resident said quietly to her. 'I'm afraid beyond that is forbidden territory at the moment.'

'Why is that, Sir Harry?'

'Ruling from the India Office. They say there's been too much meddling in Arab affairs. So our administrative officers have been recalled from the entire hinterland, just at a time when we were beginning to establish a really solid liaison with the tribes. Our mere presence there was enough to demonstrate the British style of things. Fair play and honest dealing, the idea that you could have a better life by trading and tending your crops, than by this incessant bloodletting. They look to us for leadership, you know, whatever they say in London.'

'I absolutely agree, sir.' Geoffrey's voice was raised from further down the table, with that faint slur in it that too much wine always produced. 'What we need in Aden is more of the Indian style of British rule. Set no boundaries on our territory. Rule with a tight rein, and a touch of the whip hand where necessary. Let the natives know who's master, I say, instead of this namby-pamby approach.'

Rose flinched. She was not used to servants remaining in attendance at a meal and she could not help glancing up at the dark faces hovering in the shadows. Their expressions remained impassive. Did she imagine it or did she catch the flicker of an intent gaze, swiftly turned aside, from one of the older bearers, a squat heavy-jowled Indian with a complexion that was almost black?

Dessert had been served and the other guests waited for His Excellency to raise his spoon so that they too could start to eat. But he remained quite still, frowning down at his plate. Then he looked across at Geoffrey.

'I'm afraid you've got the wrong end of the stick, Chetwynd.' His voice was cold. 'We don't go in for that kind of thing in Arabia. We may officially be a province of British India, but that's just an aberration of history, and it won't last much longer either. The Raj style of autocratic regime won't work in Aden, I'm afraid. The Arabs will never recognize themselves as subjects of the Queen – why should they? They have their own rulers, their own god, and they see themselves not just as equal to us but superior even, when it comes to surviving the rigours of desert life.'

'Quite right too,' interjected Nicko quietly.

'Then what are we supposed to be doing here at all, if that is the position?' asked the Colonel.

'In your case, maintaining the garrison – showing the flag, that is. And you're also training a body of local troops – valuable work – and keeping the imperial sea routes safe for trade. Don't forget that Aden was captured in the first place because it was needed as a vital coaling-station on the voyage to India and back.'

'Pax Britannica,' said the Major, sticking a convenient label on the discussion.

'Quite so.' The Resident had raised his pudding spoon but only to mark out an imaginary frontier with it across the polished mahogany. 'From an administrative point of view, peaceful penetration should be our aim, the establishment of a real protectorate stretching right up to the Yemeni borders.'

His normally impassive face was alight with enthusiasm as he looked around the table.

'If only the powers-that-be would adopt a more imaginative policy in Arabia, instead of fighting shy of every advance by the sultans and the sheikhs! Then the whole country would unite under our influence. They don't seem to realize that we have a special relationship with the Arabs, a natural affinity if you like. We laugh at the same things. We enjoy each other's hospitality. There's a fund of goodwill, if only we were free to trust ourselves to it.'

He sighed and attacked his caramel cream. 'God knows we've spurned endless opportunities.'

There was a pause while his guests also consumed their puddings. Looking across at Geoffrey, Rose saw him leave his helping untouched, staring down at his plate with a sulky expression. Next to him, the Danish missionary lady spoke up for the first time.

'What about the Turks, Your Excellency? Do you not risk a clash with them if the British set themselves up in the hinterland? After all, the Yemen is part of the Ottoman Empire.'

'I am aware of that, Miss Largesen.' The Resident's polite tone was edged with irony. 'But believe me, there will be a clash sure enough if this wretched war breaks out.'

Rose had the feeling that, far from forgetting the presence of the German commander, seated at the top of the table, Sir Harry was deliberately addressing himself to him in the hope of invoking some response.

Grashof picked up the challenge with a wide blue stare. When he spoke, Rose was amused to notice that he employed the same loud, slow voice as the British did when addressing foreigners.

'I know little of international politics, Your Excellency. I am a mere sailor. But do I understand you to mean that, conflict arising, Turkey would align herself with the Central European powers? And thus your faithful stipendiaries, your sultans and sheikhs, would naturally support their fellow Muslims, rather than the British?'

'I'm not absolutely certain of that, Herr Kapitan.' The Resident sounded as if they were discussing cricket teams. 'His Highness the Sultan of Jehal, Sir Ahmed Bin Seif, is after all a Knight of the British Empire. He has told me himself that he thinks England the most worthy of the foreign powers to hold sway in Arabia.'

'The old chap is a firm friend of ours, that's for sure,' said the Major languidly.

'Give him another five guns to his official salute, sir, and I'll guarantee he'll actually muster his troops alongside ours.' chaffed the ADC.

It was Eleanor Rawlinson's voice that reminded her husband of his duties as a host.

'Surely this is not the time and place to talk about war. As if it was a foregone conclusion!' Her long jade earrings swung energetically to and fro and her eyes flashed as she gestured around the table. 'Look at all the different nationalities sitting here this evening. What quarrel do we have with one another, for goodness' sake?'

The Resident squared his shoulders, as if pulling himself together.

'Especially when we are about to drink the loyal toast,' he said.

He gave a signal to the head butler, standing behind his chair. The savoury plates had already been cleared and any crumbs decorously whisked away by the bearers, wielding tiny table-brushes and brass pans. With a flourish, the cut-glass port decanter was placed in front of His Excellency. As he poured a generous measure, first for himself, and then for Rose next to him, he looked directly across at the Commander.

'Your High Sea Fleet is in the special charge of Kaiser Wilhelm, I'm told, and he of course is cousin to our own beloved King. Shall we put our trust for peace in that?'

'Let us do so indeed,' the Commander replied. 'Let us remember, though,' he added gravely, 'all depends on Russia. If the Russians mobilize . . .' He broke off with a shrug of his shoulders.

To Rose, these exchanges were too esoteric to be immediately understood. But she was aware of a strong undercurrent of drama that made her blood tingle. She looked around the circle of faces, judging their different expressions, the foreigners wry and cynical, the military alertly jolly like a rival team, ready for the whistle to blow.

Beattie judged it the moment for a joke.

'Perhaps the Captain has been assigned to capture Aden as a start to hostilities. We had the *See Adler* in last week, and the *Kondor* expected on Monday. Looks as if we're encircled, eh, Herr Grashof?'

The Commander smiled. He was sweating heavily.

'I wish to assure all present that next to the Germans, the British are the best people in the world. In every port I call,' he went on, addressing the table at large, 'my men are playing the football with British sailors and soldiers. Last year we lost every match. Here in Aden this afternoon we scored a draw. That is balance of power. Everyone is happy. Maybe it is a symbol.'

The Resident was on his feet, his glass in his hand. All rose stiffly to their feet and there was a respectful silence.

'To the health of our King Emperor.'

'The King,' said everyone softly, as they drank.

'And to every tie of kinship and friendship between us,' Sir Harry said, raising his glass again, this time in the direction of the Commander.

'British and Arab also,' he added quietly to Rose as they sat down again.

Rose was not allowed to sit for long. A glance from Lady Rawlinson summoned her to follow the other ladies. Rose was the last in the decorous file that made its way upstairs.

'What are you wearing to the parade tomorrow?' the Major's wife demanded as they stood together before the mirror in Lady Rawlinson's bedroom. Under the general chatter, Rose had been trying to gauge if the sounds from the bathroom meant that Mrs Beattie was soon to re-emerge. It was difficult to tell in a place without any proper plumbing. Instead there was an awful commode thing that everyone called a thunderbox. It was fixed to an outside wall with a trap-door at the back through which the unfortunate sweeper made his collections under cover of darkness, something Rose tried not to think about on such occasions.

'I myself had ze worst experience imaginable!'

The shrill tones of the Frenchman's wife greeted Rose on her return to the bedroom. A buxom lady with a strong suggestion of artificial colouring about both face and hair, she had consumed more of the Resident's wine than was perhaps good for her, Rose thought.

'Z'stupid fellow open the door behind me when I am still sitting. Beg pardon memsahib, he say, while I am falling down to faint.' She shrugged her shoulders. 'We get new sweeper straight 'way, of course. Who can face z'old one after zat, I ask you?'

She laughed merrily. The Englishwomen exchanged pained diplomatic smiles. Thunderbox jokes were part of the social currency, but *not* at a Residency dinner party. Mrs Beattie steered the conversation safely back to clothes.

'So what are you wearing tomorrow, Mrs Chetwynd?'

'Some brand-new London creation, just to show how out-of-date we poor exiles are!'

Mrs Wilson had a distinctly spiteful edge to her smile, as Rose had noticed earlier.

'I shall rely on Lady Rawlinson for advice,' she replied sweetly. 'She has such taste in everything.'

'Thank you, dear girl,' said Eleanor in the doorway, come to summon them down to coffee. 'That's something we will settle when our guests have gone.'

As a reminder of the time – only ten minutes to go to the ritual leave-taking hour of half past ten – the remark was not lost on the Colonel's wife as senior lady. By eleven o'clock, with the house empty again and the servants closing the shutters downstairs, Eleanor was standing in front of Rose's wardrobe, pondering the choice for tomorrow.

'This one I think.' She reached unerringly for the pale blue Indian muslin. 'You've no idea how hot it is out there, even at seven in the morning.'

'And the hat?'

'The largest you have. And don't forget your parasol.'

7

LADY Rawlinson was right, as usual. Although the sun had only been up for an hour, the iron chairs laid out on the public square were already uncomfortably warm. All around the dusty arena, throngs of natives had gathered to watch the strange and famous ceremony in honour of the King Emperor. At the front was the phalanx of seats reserved for the European community and their wives. Amongst these particularly, there was a ripple of interest as Rose and Geoffrey took their places in the first row.

The Chetwynds had come ahead of their hosts in the official motorcar, which already showed signs of wear and tear after just one year's service in Arabia. The Resident and his Lady would make their appearance in the carriage at 7 a.m. precisely. From the strange edifice known as the Clock Tower, a sort of miniature Big Ben that stood on the peak above the bay, Rose saw that it was still only ten minutes to the hour. Not that she minded the waiting. Already she was caught up in the air of expectancy, the colour and movement of the huge crowds that encircled the parade ground with those extraordinary purple cliffs rising behind. But the discomfort of the hot iron pressing through her thin dress was disturbing. So was the damp itch of stockings and gloves, no doubt encouraging the prickly-heat rash that already threatened. The chin-strap of Geoffrey's helmet was obviously giving him trouble. He ran his fingers round it with a faint grunt, then resumed his immobile pose, staring ahead. On the other side of him, Rose caught a glimpse of Mrs Beattie and Mrs Wilson in their wilting hats and almost identical voile dresses.

Then the band struck up and Rose forgot everything else. 'Sussex By The Sea', the soldiers were playing, thumping and blaring from their stand under the acacia trees. For some reason it seemed to bind together all the strangely assorted elements of the scene before her – the bright bedecked ships at anchor in the glitter of the bay, the cavalry camels drawn up and waiting in the courtyard opposite, the bobbing tide of red turbans as the Government Guards came marching into place on either side of the dais. At the far corner of the square, there was a fluttering of saris in the purdah enclosure, Indian butterflies among the black-cocooned shapes of the Arab women. Then from the whole swarm of spectators there rose the sound of clapping, respectfully subdued but odd-sounding still to English ears, as the Residency carriage rounded the bend from Steamer Point.

Rose had not seen Sir Harry before in his official regalia. The white plumes in his helmet set him apart, like some species of rare and brilliant bird, as he took his place on the dais. From Geoffrey next to her and from the rows alongside and behind, there was the clicking of spurs and swords, the mingled smell of sweat and eau-de-cologne as British officialdom and their wives rose to their feet. The thud of the cannons from Navy House, sounding out the viceregal salute, seemed to stop Rose's heart. Dust and smoke drifted upwards, following the spirals of squawking crows. As the band broke into the National Anthem, she was startled to find how proud she felt, not just proud but tearful. Some inkling of the romance of Empire, even here in shabby Aden, touched a spark that had no rational explanation, and Rose was never to forget it.

Taking her seat again, she noticed that the place next to her was still unoccupied. Further along there were more unoccupied chairs.

'Who is missing?' she whispered to Geoffrey.

'Native rulers.' He nodded towards a procession of picturesque figures who were making their way towards the dais. 'Honouring their treaties, paying their respects to the Crown. And making sure of getting their baksheesh in return, the beggars.'

He spoke in an undertone, but someone chuckled in the row behind. Rose turned and saw that the ladies had raised their parasols again and were fanning themselves with expressions of unmistakeable boredom.

The cannons began to boom again.

'And of course each one gets his royal salute depending on how important he is, I gather. Or rather, thinks he is,' Geoffrey added languidly.

Rose counted up to fifteen as the first of the rulers stepped before the Resident. A handshake and bow were exchanged, and then the younger Arab, waiting behind, went through the same ritual.

'His Highness Sir Ahmed Bin Seif, Sultan of Jehal.' Announcing the rulers from the top of the steps, Algie's voice wavered a little on the Arabic pronunciations. 'And the Emir of Jehal.'

Rose noted with some alarm that the Sultan, on stepping down again, was now approaching the empty seats at her side, as directed by one of the ushers. With his towering turban and long grey beard, his gold-embroidered cloak billowing around him, he was the most imposing-looking personage Rose had ever set eyes on. With an impassive face, the old man brushed past her. The younger man behind him paused, then took the seat next to her. That was frightening enough, she decided, glancing down at the great curved dagger slung casually in his lap. The bright gold of the scabbard was inlaid with cornelians and rubies. Under the edge of the tasselled sleeve there was an incongruous glimpse of a gold wristwatch. She was just deliberating whether she could risk a quick sideways look at his face when a soft voice broke in.

'Good morning, Mrs Chetwynd. Does it remind you of the fancy dress on the *Medina?*'

The Emir was staring straight ahead, smiling faintly. But even in profile, there was no mistaking the face of Hassan Karim. The silky folds of the green turban, with its long peacock tail, only emphasized the broad cheekbones and the slanted eyelids she had noticed on first seeing him as he came up the gangway of the ship. That memory now seemed to belong somewhere in the remote past, like everything else that had happened to her before arriving in Aden.

'Mr Karim?' The name sprang out before she could correct herself. Amazement and disbelief made it difficult for her to say any more.

'Only when I travel,' he murmured. 'It saves a lot of fuss, you see.'

He was smiling properly now, turning to look at her. 'I hope you will forgive me for being so – so secretive?' With his accustomed air of courtesy, he put out his hand. 'Now I must introduce myself all over again. I have half a dozen names to choose from. But Hassan is how I am known to my friends.'

As they shook hands, Rose was aware of a stir of curiosity in the seats behind. Next to her, Geoffrey leaned forward and more introductions and explanations took place in undertones. Rose could see Geoffrey was pleased by the incident, no doubt because of the political kudos to be gained by some kind of social connection with the Sultan's family. The Sultan himself remained aloof from these exchanges, staring ahead with a look of sleepy disdain.

'It is better I do not introduce you,' Hassan whispered. 'My father has not yet accepted the custom of shaking hands with women.'

All this time the cannons kept up their percussions as the rulers processed past to pay their respects to the Resident, and Hassan Karim delivered a mischievous commentary on them in Rose's ear. Judging by appearances, they seemed a motley bunch. The Aulaki Sultan, for instance, had arrayed himself in a pinstripe European jacket and a native kilt in bright cotton, with a pair of red socks to match.

'Richest man in the Protectorate,' Hassan murmured, with an expressionless face. 'Keeps a fortune under his bed – Marie Thérèse dollars wrapped up in old sugar bags.'

Behind him came a wizened little creature who was bare to the waist and daubed with blue indigo. Long elf-locks hung beneath his turban and bands of cartridges were slung from his shoulders. According to Hassan Karim, he ruled over thousands in his tribal kingdom up in the Yemen mountains.

'Best shot in Arabia too. You have to be careful to keep on the right side of him.'

A fat man in an embroidered skullcap and long white robes was the last to cross the dais, accompanied by a larger than usual entourage. Hassan Karim's face hardened.

'This man, Abu Mohammed, rules the state next to ours. He may look like a saint but he causes us much trouble, and the British too. And the wretch has the most beautiful daughter, I hear.' He glanced wryly at Rose. 'Like all princesses, she is kept locked up in a tower, lest the gaze of such as myself should fall on her.'

'Will she not marry, then?'

'Only when her father decrees.'

The Resident had taken his seat again, and there was a brief lull in the proceedings.

'How strange all this must seem after Cairo, Your Highness,' Rose ventured to say. She hoped she had alighted on the correct form of address. She could not help adding, 'You were at the university there, as you said? Or was that also part of your disguise?'

'Of course I was there,' he replied indignantly. 'But I felt my father needed me back. There is so much to be done in Jehal. You will see for yourself, though. You must visit us, visit the ladies at the palace.'

'I would like that very much, Your Highness.'

The prospect of such an adventure filled Rose with elation. This encounter was, after all, an adventure in itself. Standing next to the Emir, as the clash of cymbals brought them all to their feet, she suddenly felt not just a mere spectator, but a part of the whole occasion. The camel corps that led the parade was a sight to catch at your throat. The loose swinging trot of the great beasts and the small dark riders perched stiffly aloft, pennants fluttering from their lances, stayed in your mind even as the others came on from behind – the black and khaki of the infantrymen, sandals flapping in the dust, then the gleaming flanks of the cavalry horses, ridden by the British officers with their Arab grooms, the *syces*, running alongside. At the back stalked a formation of the Bedouin Legion, rifles on their shoulders, barefoot and arrogant in their desert robes and headshawls.

'They are from the Hadramaut,' Hassan Karim told her. 'In the Eastern Protectorate.'

Most touching to Rose was the sight of the army mules bringing up the rear, pulling Maxim guns behind them. After the flourish of the other contingents, there was something pathetic about the small scruffy creatures, patiently plodding along, with little bonnets tied over their ears to shield their eyes from the glare.

Now the parade was moving away towards the far side of the square. The marching feet and hooves and the turning wheels carved deep tracks in the dust, and the air was full of the prickly smell of gunpowder that reminded Rose of the Guy Fawkes parties of childhood. In the shade of the trees stood a statue of Queen Victoria, dominating the *maidan*. Someone had hung a garland of marigolds around her neck, bright gold against the streaks of green verdigris. Here the procession had come to a halt. Slowly the colours were dipped and a single bugle floated out the notes of the Last Post. Rose's fingers felt for the handkerchief in her purse. Surely she wasn't going to cry! At her side, she was aware of Hassan Karim watching her out of the corner of his eye.

'It is a proud feeling then to be a part of the Empire?' he said in a low voice, as the parade began to move away again.

'I suppose it is, even so small a corner of it as Aden.' She was ashamed to hear the catch in her voice.

'I'm afraid it is all the fault of my family.' He was smiling again, this time with an expression of irony. 'It was my grandfather who gave Aden to the British in the first place. Sold it rather, I'm glad to say. But I'm still not sure if it was the right thing to do.'

They were taking their seats to hear the Resident read the Empire message from the King. As Rose leaned back, she winced at the touch of the hot metal through her dress. At the same moment, Hassan Karim took the embroidered stole from his shoulders and slipped it over the back of her chair. It was a movement so deft it could hardly be noticed.

'Thank you,' Rose whispered. She felt herself blushing.

On the other side, Geoffrey shifted irritably. 'I trust your conversation with the Emir will not be continued during His Excellency's speech.' His voice in her ear had the edge of venom she knew too well.

Sir Harry's address went by without her registering a single word of it. No doubt everyone else had noticed her bad manners, and marked her out as an ignorant newcomer.

Then they were standing for three cheers for His Majesty and it was all over. Geoffrey's hand was on her arm, maliciously tight, as he drew her to walk out ahead. It seemed it was of the utmost importance to be the first of the official guests to follow in the wake of the Rawlinsons. There was no time to make even the briefest of farewells to the Emir, as they walked quickly to where the Residency car was drawn up in the shade at the head of the line of traps and broughams. But they had no sooner climbed in than it was evident something was wrong. Ali the driver feverishly pulled out one lever after another. There were muffled curses. But the engine only growled and stuttered, then died away completely.

'For heaven's sake!' Geoffrey exploded, as the man sprang out and began kicking the wheel in a fury.

'Motorcar no good for Aden, sahib! Every day this engine go sick. Too much trouble, too much trouble,' he grumbled to himself.

Among the flock of British making their way past with barely concealed looks of amusement, Rose saw Hassan Karim. Now he was standing at the car door, smiling gravely as usual.

'My father and I would be only too happy to take you back to the Residency in our motor, Mr Chetwynd.'

'I'm afraid we are not returning to the Residency, Your Highness. We have arranged to drive out to our new house at Sheikh Othman. It's very kind of you, though,' he added, obviously torn between irritation at his humiliating position and the politeness demanded by protocol.

'But that is even more simple. It lies on the road to Jehal which we are now taking ourselves.'

'Very kind,' Geoffrey repeated stiffly. 'Thank you.'

The Emir waved towards the gleaming green automobile drawn up outside the Crescent Hotel on the other side of the road. A group of half-naked tribesmen seemed to be guarding it, their hands on their daggers, their faces fierce and watchful. As the Emir approached, they crouched to kiss his hand and knee, before crowding around to inspect the British couple more closely.

'It is my pride and joy,' Hassan Karim said, laying his hand on the bonnet. 'A Sedanca de Ville. I ordered it when I was in Cairo. It has only just arrived.' He grimaced towards the figure in the back seat. 'My father is still convinced it is possessed by a *djin* – a devil.'

The chauffeur was holding open the door. Hassan Karim turned to Geoffrey. 'Perhaps if you could sit next to the Sultan.'

As her husband got in, the Emir said quietly to Rose, 'Fate seems to favour these breakdowns.'

For a moment she was horribly startled. Was Hassan Karim not to be depended on after all to keep the harmless secret of the Port Said fiasco? But as they settled into their seats, his eyes met hers with a look that was both teasing and reassuring. He turned away again to introduce them to the Sultan, who was studying each in turn with keen concentration. Close to he seemed not quite so forbiddingly old, but even more autocratic in manner. She was careful not to put out her hand. Instead she simply smiled her pleasure at the encounter and murmured a few words of thanks. To her surprise the Sultan's face broke into a sudden smile of great charm, reminding her of Hassan.

'You are welcome,' he replied, in slow precise English. Then his eyes closed, as if to shut out the distasteful experience of travel by automobile as they sped along through clouds of dust, away from the European settlement.

For the rest of the journey he remained seemingly asleep, apart from the movement of the amber prayer beads strung around his long brown fingers. It was left to the Emir to keep the conversation going.

'Did you know this is where Noah is said to have built the ark?' He indicated the brightly-painted dhows on the crowded beach where the carpenters were drifting back to work. Then he looked up at the rocky pass behind. 'And somewhere up there rests the body of Cain, so the story goes. He who murdered Abel.'

'But that is the Bible surely,' Geoffrey interrupted. 'Not Muslim history.'

'In this part of the world, the two intermingle,' Hassan Karim replied. 'Higher up are the water reservoirs, very old, built by the Queen of Sheba, no less.' He laughed. 'There are even some who say that Aden was Eden. But that's harder to believe.' He nodded out at the expanse of rock and sand. 'It's a volcanic crater, of course. Crater is what the British call the native town.' He turned to Rose. 'The bazaar there is a fine place for silks and gold. But you've already explored it, I suppose.'

'I'm afraid not.'

'My wife has been ill,' Geoffrey said sharply.

'I'm sorry.' Hassan Karim studied her face with an expression of concern. Then he turned to Geoffrey again. 'I trust you forgive my incognito role on board the *Medina*?'

'Jolly good trick,' Geoffrey replied, with an attempt at bonhomie.

'You will be happy in Arabia, do you think?'

'I hope so. It's very different from India.'

'Ah yes. India.'

Silence fell. They were driving towards the desert now, past the remains of an old railway line with only the occasional thorn bush on the horizon. In the hands of the immense Negro driver, the Sedanca plunged through the sand-ruts like a whale at sea. Rose started to talk about their house. Today they were just taking measurements, inter-viewing servants and so on. She had not yet seen the place but Geoffrey said it seemed quite decent, very old-fashioned with plenty of room, and a garden too.

'Of course. It is at the oasis,' Hassan Karim replied. 'There are gardens everywhere. It is quite a large local settlement.'

'You know the house, then?'

'Very well indeed. It was originally the home of a Yemeni merchant, a

71

friend of the family. So it is in the Arab style and will be cool in hot weather. There it is now.'

He pointed ahead to the date palms clustered along the track. On the right, surrounded by trees, a tall stone house came into view, with faded green shutters and a trellised verandah. The car swung in through the gates and up an overgrown drive. In the shadow of the doorway, the *chokida* stood on guard waiting, the keys in his hand. As Rose got out she was enveloped by a sharp powerful scent which she did not recognize.

'Jasmine,' Hassan Karim said, leaning out of the window. 'It grows everywhere in our garden at Jehal too.' He shook hands with Geoffrey. 'You will be visiting us there very soon, I hope. We are not far away.'

'Many thanks.' Geoffrey was brushing away the dust from his uniform, looking around at the Arab rooftops beyond the walls. 'We are rather isolated out here. But the Resident was keen I should be based near the frontier, keep in touch with the Protectorate and so on.'

All of a sudden, the Sultan leaned forward blinking.

'You will be number two to Sir Rawlinson then?'

'That is correct, sir.'

'A powerful man.' Delicately he extended his hand, first removing the prayer beads. 'Next time we will talk.'

Standing by the car Rose realized she was still carrying the Emir's silk shawl.

'I'm so sorry.' She moved to give it to him, but he simply waved his hand.

'Now it is yours. Something to say welcome to my country.'

The windows were drawn up by the chauffeur, and slowly turning, the car moved out of sight down the drive again.

Rose stood still for a moment, trying to absorb the conflicting impressions of the last two hours. Then she noticed Geoffrey's expression of impatience as he waited on the steps.

She took a deep breath. It was time to go into the house.

❧ 8 ☙

'BEG pardon, memsahib.'

It was a summons that Rose had come to dread, though it was less than a month since they had moved into the house. Without raising her eyes from the letter she was writing, she could see the faint smile on the bearer's face, that sly, supercilious expression, as he stood in the doorway waiting to speak to her. She had disliked him from the moment she had first noticed him at the Residency dinner party. Even then, the way she had caught him scrutinizing her across the table had warned her that he had some special interest in her. The next day, Geoffrey had introduced him to her.

'Rose, this is Ram Prasad, my bearer from India. Only just landed here with the regiment, and ready to start work for us as soon as we move in, eh R. P.?'

'Yes, sahib. Right, sahib.'

The man grinned up at him, revealing teeth stained scarlet with betel-nut juice. He was squat and exceedingly dark. There was a quality about his ugliness that Rose found almost sinister. She was surprised at Geoffrey's geniality. More often than not, he kept his eyes averted when speaking to servants and his tone was curt. But now, something like a glance of complicity was exchanged between the two.

From then onwards, Rose left it to her husband to issue instructions as to the setting up of their household. It was only in the mornings, when Geoffrey was over at Steamer Point at the government offices, that Rose found herself unable to escape from the odious creature. The other servants were no problem to her. There was an aged Somali cook of apparently immense experience who kept to his dungeon-like kitchens, and a cheerful little sweeper called Mohammed. These she had engaged herself, and regarded somchow as allies. The actual process of selection, though, had been an ordeal she would never forget, chiefly because of Ram Prasad. As he hustled the candidates in and out, each one clutching a tattered chitty from a previous employer, he wore the sneering look that had now become so familiar to her. Once or twice, greeting them, she tried out a few words from her small stock of Arabic. Ram Prasad shook his head and spat briefly over the verandah.

'Best for memsahib to speak Inglees,' he said afterwards. He slapped down a stack of her books in a way that especially irritated her. 'No use for to talk like these low-caste people.'

'That is my business, Ram Prasad,' she said sharply. 'I mean to learn the language as soon as possible.'

The air of brooding resentment that this rebuke produced was worse than the sneers. It permeated everything he did about the house while Geoffrey was not there. When he unpacked her delicate rose-patterned china, he clashed the cups together in a way that set her nerves on edge. Her glass of lemonade was brought to her in his fat, nail-bitten hand, as if the usual drinks tray was something reserved for sahibs only. He had a way too of simply staring back at her, blinking like a toad, whenever she asked him to do the simplest thing. Then he would turn on his heel and pad away without even a reply. When she told Geoffrey, he simply laughed and said no bearer who had worked for bachelors took easily to dealing with a memsahib.

Now here he was in the doorway, ostensibly at her service, but exuding the same air of unspoken insolence that made her feel a stranger in her own house.

'What is it, Ram Prasad?'

She struggled to sound polite, dabbing with her handkerchief at the trickle of perspiration that always ran down her arm on to the paper when she was writing. The words 'Dearest Mother and Father' were badly smudged, she noticed.

'Memsahib, here is Saleh,' Ram Prasad replied.

He turned and beckoned to someone on the other side of the door. A slender boy of about fifteen sidled in gracefully with downcast eyes. Long elf-locks hung about his shoulders, bound at the forehead with a bright-coloured twist of cloth in the way of the up-country tribes. The face beneath was beautiful and sharp as a cat's, as he glanced coquettishly across at her through thick black lashes.

'Saleh come to work, memsahib,' Ram Prasad went on.

'Surely we don't need anyone else,' Rose said stiffly. There was something about the boy's manner she found disturbing, the way he leaned at ease against the wall, gazing about the room while he played with the blue amulet that hung from his neck on a leather thong.

'Saleh is very good garden-boy. He was been learning good Inglees too. At the garrison.'

There was a pause. Rose willed herself not to look away first as Ram Prasad's bulging eyes fixed themselves on hers.

'Sahib know him.' There was a note of finality in his voice. 'Sahib say Saleh stay here.'

74

Rose turned back to her desk and picked up her pen again. 'I shall speak to sahib about it when he comes home.'

'Thank you, memsahib.' It was the boy speaking, his enunciation soft and careful. She was aware of him slipping out of the room. Ram Prasad remained motionless, arms stiffly at his sides.

'Upstairs ready now, memsahib. Everything unpacked.'

'Thank you. I'll come and see.'

Furtively, she slipped on her shoes under the desk and saw from his glance that this move had not escaped him.

With the thermometer around the hundred mark, she had taken to leaving off her stockings when she dressed in the mornings. The temptation to walk around barefoot was sometimes even harder to resist, despite the threat of scorpions. Ridiculously she found herself envious of Ram Prasad's dusty soles slapping across the tiled floors as she followed him up to the bedrooms.

Already Rose loved this part of the house. Its Moorish arches and thick white-plastered walls always kept out the worst of the heat. The fretwork carving around the verandah pillars threw shadows like cobwebs over the floors of cracked red ochre. Through the shutters, where the blue-green paint was peeling away, you could see the dome of a saint's tomb through the palm trees, and behind it a fragment of sky of the same Arabian aquamarine. Unlike the Residency and the other houses of the British, this place was miraculously free of the stamp of colonial life. A sense of the Muslim past was strong. Carved wooden screens divided the upper rooms where the women had lived and the sleeping quarters on the roof. Just yesterday Rose had come across a small stone incense-burner, very old, left behind in a cupboard, but with the ghost of its musty fragrance lingering still. Most of all, she cherished the brass oil-lamp hanging in the hall with its graceful arabesque designs, silhouetted by day against the open doorway, glowing by night when the flame was lit. Geoffrey threatened electricity. But she would fight for the lamp, whatever happened.

There were four rooms upstairs. Two were only large enough to be used as a study for Geoffrey and a sewing room for herself. The other two were lofty and spacious, one looking out over the desert, the other facing the distant view of the bay and the Steamer Point settlement. Waiting on the verandah, Ram Prasad opened the first door with a flourish.

'Sahib's room.'

Rose was startled. She already thought of this as 'their' bedroom. Here she and Geoffrey had slept since their arrival. Two spartan beds had been provided by the Public Works Department, and she had placed them at either end of the room under the two long windows, partly for the sake of coolness, partly for what she termed in her mind as 'privacy'.

'Sahib's room?'

She walked past him, feeling a prickle of pure hatred at the back of her neck. A quick glance showed her the rearrangements that had been made. Only one bed remained and on it was folded Geoffrey's sleeping sarong.

'Where is the other bed?'

'Is moved to bedroom number two.' He sighed. 'Memsahib's room.'

She stood quite still, looking round at the chest of drawers where Geoffrey's ivory-backed brushes, initialled in silver, had been laid out alongside his leather collar-box and stud box with the precision of an altar arrangement. Across the room, his favourite canvas chair with its footstool and folding table were set out beneath the window to catch the breeze.

'Who told you to do this?' Once again with her back to the bearer, she forced herself to speak at a natural level. The effort of it made her tremble.

'Sahib say this morning.'

From the edge of triumph in his voice, she knew it was true. Yet even last night, for the first time in weeks, she and Geoffrey had been intimate in this very bed. At least, he had called out to her in the dark, and then in a whisper he had insisted upon a physical act which obviously gave him satisfaction but which she herself, remembering the pain, shrank from defining in her mind even now. You could not call it love-making. But she had assumed it was his idea of expressing love. Besides, she was grateful for the release of tension it brought between the two of them. At the breakfast table, he had even kissed her goodbye as the shabby little gharry pulled up at the door to take him to Steamer Point. How strange men were, she thought.

Glancing round at Ram Prasad, she had the sudden appalling idea that he could read exactly what was going on in her head.

'If number two room is mine,' she said quietly, turning to face him, 'where will our guests sleep when they come to stay? I have already ordered two spare beds from Government stores.' She folded her arms and felt her heart beating furiously. But he was not to be trapped.

'Sahib Chetwynd is not liking strangers in his house.' He shook his head firmly. 'This I know from Bombay. Five years I was with sahib. He was like my own family. Everything I do for him as if he small boy.'

His eyes had strayed to the wall behind her. Moving across, he straightened the frame of one of the photographs that he had unpacked and nailed up around the mirror. Rose had not seen them before. They seemed to be the usual regimental groups, polo teams with Geoffrey at the centre in topee and spurs, a drinking party on a verandah. On more than one, Ram Prasad himself was to be seen, a shadowy figure standing stiffly to one side, or sitting cross-legged in the front with the other servants.

'But in India, sahib had many friends,' Rose persisted.

Back in the doorway, Ram Prasad gazed out across the verandah, his face a blank again. 'Is different,' he said.

Studying the photographs more closely, Rose's attention was caught by a young man standing next to Geoffrey in front of a swimming pool, and again lounging on the verandah steps. He was dark-skinned, half-caste perhaps, which was odd. But it was the beauty of his looks that struck her, and reminded her at once of someone else. But who? Then Saleh's face came back to her, that sly, heavy-lidded look he had given her. It was not an exact resemblance, but the type was somehow the same.

'Memsahib finish?' Ram Prasad was shifting from foot to foot impatiently.

All at once Rose was desperate to be alone. 'I'm going – going to my room. You can bring my coffee up there, please.' She picked up the whisky decanter that had been placed on the bedside table by the water jug. 'This belongs on the sideboard downstairs, surely.'

The man hesitated for a second, affecting to look surprised. Then silently he took it from her, turned and disappeared through the shutters at the end of the verandah.

Rose felt a sense of exquisite relief, like the release of a physical pressure at the base of her skull. Walking into the next room she saw that all was in irreproachable order, her bed made up with her favourite embroidered cover from home, her toilet-boxes set out on the dressing table, her clothes hanging neatly inside the wardrobe. She half-closed her eyes and tried to imagine the biscuit-coloured walls a cool pale blue, with her Botticelli prints where she could see them on waking. Her first impression of this room had been as a nursery. In her mind's eye she had seen the white muslin curtains to keep out the glare, the string bed for the ayah to sleep on behind the screen partition. Now, all she could think of were those photographs of Geoffrey's. Nothing else had driven home so sharply the fact that his real life was a closed book to her. Always, it seemed, she was the outsider, cut off from the thoughts and passions that secretly drove him and made him the person he was.

The last hour had left her exhausted, not just the episode of the bedroom, but the confrontation with Ram Prasad over the garden boy. Wearily she kicked off her shoes again and sank down into an old wicker chair someone had left out on the balcony at the back. A faint scent of sandalwood came from the cushions, making her think of the Arab women who had shared this part of the house. They lived isolated lives, yet managed to be happy, no doubt.

How slowly time seemed to go though, in a place like this. Perhaps it was because one got up so early, while it was still cool. There were a hundred and one things she ought to be doing. Mrs Beattie had sent a note to say she would take her into the Crater bazaar to choose some material for the tailor to make up into some morning dresses – the elaborate cut of English 'summer' outfits made them stifling in this fierce heat. She also had to buy material for curtains. There was Mrs Davies, the medical officer's wife, waiting to hear when she would join the roster of English ladies who handed out milk powder at the infants' clinic in the native quarter. Looming over everything was the thought of hospitality owed. Sometime, somehow, she must organize a Sunday luncheon or a dinner party for the small circle of officials and wives who headed the protocol list, not least, of course, the Rawlinsons themselves. And she still had calling-cards to leave at some of the garrison bungalows.

Yet between these commitments and herself, a dreadful lethargy intervened. It was like being enclosed in a glass bowl. She saw this outside world in clear detail, but it was somehow impossible to break through and become part of it. It was the climate of course. Everyone said one could do nothing at this time of year except lie back and swelter, and try to quench an unending thirst. Yet the Arabs themselves seemed unaffected. Here was the rumble of the camel cart coming up through the gates, bringing the regulation half-dozen barrels of well-water for the day – which meant it was eleven o'clock – the driver and the porters chanting and caterwauling with the energy of madmen. The postman had already been. An exuberant young Somali in a red fez, he had a way of ringing his bicycle bell as he circled the steps until she went out to bid him good morning, an exchange that was inevitably cut short by the appearance of Ram Prasad. The post was a landmark, local mail in red-sealed envelopes, letters from home on mail-boat day. Last week she had been thrilled to have a letter from Cynthia in India, promising a reunion on her way back to England for the hot season. There was also one from David Trevelyan asking her for her first impressions of life in Aden. She really must write back today – but what would she say?

Staring out over the stone balustrade, Rose could hear the chatter of the servants' families in the compound below, the clink of pails as the washerman squatted down to the daily pile of sheets and shirts. Everything beyond the house was perfectly still. The view was like a painted canvas, the dark line of date palms spiking the blue sky, the prayer-flags hanging limply from the mosque and the ochre walls of the town beyond, all varnished over with the unbearable brilliance of the sun.

Lazily, her eyes followed a moving speck along the horizon. Something shimmered against the desert. Slowly it resolved itself into the shape of a green limousine rolling across the furrows of sand towards the border road, a cloud of dust billowing in its wake. The Sultan's Sedanca was making its way from Jehal to the royal palace at Crater. She had seen it go this way before but it was always a startling sight, especially if the green and white standard was flying in front. It gave her an odd little jump of pleasure to think that the Emir might be inside with his father, looking across at the house and perhaps remembering his suggestion of a visit to Jehal.

Today there was no flag. The car disappeared behind the trees. Then to her amazement, it reappeared at the bottom of the drive and turned in through the gates. Her instinct was to run down to the front door. But she made herself stand back and watch as the chauffeur handed a letter to Ram Prasad. There was a brief conversation and the car moved away again.

The five minutes that elapsed before Ram Prasad came upstairs seemed very much longer to Rose. When he put the coffee tray down beside her, she was seated again on the balcony at the back. Languidly she took up the envelope propped against the cup.

'From Jehal. The Emir send by car.' In spite of himself, the bearer sounded impressed.

Even then she waited until he had disappeared before opening it. It was stamped with a green seal in the shape of a turban and inside, the notepaper was of pale green with the insignia of the crossed daggers at the head. In contrast to these splendours came six typewritten lines, the letters blurred and somewhat at a slant. Her presence was requested at lunch the following day, it seemed, after which she was invited to meet the ladies of the Sultan's family for tea. In the bottom left-hand corner there was a signature in a round schoolboy hand: 'Yours sincerely, Hassan Bin Seif.' Over this, Rose pored with special delight. Obviously the Arabic way of writing from right to left was hard to put aside even for an accomplished student of English.

Her friend had not forgotten his promise then. In an instant, languor had fled and she was searching through the wardrobe for her favourite afternoon dress, the rose-printed crêpe-de-chine with suitably flowing sleeves. A stitch in the hem was needed where Nur, the cook's daughter, now enrolled as ayah, had been ironing it with more enthusiasm than delicacy. Only as she bit off the thread did the awful thought strike her. What if Geoffrey raised objections? Moreover, how was she to travel to Jehal? No mention was made in the note of any transport arrangements.

This was, not surprisingly, Geoffrey's first observation as he surveyed the letter over lunch.

'So how are you expected to get there? I notice I have not been included in the invitation.'

'I imagine it's a wives-only affair,' Rose suggested, crumbling the bread on her side plate. The helping of mince and poached egg before her was almost untouched. Under Geoffrey's instructions, so much salt was added to the dishes – 'vital to supplement sweat-loss' – she often found them inedible.

'Damn! And of course it's tomorrow, isn't it? Typical last-minute Arab shambles.' He flung down his napkin. 'I suppose you haven't replied to the thing?'

Ram Prasad moved silently around the table, taking as long as possible to change the plates.

'The car didn't wait. Besides, I had to ask you . . .'

'Damn right, you did. For all I know, it may be completely against official policy for wives to attend such functions.' He drained his pink gin and pushed back his chair. 'There's nothing for it. I shall have to consult the Resident.'

At that moment, the telephone bell rang in the hall, a rasping succession of notes like a broken-down alarm clock. The system had just been installed and connections so far were restricted to a mere half-dozen members of the 'top brass', as Geoffrey called his colleagues. Certainly Rose regarded the instrument as being for official use only, nor would she have thought of approaching it herself. To her surprise, Geoffrey turned from a brief conversation to announce that the call had been from Lady Rawlinson. She saw at once that his mood had changed.

'Apparently she has also been invited to Jehal. Just the two senior wives, I suppose, as there's to be a visit to the harem. She says she will call for you in the Residency gharry at noon. So that solves the problem.'

He consumed his rice pudding in half a dozen gulps. Afterwards, dabbing at his moustache, he glanced across at her sharply.

'Who knows? You might pick up some useful gossip from His Highness.'

'The Sultan or the Emir?' Rose asked.

'The Sultan, of course. The Emir's just a boy, no influence at all.'

'But it seemed to me . . .'

'It seemed to me.' Geoffrey's voice crudely mimicked her own. 'I'm not interested in your opinions, dear girl. I simply want you to listen, ask a few questions if necessary. To put it simply, who would he side with if there's a war, the Turks or the British?' He lit up a cheroot and drew on it briskly. 'It's my opinion he's already plotting with his Muslim friends to make an assault on Aden when the times comes. Jehal is the ideal springboard for an attack on the garrison. The old man's probably resented the British presence ever since they flew the flag over his tinpot little kingdom.'

'But he's in treaty with the British. They've pledged to defend him from any enemy attack. Why should he betray his protectors?'

Geoffrey merely yawned as he stretched himself out on the long-chair on the verandah. 'Niggers stick together, don't you know,' he drawled. 'Blood's thicker than water. And money's thickest of all. I can tell you there are paid-up secret agents of the Turks operating not just in Jehal but in Aden too. If I had my way I'd have a few spies of my own out there, like we did in India.'

Before closing his eyes, he shot another of those sly sideways glances in Rose's direction.

'There are times, though, when a friendly go-between is the best kind of agent of all.'

❧ 9 ❧

'My dear Rose,' Eleanor said laughing, the next day. 'What absolute nonsense! Does he really see us as a couple of government spies?'

Rose laughed with her, the two of them sitting demurely side by side in their flowered dresses at the back of the carriage, as they set off for Jehal. Chiffon scarves tied over their hats and under their chins protected them from the dust. Their parasols kept off the worst of the sun, fringes fluttering in the hot salt breeze. To put up the leather hood of the carriage would have made the heat unendurable.

She had not meant to mention her conversation with Geoffrey, but the implications of it had worried her ever since.

'Perhaps he was joking,' she said, wishing it was so.

Eleanor shook her head. 'I'm afraid Geoffrey is living in India still – all those secret societies and plots against the Government. This is Arabia, remember.' She waved a gauzy arm at the endless succession of sand dunes rolling away on either side of the rough track that constituted a road. 'And this is the heart of Arabia. We call it the Empty Quarter. The Arab name is Rub-al-Qali, Desert of the Flame, altogether more romantic, don't you think?'

'Rub-al-Qali.' Trying out the sound of it, Rose felt again that quickening of the imagination she had experienced in London. She sniffed the dry gunpowdery smell of the desert, looked up to see a hawk drifting high in the blue, and heard his melancholy cry falling through the clear air. The shimmer of the far horizon was like the opening of a giant door, just a crack, but with the promise of another world awaiting her on the other side. Out here, Rose felt she could breathe freely. There were no boundaries to where one might go and what one might find.

She turned to Eleanor. 'It is exciting, isn't it? A different country . . . Exploring . . .' She tried for words, but nothing quite expressed her feelings.

Eleanor pointed to a cluster of huts ahead. A wooden pole, painted red and white, was suspended across the track.

'This is a different country, Rose. From now on we are in Jehal, and only at the invitation of the Sultan.'

She raised her hand to the tribal guard in a green turban who stood back and saluted as the barrier was raised. Once again the driver urged on the bony little horse from his seat in front of them.

'You've been before to Jehal?' Rose asked her.

'Just once, quite a while ago. European women are not often invited. It's something of an accolade.' She looked quizzically at her companion. When she was not smiling, a tiny tracery of white lines fanned out from the corners of her eyes, Rose noticed. However hard they tried to keep out of the sun, the Englishwomen who had spent longest abroad all had this sallowish tinge to their complexions.

'Not a little to do with your youthful charms, I imagine,' Eleanor went on. She put a hand on Rose's arm. 'You'll be careful, though?'

'Careful?'

'Not to get too involved. I mean, we have to remember the line between us and them.'

It sounded as if she was describing some kind of game. She paused, noticing Rose's expression, then tried again.

'All you have to remember is to keep off any political topics. That's where things can get muddled. As for friendship . . .' She looked down at her rings, smoothed out the gloves she was carrying. 'That's surely a thing to be treasured all the world over.'

Rose was trying to concentrate on what her friend was saying. But at the same time she was intently recording in her mind the landmarks of the journey. Under a solitary thorn tree, a huge Ali-Baba water pot had been left in the shade, no doubt to sustain the weary traveller. They passed a procession of camels trailing their loads of green stuff behind them like peacocks' tails. Ahead rose the turreted walls of a desert town, encircled by palms.

'Jehal!' cried the driver, pointing his whip. 'See Jehal!'

The sight of the carriage brought people running from the outlying houses, small rough-built shelters with patterns of leaves and flowers outlined in red and black against the whitewash. The women that stood at the side of the track, calling out to them, were objects of decoration too, dusty headshawls drawn back to show black-rimmed eyes and flashing teeth and the glint of coral and silver ornaments. As Eleanor said, what a pleasure it was to communicate with a smile again, after the veiled faces of Aden.

Now the track widened into a rough road and they were plunged into the town itself. The smell was the first thing that greeted them, and next the flies. It was Port Said all over again, thought Rose. Then there was the noise, the jangle of raised voices, clattering dishes and bleating goats. Along the central lane of the bazaar, the tiny shops and coffee-houses were pressed together like a concertina. Awnings of ragged sack-cloth made a patchwork of shade over every alleyway where people jostled to talk and eat, and buy and sell. In one dark cave Rose caught a glimpse of men weaving bright cloth at a long treadle loom. In another, a fat silversmith squatted amidst a clutter of daggers and swords, looking up in astonishment at the vision of two English ladies under their parasols. They rounded a corner where children were crowded around a sherbet-seller, his barrow laden with jars of lurid green and yellow. Running and whooping they surrounded the carriage, clinging to the doors with small sticky hands until the driver brushed them off with his whip like so many flies. Amidst the excitement, people seemed to pay little attention to the tall elderly man who was striding towards them down the middle of the road, completely naked. He had a dignified air and was singing loudly to himself, looking neither to right or left as he passed them by.

'He is the mad,' said the driver. 'Everyone knows him.'

Rose and Eleanor, both very pink in the face, struggled to regain their composure. Fortunately, there ahead of them was the palace, eclipsing every other impression. Privately, Rose had imagined domes and minarets and doors of bronze, in the style of Omar Khayyam. Instead, she saw a large cream-painted edifice that resembled nothing so much as a high-class Victorian seaside hotel. From the topmost gable a flag with the royal crest gave formal notice that the Sultan was in residence.

All at once Rose felt extremely nervous. She still had a vivid recollection of the haughty figure, withdrawn into his corner of the car, after the Birthday Parade. How did one behave as a guest in his kingdom? Her knowledge of Muslim etiquette was still sketchy in the extreme.

'Don't worry!' Eleanor patted her hand. She had a way of reading one's thoughts that could be disconcerting. 'Just watch me. And when in doubt, just keep quiet and smile.'

From then on, Rose's impressions seemed to gather speed, blurring and overlapping just when she was striving hardest to commit to memory everything that happened. One minute they were being welcomed on the steps by a stout and charming gentleman with long black moustaches, who spoke excellent English. The next, she and Eleanor were alone again in a lofty salon lined with velvet divans. To set foot on the exquisite Persian carpets seemed to be a sacrilege. Rose found herself walking round them, as if she were keeping off the grass in an English park. Texts in Arabic, embroidered in scarlet and green, hung from the walls. But her attention was diverted by the sight of the little gold lectern by the window. On it rested a book with a silver clasp, brilliantly bound in lacquer and jade. Perhaps it was some kind of visitors' book? Without pausing to think Rose put out her hand to open it – she was still wearing her gloves, of course – when a voice from the door made her stop.

'Please forgive the delay!'

Rose turned to see someone she took at first to be a servant, despite the excellent accent. Then with a shock she recognized the Emir Hassan, wearing the kind of clothes she had never seen him in before, a faded khaki shirt tucked into a tribal kilt of bright checked cotton. His legs were bare, shiny brown and muscular, with a pair of old sandals on his feet. Only the turban was familiar, green silk with one end trailing on his shoulder, the other twisted in the usual dashing cockade at the back of his head. She realized suddenly how young he was. It made her feel ill at ease somehow, to be in her dignified memsahib's disguise.

'Welcome to Jehal.'

He bowed to them in turn, then walked to where Rose was standing. Behind his smile, she sensed a curious tension.

'I see you have found the most important item in the palace.' He looked down at the book on the stand. 'Our family Koran. It came from the court of the Emperor Suleiman. So it is almost four hundred years old.'

'It's very beautiful,' said Eleanor.

'I'm only sorry you may not examine it. It is forbidden for any but a Muslim to touch it – something sacred, you see.' He was looking at Rose now, intently, as if willing her not be offended. 'You do understand?'

'Of course, Your Highness.' She heard her voice tremble. Blood rushed to her face. It was as if she had stepped back from a precipice.

'Hassan, please.' He turned to Eleanor with his usual shy grace. 'Lady Rawlinson, it is too long since your last visit.'

'It is a great pleasure to be here again, Your Highness.'

There was a pause. Then he clapped his hands and laughed. The moment of tension was gone. 'But that's enough of ceremony. Today is a holiday for me, and we are to have a picnic lunch. That's why I am in my Bedouin clothes.' He led the way through the door. 'There's so much to show you.'

Hassan's spirit of enjoyment was infectious. Rose and Eleanor exchanged looks of relief as they followed him on a tour of the ground-floor rooms. Along the main corridor smiling servants watched and waited in the doorways. On the walls hung ceremonial swords and banners and a series of life-size portraits that were obviously touched-up sepia photographs.

'Painting a human likeness is not allowed in the Muslim religion, as you probably know. But my father decided that the camera was different, so he had these enlargements made of everything he could, just a few years ago.'

The stern, bearded figures of nineteenth-century rulers in their robes and frock-coats reminded Rose of family photographs at home in Wales. At the end of the gallery she noticed the picture of a very small boy in the unlikely costume of Little Lord Fauntleroy, complete with lace collar and velvet cap. She couldn't help smiling, for she guessed already who it was.

'I was in London with my father for the Diamond Jubilee of Queen Victoria,' he told her. 'I was not allowed to attend the state ceremonies, of course. But I remember the crowds and the shops, and dressing up in all those funny clothes when the photographer came to the hotel.' He laughed.

'How old were you?'

'Just three.' His eyes were teasing. 'I believe you are calculating my age, Mrs Chetwynd?'

Rose had already done so and found it to be twenty. The fact that he was only two years older than she was gave her confidence again.

'Please call me Rose,' she said, impulsively. 'It's only fair.'

For a moment, it was as if the two of them were alone and somewhere else, the smile that passed between them seemed to hold them so fast. She had to make an effort to remember Eleanor standing just behind, looking, as ever, politely interested but with that tuck at the corner of her mouth that Rose called her 'Excellency expression'. Rose felt it was a warning signal, as if she were dangerously close to crossing that mysterious line between 'us' and 'them'.

'This is your English room, Your Highness, I seem to remember,' Eleanor said, moving on to the next doorway.

'You are right, Lady Rawlinson. And I want you to see my father's latest acquisitions.'

The Emir was all attention again, leading the way into a large salon that seemed to belong to another order of things altogether. Against the walls, huge sideboards of fumed oak were arrayed with silver sporting trophies and serving dishes. Plush sofas, the size of small elephants, were herded together around a black marble mantelpiece. The ornate brass fireplace below seemed to be purely decorative, with no sign of a chimney, Rose noticed. Plush chairs, with lace antimacassars, were flanked by the kind of pedestal side-tables favoured by Rose's mother. A forbidding glass bookcase was crammed with encyclopedias and leather-bound reference sets which had obviously never been opened. Strangest of all was the Turkish-patterned linoleum which gleamed across the entire floor.

'My father liked the design. Said it was so much more hygienic than carpets.'

They all laughed. On either side of the long windows, with the view of the desert beyond, hung two very dark oil-paintings of parklands and deer. Once again Rose had the impression of some never-never England lovingly enshrined in the Arab imagination.

'The Sultan ordered everything from Harrods, the whole lot, when he was last in London,' Hassan told them. 'It was the Coronation of King George. I was in Cairo at university, of course.' He glanced up wryly at the picture of His Majesty over the fireplace. 'Not really my taste, I'm afraid.' Then, turning quickly to Eleanor, 'No disrespect to the King, of course. I mean the whole room.'

'Of course,' Eleanor smiled. 'It's not a very good portrait, is it?'

He went over to the French windows. Waiting outside, a servant bowed and opened them, and Hassan ushered them on to the terrace.

'Remember, we are having a picnic. We can walk to the gardens this way.'

Outside the scent of jasmine and white canna lilies in tall stone jars flooded towards them in the hot sun. Rose looked up at the wing of the palace that ran alongside. The top storey was fronted by a screen trellis and behind it she thought she could detect movement here and there, faint sounds like the twittering of an aviary.

'The harem is watching us,' Hassan said in a low voice. He glanced up with an indulgent shrug. 'Whenever I have visitors I am instructed to bring them out on the terrace so that they can have a jolly good look.'

Rose felt a qualm of guilt. How they must hate to see her walking freely with an uncovered face. She was also consumed by curiosity.

'I thought the women of these parts went about unveiled?'

'The ordinary people, yes. The upper classes never.'

'And these ladies are your family? Your mother, sisters . . .' She hesitated. 'Your wife?'

He threw up his hands in mock alarm. 'No wife! Not yet!' He hurried them on. 'Anyway, you will be meeting them after lunch. But now my father is waiting.'

Rose had almost forgotten about the Sultan. The thought of confronting him made her nervous again, so that she barely noticed the gardens – bougainvillea, shaded paths, a banana plantation. They came to some tall palms. The Emir stopped, held out his hand for a rifle from the attendant trotting behind, and took aim into the branches. The next minute a bunch of green coconuts came cascading down into the bushes.

'Good to drink when one is hot,' said Hassan, slashing the top off the largest with the dagger from his belt. He passed it to Lady Rawlinson, who took a token sip, and then to Rose. She was unprepared for the way the sweet colourless liquid gushed out in all directions when she tilted it to her lips.

'Absolute dynamite if you're not used to it,' Eleanor murmured in her ear, dabbing at Rose's dress with her handkerchief. 'No handy thunder-box here, either.'

The Emir was strolling ahead, his rifle hitched casually across his shoulders. He had taken off his turban and tossed it to one of the servants, like a schoolboy getting rid of his cap. Now he turned round and waited in the shade for Rose as she followed a few paces in front of Lady Rawlinson. He was staring at her with a sudden intentness. Bronze against the green of the leaves, the wide vivid face with its Tartar cheekbones and heavy-lidded eyes printed itself on her mind as something rare and precious. She could feel the moment branded on her, almost like a burn. As he looked at her, Rose knew she too had been recorded in the same flash, her hat in her hand, fanning herself, caught in the stillness. A radiance hummed between them, dazzling the mind. Everything else was blotted out. Only a second had gone by.

'Oh look! The tennis court,' Eleanor called out, and the moment was over. Yet everything was changed. Walking past him down the path, Rose felt the air between them tremble.

'Rose,' he said in a low voice. The tone of it was urgent and astonished.

She bent her head and walked on, feeling the servants' eyes upon them. There in the clearing was indeed a tennis court, somewhat overgrown, shadowed by tall mango trees with the fruit upon them turning from green to rose. Two small boys were knocking a ball across the ragged net. Seeing the Emir, they came running across, shouting in Arabic.

'These are my nephews,' Hassan said. 'Abdul and Wadia.' But his eyes were still on Rose with such a look of joy she was frightened. The boys shook hands politely, first with Lady Rawlinson and then with her. Rose was aware of the huge effort she must make to remember her role in the world of appearances, especially now when everything she did as a stranger was under scrutiny.

'There is my father.' Now Hassan was playing his part again too, leading them towards the Sultan.

It was an unlikely setting for the paramount ruler of Southern Arabia, a cross between an English summerhouse and a village cricket pavilion. Seated tailor-fashion in the entrance was the bearded figure Rose remembered so well. This time he was wearing a high-buttoned jacket of cream linen and a kilt like the Emir's, mysteriously transformed from Eastern potentate to rural squire.

At the sight of the English ladies, he unfolded himself in a single supple movement. As he stood tall and straight-backed to greet them, Rose realized he was not an old man at all, merely middle-aged.

'*Ahlan wa sahlan!* Welcome to Jehal! Lady Rawlinson, it is an honour that you visit us again. Mrs Chetwynd I also know.'

Rose felt herself swiftly scrutinized, before the Sultan's gaze was hooded again. Half a dozen courtiers stood behind in a semicircle, grizzled men in bright turbans, hands on the daggers at their belts. Rose

88

now recognized this as the kind of casual stance an Englishman adopts when he puts his hands in his pockets. There too, smiling broadly, was the moustached person in the long white robe, the Vizier who had greeted them on their arrival.

They had been playing a game, the Sultan explained in his slow guttural English. He indicated the board on the ground with its stack of counters. These had to be directed into each corner. He laughed. There were many rules, but it was more restful than tennis.

'My father did try to play once or twice with our English guests,' Hassan murmured. 'But he thought it was like cricket, and all you had to do was hit the ball as hard as possible.'

'We ran to fetch the balls,' piped the smaller of the nephews, grinning. 'We ran very far. We got too tired.'

The Sultan gave him a playful pinch on the neck.

'You play tennis, Mrs Chetwynd?'

'A – a little, Your Highness.'

'The next time, you and Lady Rawlinson will play and we will watch. And billiards?' he went on, unexpectedly.

'Billiards?' Rose repeated, startled.

'Hassan did not show you my billiard room?'

This, it emerged, was the amenity of which His Highness was most proud. But there were other Western-style innovations, one of them in this very garden.

'Just a short walk,' explained the Vizier, as they all followed the Sultan in procession further along the path. Rose and Eleanor were now rather thirsty and very hot. There was no sign of the picnic site. The low whitewashed dome just ahead looked more like an ancestral tomb, or a private mosque perhaps.

The Sultan had stopped at the entrance.

'Waterworks,' he announced with pride. He pushed open the door and waved his hand at the tangle of pipes and cisterns within. 'At Jehal we have oasis. We have wells. Now Petro brings the water to us.'

'Petrovich' was an engineer, it seemed, a Russian Jew who, fleeing the Revolution, had travelled the Arabian peninsula and finally made his home with the Sultan. Alas, today he was in Aden.

'But you will hear his music,' His Highness added mysteriously.

At that moment, as if by magic, there came through the trees the sound of – could it be? – a small orchestra, brass and strings, playing something that sounded decidedly like 'The Blue Danube'.

'It is our band,' Hassan told them, smiling at the visitors' disbelieving faces. 'The Jehal Royal Band. Petrovich is a great musician. He brought his violin with him, collected together all kinds of other instruments from the army in Aden, and taught the Bedouin how to play. He writes his own music too. There is even a Jehal national anthem.'

The Sultan was leading the way through the date palms. In a clearing there came into view the kind of transformation scene that reminded Rose of a very superior pantomime. The genie had rubbed his lamp and there, amid the oleanders and the bougainvillea, was an elaborate alfresco dining salon. Turkish carpets covered the grass and in the centre stood a large table with a white damask cloth. Silver and crystal twinkled among banks of pink roses. Behind the Chippendale chairs stood a small regiment of palace servants in their white tunics and green silk turbans and cummerbunds. From the charcoal braziers in the far corner rose the scent of meat cooking. A blue haze of smoke shimmered like a mirage. And there under a large acacia tree was the band, twelve or more tribal guards, splendid in tarbushes and gold braid. At the sight of the Sultan, they rose to their feet and broke into a march. With the rousing crescendo of bugle and drum-roll, Rose felt transported to tsarist St Petersburg.

'I think it's the national anthem,' Eleanor murmured in her ear. Everyone else stood quite still except for a white gazelle with a red ribbon round its neck that had wandered in from the neighbouring paddock. The last note died away and the Negro butler struck three times on a large brass gong. The Sultan turned to his guests.

'Welcome to our picnic. It is informal, so please excuse.'

Rose and Eleanor exchanged smiles of childish delight as they took their seats on either side of him. Hassan was placed at the other end, hedged in by courtiers and companions who seemed to have grown in number since they had arrived at the gardens. She saw he was observing her with that quick glance beneath lowered lids that struck at her heart. At the same time, he continued talking to those around him. When the food was put upon the table, all conversation ceased. The cutlery was left to the ladies. Brown fingers dived into the bowls of yellow rice and lamb glazed with honey. On Rose's left, the Sultan's Vizier, whose name was Abdullah, delicately tore off the breast of a small fowl and laid it on her plate.

'Sand-grouse,' he said. 'The Emir shot them himself this morning. He was determined you should have them on your first visit.'

'It's good,' Rose replied truthfully. She was very hungry and all the food tasted marvellous, spicy and strange. Glasses of iced mango juice appeared while bamboo fans, wielded by the servants, wafted the flies away. When the dessert arrived, the choicest bunch of grapes was presented to her by her neighbour.

'I am a mother bird,' he said, laughing. But his glistening black eyes were serious. 'I am glad you have become acquainted with the Emir. Like

90

him I have lived in Egypt, and returning to life at the palace is not easy. He is in need of good English friends.'

'I am glad too,' Rose said, uncertain how else to respond.

'And I hear you like horses?' he went on.

'I do indeed.'

'Then we shall arrange some riding for you. The Sultan's stables are the best in South Arabia.' He beamed at her, mopping his plump face with a red silk handkerchief. 'And I am the best rider. I myself taught Hassan how to ride. But today there is no time.'

He indicated the two small boys sitting cross-legged under the oleander hedge. 'They are waiting to take you to the harem.'

'Just one hour,' Hassan called to the ladies. 'All that gossiping and you will be exhausted.'

He yawned and stretched in his chair like a cat.

'Don't you envy us?' He indicated the rugs laid out in the shade, the brass hookah alongside. 'Now we shall sleep.'

❧ 10 ❧

SOMEHOW Rose found it ridiculously hard to leave. It was like breaking a spell to step out of that circle where Hassan's presence was so disturbingly strong. As they followed their escorts down the path, she turned to look back for a second. She caught a glimpse of him lying against some cushions, his head propped in his hand, and knew his eyes were also on her.

'Oh, to sleep,' she heard Eleanor say, as from a distance. 'It's so hot.'

Rose searched her mind for a suitable response.

'Imagine sinking into a cool bath.' She tugged at the damp sleeves of her dress. 'Isn't that what they do in harems?' she went on rapidly. 'Bathe you in asses' milk?'

'Only in the *Arabian Nights*. Nothing like that at Jehal.'

They were passing beneath the trellised wing of the palace. This time, instead of a low twittering sound, they heard a swelling tide of ululation from the women inside. It had an exuberance about it that aroused Rose strangely. It expressed everything she felt about that unspoken exchange in the garden. It was so powerful and so mysterious, and yet it only acknowledged the secret bond that had been there right from the start.

Under an archway at the back of the house, the boys stopped. One of them pulled twice at a frayed bell-rope.

'The women stay here,' he said importantly. 'They will come for you.'

There was the sound of bolts being pulled back and the door was opened a few inches. The boys saluted and fled. The next minute the two women were drawn inside by unseen hands. There was very little light and a strong scent of sandalwood. A veil flicked past Rose's cheek with a bat's-wing touch and, out of the soft jostling, came a high-pitched squeaking and gabbling. Then a lamp appeared.

Looking up, Rose saw the whole staircase lined with women leaning over the balustrade, laughing, clapping, beckoning, while the trilling rose and fell.

'These are the family slaves, the serving women,' Eleanor whispered, holding Rose tightly by the arm. 'They want us to go up.'

A young girl in a red shawl took Rose by the hand, another seized Eleanor and together they were swept up the stairs. At the top Rose fully expected to see a large Nubian, guarding the inner door with drawn sword. Instead, there was a kind of nursery gate, such as Rose remembered as a child placed to prevent her from falling down the stairs. Two large black eyes peered over at her, and the jam-stained mouth of a very small boy smiled uncertainly down at the strangers. A wail was cut short as the infant was swung aside by a pair of female arms. The gate was opened and Rose and Eleanor were ushered inside.

The change of atmosphere was startling. They were in a long, lofty room with a great deal of glass and gilt and brocade, but impersonal, rather like the reception hall of a grand hotel. Upright sofas lined the walls and on the sofas, swathed in rainbow colours, were seated some twenty or so ladies, poised to inspect the visitors.

Could they all be the Sultan's family, Rose wondered, as a tall handsome woman came forward. She was smiling, but it was hard to see behind the smoked glasses she was wearing.

'I am Nabiha. My English is best so I make introductions.'

The words mother, cousin, sister, aunt, bobbing up in a sea of Arabic, meant that they were indeed all family. It was a strange sensation to have one's hand taken in soft, henna-painted fingers and gracefully sniffed at in the customary style of greeting. The faces of the older women, tightly framed in folds of silk, were as formal as icons. The younger ones reminded Rose of the girls in Egyptian frescoes with their plaited manes of black hair twisted through with amber and silver beads. The scrutiny of kohl-encircled eyes in pale powdered faces was so intense as to be unnerving. Rose felt some of her confidence ebbing away, especially when a formidable person in a black Chaucerian wimple beckoned her to sit beside her. Silver keys jingled from a cord at her waist. Her face, under the fat, had Hassan's cheekbones and slanting brows, or so it seemed to Rose when she was told that this was the Sultan's wife. Fingering Rose's rings, she fired off a series of questions in Arabic. Others followed suit, as Nabiha translated.

'Where is your husband?'

'How many children?'

'The Queen Mary, do you know her?'

Excitement mounted. Tattered copies of English fashion magazines were produced from under the cushions. Did Englishwomen always wear such strange garments under their clothes, one of them demanded to know, pointing at a corset advertisement.

From the other side of the room, Eleanor came to the rescue.

'Dear Nabiha, honoured Sultan's lady. Might we have dancing, like last time?'

Shrieks of gaiety greeted the idea, as if it was totally novel. From the servants' corner, tiny drums were produced and a tambourine. Clapping and singing, they called to the Sultan's wife to begin. After a moment, with smiling dignity, she took the floor, hand in hand with an exquisite doll-like creature of about fourteen or fifteen, and they glided to and fro in a slow minuet.

'She is Miriam, the cousin of the Emir Hassan,' Nabiha told them. 'Next year, they are to be married.'

As Nabiha spoke, the girl came fluttering past and, seizing Rose by the hand, drew her into the dance. Laughing and protesting, Rose succumbed. The queer jolt she had felt at Nabiha's words died away. Inches away from her, Miriam's eyes held hers, alight with pleasure and curiosity, as the circle of women pressed around them, beating time and urging them on. Now everyone was dancing, Eleanor too, and the room that had been so still was a whirling kaleidoscope, as the drums throbbed louder and the song wound up and down, round and round, like a snake with no end.

'I have to sit down,' gasped Rose. 'I am quite dizzy.'

Together, she and Eleanor collapsed on to the cushioned divans on the verandah and were surrounded once again by the women. Even the Sultan's wife was breathless, fanning herself as she gave orders, shaking out her long plait of hair, which was not grey, Rose noticed, but a brilliant red. Tea was produced, together with a large tin of Huntley and Palmer biscuits and a Dundee cake.

'London tea,' said the girl who was to be Hassan's wife. She giggled. They were her only words of English. Then proudly she held out a large emerald ring for Rose to admire.

'She is lucky,' Nabiha said. 'She can see the man she will marry, because they are same family. They cannot be alone, of course, but it is better than being given a husband you have never set eyes on. Purdah.' She laughed. 'It will change.'

'Except for you, Nabiha,' Eleanor said. 'Are you still being brave, going out with your husband without the veil?'

'I try,' said Nabiha, with a shrug. 'Like you in England, asking to get the vote.' She had taken off her glasses – 'from Egypt, my eyes get sore in hot weather' – and was surveying Rose thoughtfully.

'You are a very beautiful girl. Something different, eh, Lady Rawlinson?'

'Rose is very young,' Eleanor said carefully.

'You may be lonely at your house,' Nabiha went on. 'I live not far away. Perhaps you will visit me sometimes.'

'Thank you. I would love to.'

To be like the others, Rose had slipped off her shoes. How pleasant and relaxed everything now was. The world of men was far away. Hassan's mother had brought out an embroidery frame and was peacefully stitching away at a hideous pattern of pink and orange flowers. For a moment Rose was reminded of her mother's Women's Institute circle at home, as the sweetmeats were passed around and the cups clattered away. She felt almost drowsy. But Eleanor's hand was on her arm.

'Could we perhaps. . . ?' she was asking Nabiha. 'Is there. . . ?'

'Of course. I will take you.'

Escorted down the corridor, they were shown into a bathroom. This was surely the showpiece of the Sultan's modernization schemes. Bath, washstand and lavatory were all of gleaming marble. None of the brass taps, however, seemed to produce any water. Further investigation revealed that the elaborate network of pipes was for surface decoration only. The plumbing system devised by Petrovich had yet to penetrate this part of the palace, it seemed.

Within seconds, however, there was a knock at the door. A serving girl appeared carrying a ewer and jug in blue-patterned china. The water inside was cool and rose-scented, the towels still bearing their Harrods labels. And then, behind a curtain, they discovered the usual hole in the floor, which was a relief to both of them.

Eleanor looked at her watch. 'It's over an hour. We must go down.'

Rose was standing at the mirror, dabbing her wrists with perfume from one of an array of large glass bottles. Her dress was looking distinctly limp, still spotted here and there with coconut milk. She remembered she had brought in her bag the silk shawl given her by Hassan. She unfolded it and tucked it around the neckline. The silvery turquoise colour at once lit up her eyes. A secret happiness flowed through her. In just a few minutes she would see Hassan again.

Following Eleanor back through the salon, saying goodbye to the ladies, Rose was aware of new interest.

'They are saying the Arab style suits you well,' Nabiha said. She took Rose by the arm affectionately.

It was given to me by the Emir, she was about to tell her. But something stopped her. Perhaps it had been recognized already, though nothing was said. Amidst the smiles and handshakes of farewell, the promises to return soon, she came face to face with Miriam. The girl's gaze fixed on the shawl. As if in admiration, she reached out to finger the gold fringe. Then she looked up at Rose with a flash of furious brilliance in her eyes. The challenge of it was so naked and so intimate that Rose flinched. But it only lasted a second. The young nephew was plucking at her sleeve, telling them they must hurry, the Sultan was waiting.

Eleanor had noticed nothing.

'You were a huge success,' she chattered, as they hurried in the wake of their guide along some inner corridor. 'Nabiha took to you especially. Charming woman, and highly intelligent. Her husband is a Persian, very good family, banking and business. She will be a useful friend, such a help at purdah parties.'

Once again, Rose was about to speak, to confide something of her emotional turmoil – a mixture of bewilderment, elation and fear. But it would all sound too silly. Even in her own mind, nothing was clear except an overriding picture of Hassan. More then anything else, she wanted to be near him again, watching his face, waiting to hear the change in his voice as he spoke to her. The power of this secret compulsion was so strong that when she caught sight of him waiting with the others, she felt almost faint.

It was a great shame the visit must be so short, the Sultan was telling them both, but the car was waiting. Once darkness had fallen, it was a danger to drive across the desert. From the balcony where they were standing, he waved his hand at the lowering sun, then turned to Eleanor.

'Lady Rawlinson, I have not asked about your husband. I wonder if I might visit him very soon? There is the urgent matter of the Turkish border to discuss. They seem to be on the move, bringing up soldiers . . .'

He led the way to the stairs, with a gracious gesture to Eleanor to accompany him. The Vizier Abdullah and the rest of the party ceremoniously followed in their wake.

For Rose, all her senses had become concentrated on the corner of the balcony where she and Hassan were now suddenly alone. The sky beyond the arched wall was a luminous green. Against it, Hassan's face in profile shone like the face on a coin, antique and remote. There was a space between them as they stood side by side, looking out at the long shadows of the palace towers on the sand.

'Rose.' Once again there was that note of wonder in his voice, which had dropped to a whisper. 'What are we to do?'

He was willing her to turn towards him. But she was looking down at her hands, lying so close to his on the warm stone. He was looking down too. The movement he made, linking his little finger with hers, was so fractional and so tentative she could hardly believe the violence of feeling it unleashed in her.

'You mustn't,' she said. Her heart was knocking almost painfully.

'But you know it, don't you? Don't you?'

His voice was harsh now, full of urgency. Both were aware of the minutes racing away, the others waiting below. He took her hand in his tightly.

'Tell me. You must.'

'Yes,' she replied, so quietly it was little more than a breath. 'I know it.'

Quickly he turned her hand over and kissed the pulse-line between the wrist and palm. The vulnerability of his dark head bent in front of her pierced her strangely. There was the sound of a servant moving about inside. In the fading light, the lamps of the car came winking towards the palace doorway below. Rose stepped back.

'No more, ever again. It's madness.'

Clumsy with shock, she hurried towards the staircase, pulling the shawl around her shoulders. Behind her, he touched the silk on her neck.

'Mine,' he said, with such tenderness she felt tears springing.

From below, a voice called out in Arabic. There was an instant in which to compose herself as she walked down into the hallway.

'The sunset at Jehal is so much more beautiful than Aden,' she told Abdullah, surprised at her own resourcefulness.

The Sultan was still deep in conversation with Eleanor. He smiled at her. 'You have seen everything then, the old and the new. And one more thing!' He pointed to the telephone. 'Even the voice that speaks on the wire.'

'At first, my father would not have it,' Hassan told them teasingly. 'He thought it might bring the voice of the devil into the house. But then Abdullah suggested the Imam of Jehal should speak a prayer into it first, to make it clean. Now he is satisfied. Yes, father?'

Everyone smiled, but the Sultan preserved his dignified expression.

'You also have one of these machines?' he asked Rose.

'Yes, we do. But it is really for my husband . . .' Her voice faltered. Hassan's eyes were on her, his face alight.

'Next time, I can deliver my invitation in my own voice then,' he said. 'If you will permit.'

'I think that young man has a crush on you,' said Eleanor, as the car turned into the drive. She tucked a wrap around their knees. A cool breeze had sprung up. 'He couldn't stop looking at you.'

Before Rose could reply, the car shuddered to a halt. The driver pointed to the verandah. Hassan had vaulted over the rails and was running towards them. He was carrying a large bunch of flowers, two bunches in fact.

'The servant forgot to give them to you. I had them picked specially.'

He pushed them into their laps. Rose was nearest the door, and she felt his warm breath on her cheek.

'Jasmine from Jehal – and roses, for Rose.'

'What did I tell you?' Eleanor murmured, as they drove on again. She wore the same expression Rose had seen on Abdullah's face, a fondness mingled with apprehension. In the dusk, it was like the shadow of something that lay ahead, as yet unseen, the first small cloud of a gathering storm.

PART TWO

Hassan

1

LOOKING back years later, it would be easy to recognize one particular day as the turning-point. The strange thing was, Rose knew it at the time, even before anything special had happened to mark it out. That sense of being moved along by events outside her control was unmistakeable.

Of course, Race Day was a landmark in itself. Next to the King's Birthday it was the chief event in the Aden social calendar. For weeks beforehand, Rose had heard it discussed with a passionate intensity. Which owners would be riding? What hat were you wearing? Who was lunching with who beforehand? The race parties were evidently more important than the actual races.

'I have sent an invitation to the Emir.'

Geoffrey's announcement came out of the blue as she sat out on the verandah after dinner one evening, playing patience in the lamplight. He stood in the doorway smoking, a file of papers in his hand.

'The Emir?' Rose put a card down carefully, not looking at his face.

'The Sultan is going with the Residency party. It seemed appropriate that the Emir should come with us. After all, we do owe him hospitality, in case you'd forgotten your visit to Jehal.'

That was a whole week ago, Rose wanted to say, another time and another place, something locked away now for ever.

'I thought you didn't much enjoy Arab company.'

'I don't. But apparently the Races is one of those occasions when we all intermingle.' He underlined the word mockingly. 'Besides, as I told you before, this particular friendship could be useful. Especially the way things are going.'

What things, she was about to ask? But Geoffrey was giving instructions.

'So drop a card to the Beatties and get them to come. Richard and I will be riding together in the owners' race anyway. That Greek chap – Athenas or whatever – he might help to break the ice.' He slapped the papers against his leg irritably. 'And for God's sake get the cook to put on something a bit more presentable than his eternal beef stew. The fellow could do with a boot up the backside, the way he slacks around the place.'

The next morning, the telephone rang. As usual, Ram Prasad went to

101

answer it. She heard a note of deference in his voice, unpleasantly false, and knew at once who was at the other end.

'Sahib is out at office, sir,' she heard him say.

Standing against the landing banisters, directly above the hall, she willed herself not to move.

'Can take message, sir?'

There was another pause. Rose felt sweat springing under her cotton dressing-gown. All at once, she walked downstairs as if in her sleep, without being aware that she had changed her mind.

'Wait please,' Ram Prasad said reluctantly. 'Memsahib is here.'

She flinched as she took the receiver, which was damp from his grasp. The man remained just a few feet away, half-smiling, his protuberant eyes still fixed on hers.

'That is all, Ram Prasad,' she said in an undertone.

She waited while he turned and padded out on to the verandah. From the instrument came Hassan's voice, as close as if he were standing beside her.

'Mrs Chetwynd? Rose?'

'This is Mrs Chetwynd.'

'Rose, is it really you?' She heard him swallow. 'You sound so – so very formal. Is anything the matter? I have been so longing for a chance to talk. I have thought of nothing else.'

'That is very charming,' she began, but found it difficult to continue. Something had given way in her at the intimacy of that voice in her ear. She felt it vibrate against her skin like a bee in a flower. What a treacherous invention the telephone was, she thought, as she heard him murmur again.

'Just to speak to you, Rose.'

Her eyes were on the doors leading on to the verandah, folded back now to admit a breeze. Something flickered against the glass, the reflection of Ram Prasad's shirt. Her heart jumped painfully.

'I expect you are telephoning about the lunch party, Your Highness,' she heard herself say.

'Rose, I have been trying to get through to you every day since we parted.'

'I'm afraid I have been out a great deal.' It was true. The first morning had been the worst. Ram Prasad had been out, and she had shut herself into the bathroom so that she would not hear the bell ringing on and on. After that, she had made herself as busy as possible, helping at the milk clinic, shopping in the bazaar, learning mah-jongg with the wife of the French Consul.

'Twice I left a message with your bearer,' Hassan went on.

Rose's heart contracted again, this time in anger.

'I was very careful. I asked for either you or your husband. Did the servant not tell you?'

'No. But it is probably the best thing,' she said in an expressionless voice. She was tracing with her finger a spiral pattern in the gritty sprinkling of sand that had drifted through the shutters on to the table.

'In just three days I shall see you, Rose. I'm coming to lunch, remember. Can you really pretend you don't care?'

There was a pause. Rose said nothing.

'Oh, and Abdullah will be with me. The invitation said my ADC might accompany me.' He laughed. 'Your military husband imagines that even in Arabia we have such things. Tell him I bring the Vizier Abdullah Bin Fahzi, a descendant of the Prophet like myself.' Another silence. 'I'm only joking, you know. Do you like racing?'

'It sounds – exciting,' she said stiffly.

'I shall be riding myself, in the owners' race. His voice dropped to a whisper. 'Do you want me to win for you?'

Rose's eyes were fixed on the door. Once again the reflection moved.

'We expect you on Saturday then, Your Highness, about noon. My husband will be delighted you can join us. Until then . . .'

Replacing the receiver, Rose moved quickly across to the verandah.

'Why are you spying on me?'

Ram Prasad was slipping away, spider-like, along the passageway. He turned with a reproachful expression, a dusting cloth in his hand.

'Spying, memsahib? I not understand.'

'And why do you not give me the message from the Emir?'

He shrugged his shoulders. 'Message is for sahib. I tell the Emir to talk to the office. These people are not to trouble the sahib at his home.'

Rose felt her throat tighten with a helpless fury. She pulled her robe closer around her as she saw the boy Saleh appear at the far end of the verandah with some papers in his hand. Geoffrey seemed to have adopted him as an interpreter these days. He said it was a crime to waste an educated youth on garden work. He had even bought him a tunic and *futah* to wear, like a government clerk, and two or three times a week the young man sat with him in his study, giving him lessons in Arabic. Apparently the Resident had insisted that his new Political Advisor must learn the basics of the language as soon as possible.

Although the young man was always perfectly polite in his manner with Rose, she could not pretend she liked him. There was a softness about him that was at the same time threatening. His astonishing good looks had a strangely feminine quality which aroused in her a kind of resentment that sometimes felt like jealousy. Rose did not analyse these feelings, but

103

they had a disturbing effect on her. Even now, as he stood before her waiting to speak, there was a faint musky perfume about him that irritated her senses beyond reason.

'*Khatun.*'

'What is it, Saleh?' His manner of addressing her with the Arabic 'lady', rather than the usual 'memsahib', seemed to detach him subtly from the servant class.

'You have His Highness coming to your party, sahib say. I may be of help in the conversation.'

'There is no need, Saleh, thank you. The Emir and his minister speak excellent English.'

The heavy eyelids, rimmed in kohl, were delicately lowered. 'Chetwynd *sidi* say to stay near in case of need.' He smiled slyly. 'Something may be said by the guests in their own language that they do not wish Government to hear.'

Rose saw Ram Prasad nod approvingly. It seemed the matter had already been decided.

When Saturday came it was the presence of Saleh that unnerved her more than anything else. It was as if he alone could see through the immense efforts she had to make to appear calm and detached. On the arrival of the Emir, Geoffrey was at the door to meet him. Inside the hall, Rose extended the formal hand of the hostess. As Hassan took it, she felt a quick secret pressure that seemed to run through her whole body. She looked away and stepped back murmuring a few words of welcome, and found Saleh at her elbow smiling.

To her embarrassment he ducked down to make the traditional greeting of subject to ruler, taking the Emir's right hand and kissing his knee. Then he performed the same ritual with Abdullah who followed behind. Finally, with a flourish, he took Hassan's silver-topped cane, placed it in the stand, and took up his post seated cross-legged in the verandah doorway.

'Who is this fellow?' Abdullah asked Rose in an undertone.

'He came as a gardener. Now he is more a secretary – Geoffrey's assistant really.'

She saw Hassan and Abdullah exchange a look that she did not understand. Then they went forward to meet the Beatties and Athenas. The usual kind of Aden chatter began, stilted at first, with the punkah creaking overhead and the Europeans on their guard. Soon Hassan was making them laugh with an account of his training sessions with his new mare, bought from the Hadramaut Sultan.

'She is a handful, but she is beautiful,' he said, his face alight. He held up his hand with thumb and forefinger delicately poised together in a gesture of perfection. 'I call her Azziza. I will ride her today.'

As he talked, Rose studied his appearance in snatched glances, meanwhile carrying on a conversation with Maud Beattie as to the importance of comfortable shoes for sporting events. How dark he looked today, how alien, amidst the flowered cretonne and Constable prints of her drawing-room. His gold-embroidered *abba* almost hid his English linen suit. In profile, framed in a cream and gold turban, the line of the face was Pharaoh-like with its flared nose, full lips and slanted eye. For a moment it seemed impossible that she had ever been close to this ornate stranger with his hidden life of Islamic ritual – the daily prayers and the Ramadan fasting, the shadowy secrets of the divan and the harem. She felt overcome by the extreme incongruity of his presence in her life, and hers in his. Even friendship between them must be an illusion, a mirage that had no basis in reality for either of them.

Meanwhile she must see what was happening to lunch. As she passed him to go to the kitchen, he brought out a silver cigarette case.

'Do you mind?' His eyes held hers, telling her to remember Jehal. 'A bad habit, I'm afraid. Do you, Mrs Chetwynd?'

As he held out the case to her, his fingers touched hers. The tiny point of contact fused between them like a live wire. This was reality then, Rose thought. It was the everyday life of appearances that was the dream perhaps. The contradictions revolving in her mind made her dizzy for a second. Once again she was aware of Saleh sitting cross-legged and watchful in the doorway. If the mask had slipped, he had seen it.

When she came back, the boy was squatting by Geoffrey's chair. Geoffrey's hand was on his shoulder as he gave him directions about the riding kit to be put into the car. Then he disappeared, only to reappear later to serve at table alongside Ram Prasad.

'What a fine pair!' Abdullah said to her behind his hand. 'Beauty and the beast!' He rolled his eyes and stifled a laugh.

Rose at once felt the tension lift. Her old light-hearted self surfaced again. The day was to be enjoyed. There was no danger as long as she kept control of her emotions. Around the table all was going well. The salmon in aspic had set perfectly and Athenas was regaling them with stories of his travels in Somaliland. Even Geoffrey was at his most sociable, though she wished he would change to wine instead of refilling his whisky glass, especially in the presence of Arab guests who drank no alcohol at all.

It was the mongoose that somehow changed everything. He was a small half-grown creature called Tikki and he was Rose's pet. Against all opposition from Geoffrey and Ram Prasad, she had taken pity on him when he was brought to the house in a basket by a Yemeni rug-seller.

Rose had had a large cage built for him from which he emerged for exercise and food. He was now quite tame and used to human company. Rose adored his swift looping movements and the perky intelligence of his whiskered face as he stood up on his hind legs to survey the lie of the land.

'He reminds me of a tame ferret one of the gamekeepers used to keep at home,' she told Hassan and Abdullah. 'When I was a child, I always wanted one of my own.'

Tikki had a way of springing into her arms and nestling up under her chin, especially when Geoffrey had been taunting him with some silly trick or other. Today Geoffrey had been amusing his guests by substituting a saucer of gin for the animal's usual water. As Tikki clung to the curtains, he spurred him on like a ringmaster, making him jump from one piece of furniture to another before he escaped on to the verandah.

Now, just when the main course had been served, the little beast reappeared at the window, scenting food. Made rash by alcohol, he sprang for Hassan's plate, neatly removed the roasted quail that lay on it, and made for safety on top of the bookcase to consume his catch.

The lunch party exploded in laughter. There was a round of applause. Everyone thought it was part of the entertainment, everyone except Rose. Only she saw Geoffrey's face whiten as he flung back his chair. With a savage exclamation, he turned and snatched his riding crop from its hook on the wall.

'Geoffrey! Don't!'

The first blow had caught the animal across the face. Terrified, it cowered into its corner. Then as a second lash fell, it reared up, hissing horribly, teeth bared and eyes starting.

Everyone sat silent, rigid with horror.

'So you'd go for me, eh, you little bastard?' Geoffrey was smiling, but his voice was thick with rage. 'I'll teach you to steal food from a guest.'

'I assure you I shall not go hungry,' Hassan put in quickly, trying to defuse the situation. He indicated the serving dishes on the sideboard. 'There's plenty more here.'

Rose glanced at him gratefully and pleaded again.

'Geoffrey, I beg you to leave him. It's only because of the gin.'

Ram Prasad had emerged from the kitchen and stood gleefully blocking the animal's path of escape with Saleh behind him.

'Try again, sahib.'

This time Geoffrey caught the mongoose across the front. With a high-pitched scream it leaped to the floor and crouched there. One of its front legs was obviously broken.

Rose lunged forward. But before she could reach the animal,

106

Hassan had gripped her by the arm. She heard him swear softly in Arabic and was frozen by the look of horror on his face.

'Don't be silly,' said Major Beattie, aroused for once from his bluff complacency. 'He'll go for you. He's mad with fear.'

'Just think of what they can do to a cobra,' Mrs Beattie faltered, shrinking in her chair.

But the mongoose, in a long loping bound, was gone into the garden.

There was an awful hush. Slowly the guests turned back to their food. Only Hassan was staring across at Geoffrey, who was back in his chair again, swilling the rest of his whisky.

'Animals do not like the whip,' Hassan said in a low voice.

'Perhaps not, old chap,' Geoffrey drawled. 'But it gets them moving all right.' For a second he raised his eyes to meet Hassan's. 'You wait and see.'

This exchange was still hanging in Rose's mind two hours later at the Sports Club. Trying to compose herself, she leaned forward in her seat to watch the horses being led up for the owners' race. Ever since the mongoose incident, the day had acquired the ominous unreality of a bad dream. Poor Tikki had disappeared into the undergrowth without trace, and there had been no time to set up a proper search for him. Here at the racecourse, she found that the very brilliance and animation of the scene around her grated on every nerve. The dusty arena, ringed by desert, shimmered in the afternoon heat. The flagged markers of the golf course beyond the pavilion were lost in a swarm of Arab townsfolk in bright new shirts, and up-country tribesmen, bristling with daggers and rifles, who had travelled hundreds of miles for the great occasion.

Even in the members' stand, the usual protocol was relaxed. Rose and her guests were in the front row, close to the canvas chairs set out for the Resident's party. But here and there, shaded by awnings, groups of Protectorate rulers lounged and chatted in their most elegant silk turbans, surrounded by the hubbub of all the business bourgeoisie of Aden: Italians, Germans, Parsees, Egyptians.

'How wearing a hat does make one's head ache,' complained Mrs Beattie.

Rose nodded. Her whole attention was focused on the string of horses making their way from the paddock up to the starting post. There were only eight riders, Hassan at the front, a vivid figure in green silk shirt and turban, and Geoffrey last in the line.

From his seat on her other side, Abdullah handed her his binoculars. Now the horses were pacing and rearing behind the starting rope. The crowd fell silent. In the instant before the rope went up, Rose caught Hassan's face in the lens, suddenly magnified as if he were standing in front of her. He seemed to be looking directly at her, smiling a little, his eyes creased against the glare of the sun.

In her impatience, her fingers slipped on the screw and the glass moved fractionally to the left. There at the front of the onlookers, she saw Ram Prasad stepping forward to hand something up to Geoffrey. Even without seeing it clearly, Rose knew it was his whip, a new one, 'good and sharp', he had described it. Whips were not exactly forbidden on the course, but among the British it was felt to be more sporting to ride without. Hence this business of having one slipped up at the last moment.

As the starter's flag went down, and the horses streamed away, Rose felt sick.

'Richard's got off well,' Mrs Beattie said excitedly. She was following the race through her own glasses and was obviously one of those women who jumped up and down from start to finish and never stopped gabbling. Rose was rigid with concentration. She offered the binoculars back to Abdullah but he motioned to her to keep them.

Geoffrey was using the whip on his horse, even as he came past for the first time, close to the rails. Then all of a sudden Hassan and Geoffrey were out in front, riding close together as if there was no one else in the race. Crouched low in the saddle, Hassan seemed to be part of the mare. The long white mane flew back against his face, and the scarf of the green turban streamed out behind. His bare legs pressed against the chestnut flanks. Geoffrey, on the other hand, rode like a machine designed to extract the maximum speed from the animal beneath him, a powerful black stallion from the regimental stables. He stood high in the stirrups, the reins pulled up short, his left hand lashing relentlessly against the animal's hind quarters.

Something like a groan came from the Arabs pressed around the rails. Rose could feel them willing Hassan ahead as the two men came up towards the post, neck and neck.

'Come on, Chetwynd,' someone called from the seats behind in a perfunctory way.

She heard Abdullah say something in Arabic under his breath.

At the same moment, Geoffrey drew ahead ever so slightly. In one movement, he crossed in front of Hassan who was on the inside of the track. As he did so, Rose brought her glasses closer and saw his whip flick backwards, not on his horse this time but directly into the face of Hassan's mare. What happened next had, for Rose, an awful, slow predestined quality about it. In fact, it only took two or three seconds for the horse to rear up with a shrill whinny of fear, throwing Hassan to the ground.

'Oh God!'

She had cried out before she could stop herself. She was aware that Abdullah had caught her warningly by the arm.

'He's all right. He's clear.'

Hassan had indeed rolled out of the way of the horses, and miraculously was on his feet again. He staggered a little as he brushed himself down. The mare was up again too, looking unhurt. Hassan caught hold of the bridle and drew her close, soothing her and examining her. Geoffrey passed the winning post alone. But the roar of the crowd was one of anger while the other riders came in unnoticed.

'Did you see?' Rose turned to Abdullah. She was trying in vain to stop herself trembling.

Abdullah wiped his forehead. His plump face was set with fury.

'You didn't need binoculars for that. Do not get up,' he went on in a low voice. 'I am going to the Stewards' Box to appeal.' He paused. 'Your husband – I'm sorry.'

Rose shook her head. Her eyes were on the riders, disappearing into the club stables.

'Too exciting!' Mrs Beattie's voice quavered. She looked uncertainly at Rose. Voices hummed around them.

'Damn fool!'

'An accident, wouldn't you say?'

'Hell to pay, if not. Things could turn nasty.'

All eyes turned to the Resident in his seat in front. But something was happening there that seemed to have nothing to do with the race. A motorcyclist, covered in dust, had roared up from the roadway. The ADC took from him what looked like the yellow envelope of a telegram.

Now there was a new wave of interest in the stand. For a few minutes the Resident's head was bent over the piece of paper, as though he were unable to decipher it. Then he spoke swiftly to the ADC, who hurried over to the officials in their box. The next minute he was back with a loudhailer in his hand, an old-fashioned funnel affair used to announce the races and the results.

The club suddenly fell silent as Sir Harry rose to his feet.

'People of Aden.' His voice rang out clearly over the course. He turned slightly to the seats behind him. 'Army officers and colleagues in Government. I have just received grave news from London. I feel it my duty to pass it on to you immediately. His Majesty's Government has issued a declaration of hostilities in Europe.' He paused. 'Great Britain is now at war with Germany.'

❧ 2 ❧

ROSE felt neither shock nor excitement. The events of the last few minutes seemed to have drained her of all emotion. The crowd was tense and silent, waiting to hear what the war would mean to Aden.

'Further communiqués will be issued by Government as to the war measures to be taken locally,' the Resident went on calmly. 'In the meantime a state of emergency will operate.' He looked around the gathered faces of so many different nationalities and creeds, as if to draw them all together. 'I know the King can count on the loyalty and support of every one of his subjects, here in this Arabian cornerstone of Empire, guardian of the imperial routes.' His voice shook a little.

'Three cheers for His Majesty!'

The hurrahs burst out like a rainstorm over the hot, dusty arena. The English were standing now, the men shaking hands for some reason, the women chattering shrilly. Algie Warrington-Boon came loping over towards them.

'If you will all come into the tea tent, Sir Harry has a few more things he would like to say.'

Rose was swept along by the others. Going into the marquee was like finding yourself suddenly back in England. A greenish light filtered through the canvas and the tables were laid for tea – cucumber sandwiches on crested china, silver urns reflecting the starched white cloths. More silver gleamed on the dais where the trophies had been laid out for presentation by the Resident at the end of the day. Here and there the committee ladies had arranged stiff vases of white canna lilies and purple bougainvillea, the only flowers that flourished in the parched gardens of the British bungalows.

Rose stood by the entrance for a moment as the other official guests came trooping in, excitedly but demurely like a Sunday School outing. Her lunch party had now quite disintegrated. Neither Geoffrey nor Hassan had reappeared. Mrs Beattie had joined a group of wives, and Athenas was engaged in a grave conversation with two shipping agents. Then she felt her hand taken. There at her side was Nabiha, drawing her out of the crush to sit at a large table in the corner.

'We are here. Please join us.'

The words 'we are here' made Rose feel strangely reassured, though she looked round the circle and saw only Arab faces. The up-country sheikhs she had noticed before were there, and one or two of the local religious leaders in sober white robes and skullcaps. She hesitated for a moment out of shyness. The ring of dark eyes studied her curiously, carefully. A thin grey-haired man in a cream linen suit smiled up at her, pulling out the chair next to him.

'You are welcome, Mrs Chetwynd.'

'This is my husband Farid,' Nabiha said on her other side. She still held Rose's hand, smoothing it lightly. Rose was reminded of schooldays. Once they were grown-up, English women never seemed to touch each other if they could help it, apart from those hen-like pecks they bestowed on thin air, cheek to cheek, for purely social reasons.

'Our friend had a fall,' Nabiha said in an undertone. 'Something bad happened.' Her lustrous melancholy eyes watched Rose's face.

Rose looked down in her lap, opened and closed the clasp of her grey silk bag. 'I am ashamed.'

'My dear, it is not for you to feel blame. Men behave like this sometimes. Besides, it is all forgotten now with this war news.'

Releasing Rose's hand, she nodded towards the entrance of the tent where Sir Harry had appeared with Eleanor at his side. Behind him was Major Beattie with Geoffrey, still in his riding clothes. The Resident's expression was serious as he took his place behind the official table, looking like the local squire at a country fête with his well-worn Norfolk jacket and shooting stick.

Everyone stood up as he came in, British and foreigners alike, but he motioned them into their seats again. More newcomers clustered in at the doorway. With a start, Rose saw Hassan's face turning to search for hers, in just the same way as he had turned to look for her through the crowd on the dance-floor of the *Medina*. Unobtrusively he slipped into a chair opposite her. Now he had found her, he was careful to do no more than nod politely in her direction. Rose looked away guiltily, her heart beating fast. She tried to concentrate on Sir Harry's words.

'We have had no specific instructions from home as yet,' he was saying. 'Of course, Damascus, Cairo, Khartoum – these will be the centres of operations in any Near Eastern campaign. In Aden we have to remember we are pretty much of a sideshow.'

One or two young officers shifted restlessly at a nearby table, stretching out long-booted legs in front of them.

'This is a European war,' Sir Harry went on. 'Britain's motive has been to come to the aid of Belgium and prevent further invasion by Germany. But after the Balkans campaign the Turks may be eager for revenge. If

111

they come in alongside the Germans, things may take on a very different complexion in the Arabian peninsula. We shall have to wait and see.'

He paused, glancing from one side of the room to the other, his blue eyes very bright in his square, brick-red face. Rose was suddenly aware of her isolation from the other Europeans. It was as if she had lined up on the wrong side of a children's party game.

The Resident was rallying himself for some kind of peroration. Sitting beside him, Eleanor watched him with a strained intensity.

'Our own role in Aden is a simple one. We are both fortress and port, always have been. Our prime aim will be to keep the shipping lanes open to India and repel any attempt at aggression by the German Navy. Civilian conscription will not be practical, but the army will be put on a war footing. Extra native recruits will be put into training and our defences reinforced – dependent on funds from the War Office, of course.'

He looked down at some notes he had made on the back of the yellow envelope.

'We'll be on short supplies, of course. We must learn to ration ourselves, take in as much as possible from the hinterland. This is a matter I shall be discussing with the up-country rulers, as well as our position vis-à-vis Turkey. Her stronghold in the Yemen is only a hundred miles away, almost on our doorstep.'

Sir Harry's eyes were on the Arab contingent. One old sheikh leaned forward, cupping his ear with his hand, his arms resting on a tall carved staff studded with onyx. The fat young man next to him seemed to detach himself from the Resident's gaze, Rose noticed, leaning back and smiling faintly to himself, his turban tilted over his eyebrows. Hassan's face remained a mask, private and aloof. On the dais, Eleanor leaned forward and murmured something to her husband.

'Ah yes.' Sir Harry allowed himself one of his battered little grins which made his scar crinkle up and disappear into his beard. 'The gentle sex.' This time his eyes rested on Rose and she felt herself blush.

'Although I foresee a swift end to this war – little action in our own corner of the ring, you might say – nevertheless we must be concerned for the safety of our wives and families. And our womenfolk, of course, will be anxious for the safety of children in England, and other relatives. There is no suggestion of a formal evacuation scheme. But I should perhaps remind you that ships will still be leaving from India for England with room for civilian passengers, for the next few weeks anyway. Passages should be booked at once, I suggest, for those of you who decide to return home during the present crisis.'

Her head bent, Rose smoothed out a crease in the tablecloth in front of her. A pulse was jumping in her throat. A way of escape had just been offered her, escape from her marriage, and from the emotional danger-zone into which she had strayed with Hassan. But would she take it?

Major Beattie was on his feet now, urging that the race meeting should continue to the end. It was vital to preserve the appearance of normality before the native population. There would be no presentation of trophies, but winners should collect their cups at their own convenience.

There was another burst of applause as Sir Harry made his departure with Eleanor. From the dais, Geoffrey was beckoning her over. Rose knew that if she ignored the summons, he would be forced to come to their table. With visibly bad grace, he did so, standing stiffly behind her chair. He nodded briefly in the direction of the Arab faces opposite.

'Sorry about your fall, your Highness,' he said to Hassan, in an offhand way.

'No harm done, Chetwynd.'

Hassan's voice was a deliberate echo of the Englishman's tone. Rose wondered if anyone else had noticed. Geoffrey turned to her sharply.

'I have to go back to the Residency for a short conference. You will stay for the rest of the races? I'm sure the Beatties will take you home.'

'Let that be our pleasure, Mr Chetwynd.' Nabiha's husband was on his feet, extending a graceful hand by way of introduction. 'Our house is not far from yours. I have my carriage and my driver here.'

'Thank you, but . . .' He looked at Rose.

'If it's no trouble. I would be happy to go with Nabiha and Farid.'

There was a pause.

'Perhaps you will collect my cup for me, then,' Geoffrey said.

'I think it would be best if you took it yourself,' Rose heard herself reply in a distant voice.

'Very well. I shall see you later.' Once again he gave that cold little nod and then was gone.

With a tinkling of bracelets, Nabiha adjusted her gold silk shawl and brought out her race card.

'It's the camel race next. Have you ever seen one?'

'Never.'

Together they joined the procession of people making their way out to the course again. From behind Rose heard Mrs Beattie call her name.

'Isn't it exciting? When will you be sailing? We might have some fun on the boat.' That stale-smelling lavender cologne she used enveloped both of them as she took Rose's elbow with a playful pinch. 'Let's go back to the paddock and put a bet on with that little Jewish tout.'

Rose tried to draw back. 'I'm with some friends, actually.'

'I say, you poor thing.' Maud Beattie's eyes rounded in the direction of

Nabiha and Farid waiting a few yards away. She fanned herself vigorously with her gloves. 'Are you stuck with them?'

'No,' said Rose. 'They're stuck with me.'

Mrs Beattie brushed this aside. 'You don't have to, you know,' she whispered conspiratorially. 'Normally they're not allowed at the club at all – except on open days. Besides, you've done your stuff having the Jehal lot to your lunch party.'

This was said almost as a rebuke, Rose felt. She was hot with anger, but knew it was pointless to respond.

'I must go. Sorry.'

Turning away, she caught up with Nabiha.

'Are the others joining us?' she asked her. She was determined not to look over in Hassan's direction. The next minute, he was there in front of her, holding out his hand to her as if she were a stranger.

'Please accept my thanks. It was a most enjoyable lunch party, Mrs Chetwynd.'

'You are leaving, Your Highness?' she forced herself to ask politely. The pang of dismay she felt was almost as sharp as a physical blow. Were they to be enemies then, simply because of her husband's behaviour?

'My friends and I – we have to talk.'

He indicated the young sheikhs and the old man with the staff. Without appearing to, they were watching the conversation like hawks.

'For our people this war could be a serious matter. Jehal is the paramount state. They have to know what our policy will be towards the Turks and the Yemen.'

As he spoke he looked past her at the cluster of tribesmen beyond the paddock barrier, squatting patiently in the dust. Rose felt herself dismissed, an incongruous intruder on ancient territory.

'Of course,' she murmured. 'Please don't bother.'

With a serious face he had turned away before she had finished. Holding herself very straight, Rose walked to the stand where Nabiha and Farid were sitting. The scene around her was as if nothing had happened. The sun beat down, lower in the sky but dazzling still. The memsahibs teetered up to betting booths in their hobble skirts and flower-piled hats to put on a sixpenny bet 'just for a lark', while the Englishmen sweltered in their tweeds and bowlers, making believe they were in the paddock at Cheltenham.

As Rose sat down, a group of pink-faced young subalterns in the row behind raised their glasses to her admiringly. They had armed themselves with bottles of champagne from the bar and were obviously celebrating the prospect of 'having a go at the Boche'.

'I'm off on the next boat,' Rose heard one of them say. 'Back to the regiment. Otherwise we'll miss the whole show.'

'Better hurry,' drawled another. 'It'll be all over by Christmas, you'll see.'

'Let's hope the Germans don't come sailing down the Canal. Can't see this bunch of Gyppos standing up to their artillery.'

'Jove! They can handle these beasts, though,' said the first, a note of unwilling admiration in his voice as he surveyed the preparations for the camel race.

For a moment the sight distracted Rose from her thoughts. With cries of *'Barak! Barak!'* the Bedouins were trying to get the camels to couch, to keep them behind the starting line. Meanwhile the animals kept up their own cacophony of grunts and roars. Each was adorned in a more bizarre style than the next, brass bells jangling from their necks, their saddle-cloths hung about with fringes and tassels and feathers.

Then at the pistol, the dust swirled from the great splayed feet as they lumbered up and stretched out their legs, to trot slowly at first, then gathering speed. The hoarse cries of the young riders, perched so high aloft, urged them on, and drums and tin whistles among the crowd kept up a furious accompaniment.

But even as the ululations of the women rose ecstatically to greet the winners, Rose's mind was away again, tracing and retracing the events of the day. Try as she might, she could find no pattern in it, no sense of direction. It was as if some carefully arranged board game had been thrown up in the air and come down again in total chaos. A violent headache seemed part of this sense of disintegration. She took off her hat and fanned herself wearily, not caring that her hair was coiling loose from its pins at the back of her neck.

'Such a lovely colour,' Nabiha said, watching her.

Rose smiled, remembering Betty at home. 'I have to keep it out of the sun.'

'You are tired now. I think we should go back to our house and have some cool drinks out on the terrace, maybe something to eat.'

'You're very kind,' Rose said, touched, as they made their way out. 'But I think I should go home.'

'We shall see. Here, take my dark glasses. The sun is at its worst as it sets. It goes straight into the brain, they say.'

'What about you?'

'I have my purdah,' Nabiha laughed. 'It's very useful, you know. Like pulling a blind down.'

'Sometimes even Nabiha gets tired of the men staring at her,' Farid said teasingly.

As they drove away in the little carriage, with Farid sitting opposite, Nabiha drew out a veil from beneath her headshawl and slipped it over her face. Suddenly she was a shadow person, like all the other women of Aden. It was as if her whole personality had been extinguished by the square of black chiffon. They did not speak for the rest of the journey. Rose was grateful for this and for the smoked glasses, which were also a kind of mask. She could feel tears threatening. If she could only fight them back, she would not have to explain them to herself.

They turned in through the gates of a tall white house.

'You will feel better when you have rested with us for a while,' Farid said quietly.

Rose did not even try to demur. Geoffrey would be home soon, but she could not bear the thought of seeing him just yet. Here she could speak that other name freely, as between friends, and perhaps find some calm for the turmoil inside her.

'I'm afraid Hassan – the Emir – will not forgive my husband for what happened,' she said. They were sitting out in the scented cool of a cluster of lemon trees at the back of the house. She bit her lip to stop it trembling, horrified that she was so affected. She tried to go on. 'I had thought we were friends. But as we left, his manner was . . . he seemed rather . . .' The words died away.

'His Highness has many things on his mind,' Farid said with a hint of reproof. He sat back pressing his thin brown hands together, very much the diplomat in his neat cream suit. 'His father relies on his judgement. This war could give the Turks the chance they are waiting for, you see. If they invade Jehal, they could make him a prisoner in his own country.'

'The British will have to support him,' Nabiha said. 'His own army is not enough.'

'Of course.' Rose felt overcome with guilt. 'What will happen here in Aden?'

Farid shrugged his shoulders. 'Turkey may like to reclaim her old territory in the tribal states. But I don't believe she would take on the British garrison and the British Navy – *In'Shallah!* Besides, the Caliph may decide to remain neutral. We can only wait and see.'

'You will not leave Aden, Rose?' Nabiha asked. 'Even if some of the other wives do?'

'I don't know,' Rose said falteringly. 'It depends on my husband.'

'You will perhaps be safer here than in England?'

Rose nodded. But there is another kind of danger, she wanted to say, a scandal that would destroy us all.

In silence she sat back against the cushions of the long cane divan and sipped her sherbet drink. There was a marvellous stillness about Arab company, she thought. In between the conversational crescendos, friendly silences would descend with no need for explanation. Even now,

116

unknown presences were moving about inside the house. From time to time a shadowy figure appeared – an unexplained young man, or someone's cousin – and disappeared again after a brief whispered conversation with Farid or Nabiha. Rose felt no need to establish her presence in the English way. With half-closed eyes she watched the moon sail up through the palm trees like a distant air-balloon. From the courtyard behind came the faint splashing of a fountain. It took Rose back instantly to Leighton House, with her friend Trevelyan holding forth in his charming voice about the Arab passion for water. Even their word for blue, the blue of the Persian china, meant 'the watery colour', he had said. She must ask Nabiha if it was the same in Aden.

Magically, the sense of pressure seemed to be lifting from her. Nothing had to be decided here and now. Things might even decide themselves. Perhaps, after all, nothing had really changed.

A servant girl slipped out of the shadows with dishes of pistachios, almond-flavoured fragments of chicken and small savoury pastries, setting them out on the low tables near to hand. Then, gracefully, she crouched to remove Nabiha's sandals.

Leaning back at the other end of the divan, Nabiha groaned with pleasure as the girl massaged her feet.

'It's so cool out here,' Rose said dreamily. She nibbled again from the dish of chicken. The lunch-party fracas had left her hungry, she discovered.

'Wait till you go up to Zara,' Nabiha said. 'Our house in the mountains there is like Paradise! We shall all go and stay when it is too hot in Aden. You wait and see.'

Bowls of jasmine-scented water materialized for the washing of hands. Somewhere in the house a gramophone record was playing an Egyptian love-song, a throaty woman's voice, dark and tragic to Rose's ears.

Farid hummed softly, smiling to himself.

'It's true,' he said after a while. 'We must not allow the present crisis to rule our lives. Our days are to be enjoyed. Hassan particularly must not become too embroiled in politics. After all, he is a young man. He has his marriage to look forward to.'

Rose told herself that she knew perfectly well about Hassan's betrothal. It was absurd the way this reminder should jar on her so, like a discordant note.

'When he comes here as a guest,' Farid went on, 'we must give him a chance to escape from the pressures of government. That is what friends are for.'

As if his words were some kind of cue, there came the sound of a motor

117

in the driveway. Suddenly revitalized, Nabiha sprang up and began to straighten the cushions and push back the tables.

'Perhaps that is His Highness now, coming from the Club.'

In her mind's eye, Rose saw Hassan framed in the doorway in his ceremonial turban and robe. When he appeared bare-headed, an English jacket over his jodhpurs, she was taken by surprise. He looked very tired, with dark circles under his eyes. At the same time he appeared to be charged with nervous tension. He looked across at her almost angrily, so that she put up her hand as if to defend herself.

'What will you have to drink, dear boy?' Farid began. But Hassan shook his head.

'I have come to take Mrs Chetwynd home.'

These words seemed to have been prepared beforehand. He spoke with a touch of defiance, stammering a little. Farid glanced at him warily.

'There is no need. The carriage is still outside.'

'I am on my way to the Aden palace,' Hassan replied. 'I go past the house.'

There was an awkward silence. Nabiha smoothed it over, coming forward to Rose with a laugh.

'You must not keep your chauffeur waiting then.'

Rose got up and they made their farewells at the door.

'It is true,' Hassan said. 'I am chauffeur this time. My driver has gone to Jehal with Abdullah to spread the news.'

He touched her elbow as he helped her into the front seat and she shivered. The moonlight was so strong, everything stood out in sharp black and white: the gloss of the bonnet in front, the sandy road, Hassan's hands on the wheel and his face beside her. He was driving badly, wrenching at the gears so that the car bucked and swerved like a highly-strung horse.

Rose wanted to ask him about his fall. But as she began to speak, he shook his head.

'Not yet.'

Round the next bend, a cluster of thorn trees rose out of the verge, making a pool of shade in the silvery glare. Hassan turned the wheel abruptly and brought the car to a halt. In the dim light his face as he turned towards her was only a blur, but the wide-apart eyes were bright as a cat's.

'I had to see you alone.'

'I was so frightened when you fell.'

They both spoke together.

'I saw what he did,' Rose went on. 'You would have reported it, if the news of the war hadn't come through?'

'I would not. It would have brought shame to you too, or even worse. I know that kind of Englishman.' He hesitated, then put his hand on her arm. 'Does he beat you?'

The tenderness in his voice made her weak. She shook her head.

'Not really. He is – rough.'

He looked away, staring ahead at the bleached expanse of desert.

'You see,' he said, 'I know why he wanted to bring me down. He hates me because of us.'

'Us?'

'He's mad with jealousy. He can read my eyes when I look at you. He can feel the force between us that pulls us together.'

'No, no. You're wrong, Hassan. It's not like that with him.'

How could she explain the strangeness of her relationship with Geoffrey? Before she had time even to try, he turned suddenly and seized both her hands in his.

'He thinks I will steal you from him.' He tightened his grasp. His face was very close to hers, and his voice trembled. 'I will not steal you. I will only take what is mine.'

Almost violently, he pulled her to him, turned up her face and pressed his mouth down on hers. It was not so much a kiss as a declaration. The shock of it made her draw back, staring at him. His lips were parted. She could see the gleam of his teeth and feel his breath on her cheek. He placed her hand on his breast, slipping it under his shirt. His heart was beating as if he were running a race.

'And you will take what is yours, Rose.'

For a moment she let her hand rest on the warm skin. She wanted to caress it, touch the hollow in his throat. But once again she drew back, frightened by the powerfulness of this instinct. She whispered his name and watched the radiance break on his face.

'Hassan. I cannot. You know that.'

He did not reply, but took her head in his hands and kissed her again, a long kiss that turned this way and that as his mouth opened on hers. Rose experienced an unbearable sweetness in her submission to this embrace. There was something so simple and truthful about it, something that could not be denied.

But then, impatiently, he gripped her by the shoulders. With an urgent movement, his body closed in on hers. His face was pressed hard against her face, so that she could no longer look into his eyes.

All at once she had a sense of panic. This was no longer Hassan but a man she scarcely knew, making the kind of inexorable demands that a husband made on one, bringing the bewilderment and humiliation she knew only too well. Once you lost control, you lost yourself. At this very moment, the delicate precious understanding between them was in the process of being destroyed, and anarchy was taking its place.

'*Habibi*, Rose *habibi*.'

His lips were moving against her ear, whispering endearments. The harsh delight in his voice disturbed her more than anything else. With a drowning sense, she pushed to free herself, beating at his shoulders. The familiar phrases she had heard so often flashed through her mind. She was being taken advantage of, she had allowed herself to be cheapened, and all because she was such an impulsive and foolhardy creature. Tomorrow, no doubt, he would boast of this to his Arab friends.

'Let me go! Let me go at once! Are you mad?'

With a quick indrawn breath, he released her as violently as he had taken hold of her.

'You stupid girl!' He spat the words at her. 'Why must you be so – so English?'

'And why must you be so arrogant? Behaving like a sheikh in a penny novelette!'

They stared at each other aghast. On Hassan's face despair struggled with anger.

'Can't you see what has happened? Can't you see we have fallen in love?'

'And that gives you the right to behave as if I were one of your harem slaves?'

His hand was still on her arm. He snatched it away as if it had been burned. She heard him curse to himself. But his eyes would not let her go.

'You think this is a game then, a game with some neat set of rules? As if I am not staking my whole life by loving you! You and your English daydreams!' Wildly he leaned across and flung open the door. 'Go to your precious husband then! See what happiness he can give you!'

Half-falling, half-jumping, Rose was out of the car and running across the sand. The house was less than a hundred yards away. She could see the lights between the trees. Only the sand was pulling at her, slowing her down and making her stumble.

Blinded with rage and tears, she bent and snatched off her shoes. Looking back, she saw no sign of Hassan. The car was still in darkness. She pictured him sitting there, trying to recover his self-control. Somehow it was typical. No Englishman, however gravely insulted, would let a woman go without delivering her to her doorstep first.

Then, as she started walking again, the sand deliciously cool under her feet, she had a sudden sense of triumph. It had been a narrow escape, but ahead lay safety. However badly Geoffrey behaved, he was still her husband, the vital passport back to the right side of the frontier. Perhaps

Hassan was afraid of him, in fact, and that picture of the jealous revengeful husband was the true one. Underneath the terrible moods, could it be that Geoffrey loved her after all in his own way? While everything else crumbled around you, marriage at least was a fact of life, something you had to work at and make the best of. It was what everyone said. Besides, what else could she do?

She was at the gateway now. As she paused to compose herself, she saw the *chokida*'s lamp come bobbing towards her.

'Memsahib?' Fortunately he sounded as if he had been fast asleep.

'The motorcar dropped me outside the gate. I wanted to walk a little, get some fresh air.'

Only half-understanding, he nodded, surveying her in a fatherly way as he shepherded her up to the front of the house. Geoffrey's car was in the compound, but on the ground floor the rooms were shuttered for the night. No other servants were to be seen. Geoffrey was no doubt sitting out on the back verandah upstairs, smoking and poring over his various emergency directives. From what he had told her last year, he would hope for active service with his regiment, perhaps a posting to Damascus or Cairo. Would she go too? If not, what was to become of her? No doubt Geoffrey, as usual, had everything planned already, down to the last detail.

For a moment she stood in the hall, quite still. She was deliberately fighting back the revulsion she still felt when she recalled two things – Tikki's face as Geoffrey cornered him with his riding crop, and Hassan's mare rearing against the whip as they came up to the winning post in the third race. Whatever happened, she must be brave enough to charge Geoffrey with both these acts. She had to find out if it was alcohol alone that had fuelled such madness. Then it might be possible to start again together with a clean slate, or at least to slowly close the awful gap that had grown between them.

She hurried up the stairs. On the landing, she remembered the shoes she still carried in her hand. As she stopped to put them on, she sprang back with a little cry. The figure of Ram Prasad had emerged from the shadows. He stood on the stairs above her, as if blocking her way.

'Sahib is in his room?' she asked quickly, to cover the shock. She was struck by the uneasy expression on his bloated features.

'Sahib is sleeping.'

He did not move, as if willing her to turn in the direction of her own room. With a sudden rush of fury she brushed past him.

'I will see.'

'Very well, memsahib. You will see.'

She looked back and saw him smile almost gloatingly.

121

'You are not needed, Ram Prasad.'

'Very well, memsahib.'

With that sideways scuttle of his, he disappeared down the stairs. She could hear him mumbling to himself as he went. Perhaps he was losing his wits, she thought. She would speak to Geoffrey again about him.

As she went along the verandah, the sight of familiar objects was reassuring. The fringed lamp on the table, the stack of books she had been going through the day before – Arab history from the library – all helped to calm her nerves and restore her sense of identity. Noiselessly, in case he was asleep, she opened the door of Geoffrey's room.

❦ 3 ❧

THE room was empty. Yet somehow everything about it seemed charged with a special significance, like a stage set when the curtain rises. On a chair near the door hung Geoffrey's army jacket. Perhaps Ram Prasad had been cleaning it. The leather belt had been freshly burnished and the buttons glinted in the lamplight.

At the sight of it there flashed through her mind a picture of the station platform in Wales and the two of them boarding the train for London in the hot sunshine. Tied in with that picture was the inner certainty she had felt of belonging to Geoffrey for ever. The uniform was part of the glamour of his physical presence, and of the whole entrancing sensation of being in love for the first time, with one's life under the control of that mysterious 'other' from now on. Had it all been wiped away? Or was there still something left to retrieve, if she tried hard enough?

On the dressing-table a framed photograph of herself in her first evening dress smiled back at her like an encouraging friend. In the corner the mosquito net was down and the coverlet smoothly folded back on the bed she had not shared with him for more than a month.

Perhaps now the weather was hotting up again, he had started sleeping out on the roof. There were mattresses up there, and latticed screens where the Arab women had been safe from intrusive glances from the compound below.

Rose crossed to the swing shutters on the other side of the room. The mirror on the chest of drawers caught her half-way, a strand of hair fallen loose, her face shining in the heat. For a moment she stood motionless and touched her lips, still feeling the bruise of Hassan's mouth there.

Then a sound came from somewhere outside.

Pulling herself together, she stepped out through the shutters on to the back verandah. A flight of wooden steps led up to the flat roof. Looking up, she saw a light up there, a small night lamp that glowed behind the white canvas blinds of the trellis. Laughingly, she had once called it his cage, this pagoda-like retreat of his. Every evening, when the sun had gone down, the servants would sprinkle the curtains with water so that even a faint breeze would give an illusion of coolness.

As she stood there, the sound came again. It sounded so like some kind of caged animal that she caught her breath, remembering Tikki. The low whimpering died away and the silence brought her to her senses again. Geoffrey was indeed ill, lying up there in pain.

But even as she was about to call out, the skin on the back of her neck prickled warningly. Her foot on the step, she stood rigid and listening. What came now was a laugh, a laugh of secret pleasure, soft and sly. There was a low voice, Geoffrey's, and then another's, whispering in reply.

The blood beat so hard in Rose's head, she thought she would faint. The second voice was an Arab's, Saleh's voice. As if to drive home an unthinkable truth, there was a movement behind the canvas and Rose saw two shadows rise against the light, the unmistakeable shape of two bodies that met and turned and sank again.

'Wait. So hot, I sweat too much,' she heard Saleh say pleadingly.

'Hold still, damn you!'

It was the thick excitement in Geoffrey's tone that Rose knew so well. A hand reached out and pulled back a chink in the curtains. She caught a fractional glimpse of naked flesh, brown and white, entangled in the flickering light, a black head and a blond one bent close together.

The voices began again but there were no words this time, only the sounds. Crouched there at the bottom of the steps, Rose covered her ears against them. As in a nightmare she seemed unable to move.

From above the light was extinguished.

Stumbling now to get away, Rose snatched at the handle of the shutters. At the same moment she heard Geoffrey call out.

'Ram?' There was a pause, then with a sudden edge of tension in his voice, 'Rose?'

But she had gone running along the front verandah and into her own room at the other end. With shaking fingers she slid the bolt on the door and stood motionless on the other side. Bare feet padded close, then stopped. There was the sound of whispering, then laughter again, stifled with a gasp. Someone went downstairs, lightly and quickly.

On the other side of the door she could feel Geoffrey's presence, the rank physical threat of it. A mad impulse made her want to beat the door with her fists close to his face, but she fought it down.

'Rose,' he called. 'Let me in at once.'

She did not reply.

'Rose! I have to talk to you.'

Three times he called her name.

When she heard him finally turn away, she waited until his door closed before she forced herself to move. Running into the bathroom, she was violently sick. But even after she had washed her face and flung herself down on the bed, at first she could feel nothing at all. There was just a mindless racing in her brain, a circular pattern of question and answer that went round and round like a crazy machine.

Slowly and with a sense of infinite relief, she began to cry. There was no sobbing, just the sensation of burning hot tears that rolled unchecked across her face and on to the pillow. In her breast a long silent scream rose and died away.

Afterwards she found herself sitting up on the edge of the bed with her head in her hands. She was struggling to make sense of what she had witnessed. Men who took other men as lovers – she knew there were such people. But this man was her husband. Could a thing like that happen just once, on an impulse?

Even as she put the possibility to herself, she knew it to be untrue. The scene on the roof locked into a pattern – or rather, it was the missing piece of a pattern – that was Geoffrey's past. There had been no open scandal in India, merely a hushed-up affair, covered over for the honour of the regiment. A new posting was the obvious way to salvage a reputation, and marriage would be even more effective. It could not be just any wife though. In order to meet the situation, she had to be young, inexperienced, trusting and impulsive.

Staring into this mirror of herself, Rose felt a stab of outrage. What a perfect fool she had been, ignoring every warning signal, from the first hints in London to the arrival of Saleh himself with his coy and superior airs. The glances of older women, the young man in the photograph, the obvious complicity of Ram Prasad, were all links in the same chain of deceit.

Without thinking about what she was doing, she stood up and feverishly began to take off her clothes, throwing them in a heap in the corner as if to rid herself of the overpowering sense she had of being somehow soiled. Every instinct she had tried to fight down in her relationship with Geoffrey had been right. She had been guilty of wilful self-delusion, closing her eyes to every indication of his cruel and perverted nature. Daydreaming was the word Hassan had used, and it was the one truthful thing he had said. She had been daydreaming her life away, constructing cardboard settings to shield herself from reality, refusing to look beneath the surface for fear of what she might find out, about herself as much as about the people around her.

In the bathroom the ayah had filled the copper bath with water. Now she sank herself into its coolness and tried to concentrate her mind on planning a practical way out of the nightmare.

There was nothing to be saved out of the present crisis. Everything had been a terrible mistake, not just her marriage but her ideal of Arabia too.

The schoolgirl fantasy of a special destiny for herself in an unknown land was pathetic and ridiculous, and dangerous too. It had led her into a confrontation with a young man who had declared himself in love with her and tried to seduce her. Such an appalling misunderstanding was again the direct result of her own ignorance of the real world. She was nineteen now, she told herself, going on for twenty. As a wife she knew about the workings of the male body, the rigours of a miscarriage, and the duties of running a colonial household. But inwardly, she was no more a woman than a child of ten.

This awful day had brought one single piece of luck with it though – the declaration of war and Sir Harry's advice that wives might take the chance of returning to England. If she could get herself home again, the whole business of a formal separation from Geoffrey could follow later. At this moment the one thing she must do was to escape from the whole intolerable situation before things got worse. For once she must rely on herself to survive. In this way she might even learn to grow up.

Vigorously she dried herself and put on her robe. The ship the Resident had mentioned was not due for a whole six weeks. But she knew of an earlier sailing. The boat Cynthia Nunan was coming on was due to leave India in less than a fortnight. If she caught tomorrow's mail, Cynthia might even get the letter in time to book a passage for her.

Sitting at her desk, she felt the comfort of Cynthia's friendship even as she wrote the first words. She remembered her promise to make contact if ever things went wrong for her. With her usual gift for optimism, she saw them arriving in England together, perhaps even sharing a place to live until the future became clearer.

But physically she was exhausted. She had to force herself to search for an envelope and seal it up and address it ready for the post. When she put out the lamp and lay down again, misery suddenly reached out and pursued her again. Images of the day returned as before, and with them the realization of Geoffrey's presence just a few yards away, and the thought of an encounter the very next day.

Tossing and turning, she remembered that in the drawer by her bed were some of the pills the doctor had given her to help her sleep after the miscarriage. With the impatience of despair, she poured out water from the carafe and swallowed three, one after the other. Then she lay down again, slipping into oblivion almost without realizing it.

Waking next day, she scarcely knew if it was early or late. The blinds were drawn and there was a tapping at the door. Rose staggered to her feet to draw back the bolt.

'Tea, memsahib? You are sick?'

Ayah's childish face peered round at her with a look of concern. 'It is nearly noon.'

Rose dropped on to the bed again. Her body ached and her head throbbed.

'I shall stay in bed today, Nur,' she whispered.

'Best to rest, memsahib. Here, you drink.'

A chubby brown hand held the cup to her lips.

'Sahib sick too,' the girl chattered on. 'He stay in bed.'

'Nur,' Rose said carefully. 'The boy Saleh. He is often in the house alone with sahib? When I am not here?'

The girl's eyes met hers. She put her hand over her mouth.

'Ram Prasad say not to tell.' She sank on her heels at the side of the bed and leaned close to Rose. 'But memsahib. These things you should know about. Not Saleh alone, but other boys, many times. Ram Prasad bring them from the town. They get money but sometimes afterwards they come to me crying.' She looked at Rose piteously. 'I fright now, memsahib.'

In the pit of her stomach Rose felt nausea rise again. She put her hand on the girl's shoulder.

'I'm frightened too, Nur. But don't worry. No one will know you have told me.'

As the girl stood up, Rose remembered the most important thing. 'Postman has been?'

'Not yet, mem.'

Rose reached out for the letter on the table at the side of the bed. 'When he comes,' she said, 'you give him this.'

Ayah nodded solemnly. 'I go now to look for him.'

She slipped away. Rose got up to lock the door after her and stood motionless at the sound of Ram Prasad's voice. He must have been waiting on the verandah.

'Give that to me,' she heard him say.

'Memsahib say . . .' Nur's voice broke off as if she had been cuffed.

Her weakness forgotten, Rose opened the door in time to see Ram Prasad disappearing into Geoffrey's room. By the time she had put on her robe and followed him, Geoffrey had the letter in his hand. Propped on his pillows, he stared back at her as she stood in the doorway.

'What do you mean by this?' He attempted his usual tone of command. As he held up the envelope, Rose saw that his hand was shaking. 'Some secret communication, no doubt?'

Ram Prasad sat down on the floor at the foot of the bed, crossing his legs in front of him. He looked across at Rose with that smug half-smile she knew so well.

127

Goaded beyond endurance, she sprang forward and snatched the letter from Geoffrey's hand.

'Secrets! You talk of secrets!'

Close to, she could see the beads of sweat breaking through the stubble on his jaw. He was wearing only an Indian sarong and there was sweat on his chest too among the curls of blond hair. The shutters were still closed and the air was tainted with the sweet sickly odour she had smelt the night before. She wanted to fling at him all the bitter accusations that were seething inside her. But she would give Ram Prasad no such satisfaction. Besides, she sensed that Geoffrey was frightened now, and she wanted to preserve that fear.

From below there came the trill of the postman's bell.

She held up the envelope.

'I am taking Sir Harry's advice. I'm leaving for England, travelling with Cynthia. In two weeks' time I shall have gone.'

'Two weeks,' she heard him say to himself as she ran from the room.

At the bottom of the stairs Nur looked up with rounded eyes. Nodding, she took the letter from Rose and flew to the door where the postman waited.

She reappeared with a grin on her face.

'Done, memsahib!'

'Done,' Rose repeated.

At that moment the telephone rang on the ledge by the window. Nur looked at her questioningly, but Rose held up her hand. They both stood silent until the bell died away. Slowly Rose turned upstairs again.

'Don't disturb me, Nur, there's a good girl. Just some soup on a tray later on. I'll call you if I need anything else.'

Throughout the week that followed, the telephone rang every day at about the same time. Rose knew it was Hassan. She had a clear picture of him, standing in the hallway of the Jehal palace amidst the comings and goings of family and servants, willing her to lift the receiver. In Rose's house there was no likelihood of anyone taking the call. Geoffrey had been summoned away on an emergency tour of the Aden borders with the Resident and Ram Prasad had gone with him. Saleh too, perhaps, for there was no sign of him, only the faithful Nur, bringing her meals and messages.

Just before he left, Geoffrey had knocked on her door.

'This is pure childishness. I don't even know how I have offended you.' His voice was blustering, but still with that edge of unease to it.

'Are you afraid I shall tell tales?' she called back, unable to resist the temptation. 'I don't know why you should be. You've survived one scandal, why not another?'

128

She found herself calmly continuing to fold up her underclothes and pack them away in the bottom of her trunk. 'Besides, I do have some pride, you know,' she added, almost to herself.

'Where will you go in England? What will you do?'

'Make my own life.'

'What about money?'

'I have enough for my passage. You'll hear about future arrangements through my solicitor.'

On an impulse, she moved across and flung open the door. It was a pleasure to her to see him flinch, as she had so often flinched before him. She remained quite still, just a few feet away, her eyes searching him over.

'There is only one thing I want you to know.' She took a deep breath to steady herself. 'I do not care about the morals of your way of life. You will follow your own indulgences and they will destroy you in the end. But to deceive me as to our own relationship, to trick me into marrying you and then to make use of my trust for your own ends – that I can never forgive.'

'You bloody naïve little fool,' he began. He put out his hand but she sprang back as if there was a knife in it.

'If you ever come near me again . . .'

Trembling, she slammed the door between them. The last thing she heard of him was the heavy tread of his riding boots on the stairs, spurs clinking, then the sound of voices and the trap pulling away.

The next few days Rose did not go out of the house. She used the telephone to confirm details of embarcation arrangements with the harbour office. Meanwhile, she busied herself packing up her belongings: her clothes, her books, her pictures. The shelves of china and all the other wedding presents, she could not bring herself to touch. They were part of their shared life together, that horrible charade, and she wanted no more of it.

The old man in the kitchen cooked the usual meals, Ali sweeper cleaned the rooms, and Nur went about her tasks of washing and ironing, saying nothing and asking no questions. It was a strange time, a kind of limbo. All Rose's energies were narrowed down to a single goal, the need to get away while her resolve still held. No messages came from Jehal, and after the first week the phone no longer rang at noon. Once, at sunset, sitting out on the verandah, she caught sight of the green limousine with the standard flying as it came shimmering along the Aden road. A cloud of dust swallowed it up. She got up quickly and went into her room. At her desk, she marked off on her calendar the half-dozen days still left before the ship was due. The day after that, Geoffrey would be back again, according to the note he had left with the servants. But she would be gone.

Only one hurdle remained. She could not leave without seeing

Eleanor. There was a real tie of affection between them and it must be honoured. So when a card arrived inviting her to a ladies' tea party, 'to discuss ways of furthering the war effort', she wrote back accepting.

The social chit-chat of the assembly in the long white drawing room was something that had to be endured. Rose would have to wait a while for the chance of a tête-à-tête with her friend. In the meantime, over the teacups, there was an enjoyable air of drama. For the British wives it was as if the war news had injected a magical vitality into the usual hot-weather ennui. Those who were staying in Aden had banded themselves together into little committees devoted to various good works. There were bandages to be made for the Red Cross, and 'comforts' to be knitted for the soldiers in Europe. There was also the more amusing prospect of organizing hospitality and entertainment for the troop ships and naval escorts that would be calling at the port. The buzz of suggestions rose as diaries were brought out and pencilled notes passed to and fro.

At the other end of the Residency verandah were gathered the ladies who were leaving Aden, Rose amongst them. Their chief concern was to establish purely honourable motives for their decision to take ship to England.

'I simply couldn't bear to think of the children without me at such a time,' declared Maud Beattie. Apparently they were with their grand-parents at Bournemouth, in the centre of the 'danger zone' for possible coastal attacks.

'I'm quite sure the Germans wouldn't have the nerve to invade,' declared Mrs Rankin, the stout wife of the Government accountant. 'But with all this talk of airships and naval bombardments, the little mites may be frightened out of their wits.'

'Apparently women might even be needed for war work on the home front,' put in another. 'In the factories and farms and so on.'

'Really?'

One or two of the memsahibs looked dubious. Mrs Rankin announced with a virtuous glow that she intended to return to nursing.

'Where will you go?' Mrs Beattie asked Rose.

She hesitated. 'Back to Wales, I suppose.'

'What a shame, just as you were so obviously enjoying Arabia,' Mrs Beattie replied maliciously.

'Taking to it like a duck to water,' added the French Consul's wife.

'So you'll be on the *Acacia* with us?' Mrs Rankin chipped in.

'Well, actually I'm off in just a few days. I've booked on an earlier ship with a friend from India. It seemed a good idea.'

There were murmurs of interest.

'Of course.'

'Then when it's over, we'll all be back together in dear old Aden again,' said Mrs Rankin brightly.

Rose caught Eleanor scrutinizing her curiously. The guests were starting to leave, and she was busy for the next few minutes dispensing her usual vague charm and reassurances. Then when the last one had gone, she came back to where Rose had tucked herself away on the sofa in the alcove.

'I was hoping you wouldn't rush off. Thank God that's over.'

She signalled to the bearer, then sat down close to Rose and studied her face again. 'I was surprised to hear you were joining the exodus. I shall miss you terribly. What made you decide?'

Rose had already prepared herself for this question. But now, confronted by Eleanor's concerned expression, she found it hard to reply.

'It seemed best,' she began. 'Geoffrey and I ...' She broke off, struggling with a childish urge to throw herself on Eleanor's shoulder.

'Not getting on too well?' She reached out and squeezed Rose's hand.

'Badly, I'm afraid.'

'The jealous husband?' Eleanor asked teasingly. She turned away as the drinks tray was put down beside her.

The anguish of being so completely misunderstood was too much for Rose. She hid her face in her hands, huddled forward to try to contain her distress. Then she felt Eleanor's arm around her, pulling her round gently.

'Here. Drink this.'

Rose clutched at the cold glass, took a gulp and almost choked at the strong tang of gin in the lime.

With a little grimace, Eleanor had already drained most of her own drink.

'We all have our troubles,' she said to Rose, smiling wryly. 'I'm afraid this is my consolation when I'm feeling ill done to. Didn't you know?'

'But Sir Harry is so kind,' Rose said, unbelieving. 'Such a lovely man.'

'A very busy man. Totally wrapped up in his beloved Arabia. I feel sometimes I shall scream out loud if I hear the story of yet another tribal feud over wells, or women, or whatever.' Her face looked suddenly harsh and lined in the yellow light of sunset.

'Geoffrey hates me,' Rose suddenly said in a whisper. 'He should never have married me.' She looked desperately at Eleanor, searching for words. 'Never have married anyone.'

Eleanor got up to refill her glass. She walked across to the verandah rail and turned to Rose again with a stricken face.

'You don't mean ...'

'Geoffrey and another man, they were making love – like animals,' Rose went on, still in a whisper. She found she could not continue.

Eleanor came close and crouched beside her. 'Has it happened before? Can you not tell me more, Rose?'

She shook her head violently. She found her handkerchief and was holding it against her mouth, as if trying to stop more shameful words from pouring out. There was silence for a moment. Eleanor's arm tightened around her shoulder.

'I don't believe it. And yet there were stories, about India.'

Her voice trailed away. She got up slowly, then turned to Rose again with a sudden urgency.

'My dear Rose, you're right, of course. You must leave at once. You're so young. Your life has hardly begun.' She paused, looking away. 'I had thought it was some other trouble. A problem with the Emir. I'm sorry.'

'That is resolved,' Rose said stiffly. 'It was a misunderstanding, another thing altogether. I have dealt with it.' For some reason, she was unable to speak to Eleanor about Hassan. It was too embarrassing. Besides, the slate had been wiped clean and there was nothing more to be said.

The two women stood side by side, looking out at the tapering peaks of the blue coastline, so idyllic in the distance, in reality a wasteland of scorched plain and barren rock.

'This place,' Eleanor said in a low bitter voice. 'If you are unhappy, it has no mercy on you. Arabia can kill, you know.'

She looked round at a movement from the room behind. The bearer had reappeared at the door, politely out of earshot. She took Rose's arm.

'Mohammed is reminding me I have to dress to go out to dinner. About Geoffrey . . .' Her face tightened with an expression of distaste. 'I shall have to tell Harry, of course. I don't understand such things. One comes across certain bachelors who are known to be – how would you say – effeminate? But for a married man to be capable of such – such unnatural passions . . .' She broke off, blushing painfully. 'You're sure it was not some kind of drunken joke?'

'Quite sure.'

'And the other man? If he's army, his commanding officer will also have to be told.'

'The other man is an Arab, not much more than a boy.' Watching Eleanor's face, Rose was filled with a sudden sense of power. This time, Geoffrey should not escape. His life should be shattered as hers was. 'The worst of it is that there are others, all just as young. They're brought to the house on Geoffrey's orders.' She attempted flippancy. 'It's something of an Arab custom, isn't it?'

'For the British, it's a criminal offence,' Eleanor said. 'Don't you know that? Dear God.' She seemed to be trying to recover herself. 'For your sake, I doubt that Harry would set up proceedings against him. But it will certainly mean the end of his career.' She frowned. 'Not that he won't turn up again somewhere, somehow. That kind of man always does.'

Once again she surveyed Rose with her look of troubled affection.

'No, my dear. There's only one victim in all this and it's you. But you'll survive. You have spirit, you see, and you're beautiful too.' Gently, she kissed her on the cheek. 'Leave it all behind you, forget such horrors ever happened. The rest of the world is waiting for you, remember. Including some perfectly decent and delightful young men. I'm sure of that.'

In spite of herself, Rose smiled. 'You're very encouraging.'

'We'll talk again before you go, shan't we?' Eleanor said in the doorway. 'If only on the telephone. You'll call me?'

'I shall.' On an impulse, she turned back and put her arms around her, hugging her tight. 'And thank you.'

'For what, my dear?' Eleanor asked, obviously touched.

'For your friendship,' Rose said.

❧ 4 ☙

ROSE knew very well it was unlikely she would be talking again to Eleanor. She had said as much as she could, and for this release she was grateful. There was always a barrier between the generations though, however slight, especially where a difference in status was involved. Eleanor was still the Resident's wife – the burra mem, as the other memsahibs put it. It was surprising how far their confidences had gone, all things considered. But with Cynthia, it would be different. To her she could tell everything. Only then would she be able to believe it had really happened. Then in London, there was David Trevelyan. Would he think she had run away from Arabia, unable to face up to the painful process of self-discovery the place had imposed on her, just as he said it would? The truth could only be hinted at, but whatever happened, she wanted to see him again.

By keeping her mind fixed firmly on the future, Rose found she could cope with the last few days. For the most part she found she was surprisingly successful at keeping thoughts of Hassan at bay. Only at night, in dreams, did he reappear to her, alternately angry and remorseful, following her in and out of a succession of empty houses and deserted streets. Once she dreamed that he held her again and this time their embrace was tender and never-ending. Another time, she was telephoning the palace, only to be told he was very ill and had gone away and would not be returning. The voice was Ram Prasad's and the menace of it forced her awake, sweating and close to tears.

This was her last day, the day before the ship was due. She had arranged for a cab from the town to come to collect her boxes first thing the next morning. She would follow later with her cabin baggage. She had promised Nur she could come with her on board as a special treat to see her off. Today, all she had to do was to call on Nabiha to say goodbye. She thought of Nabiha as her only real friend in Aden, apart from Eleanor, and so far she had told her nothing of her decision to leave. In this way, Hassan himself would be the last to know, indeed might not hear the news at all until after she had sailed.

As she bathed and changed, she tried to visualize his reactions. Perhaps, with that Buddha-like fatalistic smile she had often seen on his face, he would simply shrug his shoulders and turn back to his affairs.

134

Perhaps, in private, he would give way to male fury at this final humiliation. But his mood would soon be sweetened by the blandishments of his womenfolk, not least the doll-like creature who was to be his wife. What did any of them care about such transient figures as herself? Within a few weeks, it would be as if the delightful young Mrs Chetwynd had never existed, and the next English newcomers would be made just as welcome on their visits to Jehal.

Today, it was almost as if she had gone already. Standing by the verandah, still in her peignoir, she felt herself removed from the view like a figure that has been painted out of the corner of a landscape with a few swift strokes of the artist's brush. There was the familiar line of the palm trees and the white dome of the saint's tomb, but she was no longer part of it. Even the weather was different. There was a curious stillness in the air and the turquoise blue sky had taken on a dull pewter tinge. As she stood there she was on the defensive, ready to beat down the faintest stirrings of regret at leaving Arabia. But only one memory slipped through the barrier – Hassan's face as he stood on the path in the Jehal gardens, staring at her as if he had been shown a miracle.

The absurdity of it! That was the trouble with romantic imagination, Rose thought. It could catch you unawares and delude you into believing anything. But as her father would say, no experience was wasted. You built on it, brick by brick, to make a better self.

Already, she was deciding in her mind how much and how little she would say to Nabiha. She would avoid any hint of a scandal. Hassan's reputation would be left intact, and Geoffrey's betrayal was far too complex to even touch on with someone she was only beginning to know. Besides, she had no idea how an Arab woman would react to such things. The simplest thing was to claim her departure as Geoffrey's idea. Nabiha would perfectly understand that.

Even as she was formulating the words, she was startled by sounds on the drive. The *chokida* must be bringing the trap round already to take her to Nabiha's. It must be later than she realized.

She leaned out to look and caught her breath. Down below three horses were waiting, a tall black one in front and in the saddle the familiar figure of Abdullah. Alongside on a grey, she recognized another personage from Jehal, a small bearded sheikh with a dagger at his waist. The horse at the back was unmistakeably Azziza. She was riderless and a *syce* stood holding the reins.

Taken totally by surprise, his first instinct was to draw back out of sight. But Abdullah's sharp eyes had already seen her.

'Rose!' He called out the name in the Arab way so that it sounded like a drum-roll. 'Had you forgotten? Are you not ready?'

'Abdullah!' she called back faintly. 'Ready for what?'

'For our ride, of course. It was today, remember? You are to be introduced to Azziza. Here she is, waiting for you!'

'But I can't,' Rose replied falteringly. 'I have to go to Nabiha.'

'Nabiha! Pah! She is still sleeping. We will go there later.' As usual, Abdullah swept aside all objections. He peered up at her impatiently. 'Surely you have not forgotten.'

Rose racked her mind. It was possible, in view of all that had happened, though Arabs seemed to be wonderfully vague about dates and times.

'I thought it was next week,' she replied, fencing.

'This week, next week, why worry! Here we are, and the day is perfect for riding, cool like England.'

There was no alternative, it seemed.

'Just for a little while then. Please go inside and sit down. I have to change.'

'No sidesaddle,' Abdullah shouted as he swung himself down. He laughed. 'You will wear trousers like the Turkish ladies?'

But Rose was already in her room, pulling on the full blue skirt, somewhat faded, that she had laid out on the bed as a present for Nur. She snatched a shirt out of the trunk, furious at the rearrangement to her carefully thought-out schedule. Even so, she felt a pang of guilt. Could she really have left without saying goodbye to Abdullah, whom she liked so much and who seemed always so concerned for her welfare?

'It's a good thing you came,' she said as she joined them downstairs. 'I'm leaving tomorrow.'

'Leaving?' Abdullah looked puzzled. 'For where?'

'England. Many of the wives are going.' Remembering her decision, she added, 'My husband thinks I should. I'm sorry.'

The little sheikh was glancing from one to the other, scenting drama. Abdullah was frowning.

'His Highness also will be sorry. He wanted to be with us today but he had business. Instead, he sent Azziza for a surprise.'

'Please thank him. Do I need a hat?' she asked.

Abdullah shook his head, still bemused.

'There is no sun. Strange weather today.'

Outside, the warm scent of horseflesh acted on Rose like alcohol. In that instant, she was back home at Glyn, leading her favourite pony out of the stables.

'You lovely thing,' she said, stroking the mare's soft nose. She took the reins from the *syce* and turned to see Abdullah watching her with a mournful smile.

'You and she are friends already. She has spirit. She gallops well.'

'Not today,' said Rose, putting her foot into the *syce*'s hands. She swung herself up nimbly, pushing her skirts as she settled into the saddle. 'I have to be back soon.'

'Just a trot on the beach then.'

Abdullah led the little procession at walking pace around the garden wall and over the line of sand dunes at the back. Rose had not been this way before.

'Is the coast so near then?' she asked in surprise.

From behind, the sheikh chuckled and said something in Arabic.

'He says you English women live like prisoners,' Abdullah told her. 'You do not know what is beyond your own compound.'

It was true. The sudden sense of freedom took her breath away. There beyond the dunes lay the unbroken sweep of the sea, the thin line of foam curving away from the land as far as the eye could see.

As they paced towards it, that half-forgotten holiday feeling of childhood came back to Rose. The sand here was pale brown, firm and flat under the print of the horses' hooves. Suddenly the Arabian shore was the English seaside, right down to the tang of salt in the air, and the odd little breeze that flicked up the edge of Azziza's cream mane.

'What a marvellous place to ride!' she called. Almost without thinking, she pressed her heels against the horse's side. With a joyful shake of her head, Azziza broke into a canter. Then, a little too suddenly for Rose's taste, she quickened to a gallop, overtaking both Abdullah and the little sheikh. The *syce*, who had been running alongside, fell behind with a whoop. Pulling at the reins, Rose was suddenly terrified that she had lost control. But Abdullah was only laughing, keeping up just behind her.

'She knows where she is going!'

About fifty yards ahead on a rocky outcrop, another horse and rider had appeared. They were obviously the cause of the mare's excitement. To her relief, the man dismounted and came towards them, waving his arms.

'Azziza!' he called. And then in Arabic, 'Slow down!'

At the same moment, Rose recognized both the figure and the voice. Sure enough, just behind, parked at the end of the track, was the familiar green car with a flag on the bonnet. Meanwhile, the horse was still moving fast. Hassan had to stand in her path to make her check and swerve so that he could reach out to grab at the bridle and bring her to a halt.

The wave of relief Rose felt blotted out other emotions. Hassan was cursing the horse in an affectionate way.

'I told Abdullah she was too frisky today.' He looked up at Rose. 'I thought I had better be here to see, just in case.'

'Once they get out of control . . .' she began breathlessly.

137

'Out of control!' Hassan echoed. There was a hint of mockery in his smile. 'Simply cannot be allowed, can it?'

Rose stared down at him. How could he adopt that frivolous tone? The last time she had seen him, he had been almost as distressed as she was. But before she could reply, the others had caught up with them.

'This is fortunate!' cried Abdullah, still puffing a little.

'You mean you could not have overtaken the lady?' Hassan replied teasingly. 'You, the greatest rider in South Arabia?'

'My horse is lame today,' he said with dignity. The sheikh was laughing, but Abdullah's face was serious.

'Fortunate that you could join us after all.' He was speaking to Hassan. 'Another day and Mrs Chetwynd would no longer be here.'

'Indeed?'

The change in Hassan's expression was so marked, Rose felt an even greater confusion.

'I'm leaving for England tomorrow.'

She was busy rethreading a loose buckle on the rein. 'In fact, I should be finishing my packing at this moment.'

She smiled across at Abdullah. 'Then I thought that a short ride in the desert with my friends was the right way to say goodbye to Arabia.' She paused. 'I was told you would not be joining us, Your Highness.'

'I changed my mind.' There was silence. 'Let us have that ride into the desert then.'

His voice was harsh. Back in the saddle he sat bolt upright, staring ahead, his mouth set at the corners.

Sensing the tension, Abdullah said quickly, 'You go ahead, Your Highness. We will ride round by the road and meet you at the point.'

As the sheikh said something in Arabic, Abdullah nodded.

'He's right. We must not be long. The weather is changing.'

'Very well.' Hassan spoke without expression. 'Tell the driver to be there with the car so that he can take Mrs Chetwynd home. Her time is precious, after all.'

The last words caught Rose on a raw nerve, as they were intended to do.

'I suppose it would be too much to expect you to apologize for your behaviour the other night,' she said in an undertone, as they walked their horses away. 'As any Englishman would,' she added.

'I am not an Englishman. And I am glad I am not.' He held his head high, disdain marked clearly in the jutting line of cheekbone and jaw. The arrogance of his expression maddened Rose still further.

'You need not think I am leaving Arabia on your account. My going back to England is my husband's decision.'

'Your husband!' The scorn in these two words matched the look he gave her as he turned round sharply, the wind plucking at the fringe of his turban. 'And did he also forbid you to answer the telephone in case it was I at the other end? Did he order you to send no message to me of any kind about your leaving, even out of courtesy?'

'No,' Rose said coldly. 'Those were my decisions.'

They spoke no more, riding on side by side without a look or a word. The horses knew one another well and kept close, ducking their heads in play, so that the two riders brushed together from time to time. The accidental touch of Hassan's knee against her skirt was beyond enduring. It set up an agitation that seemed to spread through her whole body. In vain, she jerked the reins in the opposite direction.

'Please keep your horse away from mine,' she said, gritting her teeth.

But Hassan's eyes were on a group of fishermen hurrying along the water's edge. She saw him adopt what she thought of as his princely look, aloof but kind, as they bent to greet him. One of them, handsome in his rags, smiled wickedly up at Rose and said something in joke. The others cut him short. They had something to tell the Emir. There was a storm coming. They had seen sand blowing up on the horizon. It was no time to be out riding. Rose's Arabic was limited, but there was no mistaking their meaning.

Hassan nodded and they ran on, their catch of fish swinging from their shoulders. He looked round at the line of desert stretching away to the Empty Quarter. The light had become a dull, sulphurous grey. The air seemed to be turning to dust before their eyes. Both of them heard, thinly in the distance, a long high whistle like an approaching train.

He turned to Rose, his face grave.

'We must gallop now. Look out for a building on the left, an old shack of a place. We should do it.'

As he spoke, there came the first lash of the storm, a blast of wind that was spiked with sand. Instinctively Rose tightened the reins and crouched low over the mare's neck. She saw Hassan's hand reach out for the scarf around her neck. He was telling her to wrap it over her face.

'Don't be afraid.' His voice was muffled by the folds of his turban which he had wound across mouth and nose. Only his eyes were visible, narrowed to slits against the sand. 'Just stay close and keep your head down.'

The horses need no urging. The only sound was their frightened panting as they stretched into a gallop, hooves silent on the whirling carpet beneath them.

The wind was behind them now, whipping them on. All around, the daylight was eroded by what looked to Rose like a London pea-souper on a gigantic scale. But this was slow-drifting vapour that rolled up around them. There was a force behind it that seemed almost demonic, sucking up great spirals of sand and slashing them into horizontal sheets of dust with edges of steel. Through the thin cotton over her face, Rose felt she was choking. All she could see was the dim outline of Hassan just in front. His arm was raised and he was pointing ahead. Rose could just make out, about a hundred yards away, the shape of a small house crouched against some thorn bushes, as if taking shelter.

Hassan's voice floated back to her. 'Come on!' He raised his hand above his head as if brandishing a spear. She heard him give a triumphant kind of cry.

'Bas el awl! Bas el awl!'

Then they were plunging through the drifts towards shelter. A thatched lean-to at the back seemed to be protected from the worst of the gale. Tethering his horse to the wall, Hassan led Rose's mare alongside and helped her down. He had snatched his turban away. Under its mask of sand his face looked oddly exuberant.

'You were enjoying yourself!' Rose exclaimed, gasping.

'It's just the Bedouin way. You shout to do battle with the storm devils.'

But all at once her legs were trembling violently and she had to lean her face against the saddle. As she clung there, she felt a reassurance in the sweating solidity of the animal. Behind her, the wind whipped at her skirts.

'We'll be safe here,' she heard Hassan say.

She was aware of him taking her by one arm and leading her inside the house. The door leaped back behind them with a crash. Hassan bent to fasten the wooden peg at the bottom. Rubbing at her eyes with her scarf, Rose saw a low dim room, a shuttered window still intact.

'Sit down. You're shaking all over,' he told her.

There was a decrepit wicker chair in the corner. She dropped into it like a stone and covered her face with her hand, fighting to breathe normally again. When she opened her eyes, she looked round in disbelief. It was only a rough little place with half-plastered walls and a boarded floor, but it had the feeling of something foreign. An English beach-house, that was it, long disused. Dust lay thick on the deal table and a couple of rickety deck-chairs. There was a string-bed in the other corner, cooking pots, a primus stove, and the broken glass shade of an Aladdin oil-lamp.

'What is this place?' she managed to say. It was hard to speak. Her throat felt parched with sand. 'Who lives here?'

'No one.' He was leaning against the window with his back to her. 'Some Government officer had it built for himself. He used to come out here to ride and shoot, acting the Bedu in the usual way. I expect he got a better posting somewhere, left Arabia behind him like they all do. You too, Mrs Chetwynd,' he added, over his shoulder.

'That's not fair,' Rose said, stung. 'I am – forced to leave.'

'I don't believe you.' He had turned to face her, his eyes on hers.

'The war has changed everything.'

'Everything? Even the way we feel for each other?'

'You changed that,' she replied bitterly. She was fighting back a sense of panic at this confrontation. It was something she had never intended, nor even imagined. She looked at her watch. 'This is ridiculous. I have so much to do. How long must we wait?'

For answer he pulled back the shutter and motioned her to look. The sand was gusting past like a blizzard. Every now and then the wind rose in a crescendo and tugged at the little house so that the walls seemed to quake.

'This is the time of the year for sandstorms. It can last like this for hours.'

'Perhaps they'll come to look for us?'

Hassan shrugged. 'Abdullah will think we made for home half an hour ago.'

Abruptly he moved across to sit down at the table, as if to put more distance between them. 'I was stupid. We should have turned back. But I couldn't . . .'

He faltered and stopped. Rose saw his face struggling with emotion. She turned away quickly. When she looked back, he was bent forward over the table with his head in his arms.

'Hassan?' She moved towards him, then froze, holding her breath. 'You couldn't . . . ?' she prompted.

He did not reply. Under the sand-spattered shirt, his shoulders were shaking, the thin hunched shoulders of a boy they seemed to her at that moment. Somehow the pain of seeing him like this was not to be borne. No power on earth could prevent her reaching out to him. Fearfully, lightly, she touched his head. The tips of her fingers tingled at the contact with that crisp black hair that seemed to have a life of its own.

He raised his face with a start, staring back at her. The line of a tear had cut through the fine layer of dust on his cheek. Very gently, Rose brushed it away with the back of her hand. She felt her throat contract. She had never seen a man cry before.

'I could not bear the thought that I am to lose you,' he said under his breath. 'I do love you, you see. It has never happened to me before. But there is no doubt about it, no doubt at all.'

Rose had fallen to her knees in front of him. She wanted to bow down

141

and beg forgiveness. The terrible waste of it all, she thought. Yet behind the sorrow, a strange and powerful tide of joy was rising. She clung to his hands as if she were drowning.

'I didn't know . . . I didn't realize . . .' She raised her face to his.

'It was my fault. I was mad with impatience. The time we have alone is so short, so dangerous.'

'Hassan.' She murmured his name over and over again, like a difficult word she was trying to learn. Their voices overlapped, jumbled together incoherently. Hassan drew her hands around his neck. They kissed, so closely it had the same endless quality of Rose's dream. But it was not enough. This time she knew the truth – there was no resisting it. She and Hassan had always belonged to each other. It was not a matter of choice. A powerful compulsion she had never known before was flowing between them. Every nerve in her body clamoured to be possessed and released by that final, most intimate embrace.

'I want,' she said impatiently, like a child. 'I *want* you.'

'Are you sure?' Hassan whispered. He looked down at her with a tenderness that pierced her to the quick. 'Are we truly to be lovers then, Rose?'

'We are lovers already,' she heard herself say.

She wanted to pull her clothes away but there was no time, only time to lie down on the tattered bed in the corner. Nor did she feel any fear. The shape of his back beneath her hands was something she knew by instinct. As he entered her, she felt a rage of bliss that blotted out every moment in her life but this one. There was no such thing as shame, no consciousness of a separate self any longer, only this miraculous question and answer of his body on hers, this slow mounting pursuit of an ultimate mystery, hidden at the very core of existence.

'Together,' he whispered to her.

'Together,' she answered.

At the centre, there was a stillness. She felt her whole being stretched like a string beneath a bow. As the arrow sped home, then she cried out that she loved him, cried out almost in outrage at so violent a convulsion of ecstasy. Half-fainting, she was lost to everything except the face so close to hers, Hassan's face, drawing away now so that his eyes could seek hers again.

'Now you know,' he said in a low voice. 'Now you believe me.' His look was exultant, transported. Rose placed a finger across his lips. She could not bear for the spell to be broken. Breathless as swimmers, still face to face, they lay back on the musty pillows. She was aware of the gritty touch of sand under the cooling sweat. Outside the wind still prowled and the dust rustled in the shutters.

'So beautiful you are, Rose.'

He took up the corner of the cotton coverlet and wiped her forehead and cheeks and her breasts where the blouse lay open. She turned her mouth to be kissed. A delicious languor was still seeping through her, holding anxiety at bay.

'It is so strange, like being born again.' She stretched the length of her body against his. 'Am I a different woman now then?'

'You have only just become a woman,' he told her. 'My woman.'

'And for you?' she asked.

'The girls at the palace wanted to teach me things.' He smiled, teasing. 'But it was like playing games. Inside, I was quite cold, pretending. Do you know?'

'I know,' she said simply. 'I know very well.'

'Of course.' She saw anguish cross his face like a shadow.

He drew away from her and sat on the edge of the bed, looking savagely round at the little room. 'Why could we not have met before somewhere, anywhere. Cairo? London? Why here? Why now?'

But Rose too was throwing aside the coverlet, groping to fasten her clothing, aware all at once of reality again.

'The others may be here any moment, do you realize, Hassan? Besides, I have to go home. Tomorrow . . .'

The word died in her mouth. 'I am leaving,' she tried to say.

She was silent again, trembling. As she stood there, he reached out and pulled her close to him, pressing his head against her breast.

'Please do not go, Rose! You cannot go now! This is the most important thing that may ever happen to us, this love of ours. It changes everything, don't you see? From now on our lives belong to each other.'

She shook her head. 'Nothing is changed, Hassan. Both of us are prisoners. Our lives are separate and we are tied to them. It's hopeless, absolutely hopeless.'

She stared across at the darkening window. The sound of the storm was dying away. An awful sadness came over her.

'We have no future, Hassan,' she said in a low voice. 'It's madness to pretend it.'

He stood up, gripping her by the shoulders, forcing her to look at him. 'Listen to me, Rose. Can you really accept the idea that after today we shall never see each other again? Can you?'

Once again she shook her head. She was trying so hard to be resolute but tears welled up in spite of herself.

'Will you pledge yourself to me then? Accept our circumstances for what they are, and trust me to guide us through the best way. Anything is possible if we are brave enough and careful enough. There are friends

143

who will help us. There is time we can steal, places we can be together, I swear it. It won't be easy. But isn't it worth it?'

'Geoffrey . . .' she faltered. 'To be in the same house . . .'

'I know about your husband,' he said quietly. 'I know the marriage is over, if it ever was a marriage. But outwardly you are still the wife of the Political Advisor, just as I am the Emir of Jehal. To keep things as they are is our only hope.' He smoothed back her hair. 'In the same house as your husband, yes, but as two separate people? Do the British not make such arrangements from time to time?' he added, smiling a little. 'Say it can be done, Rose, for our sake!'

Rose felt his energy flowing into her. Held there in his arms she was so safe, so wonderfully complete.

'I could say I have changed my mind,' she said, half to herself. 'He cannot make me go. Besides . . .' She frowned, working it out in her mind. 'It is surely in his interest too, this keeping up of appearances.'

She heard Hassan catch his breath.

'You will stay, then?'

'I will stay.'

Solemnly, they stared back at one another. Then a wild euphoria swept over them and they clung together laughing.

'Ah, Rose! If I were not the Emir, I would take you away to live with me in all the most beautiful places in the East – Teheran, Constantinople, the mountains of Yemen.' He sighed and looked at her steadily. 'But you know there is only one place I have to be. I have a country to rule, after my father. It is my solemn duty. That is why we must always be patient and above all discreet. If this thing between us became knowledge, it could destroy us both. Even now . . .'

He broke off, looking at his watch.

'We should go very soon, if the storm is over. Wait. I'll see to the horses.'

While he was outside, Rose looked around at the strange place that had become their refuge. It still felt like an Englishman's room. On the hook behind the door there was even a battered old panama hat. She moved across to look at the stack of books on the shelf.

'It's just as if someone had walked out and never come back,' she said as Hassan reappeared.

'I think that's exactly what happened,' he said. He had a leather bottle in his hand which he unscrewed and handed to her. 'You must be thirsty. I'd forgotten I had it in my saddlebag.'

'How do you know?' She gulped at the dusty water gratefully.

Hassan had picked up his boots and was sitting on the bed, pulling them on.

'This Englishman, he was a friend of my family. Apparently he was a political officer who got into trouble with his superiors. For taking the Arab side in some dispute or other, I remember my father saying. So he was sent home in disgrace at short notice. The local people loved him, called him one of the tribe. He even became a Muslim, I think.'

Something stirred at the back of Rose's mind.

'Did you know his name?'

Hassan shook his head. 'I remember I was taken in to meet him once at the palace. I was just a small boy. A very big man he seemed to me, very handsome, with eyes like an Arab's.'

Rose had taken down one of the books, a faded copy of Palgrave's *Golden Treasury*. She knew what the name on the flyleaf would be, even as she turned the page.

'Trevelyan. Aden. 1899.'

She murmured it to herself, as if to make sure. It was as if the tall white-haired figure was in the room with them, surveying them both and smiling his wry smile.

'You know this man, then?' Hassan asked curiously, coming over to look.

'I met him in London. He told me Arabia was a hard place, but it would show me my real self.' She looked up at Hassan, glowing. 'He said I would find my destiny here.'

'He was a wise man then, this Trevelyan. Here, stand still.' He fastened a button in her shirt in a brisk proprietorial way. 'He learned the most important thing from his Arab friends. This idea of fate, it is a thing most English call rubbish.' He frowned at her mockingly. 'You're sure he was an old man? I can become very jealous, you know.'

She took his hand. 'Hassan, let's go now, before the others come to look. I don't want them to find us here. This is our place.' She looked at the bed and felt herself blushing. Suddenly shy, she turned to peer at herself in the broken mirror on the wall, pulling her fringe down over her forehead. 'Then we can ride back together, just the two of us. The horses, are they all right?'

'Tired and dusty, but ready to go.' He was watching her, waiting at the door.

On an impulse, she picked up the *Golden Treasury* again and slipped it into the pocket of her skirt.

'For luck,' she said. 'To go with another book he gave me.'

It was hard to leave the house. Both of them felt it. Rose knew it was something to be accepted. They had to take the hour that was given them and be grateful. Then, inevitably, the shutters must come down until the next time. That must be the pattern of their relationship if it was to survive.

145

Outside, just for a little while longer, the world was still kind to them. It was as if the storm had never been. No boat or fishing party had ventured out again though, and the shoreline was deserted. The air was motionless and glittering, the wind spent, the sky clear. Over the edge of the sea, the sun was going down behind a thin saffron-coloured veil of cloud. The golden light lay slanted across the heaped-up walls of sand that the gale had thrown up on the edge of the desert, rising in the distance like the ruins of some fantastical castle.

'Do you not pray at sunset, Hassan?' Rose asked, as they turned their horses down the beach.

'I did pray,' he replied. 'Just short prayers, when I went out to the horses. I was too shy to do it in the room. Besides, I needed water. One cannot approach Allah after making love, without washing. It is in the Koran.' He spoke simply, but with a note of pride in his voice.

'What does it say in the Koran about making love to an infidel?' Rose gave him a teasing look. But he smiled gently and shook his head.

'All these things we will talk about. Another time, another place.'

They rode in silence, walking their horses side by side, Rose's hand in his. In front of them their horses cast long shadows, delicately stepping in and out of the line of foam. The only sound was the hiss of the waves and the faint jingle of harness. Rose felt as if the two of them were enclosed in some radiant bell of glass that stretched from one horizon to the next, magically protecting them from time and change, keeping them safe where no one could touch or harm them. Every now and again they would turn to one another with a look that brushed against the senses like a caress.

'Now we two are in Paradise,' Hassan said, very softly.

Rose shivered. Dear God, let nothing change, she said in her heart, seeing at that very moment the group of figures waiting for them in the distance.

At once they drew apart guiltily. The horses quickened to a trot.

'Tomorrow?' Hassan asked.

'First thing in the morning I shall go to the ship to see my friend. I have to tell her I shall not be travelling with her after all.'

'At noon then,' he said quickly. 'I shall telephone your house and let the bell ring three times only. If you are there you must telephone me back straight away. If not, I shall try again later.'

'Very well,' Rose said. Abdullah and the others were quite close now. She swallowed hard to keep control of herself.

He turned in the saddle, just ahead of her, and looked back at her for the last time.

'Remember I love you, and shall never cease to love you. Remember, Rose.'

✵ 5 ✵

'I THINK you have put yourself in a position of great danger.'

Cynthia Nunan's expression was grave, her voice tense and low. She leaned across and placed her hand over Rose's. The two women were sitting close together in the shade of the promenade awnings on board the P&O liner. The throb and bustle of the crowd on the jetty below could have been a hundred miles away for all the attention they paid to it.

Rose bit her lip – she had not meant to tell Cynthia the whole truth. After the excitement of their reunion at the top of the gangway it was hard enough simply to break the news that she would not now be travelling to England with her friend.

'Why the change of heart at the last minute though, dear girl?' Cynthia had demanded, as they seated themselves at one of the tables where coffee was being served.

Rose could sense her trying hard not to sound vexed in her disappointment. For the first time she noticed the pallor that had replaced Cynthia's rosy complexion, the slight dulling of the curly dark fringe beneath the brim of her boater.

'Perhaps Geoffrey has reformed his ways after all?' she persisted.

Rose shook her head. 'Everything is just as I wrote you. The marriage is impossible – a nightmare.' She twisted the gloves in her lap, her heart pounding. The struggle to contain the wild new happiness she carried with her made her feel almost light-headed.

'Then why on earth must you carry on with it?' Cynthia demanded indignantly. 'The man's a beast, it's obvious. For goodness' sake . . .'

All at once, Rose could hold back no longer.

'Hassan,' she said, half to herself. Just to speak the name was to evoke the physical sense of him, the smooth brown skin of his back, the dark head pressed tight against her. Deep inside her, she felt the secret tremor of response.

'Hassan?'

Across the coffee cups, she was aware of Cynthia's startled gaze, compelling her to find words.

'You remember I wrote to you, about Mr Karim – the person we met coming out on the boat? How he turned out to be the Emir of Jehal?'

'Yes?' Cynthia was frowning now, puzzled, as she stared back.

'Well, it's really too extraordinary. I mean, it sounds so bizarre.'

She broke off, hating the forced tone of triviality. Then the words rushed out. 'He loves me. I love him. There is nothing that can be done to stop it. I've tried but it's no good. We belong to each other.' She took a deep breath. 'Hassan and I are lovers, Cynthia.'

'Rose! What are you saying?'

'It's true.'

'But it can't be!'

The horror in her friend's voice cut like a knife.

'Why is it so wrong?' Rose demanded passionately. 'Can you imagine what it is like to live without love, and then suddenly to find the one true thing forbidden to you? We want this love of ours. We want it to live, even for so short a time, even despite the dangers. I'm alive for the first time!' She snatched Cynthia's hand and placed it against her cheek, feeling it cool and dry on the hot glow of her own skin. 'Can't you see?'

'Dear sweet Rose.' Gently Cynthia reached out and pushed back a strand of the coppery hair that had escaped from its pins. She sat back surveying her friend's face with a look of tender disbelief. 'Of course I can see. The trouble is, so will everyone else.'

They were silent for a moment as the steward brought them fresh iced coffee. It was so difficult to talk amidst the swirl of arrivals and departures going on around them. Indian troops were disembarking below to the bark of English officers.

'There is no possibility of marriage, I suppose?' Cynthia asked hesitantly. 'Even if you were to be divorced? In Jaipur, one of the Indian princes has an English wife. He's Hindu of course. Things are different there, I suppose.' Her voice trailed away.

'We haven't even discussed it. Everything has happened so fast,' Rose said dreamily. 'Anyway, it's not just his religion but his position, you see. He is the only educated leader the people here have. So much depends on him. He could never turn his back on all that – which is what he would have to do if he was to commit himself openly to a European woman. A Nazarene, they call us here. And then the awful scandal from my own point of view – to go through all that! I think it would destroy us both!'

'But to be his mistress!' Cynthia's voice dropped at the word. 'If it is discovered, society will disown you both, his people and yours.'

'If we are discreet, no one will ever know for sure what our relationship is.' Rose was reassuring herself as much as her friend. 'We have to play a game, do you see. Keep to the rules. The – the difficulties will make the times we're able to be together even more precious.' She felt tears threaten and she faltered for a moment. 'You've no idea how much we love each other, Cynthia,' she went on softly. 'It's a miracle. And to think, we might never have known it.'

She bent her head and looked into her handbag. 'He sent me a note by car last night after we had parted.' She put a folded piece of paper into her friend's hand. 'It's only a line, but you'll see.'

Cynthia opened it uncertainly. 'You are the sacred flame that lightens the darkness of my life.' She read the words under her breath, then quickly passed it back to Rose whose eyes were wide and brilliant.

'It is almost a holy thing between us, you see,' she whispered. 'I can't explain.' Her fingers went up to the silver pendant in the shape of a crescent moon that hung from her throat. 'This came with the note. To the Arab, the moon is woman. Did you know?'

She felt herself beginning to babble. She was suddenly ashamed at showing the note. It was no good. Love was a secret code, not to be translated to outsiders, even your closest friend. Cynthia was smiling at her with a touch of cynicism. Or was it even envy?

'Very *Arabian Nights*,' she said crisply. 'Very romantic.'

'But that's not it at all.' Rose was still struggling to explain. 'We are just two people who have fallen in love, very young people, I agree . . .'

'And not very practical people, perhaps.' Cynthia looked down at the neat bright rings on her chubby fingers. Making an obvious effort to sound casual, she said, 'What if you should become pregnant?'

'That's not possible,' Rose replied quickly. 'After my miscarriage, the doctor told me I could not expect to conceive again.'

'But can you be sure?'

'I have to be sure.'

A silence fell between them. A blast from the ship's funnel made them both jump. People around them were making farewells. Two officers had taken up positions at the top of the gangway, politely hurrying visitors ashore. Rose stood up.

'I must go.'

The two women searched each other's eyes.

'I'm having a baby in the spring,' Cynthia said.

'Oh, darling!'

They clung together, both of them crying a little.

'Francis has rented a house for us, by the sea. Say you'll come to stay.'

'Of course. We're due for leave next year. And then . . .' She hesitated. 'Hassan plans to visit Europe. But this war – I live now from day to day. You understand.'

'And Geoffrey? There's been no time to ask you. How will you manage – when he comes back tomorrow?'

'I shall manage.' Rose lifted her chin. 'He has to accept my terms now, after what I found out.'

'Remember, you have my address,' Cynthia said quietly.

'Oh, Cynthia!' Rose remembered the other letter in her bag. Late last night she had written to David Trevelyan to let him know she was staying on in Arabia after all. She had found his little house on the beach, she told him, when she was out riding with the Emir. Wasn't that fate – *kismet*? She added nothing more. It was not the time for confidences. But perhaps he might catch a hint of the truth, knowing the odd rapport between them.

'Could you post this for me in England?'

Cynthia glanced at it curiously. 'Your elderly admirer?'

'You might like to deliver it in person,' Rose teased her. 'He's such a charmer.'

'You haven't sent him a confession? Honestly, Rose!'

'Not really. But there's a strange coincidence . . .'

The hooter sounded again. The last of the pilot boats was bobbing at the foot of the steps, waiting to return to the jetty. Rose tore herself away.

'I'll write. And take good care of yourself. Perhaps I can be godmother.'

Down in the little launch, she scanned the deck for a last glimpse of Cynthia's face. But it was blotted out by the crowds which had surged forward to the rails. Rose felt a sudden pang, as if a lifeline had been snatched away.

Stepping ashore, she was aware for the first time of the perilous isolation of her position. The usual raucous peddlers of curios and sweetmeats surrounded her. She looked up at the shabby green verandah of the club where the Union Jack hung wilting in the sultry morning air. Someone waved down to her from among the pink faces leaning out to watch the liner cast off. Mechanically, without knowing or caring who it was, she raised her hand in response. At the same moment she realized that what had happened yesterday had set her apart from everything and everyone. From now on, she was two different people – Rose Chetwynd, the conventional young wife of the Political Advisor, and Rose the beloved, who belonged only to Hassan. All her energies, every ounce of discipline had to be directed towards the task of keeping those two lives separate and self-contained.

Even now, she thought, as she walked on through the stone archway of the Customs' offices, if he should appear through the crowd on his way with his ministers to some appointment, she would simply smile, shake hands and exchange a polite greeting before moving on again. Hassan would be so much better than she at dealing with such an encounter. He had been brought up to conceal his feelings before others, to wear the mask of princely indifference. But he would teach her and she would learn. And, oh God, it was a small price to pay in exchange for the secret joy of knowing oneself loved as she was. It was like being given the power of flight, so that you felt like an angel floating high above the drabness of other people's lives. What would she not do to keep it safe, this gift that had transformed her whole existence?

'I promise,' she said solemnly, stepping into the cab that stood waiting for her, though she did not quite know what it was she was promising, or to whom. In her heart she had a vivid split-second sensation of Hassan speaking her name, summoning her up from out of nowhere. She looked at her watch and saw it was already half past eleven. In thirty minutes she would hear his voice on the telephone. More than anything, she wanted him to say again that he loved her and would always love her. But if it was not safe, if he was not alone, he would have to pretend it was a conversation of no particular importance. They would discuss practical matters of the places and times of social engagements. Only a word or a special inflection would signal their real thoughts, as the two voices merged and clung across the miles of desert wire.

'Hurry, please,' she said to the driver. The elderly Somali touched his fez in salute and slapped the reins down on the bony grey back of his horse.

'Quick-sharp, memsahib,' he called out, proud of his English.

She sat back, willing him not to talk as they drove. Tomorrow Geoffrey would be back. She would have to make up her mind what she would say to him. But now she wanted to think about yesterday, to turn over each moment yet again like the beads on a prayer-string. Closing her eyes she saw once more the tear that streaked the sand on his cheek, heard again the word 'together' in her ear, hoarsely, tenderly, as she gave herself up to him.

With a jolt the little carriage was turning onto the peninsula road. She looked out from under the cracked old leather hood and saw to the right the steep granite pass of the garrison fortress, to the left the glitter of the desert. There at Jehal Hassan was waiting for the moment to pick up the telephone. She touched the little silver moon warm against her throat, and willed him to be alone as she would be. Perhaps even this afternoon, they might be together again, riding along the beach.

At the house she fumbled in her purse, giving the driver a ridiculously large tip because she was too impatient to find the right change.

Just as she stepped into the hallway, the bell of the telephone rang. Instinctively she ran forward to the foot of the stairs to pick up the receiver but stopped herself. Hassan had said three times. Then she must put through a call to the palace and he would be waiting to pick up the receiver.

As she stood poised with fast-beating heart, waiting for the third ring to die away, her eyes were fixed on the telephone. She did not see the figure standing at the drawing-room door.

'So it seems you have changed your mind?'

She started violently and spun round. Blackness swam before her, so that she had to hold on to the banister post to regain her balance. The telephone bell had stopped.

'Geoffrey. I – I thought it was tomorrow you were coming back.'

'Does it matter?'

He came closer, staring at her. How bitterly she hated him at that moment for denying her Hassan's voice. How ugly he looked to her, with his bloodshot eyes and red shiny face, peeling where the sun had caught it. 'I think it is I who am owed an explanation,' he said roughly.

'I saw Lady Rawlinson a couple of days ago.' Rose was fighting for time, improvising on a few half-formed ideas. 'She is staying on. She wanted me to do the same. Besides,' she went on, trying to control the quivering of her chin, 'all the passages on the ship were fully booked. I've just been down to Steamer Point to see Cynthia. I was up very early.' Her voice died away. The very nearness of the man was making her feel sick. 'I need to lie down,' she whispered.

As she turned, a shadow fell across the stairs. Ram Prasad was standing above her on the landing. Under his arm he carried a bag of Geoffrey's laundry, ready to go to the washerman. The familiar smell of her husband's stale sweat hung between them like a threat.

'Good morning, memsahib.'

His voice was obsequious and he stood aside with an air of exaggerated deference. All at once she realized she had fallen into her browbeaten attitude of the past. But now things were different. Instead of fleeing, she had to stand her ground and fight. Her foot on the stairs, she turned to face Geoffrey with new authority.

'There are things we have to discuss – in your study, perhaps.'

She hurried past Ram Prasad, and stood waiting at the top of the stairs. After a pause, Geoffrey followed her. She saw that his hair had started to thin, the yellow strands parting to show the glistening scalp beneath. Even so early in the day there was whisky on his breath, as he confronted her.

'I don't believe you,' he said. 'About the ship being fully booked.'

He pushed past her into the study and flung himself into the chair behind the desk. 'They tell me you were out riding with the Emir and his chums yesterday. Don't worry – Ram Prasad can get anything out of your dear Nur with a bit of persuasion. Perhaps it was your darkie friends who put you up to staying, eh?'

He leaned forward, sneering up at her with those boiled blue eyes. Staring back at him, Rose found she had closed her hand around the cut-

153

glass paperweight on the desk in front of her. To her horror she realized that if he should reach out and touch her, she would smash the thing down on his forehead without a moment's hesitation.

There was silence between them, a silence that seethed with suppressed violence. Rose took a deep breath and removed her hands from the desk. Standing very straight, she looked past him through the window.

'I think I had better make my position clear,' she said. 'From now on, what I decide to do with my private life is my concern. This has been your own guiding rule and now it is mine. To the rest of the world I am still your wife. But between the two of us, there is nothing. We go our separate ways.' She stopped to steady her voice. 'There is just one thing. I will not have Saleh in this house again, nor any other of your boys.'

She watched him closely now, noting a flicker of disquiet pass over his face. He put a hand up in front of his mouth, pressing down his moustache.

'What the hell do you mean by that?'

'Don't try to bluster, Geoffrey. I know the truth. But I'm prepared to keep silent on one condition. That you leave me alone. So that we are only together in company, whenever it is socially necessary.'

'Playing the perfect husband, you mean?' he asked mockingly. 'What a bloody ridiculous scheme – a typical schoolgirl charade! Can't you grow up Rose, for God's sake?'

'I have grown up, that's just the point,' she whispered. Then for a moment, the tension inside her snapped. 'You fool! You're not just wicked, you're stupid too! Don't you realize that it only needs a word from me to let loose a scandal on your head, put an end to your whole precious career? Isn't it in your interest to keep up appearances as best we can?'

'And yours?' he drawled.

She said nothing, feeling the blood rise to her face.

'Well then.' He got out of his chair with something of his old swagger. 'So it's a sort of armed truce, is it? Suits me anyway. I've been bored out of my mind for the last twelve months, if not longer.' He thrust his hands into his breeches pockets and stood half-turned away from her. 'You won't be seeing much of me anyway. The Resident wants me to take up quarters at the garrison for the time being, so's to be on hand in case of emergencies. I shall be my own man there all right, shan't I?' Once again he eyed her with that look of mocking insolence. 'Ram Prasad will be coming with me, which should please you. And any other servants I may need, of course.'

Rose was unable to conceal the shock of relief. At once, she saw that Geoffrey had observed this change of expression.

'In return, old girl, there may be one or two favours you can do for me.'

154

She flinched, not just at the false endearment but at the threat implied in the words.

'This Jehal lot of yours,' he went on. 'I'm supposed to be having a meeting with them some time next week. The Resident's keen to get the Sultan to sign a formal treaty of alliance with the British, now there's a war on. Not that we expect the Arabs to join the British Army or anything like that, heaven help us. But if Johnny Turk turns against us, the rulers in the hinterland will have to stand up to him. Jehal, as usual, seems to be shilly-shallying between his Islamic brothers and his British paymasters.'

'I know nothing of all this,' Rose said faintly.

'I don't imagine you do. But at least you might exert some of your famous charm on the old boy to get him to sign on the dotted line. If he can write his name, that is. And the Emir too. He's the one who lays down the law in Jehal as far as politics are concerned, I gather. We're meeting at Perim. I think you should be there. There's a feast laid on, the usual ghastly affair that you seem to enjoy.'

'Perim?'

Rose had a mental picture of a whitewashed lighthouse on a rocky island, something glimpsed from the rails of the *Medina* an age ago.

'Belongs to Jehal officially, but we want it now. Vital strategic point for the defence of the Red Sea and all that.'

Briskly he buckled on his belt and picked up his riding stick.

'I thought you were keen to follow in the footsteps of all these other female explorers – Hester Stanhope and Gertrude Bell and all that.' He smiled at her, unpleasantly. 'Besides, it's all part of this husband and wife act, isn't it? I'm sure Sir Harry would approve.'

The name jerked Rose's mind in a new direction. All at once she was frantic for Geoffrey to leave.

'Very well. I shall come,' she said quickly, to end the conversation.

He was off to garrison headquarters, he told her, to make arrangements for his accommodation. He would be back later to pack.

Even before his car had turned out of the drive, Ram Prasad at his side, Rose was lifting the telephone receiver. At the sound of the operator's voice, she had to struggle with herself not to give the number of the palace. But Hassan's instructions were quite clear. If she missed the noon call she must wait until he tried again later in the day. Instead she asked for the Residency, trying to collect her thoughts as Eleanor was brought to the telephone.

'My dear! I thought you were sailing this morning?'

'I decided to stay after all. That's why I had to speak to you.'

'I can't believe it! What made you change your mind?' Lady Rawlinson's tone changed from bewilderment to sudden anxiety. 'Is anything wrong, Rose?'

'No, not really. Geoffrey came in today so I knew Sir Harry must be back too.' She was trying to keep the note of desperation out of her voice. 'I wanted to ask you, Eleanor, please not to tell him anything of what we were talking about the other day – about my husband. Not now, anyway.'

There was a pause. 'Are you sure about this?'

'Quite sure.' Rose spoke hurriedly. She found it was the only way she could tell a lie convincingly. 'It's just that things may not be as bad as I thought. At any rate, I mean to try. With the marriage, I mean. Running back to my mother wouldn't really solve anything, would it?'

'I suppose not.' Eleanor still sounded hesitant.

'I may have been mistaken, Eleanor, jumping to conclusions. I intend to give him the benefit of the doubt. Rifts can be healed, after all. Besides, it was harder to contemplate leaving than I had thought.' She was searching hard for a few words of truth. 'Arabia has become my home, after all. I do so love the place.'

'I envy you that,' Eleanor said dryly.

'And I knew you'd be glad if I stayed.'

'I am glad, my dear.' Her voice was warm again. 'For my own sake, I'm delighted of course. And if at any time you need to take me into your confidence again . . .'

'I know.'

'Your husband's a lucky man, that's all I can say. Otherwise he might have been packing his bags for England tomorrow.'

And I with him, Rose said to herself. No other course would have been possible.

'We women do have to trim our sails to the wind, cut our coat according to our cloth,' Eleanor went on. She gave her vague little laugh. Rose could tell she had already had her first gin-and-lime of the day.

'I must go now, Eleanor,' she said. 'Unpacking, this time.'

'Of course, dear Rose. I'll be seeing you within a day or two, no doubt. Come up as soon as you can. It's better than this wretched machine. Besides, nowadays I gather the lines are supposed to be kept for official use only.'

Shakily Rose replaced the receiver and wound up the handle to signal the operator that the call was at an end. Despite the intense humidity, her hands were icy cold. She had the sense of having put down some all-important card that would determine the whole outcome of the game.

With a sigh, she turned and went up to her room. For the next hour or so, she busied herself unpacking and rearranging her clothes. Nur darted in and out helping, full of delight that her mistress was staying and that Master and Ram Prasad were out of the way, for the time being at least.

156

But for Rose, the day dragged by endlessly as she waited to hear from Hassan. Perhaps Eleanor was right and the lines were no longer available for private calls. From now onwards Hassan might have decided it was too risky for them to talk at all.

Then at four o'clock, a note was delivered at the front verandah by a small Bedouin urchin. Snatching it out of his grimy paw, Rose felt her heart drop. It was not Hassan's writing, a woman's rather. Puzzled, she ripped it open to find a message from Nabiha.

'Dear Friend,' she had written. 'Here is a small boy from the servants' compound who has offered to run over with this faster than any of the others. The Emir asks me to let you know he had to leave suddenly for Hodeida. There was a summons from the King of Yemen to attend with his father. After one week he will be back as he must meet the Resident at Perim that day, Thursday. Afterwards, in the evening he will speak to you to make arrangements to go riding again. Please visit me soon, or I will call on you. In the meantime I am happy to be the bearer of messages. Your friend, Nabiha.'

The small boy was gently tugging her sleeve.

'You write letter go back, memsahib?'

'What? Oh no, no letter. Just say thank you to mistress.'

She read it through again. Dear Nabiha, to be so helpful. Whether she guessed the real situation, it was impossible to tell from this delicately worded missive.

The urchin still stood before her, shifting from one bare foot to the other.

'Baksheesh, memsahib?' came the whisper.

'Oh yes, yes. Wait.'

Once again, Rose was scrabbling in her purse, her mind far away. For Hassan Perim would be a calling-point on the journey back from the Yemen. So there would be no way of letting him know that Geoffrey was taking the Resident's place at the meeting, and that she would be with him.

The problems posed by this seemed to Rose to be serious indeed. Being so totally unprepared, how would Hassan react? Would the Sultan himself be pleased or displeased by her appearance?

As for the treaty, Rose knew by instinct that Hassan would be reluctant to put his country under further obligation to the British, or any other occupying power. Nor could she imagine that she would have the slightest influence on such a decision. It was typical of Geoffrey's naïvety to think she could. In fact, so far as the Emir was concerned, the greatest possible stumbling block to any kind of Anglo-Arab agreement would be the presence of Geoffrey himself.

Rose shivered. The threads of conflict seemed to be tightening around her.

❧ 6 ❧

EACH night that followed, Rose dreamed obsessively. They were dreams that were coloured by fears and premonitions, all revolving around the Perim expedition. Somehow in her mind, the place itself had acquired a threatening, sinister quality. The tiny island and the innocent-looking white tower that had been her first glimpse of Aden now became a backdrop for danger, in her imagination at least. But when the day came, such fancies seemed to melt away. It was the day when she would see Hassan again. A misty dawn had bloomed into a perfect morning. The sunshine glinted over the waterfront at Ma'alla, the air still cool, as if it could never reach the sweltering temperatures of noon. Ma'alla was the native harbour. Rose remembered Hassan telling them that the ancient boatyard was where Noah was said to have built the Ark. Certainly it was a whole world away from the British officialdom of Steamer Point. She loved the tall painted dhows, lolling at anchor among their shimmering reflections, and the sight of the great lateen sails filling with wind at the harbour mouth, bound for Muscat or Kuwait or the coastal towns of the Hadramaut. Even at this early hour the wharf was thronged with white-robed merchants flitting like cabbage butterflies between the warehouses. Carpenters were hauling timber. Turbanned Sinbads, naked to the waist, swarmed about the rigging, and the mingled scents of coffee and spices and melting tar surrounded her as she stepped out of the cab.

She had already sighted Geoffrey at the far end of the jetty, an incongruous figure in his Colonial Service uniform and topee. Next to him, she recognized Major Beattie in khaki. The two of them were ringed around by a bodyguard of native police in scarlet pillboxes.

Rose had no idea what vessel they were to travel in. Because she had been instructed to come to Ma'alla she had assumed they might be making the journey by dhow. Somewhat to her surprise, she saw, waiting alongside, an old tramp-steamer of the kind used by the Indian trading companies. As she approached the group she saw that Geoffrey was already in one of his tempers and that the shabby little vessel was the cause of it.

'It's totally ridiculous. I was told we were to travel in the Government motor launch and then at the last minute His Excellency decides he needs

159

it for his expedition to Mukullah.' He was speaking to Beattie. Both men paused briefly to salute Rose as she joined them.

'Hardly very comfortable for your wife, either,' Beattie said, smoothing his black moustache with his usual attempt at gallantry.

'I shall be perfectly fine,' Rose replied cheerfully.

In truth, she had been dreading this encounter with Geoffrey, the first for several days, and was only too pleased that his attention was distracted.

'She looks quite seaworthy to me.'

'What a thing for His Majesty's imperial representative to arrive in!'

Geoffrey was swinging his cane towards the battered hull, his voice raised in fury. The gang of coolies shifting cargo on deck paused to watch in surprise.

'Just look at it – the *Katerina*! Hardly a British name. I don't expect they can even run to a British flag!'

'Well, you've a British master at the helm anyway.'

A remarkable figure was surveying them from the bridge, a stout grey-bearded man wearing khaki shorts, a white polo shirt and a pyjama jacket decorated with four stripes. Captain Strong, as he introduced himself, immediately addressed himself to Rose. Ignoring the rest of the boarding party, he invited her to join him in the wheelhouse as the little ship got under way.

'Give you a good look at the lie of the land,' he told her gruffly, pulling out a chair for her. Geoffrey and Major Beattie had taken over the saloon with a newly-opened bottle of gin and a pack of cards. Rose was more than happy to pass the four-hour journey on the bridge.

'Difficult chap, that one!' Captain Strong remarked conversationally, lighting up his pipe, his eyes on the horizon. 'The Government fellow in the gold braid.'

'He's my husband.'

She was trying not to smile as the Captain bit hard on his pipe, his red face turning purple.

'Beg pardon, ma'am. I was under the impression you were one of the ladies from the Medical Mission. Mind you,' he added with a sideways glance at her new cream voile dress and matching hat, 'you don't look much like a Mission lady, I must say.'

'Thank you, Captain Strong.'

They turned to safer subjects, while the Arabian coastline glided by, tawny gold in the distance. The old man had seen service up and down the Nile in the Khartoum campaign. Retirement had bored him and he'd come East again to take up a job as skipper for Cowasjee Dinshaw, the Parsee merchants. Skins and hides were his usual cargo, but he took on passengers from time to time.

'Not often important ones like this, though. They're having a bit of a chinwag with the old Sultan, I gather. Trying to get him to lend a hand with the war effort.'

'I believe that's the idea.' Rose knew she had to be cautious about discussing politics. On the other hand, the Captain was obviously an old hand who prided himself on his knowledge of native affairs. 'What do you think?' she went on. 'Do you think the Arabs will come in on our side if the Turks join in with Germany?'

'Why not?' The old man's eyes narrowed as he stared ahead at the changing currents of the straits. 'It could be the very opportunity they need.'

'What do you mean?'

'The chance to overthrow the Turks at last. They've been ruling the roost from Syria downwards for centuries, remember. Now perhaps the tribes can get together and manage their own affairs. Why should they have the Turks or the British or any other damn foreigners running their countries?'

Rose laughed. 'You're quite a radical then, Captain Strong?'

'Just a bit independent in my ways you might say. Aren't you, Mrs Chetwynd?' He looked round at her with a twinkle.

'I am, yes,' Rose said defiantly. 'But may we not be able to help a country that's more backward than ours?'

'That's the idealistic point of view. What I see is change in the air. I think the Arab rulers would do anything for us if we promised them independence. They'd need gold, of course, to spur them on. And the right leadership.' He shrugged his shoulders. 'All this may be never-never stuff, perhaps. In London they're banking on Turkey to stay neutral, they say – got enough on their hands putting paid to the Huns.'

A huge Goanese appeared from below with two mugs of tea and a broad grin on his face.

'Sahibs in the saloon say too bloody hot down there!'

Captain Strong guffawed loudly. 'This old bucket was built in Kiel,' he told Rose, 'designed for trading in the Baltic. So they put the boilers behind the living quarters to keep the crew warm.' He laughed again. 'Tell 'em that's what they have to expect if they choose to travel in a German ship. That'll give 'em something to think about.'

'You're very naughty, Captain Strong.' Rose peered out at the two distant shores, Arabia on the one hand, Africa on the other. 'I remember this part from the journey out, coming out of the Red Sea. It's the Bab-el-Mandeb straits. The Gate of Tears.'

He caught the change of tone in her voice and looked at her quizzically.

'Not as far as you're concerned, I trust, Mrs Chetwynd?'

161

Rose shook her head quickly. She pointed to the shape of a small rocky island emerging ahead, crowned by a white tower. 'And that must be Perim.'

'And the famous lighthouse. Lonely old place, I always think. It's a bit like Marble Arch. Everybody goes past it, but nobody stops there.'

It was obviously a favourite remark. He paused for Rose to ply him with questions. But she was silent. There was something forbidding about that uplifted finger of stone emerging out of the emptiness of sea and sky. It was almost as if she was being warned to stay away from the place. She began to talk of other things, but the curious sense of unease she felt stayed with her until the lighthouse point had disappeared behind them. Then with a sudden jump of her heart, she saw the settlement and the jetty come into view. Anchored before it was a tall dhow flying the Sultan's flag.

'Looks as if the Jehal party are here already,' said Captain Strong. The *Katerina* was slowing down, as the engines died away.

Images of Hassan which Rose had deliberately kept at bay now flooded in. She felt a sudden panic at the prospect of the confrontations ahead. At the same time, she was filled with a delicious impatience just to see him before her again. There must surely be a chance to talk together, if only briefly. But it was an occasion when she must guard against betraying even the smallest sign of emotion.

A thin young Englishman was standing on the jetty, his hand raised in greeting. A crowd of local people swarmed at his heels. As the anchor chain went rattling down, Rose felt all eyes upon her. It seemed she was to be the first to disembark.

With a shy smile the young man reached out to help her across the deck to the rough-stone landing.

'Be careful!' he called.

Yes, be careful, Rose told herself as with a quick little skip-jump she stepped ashore.

'I'm Mrs Chetwynd,' she said, still holding the young man's hand. 'Rose Chetwynd.'

'Martin Foster, Administrative Officer,' said the young man, stammering slightly. Behind his glasses he was staring at her with an expression of disbelief. 'It's a great pleasure – I had no idea you would be coming with your husband.' He gave a smile that transformed his plain pink features. 'I was posted here six months ago and I haven't seen an English face since, let alone a female face.'

He broke off to introduce himself to the official party. Geoffrey stuck out his hand with a frown. His eyes went from Mr Foster's sandalled feet to the red cotton *keffiyeh* he wore knotted about his head in the Arab style.

162

'Do government officers usually ape the Bedouin in these parts?' Geoffrey asked coldly.

Mr Foster wilted, turning even pinker.

'I – I find the Arab head-dress cooler than a topee, sir.'

Geoffrey was now scrutinizing his crumpled white breeches and shirt. 'I'm afraid I've been laid up with a bout of amoebic dysentery until this morning, and this was all my servant could produce. My official togs seem to be still in the wash,' Mr Foster went on, with a dying fall in his voice.

'Oh, you poor thing!' Rose exclaimed. 'Are you sure you're recovered?'

Mr Foster nodded apologetically, still looking at her husband. But Geoffrey was already surveying the rocky landscape behind them. As far as Rose could see, the settlement consisted of a cluster of fishing huts and a tiny mosque. A few villagers stood by at a respectful distance.

'Where is everybody then?' he demanded.

'At the Government rest-house, sir. The Sultan and his party arrived about an hour ago. Most of the local people are there presenting the usual respects, welcome ceremonies and so on.' He indicated a rather moth-eaten camel and three small donkeys tethered nearby. 'Do you prefer to ride or walk?' he went on, glancing at Rose. 'It's only a hundred yards or so, just around the hill and there's a good track.'

'In that case, we walk,' announced Major Beattie. He swung his sword-stick briskly. 'Do us good to stretch our legs after that rotten little ship, eh, Mrs Chetwynd?'

'Certainly,' said Rose. She turned to wave to the Captain, who was spending the day on board. 'Till this evening, Captain Strong,' she called.

'Odd sort of cove,' growled the Major as they set off up the track.

'Fascinating man,' Rose replied. 'A great storyteller.'

'And you're game to believe most things, I should think,' he chaffed.

But Rose hardly heard him. Her eyes were fixed on the whitewashed building coming into view ahead of them through the straggling palms. It reminded her of nothing so much as a small fort, with its two square towers and crenellated walls.

'It looks like something out of those stories of the French Foreign Legion,' she remarked to Martin Foster, trying to hide her nervousness.

'As a matter of fact, the island was a base for the French Army back in the 1730s,' he replied eagerly. Alongside her, his face was suddenly animated. 'They were waging a campaign against the Yemen. Then at the end of the century, it was the British turn. They wanted Perim as a stop-gap against Napoleon of course. He was in Egypt, you remember, planning to invade India . . .'

'Mr Foster, do we have to have a history lesson?' Geoffrey drawled from behind. 'We're here to see what use the place is to us in this year of grace 1914.'

'Same sort of thing, though,' Major Beattie put in unexpectedly. 'Except this time the enemy is Germany.'

Rose remembered that the Major's hobby was military history. No doubt he would have pursued the subject further had he not been distracted. A band of ragged children had detached themselves from the crowd outside the rest-house and now descended on the English party with a rush. Women in black, their veils tucked halfway across their faces, surrounded Rose in a chattering mob. One of them, a girl in her teens, took her hand shyly.

'Tell them to keep away,' Geoffrey called sharply to Foster. 'Heaven knows what diseases they've got.' Rose saw the young man's face stiffen.

'Please don't,' she murmured to him. As they walked towards the house, she kept the girl's hand tight in hers. It seemed to give her courage, for now every nerve was tense at the thought of seeing Hassan. Somewhere in the thick of the throng around the doorway, a drum was pattering out a welcome in time to the beat of her heart.

Then suddenly the girl drew back. The dazzle and thrust of the crowd was behind them, and they were moving into a long, low room hung with rugs. Out of the dimness, the first thing Rose saw was Hassan's face, staring at her from among a group of people at the far end. His expression was one of astonished delight. She bit her lip to stop herself smiling too much and at the same time saw caution cross his face like a shutter. He bent and spoke to his father who was seated at his side.

It was the Sultan who took the initiative.

'Mr Chetwynd, Major Beattie, welcome to Perim.'

The tall figure in the black and gold robes stood up and came forward with outstretched hand. He made a dignified inclination of the head, while the hooded gimlet eyes darted from one to the other. 'And His Excellency? Sir Harry is travelling separately?'

'I'm afraid the Resident has unexpectedly had to leave for the Hadramaut,' Geoffrey said with a trace of the old automatic charm. 'He asked me to deputize for him. I trust this meets with Your Highness's approval.'

'Of course, of course.' The wary expression on the Sultan's face was replaced by a quick smile that reminded Rose of Hassan. 'Especially as the change of plan brings with it Mrs Chetwynd, who is already a friend of ours.'

A hand emerged from the gold-embroidered sleeve and was extended for Rose to take briefly in hers. With an amused glance at his father,

Hassan followed suit. At his touch she felt a quickening in every sense, as she cast down her eyes according to custom.

'And my Vizier Abdullah and Sheikh Mohammed you also know,' Hassan said, turning to the others in the party.

Introductions gave way to the serving of lunch, a welcome distraction. The bare tiled floor of the inner room had been spread with rugs and cushions on either side of a long white cloth, where dishes were piled high with saffron rice and flat bread and chunks of roast meat and chicken. To one side a large table was arrayed with an incongruous mixture of what Mr Foster's cook evidently regarded as European staple diet – a large baked custard, somewhat burned, and what, on closer inspection, looked very like cucumber sandwiches.

'Chairs?' murmured Major Beattie, glancing around hopefully. He touched the nearest cushion with the toe of his boot. 'Or is it hunkers as usual?'

Martin Foster swallowed hard. 'The Sultan is a stickler for tradition. And footwear to be removed also, if you don't mind, sir.'

Rose heard Geoffrey groan behind her. 'Not even a bloody fork in sight,' he whispered to Beattie.

The young officer was hurrying over to settle the Sultan in the place of honour at the top of the room.

'Mrs Chetwynd, if you could act as hostess it would be the most tremendous help.'

Rose decided that Mr Foster needed some support.

'Of course. It will be a pleasure.'

Seated on the Sultan's right, she was grateful for the usual concentrated silence that fell as the meal was sampled and consumed. In between dishes, there were the ritual enquiries among the company as to one's health and the health of one's family. Then there was the weather to discuss – hotter than usual for this time of the year, it was decided – with the drought threatening the new cotton crops up-country. Just occasionally her eyes met Hassan's, sitting at the far side of the circle. A spark flew between them and just as quickly they both looked away again.

'I prefer to eat with my fingers,' the Sultan remarked to Rose as he popped yet another neat ball of meat and rice between his beard and his moustache. He leaned towards her and lowered his voice. 'Fingers are clean but forks not always so, especially in these primitive parts. Not like Jehal, eh?'

He chuckled as he held out his hands for a nervous servant to pour a trickle of scented water over them from a chipped enamel jug. Rose was aware of being carefully studied by those darting black eyes.

165

'I hear you have been riding. Remember I told you I would be most pleased for you to try some of my horses? Was it enjoyable?'

'Very enjoyable, Your Highness. Azziza is a lovely creature.'

The Sultan's mouth curled, as he murmured something in Arabic. A sallow-faced man in a white robe, who had been introduced as an interpreter, smirked across at Rose.

'His Highness says the horse's rider is equally so.' His smile faded under a withering glance from Hassan.

'But still you have not come to Jehal to show me how to play this game of tennis,' the Sultan went on. 'And yet you promised – you and Lady Rawlinson, that is,' he added.

Rose could see Geoffrey leaning forward to catch the drift of the conversation. She was grateful for Hassan's intervention.

'Mrs Chetwynd will visit us again very soon, but she must receive a proper written invitation, Father. We *owe* her now, as the English say about their social engagements.'

Everyone laughed. Geoffrey saw it as a break in the ice to be taken advantage of, while coffee was being handed around.

'Your visit to the Yemen was a successful one, Your Highness? You found the King in good health?'

'Very good health, thanks be to God.'

'Were you able to learn anything of His Majesty's view of the war, sir?'

'Ah!' The Sultan leaned back, with a look of amusement. 'So the English have enrolled me as their spy?'

He allowed Geoffrey a moment of discomfiture. Then he became serious. 'It is simple. His Majesty regards it as a purely European war. Even if the Germans do put pressure on the Turks to move against the British, it will be difficult for Yemen to take sides.'

Hassan was looking round at the three Englishmen. Rose could see him thinking it was time to give them a brief history lesson.

'You see, the Turks have been part of our lives for centuries. Aden and Jehal, the whole of the Arabian peninsula, all belonged to the Ottoman Empire, right up to the time of the British arrival. Yemen is still part of that Empire. The King even has a Turkish son-in-law. And our own links with the Yemen are just as old – they are our closest neighbours, after all.'

'Some say the days of the Turkish Empire are over,' Foster said quietly. 'It might be the time for Arabia to rid herself of her old masters.'

'And become the slaves of new ones instead?' Hassan was smiling, but there was an edge of bitterness in his voice.

His father glanced at him sharply. 'We regard the British as our friends. We live under their wing, as it were.' He tried to lighten the atmosphere again. 'After all, my ancestors gave them Aden in the first place.'

But Geoffrey was obviously chafing at these generalities.

'The point is, Your Highness, if the Turks pushed through the Yemen borders, would you defend yourselves against them?' His mouth was working at the corners. 'Can we rely on Jehal to hold the line? Otherwise the Aden garrison itself might be in danger.'

Hassan replied for his father with an authority Rose had not seen before. 'The question is, would you give us the troops to do so? The Jehal army on its own would be no kind of match for the Turkish military machine.'

Geoffrey had reached for the black leather dispatch case that he had kept at his side since his arrival. 'All that is implicit in the treaty we have drawn up. It's a revised version of our Treaty of Friendship with Jehal, quite simple really, with the emergency measures added in case of need.' He paused, holding out the document for the Sultan to see. 'The Resident is hopeful that Your Highness would see fit to put your name to it today.'

He was about to continue but the old man put up his hand. His expression was suddenly haughty. 'You go too fast, Mr Chetwynd. I think this thing must be done in the presence of the Resident. Sir Harry is my old friend. I need to talk to him.'

'But His Excellency has expressly empowered me . . .'

Once again the Sultan interrupted him.

'Besides, I need to confer with my son. I take his advice on many such matters. Remember, his years in Egypt were spent in the study of Near East politics.'

There was an awkward silence. But the next minute the Sultan had gathered his robe about him and with a single supple movement was on his feet.

'And now,' he said, beaming at the company, 'we go on a tour of Perim, yes? That is the immediate issue, is it not? How your people can set up some kind of defence here, in case the Germans wish to follow in Napoleon's footsteps.'

'Exactly, sir.' With a quick glance at Geoffrey, Major Beattie was taking over the operation. 'It's most gracious of Your Highness to allow us the freedom of the island in the first place.'

The Sultan clapped a friendly hand on his shoulder. 'To tell the truth, I am not sure whether it's yours or mine.' He led the way out to the verandah and pointed to the blue line of the coast stretching away in the distance. 'Our borders are directly opposite, you see. But just up there is Yemen. And Mocha is a port the Germans are after – or so I hear.'

'And that would give them the Red Sea and the passage to India.' The Major's voice was urgent. 'You see, Your Highness, Perim could well be another Gibraltar. It would guard the Indian Ocean as the Rock does the Mediterranean. A few ships are what we need here, gun emplacements, a regular shore battery.'

'There's an old cannon at the point,' Mr Foster volunteered. 'Perhaps you should take a look. Water is always the problem here, of course. Government talk of setting up a distillation plant. And there are plans for a coaling station too, I believe . . .'

The voices of the rest of the company faded into the compound as Rose paused for a moment in the shade of the verandah. With sudden magical ease Hassan was alongside her, the two of them standing together, out of earshot of the others.

'Rose, darling. I tried to speak to you before we left.'

'I know. Geoffrey came back early. I had Nabiha's message.'

They were whispering rapidly, like conspirators, still gazing ahead at the group in front of them.

'And my own little message?' His voice shook. 'The note . . .'

She nodded, unable to speak. For a few seconds their eyes met and drank in delight. Then a long swelling note from the seafront made them turn away. Across the gulf, out of the glitter of the water, they could see a liner approaching. Slowly it drew parallel with the island, floating effortlessly by, a dream-like world of its own. Unknown figures lined the rails, and there was the faint sound of music.

Rose held her breath. Both of them were thinking of the *Medina* and their very first meeting.

'I remember,' she said under her breath. She looked across at the Sultan and his party, who were also watching the ship only a few yards away. 'I remember standing at the rail as we passed Perim. I saw people watching from the shore as we are today. With all my heart, I wished myself there on that island, wished freedom for myself, and happiness. Now I have them.'

'Not freedom yet,' Hassan answered. 'But one day . . .'

The snatch of a popular tune drifted back to them from the deck. It was one the orchestra had played on the *Medina* every evening over and over again, lilting, seductive, absurdly sentimental. She felt Hassan's hand move ever so slightly to brush against hers. Stealthily he linked his little finger in hers, reminding her of that first touch between them at Jehal. But now that tiny point of contact flared between them as if they were embracing again in the house on the beach. All of a sudden Rose felt weak with longing. At the same moment, Abdullah turned round from the group in front. They moved apart guiltily.

'The ship,' Hassan called out quickly, nodding towards the liner as it began to draw away. 'We are talking about the *Medina*, a sister ship I think.'

Abdullah nodded. His face was anxious, almost protective, it seemed to Rose, as she and Hassan strolled over towards him.

'We are walking to the point,' he told them. 'To take a look at the cannon, it seems.'

Nearby, Martin Foster was directing the little procession towards a winding track that bordered the sea.

'If we go by way of the lighthouse, we should shake off the crowd,' he told them. 'The village people won't go near the place.'

'Why is that?' Rose asked, curious.

'They can't understand what works the lamp. They think it's a spirit of some kind, a *djin*. Also,' he went on, 'many years ago they say there was a murder there. One of the villagers discovered his wife was making assignations with the keeper. One night the man went up there and cut their throats. Or so they say.'

'My God,' Abdullah exclaimed in Arabic.

No one said anything else as the guards in their red fezzes rejoined the party, with a solitary Indian policeman in tow. Together they all set off at a dutiful trot at the heels of the Sultan, who strode ahead like a young man. Rose and Hassan followed at a little distance with Abdullah and the white-gowned interpreter. It was late afternoon now and the sun was low in the sky. Against it rose the lighthouse, throwing its long shadow over the rocks.

'I can understand the local people not liking the place,' Rose said, forcing a laugh.

'You are becoming a superstitious Bedouin,' Abdullah told her teasingly.

'It must be so lonely at night-time. Does anyone actually live there?'

The interpreter shook his head. 'The keeper comes over at sunset, an Indian from the village, another one to relieve him at midnight.'

Ahead of them, the Sultan's party had disappeared behind a bluff.

'What a walker your father is,' Abdullah said to Hassan. 'We must catch up with them.' He hurried the interpreter to the front and quickened his own pace. Then turning, he said to Rose, 'Take your time, Mrs Chetwynd. We'll tell the others you are following with the Emir.'

'Abdullah is our true friend,' Hassan murmured, watching him move off down the path. He turned urgently to Rose.

'Your husband – how did he take the idea of your staying on?'

'He calls it an armed truce. He knows I can destroy his career at any moment if I choose. And he's ambitious, Hassan, though he pretends not to be. This treaty – it would certainly be a feather in his cap if your father signs.'

'Never mind the wretched treaty.' They had both come to a standstill, each rapt and rooted in the other's gaze. 'What about us? What does he know?'

'Nothing.' Rose faltered. 'Nothing for certain, anyway.'

He took a step towards her.

'Put up your parasol, Rose.'

She obeyed as if in a dream, holding it in front of her against the glare of the sun. The thin silk enclosed them in a golden shield. Slowly Hassan put out his hand to her cheek.

'I just wanted to touch you.' She felt his fingers tremble on her skin. 'It's torture being so close to you . . .'

'We must walk on. They will notice something.'

He put his hand on her arm. 'This way, Rose. Just for a moment.'

Raising her parasol, she saw they had reached the side path to the lighthouse. It was only a few steps to the door, which stood open.

Almost before she realized what was happening, Hassan had drawn her inside.

'Just for a moment, Rose,' he whispered again. 'Just to hold you.'

His arms were around her. She could feel his heart thudding against hers. Then she gave herself up to his kiss. The release of that moment was so intense, so exquisite, she could not repress a cry. Inside the tiny passageway, they clung together like survivors from some disaster, pressed together against the wall. Rose felt the stone encrusted with the salt of years, clammy against her back, smelled the damp rotting odour of the spiral stairway rising above them.

'The keeper – maybe he is up there.' Her voice shook as she turned her face to look up into the shadows. Far above she could see the glint of the glass dome.

'Not yet. Not till sunset.'

The door behind them had swung to. Now they were enclosed together in this dusky secret place. As Hassan drew her into a deeper kiss, his recklessness made her suddenly blind with longing. Violently she snatched open the button on her shirt and placed his hand between her breasts, where the little silver moon hung hidden on its chain.

They were motionless for a moment in their embrace. Inside the thick walls the silence was intense. From far away they could hear the faint rustle of the sea breaking on the rocks, low and rhythmic like a clock, reminding them of the seconds slipping by.

In that hush there was no mistaking the sound of a footfall above them. Someone was inside the tower. It seemed to Rose unbelievable and for an instant terror blotted out reason. She remembered the story of the murder, the woman caught with her lover. Instinctively she flung herself away towards the door, still clinging to Hassan's hand.

'Oh God! Quickly!'

But Hassan remained quite still. He was staring up at the man who stood in the bend of the stairs above.

'You little whore!' came a slow drawling voice. 'You stupid little whore!'

As Rose turned and saw Geoffrey, that hateful face looking down at them, red and mocking, something curious happened. In a flash all fear drained away from her. Instead she felt fury, an overpowering rage at the trick he had played on her.

'How dare you spy on us! You've been waiting for us, watching us!'

Hassan stepped in front of her.

'Rose, stop. Go outside. The man is mad.'

But Geoffrey was still smiling.

'On the contrary, I have simply been inspecting the premises.'

He came down the steps between them. 'Perhaps that was your intention, Your Highness? After you had finished with my wife.' He was close to Rose. She could smell the whisky on his breath from the hip-flask he always carried in his inside pocket. She shuddered as he touched her shoulder.

'Does it please you then, that skin of his? Something different . . .'

Like an uncoiled spring, Hassan reached out to take him by the throat. His other hand went to his belt.

'Get away from her,' he said, in a low voice.

Everything seemed to Rose to be happening with interminable slowness, like a scene from a nightmare. There was a flicker of steel as Hassan drew the curved dagger from its sheath. He held it lightly against the opening of Geoffrey's jacket, but not too lightly. Rose saw a tiny bead of blood break, hanging like sweat from the edge of the blade. He was panting now, his eyes brilliant.

'Why do you threaten a woman? Why can you not fight for her like a man?'

'A crime of passion, eh?' Geoffrey drew back, staring at him. 'I'm afraid that's not exactly my line.'

'Hassan, please.' She thrust herself between them, appalled at the danger of the situation. It was a place for madness. She had known it from the start.

'All the same,' Geoffrey went on evenly, 'I don't imagine your honoured father would be any too pleased to hear that the young Emir had been forcing his attentions on the wife of a high-ranking government official. Physically molesting her, in fact.'

171

'Your wife!' Hassan spat the word, his eyes blazing. 'You have no wife, Mr Chetwynd. You have no women even, only boys, young boys, brought to you against their will, secretly. How would the Resident look on that, I wonder? How would he like to hear of the fathers who vow revenge on you for ruining their sons, you, the representative of the great King Emperor?'

Geoffrey stood quite still now. Rose saw his knuckles stand out as he gripped the rail behind him.

'One man's word against another's. In Aden I think the white man's word will rule, don't you?' He looked from one to the other with that sneering expression back on his face. 'Besides, how do you propose to rescue poor dear Rose from her beastly situation? Carry her off into the desert on your great stallion?'

Hassan flinched. 'I am a free man. I could take her away with me anywhere – she would come. How would you like that, Mr Chetwynd? Shown up before your fellow officers for the creature you really are?'

'Stop it, for God's sake.' Rose stood against the wall facing them, her arms stretched out on either side. She was still shaking but her voice was clear. 'Someone may come at any time. Do you want disaster – disaster for all of us?' She turned to Geoffrey. 'And you?' she said bitterly. 'Is this the truce you promised me?'

'At least I am able to control myself in public. Your lover must learn to do the same, I'm afraid.'

There was silence for a moment. Geoffrey brought out a handkerchief. He dabbed at the speck of blood on his throat casually as if a mosquito had landed there.

'My proposal is simple,' he went on. 'I will say nothing of this – this incident, if the Emir will oblige me with a certain service.'

'Service?' Hassan looked at him sharply.

'Come back with me to the rest-house. Put your name to the treaty, and persuade your father he should do likewise.'

'But I cannot tell the Sultan what to do!'

'Say you have been turning the matter over in your mind. He will accept your advice. Besides, old boy' – he raised his eyebrows insolently – 'under the circumstances you don't have much choice, do you? Put it down to the gentle art of persuasion as practised by Mrs Chetwynd.'

Hassan studied him without expression. 'And your side of the bargain? Do you promise to leave Rose alone? You will not threaten her? You will not approach her even?' He moved closer to Geoffrey. 'Just leave her to her own life as you are left to yours?'

'That is understood. Nothing will me give me greater pleasure.'

'Very well then. The treaty will be signed.' It was Hassan's turn to mock. 'And you will earn good marks from your English superiors.'

Rose was silent. There was nothing more she could say. Events had taken charge of themselves and she was powerless. As from another world, she heard steps outside. Someone knocked timidly on the door.

'Mr Chetwynd? We are walking back now.'

It was Martin Foster's voice. Hassan saw surprise on his face as he opened the door.

'So you are here, Your Highness.'

'Mr Chetwynd and I have been discussing the situation. We can continue our talk back at the rest-house no doubt, with the Sultan.'

He walked out with Geoffrey behind him, while Rose stood in the doorway. Mr Foster waited on one side, looking at her with an expression of concern.

'Rose?' Geoffrey's voice had its usual peremptory note as he paused on the path.

On an impulse, Rose turned to the young administrative officer.

'Mr Foster, I wonder if you would be kind enough to take me back to the boat? I have rather a bad headache. I need to lie down until it is time to leave.'

'Of course, Mrs Chetwynd.'

Rose walked over to Hassan and put out her hand.

'You will forgive me, Your Highness. And please convey my regrets to the Sultan.' She paused. 'You all have business to attend to now.'

'And tomorrow?' Hassan's voice was formal too. 'I hope you will be feeling well enough for our riding engagement, with the others from Jehal,' he added.

'Yes indeed. I'm sure I shall.'

Martin Foster was still looking at her as they made their way down to the jetty. 'Are you all right, Mrs Chetwynd?' He offered her his arm. 'The old lighthouse, it is rather a queer place, isn't it? Can't say I like it myself. And then all the walking in this heat.'

'I shall be better when I lie down.'

She felt tears rising, a delayed reaction. 'Perhaps I was wrong to come in the first place.'

'Not in my opinion, Mrs Chetwynd.'

They had reached the mooring. From the bridge, the figure of Captain Strong could be seen awaiting her.

'In fact, we could not have done without you. You were a great support, under rather difficult circumstances.' The young man put out his hand with a diffident smile. 'If there is anything I can do for you in return, at any time . . .'

'Not now.' Rose smiled back at him.

She turned to look towards the cliff path above. The figure of Hassan

173

was waiting there to see her board. He raised his hand to her and slowly she raised hers in reply.

She turned back to her companion. 'But in the future, Mr Foster, who knows?'

❧ 7 ❧

ALWAYS afterwards, the lighthouse at Perim stood out in Rose's mind as a warning. If you ignored the danger signals, you could be driven on to the rocks of disaster. If you were careful though and kept to the proper channels, you stood a reasonable chance of survival.

The trouble was, Rose reflected, it was so hard to be careful. When you were as wildly in love as she and Hassan, the risks involved seemed a small price to pay for the hoarded moments of pure happiness together. The bargain struck with Geoffrey, for instance, was by its very nature a horribly precarious one. Even now, Rose knew how hateful it had been to Hassan to be blackmailed into a political corner. But he would not talk to her about it.

'Why waste time on such things,' he said, as they lay together in the beach-house the following afternoon.

This time there was no friendly sandstorm to protect them. The sun struck down through the broken blinds and there was a fever about their embraces that drove them on to a kind of frenzy. Two miles away, Abdullah would already be waiting for them at the point. The thought was a torment to both of them. Afterwards, Rose found herself crying bitterly. Hassan turned her face to his.

'Rose, *habibi*!'

'It's not fair,' she kept repeating. 'It's just not fair.'

Naked, they huddled together, clinging tight like children whose games have led them astray into a dark place. But there was no putting off the moment when they had to draw apart and prepare to leave. Rose stood in the doorway looking out as she fastened her hair up under her hat. In the afternoon heat the unending line of the dunes had a cruel glitter like broken glass.

' "While yonder all about us lie, Deserts of vast eternity." '

She murmured the lines half to herself. Behind her, Hassan's arms encircled her for the last time.

'What is this?' he asked drowsily, bending his head to hers. 'Is it love poetry?'

'Yes, love poetry. About the shortness of life. "Time's winged chariot hurrying near." '

'Winged chariot?' He laughed and shook her gently. 'I wish our horses had wings. Abdullah will be wondering what has happened to us.'

These times together were carefully judged. It would be indiscreet to ride out more than once a week. Meanwhile there was the bittersweet pleasure of being in one another's company in a crowded room for an hour or so: at a Consulate reception, a musical evening given by Arab friends, an official function such as the opening of a new school or the presentation of regimental colours.

In between came the long dead periods of total separation. Time, which slipped away so inexorably when they were together, like sand in a glass, now became a solid barrier between them. There were many days when it was not possible even to speak together, long afternoons when Rose sat out on the verandah trying to read or sketch, knowing that Hassan was only a short distance away at one of those interminable state meetings of his. It was ironical that, even with Geoffrey away so much, it was almost impossible for Hassan to come to the house. The danger of a scandal was too great with servants about, as well as the occasional visiting memsahib, card in hand, groom and trap at the gate.

Worst of all were the nights, when Rose lay alone in her neat English room, thinking of Hassan in his bachelor suite at the palace, at the centre of a hive of servants, family and hangers-on – almost a hundred people, he had once told her. Still vivid in her mind were pictures of the harem. She could not forget the supple slave girls with beckoning eyes, or the doll-like creature in spangled silks who was destined one day to become the wife of the Emir.

'Why do you distress yourself with such thoughts?' Hassan asked her when she told him of these painful moments. They were sitting together on the cane sofa on Nabiha's terrace with a large circle of Arab guests, listening to the usual Egyptian records on the gramophone. Under cover of the song, Hassan went on, 'You know quite well you have driven the thought of any other woman completely out of my mind. There is only you, Rose. There always will be.'

'You must be careful, then,' she said, teasing him. 'The women will be bound to notice this lack of interest. They will become suspicious.'

'Then I shall pretend I have become like those slaves in the *Arabian Nights* – the kind of thing you English like to read about. What is the word? Eunuch, eunork' – he pronounced the word comically, rolling his eyes in mock-terror, so that they burst out laughing together.

The others looked round curiously. Those nearest them judged it a moment when they could join in the conversation with this unconventional young Englishwoman who was able to make the young Emir seem so pleased with life.

176

'You have travelled outside Aden yet?' The question came from a young niece of Nabiha who, like her daring aunt, had defied convention to be present at a mixed gathering, and without her purdah veil. 'You must go up to the mountains, to Zara. It is very beautiful, very primitive. The Fauzis have a house there. Maybe they will take you.'

Nabiha was at Rose's side, holding out a dish of her favourite pistachios. 'I have told her about it. But now with this stupid war, who knows?'

Rose saw her glance quickly at Hassan beneath kohl-stained eyelids. But no more was said.

Five days went by before she and Hassan were able to meet again. It was a party being given on the roof of the Steamer Point Hotel by the Italian Consul. Rose was attending with Geoffrey, but on such an occasion it was perfectly acceptable for her to leave her husband's side and take up a polite conversation with the Emir. The young man was usually a guest of honour at such gatherings. It salved the European conscience to be able to ask two or three 'civilized' Arabs to their parties. Besides, the young man was known to be a friend of the Chetwynds. 'Particularly Mrs Chetwynd,' as Mrs Beattie was fond of remarking.

Hassan greeted her with a stiff little bow. He was standing against the parapet smoking a Turkish cigarette. His white sharkskin dinner jacket gleamed against the pale green sky of early evening.

'You enjoyed the music the other evening?' he enquired.

For a moment he seemed to Rose an exotic stranger again. But then his eyes forced her to meet his gaze. 'How beautiful you look tonight,' he said, under his breath.

'I enjoyed it very much. And thank you, Your Highness.'

She took a sip of her crème-de-menthe frappé. Hassan said she always chose it because it matched her eyes. In fact, it was the only drink she did not associate with the smell on Geoffrey's breath.

'Is tomorrow all right for riding then?' she asked quickly, before they were joined by anyone else.

He shook his head.

'Bad news, I'm afraid. I have heard that the army have set up a training camp all along that part of the beach. They are using the house as a base for the officers.'

Rose caught her breath. It was as if she had been struck in the face. An image of an angel with a flaming sword, barring the way to Paradise, flashed through her mind.

'Oh, no! They can't! It's our own place,' she whispered.

She struggled to retain her social façade, but tears were forcing their

177

way through. They stood in silence for a moment, Hassan slightly in front of her, in case watchful eyes were upon them.

'I can't stand this kind of thing much longer,' he said in an undertone. 'Rose.' The urgency in his voice recalled her to reality. 'There is something. If Nabiha can arrange to go to Zara, will you go with her? Can you?'

'Why not?' she replied, suddenly fierce. 'I am her friend. It is perfectly proper.' Her eyes widened. 'And you?'

'I will be there. These things can be managed. We can travel on together, escape for just a few days. It is very wild country up there and I am not known by the people.'

'But what about me? A solitary Englishwoman will hardly go unnoticed.'

'The *chador*, the veil, has its uses, you know.' He smiled mysteriously. 'Other women have found it so, before now.'

Rose was half laughing. It was difficult to take the idea seriously. 'So you are going to carry me off on your stallion after all? Off to your black Bedouin tent in the middle of the desert!'

He lifted his chin as he did when touched on the raw.

'Why do you have to make a joke of everything? Perhaps we are a joke too, you and I and our meetings?'

'I'm sorry,' she said, contrite. She was suddenly nervous of these swings of mood he sometimes revealed. 'I didn't mean . . .'

'Rose, listen. There is one problem. You will need an official pass to cross into the interior. The Resident has to give his permission. These days it may be difficult.'

He broke off as the formidable figure of Miss Largesen of the Danish Mission made her way towards them, accompanied by the French Consul's wife.

'I was just advising Mrs Chetwynd on her plan to travel up to Zara,' Hassan said smoothly with a bow to each lady. 'But I was telling her that these are not ideal conditions at present.'

'You are an explorer then?' Miss Largesen said, turning on Rose with a jolly twinkle. 'I also in my young days, working with the Mission doctors. But now I am too old for such adventures.'

'Your husband is going up on tour zen?' inquired Madame Ries.

'No, it is an invitation from Nabiha Fauzi,' Rose said coolly. 'She hopes we might have a few days at her house up there. A holiday really, a break from the heat.' She had caught a glimpse of Sir Harry through the crush. 'If you'll excuse me, Your Highness, ladies . . .'

'We shall indeed,' cried Miss Largesen, waving a finger teasingly. 'You have monopolized the Emir for too long. I need to talk to him about medical supplies in Jehal.'

Rose could feel Madame Ries's spiteful gaze following her as she moved across to where the Resident stood, glass in hand. He was listening politely to the chatter of the Italian delegation. He turned towards her with an expression of some relief.

'Rose, my dear. Eleanor was talking about you only this morning. She couldn't be here this evening, alas – one of her migraines. You must come to dinner very soon. I see a great deal of your husband, of course,' he said with a touch of stiffness. 'But not enough of you,' he added.

With his square weathered face smiling so warmly at her, his hand on her arm, it was somehow easy to plunge straight on to her request.

'Do you remember, Sir Harry, that dinner party at the Residency when I first arrived? You were talking about travel in Arabia. You said if ever I wanted to make an expedition out of Aden, you would arrange it for me.'

Sir Harry shook his head dubiously. 'I'm afraid things have changed since then.' He looked at her hard. 'Of course, if it's just a trip to Jehal as a guest of the Sultan, no permission is needed.'

Rose swallowed, screwing up her courage another notch.

'Actually it's to Zara, to stay at the Fauzis' house.'

'Aha! Old friends of mine, Nabiha and Farid!' He suddenly looked relaxed again. 'Near to my old stomping-grounds as a Political Officer. Well, as long as you promise not to get involved with one of those tribal blood feuds like I did!' He rubbed the scar beneath his beard with a wry grin. 'You've got to remember the Yemen border is only a few miles away. If any trouble with the Turks breaks out, we'll have you back here right away and no nonsense.'

'Of course.'

'Then I think we can fix things up for you.' Again he looked at her closely, this time with an almost wistful expression. 'You love this country, don't you?'

Rose nodded, not trusting herself to speak.

'Well, see as much of it as you can, while you can. Things change you know, sometimes overnight. And then the chance is gone for ever.' His hand tightened on her arm. 'Only wish I was coming with you.'

As she moved to make way for other guests eager for a word with the Resident, he leaned towards her. 'Pick a peach for me while you're there,' he whispered. 'Best peaches in Arabia at Zara! Don't forget.'

⚜ 8 ⚜

THE peaches were almost the first thing Rose saw. She and Nabiha had been travelling for two days, a period of time that had become a strange jumble of experience. There were the endless dusty desert tracks unfolding beneath the wheels of a bone-shaking motor wagonette, the nights spent in a Government rest-house and the little clapboard shack of an up-country sheikh, and then a long winding climb through the hills on donkeys. Nabiha's bearer-cum-driver was in charge of the expedition, a rugged, taciturn character by the name of Abdu. His forebears had been retainers of the Fauzi family for as long as anyone could remember. Assisted by the urchin who had been the bearer of Nabiha's note that day, he proved to be a model of resourcefulness, producing tea and food, rugs and pillows at a moment's notice out of the mountain of baggage piled on the back of the smallest donkey.

The whole trip had materialized suddenly in the usual Arab way, like the genie out of the lamp. The day after the party, there had been a telephone call from Nabiha. Now here they were, at the end of the trek, ensconced in the Fauzis' house at Zara, which was like no house Rose had ever seen before. It had been dark when they arrived. They had come through a village that was silent and shuttered in sleep. Rose herself was nodding with drowsiness, one hand clutching the rough little mane of the donkey, the other holding her shawl tight around her against the mountain air, as the little procession followed the circle of Abdu's lantern. There was a stony track up a hill, a tall building at the top, and under an archway a low wooden door with ancient iron studs. Bolts were drawn back from inside. A shapeless old woman threw herself on to Nabiha with squawks of joy. Inside, there was a little courtyard with a glimpse of chickens and straw, and a pair of glowing eyes that made Rose jump out of her skin.

Nabiha laughed as they got off their donkeys. 'It's only a goat.'

Alongside the animal smells, there was the usual faint whiff of sewage. Then Rose was taken by the hand and led in through another door. There was a lime-washed room like a kitchen, black pans hanging on the walls among bunches of dried herbs and vegetables, and sacks of coffee in the corner. Nabiha picked up a small oil-lamp. 'Take a deep breath,' she said. 'Now we go up and up.'

180

Rose counted three landings as they climbed the corkscrew staircase. On the fourth, Nabiha said, 'My room is here,' and then on the fifth, 'This is the top. There is a bathroom, such as it is. And this is yours.'

She opened a door and put down the lamp, then stood back to watch Rose's face.

'You like it?'

Rose nodded, speechless with weariness and delight. Next to the flickering light stood a glazed bowl, blue and white, piled high with yellow peaches. The whole thing glowed like a painting, set at the centre of an Aladdin's cave of clutter and ornament, flower-embroidered curtains of old blue velvet hanging from the walls, Turkish rugs on the bare boards of the floor, a low table covered with mysterious bottles of oil and scent and various small brass pots. But it was the bed that dominated the room, an amazing four-poster edifice, with an ancient crimson-tasselled canopy. Beneath it gleamed a headboard of faceted glass and inlaid mother-of-pearl, with a frieze of painted birds and trees that went right round to the foot.

'It came from my Persian grandmother,' Nabiha told her.

'Who sleeps here usually?' Rose asked, bewildered.

'Visitors like yourself. The women's quarters are always at the top of the house. If any men want to come up the stairs, they must shout out the name of Allah three times. Just to make sure the way is clear.'

She laughed, bustling about the room in her dusty black travelling cloak. With her hair tucked back into two long plaits, Nabiha was no longer the languid Aden hostess, but a country woman full of earthy energy. 'One of the wives of the Naib sometimes stays here when her husband visits Zara,' she chattered on. 'There are always plenty of clothes in the cupboard. Here.' She handed Rose a long loose garment of faded blue. 'Take this for sleeping. It will save you unpacking.'

'Nabiha.' Rose caught her friend by the hand. It was the first time they had been really on their own since the journey began. Whenever they stopped, the little rooms had been full of tribespeople eager to greet the visitors. 'You are a darling to me. It's been marvellous escaping like this. But there are so many things I need to talk to you about.'

She meant Hassan, of course. But Nabiha simply laid a finger across Rose's mouth. 'Shush. No need to talk. Just be happy. Take what God has given you.'

'But what do you plan?' Rose began again.

'We are both too tired,' Nabiha said firmly. 'Tonight sleep. Tomorrow plan.'

With a quick hug she was gone, leaving Rose with just enough will-power to investigate the dank little cell next door with the usual hole in the

181

ground. Then all she had to do was to step out of her clothes, pull on the shift of the Naib's wife and sink into the extraordinary bed.

'Sandalwood,' she thought, as the pillows gave up a musky feminine fragrance. Another scent vied with it, frail and sweet. It seemed to come from the two slit windows.

'Jasmine,' Rose decided drowsily. And then, 'Hassan,' she said to herself as sleep washed over her. She had no idea when or where they were to meet. No doubt she would be told tomorrow. In the meantime, he was there in her dreaming, leading her through a mysterious sequence of events that took them through numberless deserted houses, sometimes in Wales, sometimes in Arabia. But always time was rushing by and they were hurrying, anxious, late for whatever it was that awaited them. So that when she stirred in the bed and half-opened her eyes, the sight of Hassan in the doorway seemed to be merely a continuation of her dream. It was barely light. A pale glow came in through the chinks in the wall, falling on the slight figure that stood facing her. He was bare-headed, a sand-coloured wrap thrown over one shoulder.

'Good morning,' he whispered.

She hardly saw him come towards her. One minute he was at the door, the next he was in her arms and tenderly, dreamily, they were slipping away together into that secret country where time and place no longer existed, only the revelation of ecstasy. This time Rose thought there was a new dimension to their love-making. There was a sense of freedom to it, a glorious isolation as if they were the only two people in the universe.

'Are we really alone then?' she murmured when there was stillness again between them. They had turned face to face on the sandalwood pillows to talk.

'Alone in the house? Yes, my love.'

'But Nabiha?'

'She left very early to meet Farid at Ariab. It's a little town further to the east. Farid has business there. I came from there just an hour ago. Nabiha and I met each other half-way. She said she wanted to give us a place of our own, if only for a few days.'

Rose felt a flood of gratitude. 'She knows then?'

'Of course she knows. So does Abdullah. They call us the sheep of heaven. It's an Arab name for lovers who've lost their wits completely. It's too silly to explain.' He stroked her face gently. 'You must not be shy about it, Rose. Without such friends, nothing would be possible.'

'I know.' She gave a long soft sigh of happiness and stretched out under the embroidered coverlet with its magical patterns of leaves and stars. 'Hassan. Do we have to go anywhere today? Can we just stay here in this room?'

He laughed. 'Like castaways on an island? Yes, we can stay here as long as we like.' He slid gracefully out of the bed and stood beside her, still holding her hand. 'But I have to bath. And we have to eat and drink.'

As she stirred to sit up, he pushed her back again. 'You shall do nothing. There is a serving woman, Ayesha, who lives in the basement, one of the Fauzi slaves. She will look after us, and she will speak to no one about us. She belongs to the Fauzi family, body and soul, the way slaves do.'

'But who will she think I am?'

'She will neither know nor care, except that you are mine.' He looked at her quizzically. 'Perhaps some courtesan from Cairo or Beirut. Circassian with green eyes and ivory skin.' He turned at the door. 'Now rest, till I come back.'

Rose turned on her side and closed her eyes. A sense of bliss flowed through her like a benediction. Outside the house the day had begun. Every sound that floated up to her from that unknown world was precious to her, part of the miracle of being alone with Hassan in an unknown place. Voices called out to one another, cracked and distant, as if from one hill to the next. From closer by, she heard the chant of the muezzin in his tower calling the faithful to prayer. There was the queer pumping groan of the little donkeys in the courtyard below, the snatch of a flute being played, the clatter of pots and a woman's laugh, wheezing and fat.

After a while, curiosity roused her and she got up. Peering down from the high slit window, she felt like Tennyson's Lady of Shalott looking out from her turret room.

After the leaden heat of Aden the mountain air had a cool tingle that touched every sense. There were fields of maize and barley stretching away on either side. In their midst the village of mud houses was turned to gold by the radiance of the morning sun. On the hill behind there was a little fortress, sitting with the defiant air of a crumbling sandcastle. A hawk hung in the clear blue, a shimmering speck, and all along the twisting track to the village medieval figures went up and down, tribesmen in bright kilts and cloaks, the young boy playing his pipe, robed women with water-pots on their heads. It was like looking through a chink in time, on to a world that had never changed.

Outside the window, there was the scent of jasmine again. Rose put out her hand and encountered something smooth and round, a peach growing against the wall. When Hassan came back he found her sitting on the floor in her blue gown with her knees under her chin, her hair down her back, a half-eaten peach in her hand.

'Can't you wait for your breakfast then, greedy girl?'

He proffered a tray which bore pancake bread in a wicker dish, a chunk

183

of honeycomb, glasses and a teapot steaming with the bitter fragrance of mint.

'It was by the door,' he told her. 'Ayesha thought you were still asleep.'

They ate sitting cross-legged on the bed. A shaft of sunlight threw rosy shadows under the tasselled canopy.

'It's like being in a tent,' Rose said. 'A Bedouin tent.'

'And how would you know, Mrs Chetwynd?' he taunted her with a grin, stuffing the last of the bread into his mouth. 'Wait till you see the real thing.'

Brushing off crumbs, he sprang up and went to the window. Rose wanted him to stand there without moving, his beauty was so extraordinary. He was bare to the waist, with a length of scarlet cotton knotted about his hips. The line of his face in profile, the slanting bronze planes of cheekbone and shoulder had a power to move her now that frightened her.

But in a moment he was turning again, pulling his clothes on, talking and gesticulating. 'I have to see about mules for the journey. Ayesha will be coming to you now, to bring you your bath and so on. So be prepared.'

'You won't be long?'

'How could I?'

As he went out, he threw something into her lap. 'Say your prayers while I am gone.'

Smiling, Rose picked up the string of amber beads which he always carried with him, usually around his wrist. She was sitting on the edge of the bed, running them through her fingers when there was a tap at the door. A very fat, very black old lady, her head wrapped in a yellow scarf, came waddling in.

'Ma'salaam, ma'salaam!' She was breathing heavily after her climb, her eyes darting over Rose, as she approached with her head bent at a respectful angle.

'Ma'salaam,' Rose replied. 'You are Ayesha?'

Vigorous nods and smiles were interspersed with a torrent of Arabic, some it followed by Rose, some not.

It was hard to remember the exact sequence of what happened next. All Rose knew was that she had become the object of a series of complex rituals. First she was thoroughly drenched in scented water poured from an immense copper jug, then dried, oiled and pummelled by those fat little hands that were so surprisingly soft and deft. There was no time to feel embarrassed. Rose decided it was best to relax and accept it all, like a prize filly being groomed for a show.

All the time there was a soothing, breathless commentary from Ayesha, with occasional exclamations of amazement. The fairness of Rose's skin was being compared, it seemed, with the whitewashed walls of the little room as well as the jasmine flowers.

She found herself swathed in an enormous shawl from which her feet and hands protruded. These were then painstakingly decorated with tiny criss-cross patterns, painted on with some dark blue paste. They made a fetching effect of lace mittens and socks.

'Wallahi!' exclaimed Ayesha, sitting back on her heels to admire her work.

Then a succession of petticoats was pulled over Rose's head, and finally a robe of striped brocade. Only when a box of brightly-coloured powders and creams was provided did Rose try to protest.

'No really, Ayesha.'

But it was useless. A kind of yellow dust was being pressed over her face which made her feel like a bee emerging from a pollen-filled flower. A number of dots and circles were pasted on cheeks and forehead with the neatness of stamps on an envelope. Finally, pièce de resistance, a tiny brass urn was produced. From this Ayesha drew a pointed stopper coated with black.

'Kohl!' she cried triumphantly, demonstrating how Rose was to close her eyes while the stopper was laid along the lower lid. A delicate flick was applied at each corner to complete the encirclement.

Once again Ayesha drew back with the narrowed gaze of the artist contemplating a canvas. With a brisk nod, she brought forward a mirror and Rose was invited to look.

It was a heart-stopping moment. Some Eastern houri stared back at her. The black-rimmed eyes were huge in a face like a gilded mask. Rose smiled nervously to placate this alarming stranger and saw white teeth appear through rouged lips. In a way she was to be admired, this idol. It was beautifully done, a work of art, beauty spots and all. But the greatest shock was her hair, now being oiled and combed so tenderly. Without Rose realizing it, a shampoo of henna had been rubbed into it and what had been gold was now a rich mahogany red.

Ayesha was holding up her stained palms with cries of delight.

'Tamam! Tamam!'

Rose nodded, dumbfounded. She felt like an actress who had forgotten her lines. This disguise had imposed a whole new character upon her. Even when Ayesha had made her departure, she remained where she was, sitting cross-legged on her cushions, motionless as an icon. What would be the look on Hassan's face when he reappeared? Delight? Amusement? Annoyance?

Nothing quite prepared her for the way he stopped dead in the doorway. He drew in his breath quickly.

185

'God be praised!'

'You like it?' she asked eagerly.

He sank down on his haunches in front of her with an expression of disbelief. 'You look like a bride,' he whispered. He bent his head and kissed her knee, the old token of fealty, a gesture so instinctive it did not seem strange to her.

'Perhaps one day,' he said, raising his eyes to her again. 'Perhaps one day it will come true.'

She shook her head gently. The idea struck her as fantastical. She pulled at a package he had tucked inside his jacket.

'What are you hiding?'

'Ah, yes.' He was brisk again, pulling her to her feet. 'Please close your eyes until I say.'

Rose felt her hair lifted from behind and the touch of something cool and heavy around her throat.

'Now look.'

He was holding up the mirror. In it she saw her face framed by a splendid necklace of carved and fretted silver chains. Each link was studded with rubies, amber and cornelian, shaped like flowers.

'You know the Arab saying: A beloved woman without jewels is like a blossom without scent.'

Rose touched it wonderingly. 'But something so old, so precious! Where did you find such a treasure?'

'There is a very old silversmith at Ariab. He keeps such things at the back of his workshop. I saw it there yesterday and it seemed somehow to belong to you.' He sighed. 'Ours is not a rich family, like the Sultans in the stories. More like one of your country squires, living on our estates. Otherwise I would give you emeralds and diamonds. But there are other things I want you to have – rugs from Isfahan, silks from Damascus. You are my love and I want to spoil you.'

He took her hand and kissed it, on the palm and then the inside of her wrist as he always did. There was a soft tapping on the door, the brush of footsteps going down the stairs. Ayesha had taken food for them on to the terrace, Hassan explained.

'Well, not exactly a terrace,' he went on. He led her out through a side door, hidden behind the blue curtain. 'Just a flat rooftop really. All the houses have such a place. It's where the women can sit and take the air without being spied on. Where a wife can be undisturbed with her husband when it's too hot to work in the fields.'

The sun was indeed hot now, but there was a canvas awning over a little alcove to shade them. Someone had planted aromatic herbs in a stone box. On the wall above hung a goat's foot for luck. Slowly, imperceptibly, the day was already melting away, Rose thought, however hard she tried to hold it. There was the meal they ate, tiny sand-grouse shot by Hassan the day before, and then the siesta they shared lying side by side and hand in hand on the rug. Rose opened her eyes and once more saw the hawk drifting and mewing high above, in a sky that was already losing its brilliance.

'What time is it, Hassan?' she asked lazily.

'Time, time,' he sighed. 'Always the English ask the same question. If I told you, you wouldn't believe me anyway. Don't you know that we count the hours from sunrise, not midnight?'

'There's so much I don't know, things you said you would tell me. What about Arab women? Are they so different from me?'

He smiled slyly. 'Well if you were an Arab, you would have no hair on your body. Arab women shave themselves, you know.'

Rose was startled. 'Do you mind?'

For answer Hassan reached out and laid his hand on her. 'The only thing I mind is that we cannot be together like this every day of our lives.'

They looked at each other in silence.

'And what else?'

'Arab women are very superstitious. If you have a headache, don't tell Ayesha. She will brand the soles of your feet with a hot iron to send the *djin* away.' He thought for a minute. 'And when you have your time of the month I must never come near you. "Lest she tarnish his sword with her blood," ' he quoted.

Slightly shocked, Rose affected nonchalance. 'That's certainly a poetic way of putting things.'

'We are all poets, you know. Myself included. Wait, I will sing you something I made for my cousin's wedding.'

He disappeared inside, returning with a battered-looking string instrument that Rose recognized as an *oudh*. Without self-consciousness he sat down before her and produced a winding thread of melody seemingly without a beginning or an end. It touched her strangely to see him play, and when he began to sing very softly the sound seemed to summon up echoes of heartbreak that were almost too much to bear. All the time, his eyes never left her, as if she were the music he was reading. Quickly she got up.

'You're making me cry.'

It was almost sunset and the air was cooling. She went into the room to look for a wrap. The song had come to an end and when she looked out again she saw Hassan had laid aside the *oudh* and was washing his hands and face from the ewer in the corner. Then he knelt down on the rug with his head bowed. She kept quite still, watching, as he prostrated himself, utterly absorbed in the prayers he was repeating to himself. Finally he raised both hands, palms upturned, for a blessing. It was a moment when she realized with unforgettable clarity what she could only describe to herself as the 'otherness' of Hassan's life. This world of Islam was something totally beyond her, something she could never penetrate or even begin to understand.

Even when he tried to explain to her some of the principles of the faith later that evening, it was hard to shake off this sense of being the outsider, the infidel. What power could she compare it with in the life of a milk-and-water Anglican like herself, a *Nasara* – as the Arab children shouted after the English in the back streets of Aden.

'It is what binds us all together, you see,' Hassan said. 'Syrian, Yemeni, Persian, Egyptian. It is the real force the West can never break.' His face lit up. 'One day it will make us into the great empire we once were. But first there has to be a revolt to rid us of the Turks, to show the world how serious we are. It will be a crusade, like the crusades of history.'

'Is this what you talked about in Cairo, at the university?'

Hassan nodded. 'Egypt is where it will all begin.'

'Perhaps some of the British will support you?'

'At a price,' Hassan said. 'Do you believe a treaty is to be trusted, like the one we signed at Perim?'

'I believe a man like Rawlinson is to be trusted.'

'Ah, Sir Harry. A good man. He it was who made this possible.' They looked around them at the shadowy garden, the white oleanders clustered around the steps that led to a small pool. It was dark now and they had come down to enjoy the cool of the evening behind the high surrounding walls. Ayesha had been watering the flowerbeds. The smell of the wet sandy soil rose up with the last scents of the day. A hurricane lantern hung from an old fig tree by the door, but overhead the stars were so dense and bright they gave off a glow of their own.

'Water and gardens,' Hassan said. 'That is the Arab dream of Paradise, you know. Perhaps because they are so hard to achieve.'

'Like all the best things,' Rose said quietly.

For a long time they sat and talked at the edge of the pool, under the date palms. Rose told him of her childhood in Wales and Hassan described his terror of going to the Aden boarding-school for the sons of sultans. For the first few days he pretended to be dumb. Then, being taken home, he called out delightedly to his mother and gave the game away.

'Did you learn to swim?' he asked her.

'Of course.'

'Then show me.'

It was not really a pool designed for swimming, but just to be together in the water was a new delight. Rose was stripped to her shift, Hassan naked except for his scarlet *futah*. It was as if they were two children playing entangled in the shallows, until they began to shiver in the cool, evening air.

Climbing the stairs again, they were grateful for the warmth of the room at the top, which still retained the heat of the day. Ayesha had lit some incense in a little clay burner and its rich smoky perfume filled the air. Rose thought of her convent school and the power of that particular scent still to evoke a sense of holiness and mystery. In the mosaic of tiny mirrors around the bed, she caught a glimpse of Hassan's face next to hers, brown against white, fragmented yet joined. Then he blew out the flame of the lamp. Lying in his arms, she fell asleep with one hand curled around the string of prayer beads under the pillow.

❧ 9 ❧

In the morning they had to wake early, for this was the day they were
making an expedition to the ruins. Hassan was vague about them.
Something to do with the Queen of Sheba, people said. All this country
was part of the old incense routes, where the trading caravans had criss-
crossed from Syria down to the coast of the Hadramaut.

'We must ride through the village to get on to the track, so now you go
into purdah,' he told her as he helped her to dress.

From the cupboard, he fished out a long black *chador* that cocooned her
from head to foot. Underneath it, he tucked a black gauze scarf to cover
her face.

'How do you know about such things?' she asked in a muffled voice.

'All my life I see my mother and my aunts go through the process every
time they want to go out for a drive.' He peered at her, grinning, through
the veil. 'How does it feel?'

'Invisible,' she said. 'I like the attar of roses, though. Nabiha told me
that a woman can pick her own *chador* out of a pile of everyone else's, just
by the scent.'

There was a slight problem, she discovered, when it came to riding in
purdah. The only way was to sit on one's mule sideways, packaged into a
sort of makeshift saddle of cushions and sackcloth and hanging on firmly
to the head-rope. Hassan was only a few yards away, riding in front with
the various items of baggage.

'Food and water and something to sleep on,' he told her. 'Then we can
camp out overnight.'

Fortunately the village was crowded for market-day and no one paid
them much attention as they made their way through the jostle of the
narrow street. Rose discovered there was a curious freedom about the
veil. Beneath it you could stare, frown, smile or yawn without anyone
being the wiser, even though the passing scene became a kind of
shadow-play: the stacked-up wares on either side, stacks of maize and salt
and tobacco, the bobbing sea of turbans and headshawls, the up-country
tribesmen, bare to the waist and bristling with rifles and daggers, all went
by like a succession of badly developed photographs. At one point, she lost
sight of Hassan and panicked. But there he was again, a purposely

nondescript figure in a faded brown burnoose, beckoning her on with a truly Arab gesture of lordly indifference.

Then they were out on the open track again. Rose slipped the veil from her face and saw a rocky plateau stretching ahead, green turf underfoot scattered with tiny shrubs. Here and there flowers like tiny irises sprang up where the spring rains had fallen. Away to the south lay the sands of the Empty Quarter and always behind them the mountains. Muslims believed they had been placed there by God to peg down the earth and stop it from moving, Hassan told her. On the horizon, he pointed out a faint blue line like a slow-moving cloud.

'The camel herds,' he said. 'Soon we will see the camps.'

They had been riding for another hour before they came in sight of habitation, just two black tents, three camels and a few sheep, with the smoke of a fire shimmering in the haze. Rose had never seen anything quite so lonely in all her life.

'We will have to stop just for a few minutes, it is only polite. You had better put your veil on again. But don't worry. They're simple people. All they want to know is that we're friendly. Raids and feuds go on all the time among the different tribes.'

'And who do we say we are?'

'Just townspeople from Aden, travelling to the next village to see relations. Don't mention the ruins. They'll think there must be treasure hidden.'

As they were speaking, a figure appeared from inside the tent, a bearded, gaunt-looking man in a ragged grey robe, shading his eyes against the sun. It was a relief to Rose to see a family of small children surrounding him, instead of the band of brigands she had imagined.

'Welcome in God's name,' he called to them.

'Peace be upon you,' Hassan replied.

An older man came hobbling forward, his face wrinkled in a broad smile under the folds of his red headshawl.

'Come sit and talk. The coffee is freshly made.'

With a quick look of reassurance in Rose's direction, Hassan dismounted and disappeared inside. At the same moment a small boy, his face much covered in flies, led her mule round to the back of the tent. Here the womenfolk were waiting for her. Veils were twitched aside, eager hands helped her down, while once again Rose had to accept a shrill chorus of excited comment as the brilliant black eyes devoured her from head to foot.

Where did she come from? Where were her children? It was a new husband she had with her perhaps?

Rose tried to shrug off the cross-examination with a few of her Arabic set-pieces. Then she was taken over by a girl of about her own age who reminded Rose of one of the gypsies of Wales with her impudent smile and plaited side-curls.

'*Gahawa?*' she demanded, pulling her towards the tent. Rose could smell the ginger coffee that was brewing inside and somehow could not face it. The girl saw the hesitation on Rose's face and laughing led her round to where the animals were tethered. Within minutes she was milking a noisy female camel. She handed her a bowl of the frothing liquid and Rose drank gratefully, trying to disassociate the taste from the pungent-smelling beast.

Afterwards the girl seized Rose's hand and placed it on her stomach. Under the strings of coins and amulets, Rose could feel the unmistakeable swelling.

The girl nodded delightedly. Yes, there was a baby there, her first. She prayed to Allah for a boy. Now she put her hand on Rose with a questioning look, but Rose shook her head blushing. She was glad to see Hassan reappear.

Behind their veils, the women trilled out their farewells. As they rode away, Rose's friend called something after her.

'What is she saying, Hassan?'

'She prays you will soon have a son. That he will be as tall as his father and as fair as his mother.'

Their eyes met. Rose felt the prickle of tears not far away. As she looked back, she saw something she knew she would never forget, that cluster of figures so tiny in an immensity of sand and sky. Despite the incredible harshness of their life, these people were kind, courageous and gay. Their pride in their freedom was inseparable from the landscape that bred them. Once again, Rose had the sense of looking through a shutter at a world that had existed untouched for thousands of years, a world in which she could only be a passing onlooker, an outsider with all the tarnished self-awareness that Western civilization produced. Hassan was also a sophisticate, it was true. But he only had to shed his cosmopolitan veneer to be at home again. She had seen it as he talked to the man of his camels, seen it every time he handled a cup of Bedouin coffee, or put his bare feet on to the sand. She watched him twist his turban around his face, as the sun struck down on them with full force. They had come out of the pass and on to the plain. Ahead Rose saw a village and thought of shade. But it was only the skeleton of a village, half-buried in the dunes. The mud walls were crumbling, broken beams scattered like driftwood, and the well-head was choked with weeds.

'Who lived here?' she asked.

'Who knows? There are such places everywhere. Perhaps the people ran away in some fighting. Or the water gave out.'

Rose rested her hand on the neck of her little mule, glad of its solid life. 'It's ghostly, somehow. You feel the people are still here, watching you.'

'Come. This is where the real ghosts are.'

He pointed uphill, past a little white cairn with the plaster falling away. Hassan said it was the tomb of 'some old *sayed* or saint'. But up there, right at the top, that was where a palace had once stood. Now all that was left was a jumble of honey-coloured stones. Here and there an archway was still standing, a broken pillar fallen on its side.

'This is what I wanted to show you. They say that it was a favourite place of one of my ancestors. He used to come up here in the summer months when it was too hot in Aden.'

Neatly he tethered the mules to a thorn tree and brought out water for them from one of the saddlebags. Rose was on her knees in the rubble, turning over flints and fragments with mounting excitement.

'Have the archaeologists been here?'

'Hardly at all. I seem to remember some Germans coming to Jehal to question my father about it when I was a small boy.' He dusted himself down. 'But what is one ruin when there are so many?'

Rose was entranced. 'Perhaps the Queen of Sheba lived here. Perhaps Solomon visited her here . . .'

'Never mind Solomon and the Queen of Sheba.' He was dismantling some of the baggage. 'I am a poor Bedouin and I am hungry. Come and be a good wife. Look!' He pulled out a goat's-hair blanket. 'I even have a black tent for you.'

Rose laughed. She was tying her veil over her hair to keep out the dust. 'I don't believe you would know how to start to put one up.'

'Wait and see. At least it will keep the sun off us.'

Slung over a corner between a broken wall and a branch or two, it did indeed provide a shelter. They ate their picnic lunch in it, cold chicken and bread packed by Ayesha, with fresh figs. The water in its goatskin container had kept surprisingly cool.

After this feast they rested until the sun had crept round behind the ruins. The plain in front swam in a soft ochre light and violet shadows marked the slopes of the dunes. Sitting up, Rose remembered the sketch-pad and pencils she had stowed in her bag. When Hassan opened his eyes he saw her busy at work.

'Always *doing*,' he teased her. 'Is it so hard to just *be*?'

But he looked over her shoulder curiously. The sketch of the desert had been abandoned. Alongside it there was a drawing of a young man asleep on a rug with his turban over his eyes.

'Stealing my soul while I sleep!' He shook his finger at her. 'No good Muslim can permit it!'

She sighed. 'This landscape is impossible for an amateur.' She narrowed her eyes and stared out to where a mirage seemed to be glimmering against the blue. 'It takes hold of your whole being. But when you try to put it on to paper it just evaporates!' She laid her head on his shoulder. 'How can one feel so at home in such a lonely place, Hassan?'

'Destiny, or so your friend Trevelyan would say.' He smiled down at her. 'Perhaps he came here too.'

After a moment he got up and splashed his face from the water bag. She watched him stroll away outside the walls. She knew he was going to make his evening prayers, and that he did not always wish to tell her.

Against the stones a lizard flickered a lazy tongue for flies. She saw it watch her out of a winking eye as she sifted a handful of dust through her fingers. Something blue glinted amongst the grains, a fragment of turquoise mosaic set in clay. Soon she had uncovered several more of the tiny shards, brilliant as a butterfly's wing.

'Treasure,' she said, holding them out in the palm of her hand when Hassan returned.

'Tea,' he replied.

He piled together the sticks he had brought back with him, and rummaged in the baggage for the kettle. 'I used to be able to make fire with flints when I was little. But now!' He produced matches with the air of a conjuror, carefully adding more fuel as the flames sprang up. Rose made the tea. As they drank the smoky-tasting brew, he watched her tie the fragments into her scarf for safety.

'What else do you have there?'

'Your prayer beads.' Rose felt a qualm of guilt. Was this forbidden too? 'I love the feel of the amber.'

'Infidel,' he said, pinching her cheek softly. 'Beloved infidel.'

It was almost dark now. Hassan had lit the little travelling lantern.

'Come,' he said mysteriously, taking her by the hand.

The lamplight made a yellow circle around their feet as they climbed the dune behind the ruin. The sand was ridged in long curving ripples, so that it was like walking on the sea. At the top, Hassan laid down the rug he was carrying in a hollow scooped out by the wind.

'Now look,' he said, turning her round. Rose saw that on the horizon, a wonderful thing was happening. Over the edge of the plain, an enormous full moon had begun to emerge. With Hassan's hand on her shoulder she stood hardly daring to breathe, as slowly the great disc hung clear of the land and the whole desert was bathed in its radiance. Even the sand around them gave off a phosphorescent glow. At the same time the stars came pricking out, crowded so close together in that vast sky that there was scarcely a space between them.

Hassan blew out the lamp. Every detail of the other's face was as clear as if etched on silver.

'Rose.' His voice was so low she was not sure she had heard him. They sat down on the rug, close together. 'You will not be cold up here?'

She shook her head. She drew the shawl more tightly round her shoulders but could not stop herself trembling. She had the feeling that he had found the right moment to put into words something he had been carrying with him since his arrival at Zara.

'Do you remember what I told Geoffrey? That if I asked you, you would come with me anywhere?' He paused, looking down at the fringe of the rug he had twisted between his fingers. 'Would you?'

'Go away? The two of us?' Rose's heart seemed to stumble, then recover itself. She put her hand on his arm. 'But Hassan, where would we go?'

'Cairo. I have friends there. We could live together there with no trouble. Be free together. Can you imagine it, Rose?'

He pulled her towards him, searching her eyes. 'We can't go on like this, stealing time, making lies. It's all just pretending, like a play.'

'I know,' Rose said softly.

'You have a husband. Otherwise I would be asking you to marry me. All I can do is ask you to live with me as my wife, until you can get a divorce.' He was talking rapidly now, his face alight. 'It will take time, I know. But such things can be done.'

For a moment Rose was too moved to speak. Finally she said, struggling for words, 'What about your father? You would have to give up your life as Emir. You could never be Sultan.'

'I know. But I have decided. You have become the only important thing to me. Everything else is ashes.' Rose saw the muscle working in his cheek as he strove to control himself. 'I will talk to my father, tell him everything. There are others to follow him, you know, other young men in the family.'

Rose touched his hair at each temple. 'And can a Muslim marry an infidel? Or do I have to convert?'

He clicked his tongue impatiently. 'It is not of importance. There are civil ceremonies for people like us.'

'You will still have to be very brave, I think, to go through with it. For me it's nothing like so hard. I simply . . .' She hesitated. 'Simply make a bolt for it, shed everything.' She laughed. 'Including my reputation.'

'Would you mind that?'

195

She shook her head.

'We two, what we have together,' she said fiercely. 'How can it be compared . . .'

He stopped her with a kiss, then drew back and looked at her again.

'What about your own family, Rose? You would be giving them up, just as I am giving up mine.'

For a moment, she felt a pang. She had a sudden picture of her parents' faces at the station, Betty at the gate, the view of the hills behind. But it was only a picture, something framed and finished with. Now it was utterly irrelevant to this living present and the man who had become so precious to her.

'I could always pay them visits,' she said lightly. 'The return of the prodigal daughter.'

Hassan had brought out something from the pocket of his shirt, something small wrapped in a wisp of tissue. He held it out to her, suddenly formal.

'It is a ring.' He paused with a solemn expression. 'In Western custom, there has to be a ring, does there not, when a proposal is accepted?'

In the moonlight, Rose saw the glint of a broad silver band, with some kind of arabesque pattern in filigree.

'And this one?' Hassan touched the gold wedding ring on her left hand.

Almost without thinking, Rose pulled it off. She held it for a moment, regarding it between her finger and thumb with a look almost of pain. Then with sudden resolve she threw it away from her, far into the sand.

'Now,' she said, holding out her bare hand to Hassan. Solemnly he slid the silver ring on to her wedding finger.

'It is a little loose on you. It was my grandmother's,' he said. He kissed it lightly.

Rose shivered.

'Are you frightened?'

'Just a little.'

'Don't be. Trust me.'

'What happens next?' she asked childishly. All at once, she felt very tired.

'I will travel to Cairo alone. There will be so many arrangements to make. You will follow by the next boat. Abdullah will make all arrangements. But everything must be done quickly, in case . . .' He broke off. He was looking up at the line of mountains to the north.

'In case?'

He shook his head. 'Let sleeping dogs lie. Isn't that what the English

196

say?' He stood up and pulled her to her feet. 'And now we must sleep too. We have the journey back to Zara in the morning.'

'Nabiha and Farid will be waiting for us?'

'Yes, but we must say nothing yet. First I have to tell my father. You understand.'

Even back inside the ruins under their makeshift tent, the night air had a chill to it. Wrapped in rugs, Rose said it was like making love in England. But out there the ultimate meeting-point of his flesh in hers had an edge of savage delight to it. His claim on her, and her quiescence to it was part of a new bond. Now they could spend their happiness freely. It was a currency without end, and the future that stretched ahead of them was something that had been there all the time, if only they had known it.

'Nothing can change now,' she heard him say, his head on her breast.

'Nothing,' she told him as she fell asleep.

She thought it was the sound of thunder that woke her. There it was again, a low rolling reverberation that died away into silence. She was aware of the blanket thrown back and Hassan scrambling to his feet in the darkness.

'What's the matter?' she asked drowsily. 'Is it raining?'

He was outside the tent when a fresh sound broke through, a heavier clap this time, with an echo that thudded out from somewhere above and behind. The next minute he was tugging at her shoulder.

'Rose, quick! Get dressed! We must go!'

'But what is it? What's happened?'

For answer, he pulled her out and pointed up to the mountains. The moon had disappeared behind clouds but they seemed to be clouds of smoke. Now the darkness was split. There was a livid flash and the thudding began again.

'Turkish guns. Up on the Yemeni frontier. It's the invasion. They're going to war on us after all.'

'The lantern.' Rose was groping for the matches when Hassan snatched them from her.

'Be careful. No lights. We may be in their sight lines.'

Now they were both pulling on their clothes, bundling up the baggage on the mules. Even as Hassan took the bridle to lead her down the track, Rose saw the sky turn a dull rosy red at the edge of the pass.

'Fire?' She tried to stop her voice from trembling.

'They're moving over the border, burning the villages. I must get back to Jehal before they get that far. We have to defend ourselves.'

For a moment they turned and stared at each other appalled. Roughly he took her in his arms and they clung together.

197

'I'm sorry, Rose,' he whispered. 'It's too late for us. We've missed our chance.'

10

ROSE was glad of the rigours of that ride back to Zara. They helped to divert her from the turmoil of her thoughts. It was not just that happiness had been so violently snatched away, but that Hassan's very life would be in danger once he was back at Jehal.

'We have to go as fast as we can.'

It was all he said as they turned down the track again. The sound of gunfire had died away. Jolting along between the loose stones, Rose let the mule have its head, her concentration focused on the shadowy figure in front. There were no words between them. But she was conscious of every conflicting emotion that Hassan was enduring. When they came out on to the plain again, they were able to ride side by side. Dawn was beginning to break and in that half-light Rose glanced at his face. He was gazing straight ahead, his mouth set tight, as if some inner compulsion had set him suddenly apart from her.

She knew better than to try to break in on his thoughts. Only when they were in sight of the village did he rein in his horse, reaching out to bring Rose to a halt alongside. A yellow cloud hung across the eastern horizon as the sun came up through a haze of lingering gunsmoke and abandoned campfires. The strange saffron-coloured light charged everything around them with the sense of a storm about to break. Caught in the glow, Hassan's eyes reminded Rose of a tiger's, golden brown with pinpoints of black, as he stared up at the mountains.

'They've gone. Moving round to the west.'

'Towards Aden?'

'To Jehal.' He turned to look at her. 'We should never have come, Rose. I should never have left my father at this time.'

'But Hassan, how could you know? The invasion could have come at any time. Besides, it may all be a false alarm . . .'

Her protests died away. His hand tightened on her wrist.

'Rose, listen. I said nothing could change now. Nothing can change what has happened between us. Everything we planned will happen, just as I said.'

She nodded, not trusting herself to speak.

'But not now, not yet. We have to be patient. You do see that I can't just run away from everything now? I have to be with the Sultan, to take command at Jehal.'

Gently, Rose reached out and touched his cheek. 'You don't have to explain. There's no alternative, I see that. I will wait. We both will wait.' She heard the tremor in her voice and strove to steady it. 'Besides, it may not be for long. Everyone says the whole war will be over in just a few months.'

'As for the Turks . . .' His face was scornful now. 'Once we have the British reinforcements out there, we'll soon put paid to them, don't worry.' He stroked her hair. 'But Rose, we may not be able to see each other for a while. We may not even be able to talk on the telephone. But at least we can still send messages. You will go back with the Fauzis, won't you? I know Nabiha would want you to stay with her.'

Rose hesitated. 'I think it best I go back to my house. We have to be careful still, remember, even more careful now. I must go back to being the memsahib, just for a little while longer. We've probably started enough gossip already.'

'No one will know we've been up here together,' he said quickly. 'You can rely on that.'

She bit her lip. 'At least Geoffrey will have his hands full now. He'll be too busy playing soldiers to have time for tormenting me.'

Hassan did not answer but pulled her against him. He took her chin and turned her face to his.

'Till we meet again.'

They clung to one another as they kissed. Then she felt him break away. He had seen figures hurrying up the path from the village.

'Ya sidi! Ya Emir Hassan!'

It was the boy calling, Nabiha's urchin messenger. As he ran towards them, Rose could see Nabiha herself, following close behind on horseback.

'A message from the Sultan.' The boy crouched in front of Hassan, gasping proudly, and handed up a scrap of paper. Nabiha had pulled up alongside Rose. She threw back her *chador* to take Rose's hand, but her eyes were on Hassan, her face pale and troubled.

'It came from the signals station at Mukeiras. We have been so worried about you. When we heard the guns we thought the Turks would be on us by morning. Praise be to Allah they have gone the other way.'

Hassan nodded, still reading. There was a line between his brows that Rose sometimes teased him about. Now, idiotically, she wanted to smooth out that frown as he looked up at them.

'My father is at Aden waiting for me. We must see the Resident about the Relief Expedition. At least the Turks are taking their time, so we shall be able to prepare for them.'

'There is much fighting?' Nabiha asked.

Hassan smiled grimly. 'It seems some of my fellow-rulers are throwing in their lot with their old masters. Welcome parties rather than a leap to arms. That's all my father says, so it's difficult to tell. But it certainly sounds as if the Turkish army is gathering strength all the way.'

'So Arab will fight against Arab . . .' Rose faltered. 'If they get to Jehal.'

Hassan shrugged. 'Nothing new about that, I'm afraid. As far as some of the tribes are concerned, it's a golden chance to settle old scores.' He pulled his robe closer around him. 'Now I must go.' He was looking at Rose.

'Farid has gone ahead to arrange motor transport for you from Mukeiras.' Nabiha told him. 'Rose and I will make our own way later with the servants.'

The boy had taken Hassan's reins and was gazing up at him with a pleading expression. 'Let me come with you, *sidi.* I can run as fast as you can ride. Or I will get a mule from the village.'

Hassan laughed.

'Another time, Yussuf.' He patted his head roughly. 'Another time, maybe.'

He moved across to kiss Nabiha's hand, then Rose's.

'Be careful,' Rose said in a low voice. Her fingers clutched at his.

'I will get a letter through to you as soon as I can,' he told her.

'We shall look after her, never fear,' Nabiha called after him. Then with a final salute he was gone, clattering down the track, making for the pass at the bottom of the valley. Only the green of his turban stood out as the dust-coloured silhouette merged into the ochre landscape. In silence, they watched until the rocks hid him. Only then did Rose let the tears come. Nabiha held her tight for a moment. She motioned to Yussuf to take the bridle and lead her ahead.

'We must get back to the house. We must be ready to leave by this afternoon. It's a long trek, remember.'

To Rose, travelling back to Aden seemed to take ten times as long as the journey up. There was a sense of weary anticlimax about it, with no prospect of seeing Hassan to lighten the way. Ahead she could see only threat and confusion, however hard she tried to be hopeful.

'You mustn't worry,' Nabiha told her. 'All is in God's hands.' Her sharp eyes had picked out the silver ring on Rose's finger. 'Besides, you are a wife now, something precious.'

'Not a real wife, not yet.' Before she could stop herself, she went on. 'We were going away, you know. But now . . .'

'Dearest Rose.'

They were back in the shaky old juggernaut now, with Abdu at the wheel, driving through the outskirts of Aden. 'You will be together. It is written. When this stupid business is over.'

She waved a disdainful henna'd hand, jangling with bracelets, toward the crowds outside the native barracks. The mountain villages they had passed through seemed to know little of the Turkish moves. But here in Aden the news had obviously spread like wildfire. Abdu had to reach hard for the brakes to avoid some kind of fracas on the road ahead.

'It is the horse-cabs,' he explained. He leaned out the window and joined in the kind of violent altercation dear to the hearts of all Aden Arabs. 'The police are telling the drivers they must take off the Turkish sign from front.'

'But it is the emblem of Islam, the crescent moon,' Rose said. 'It's everywhere in Aden.'

'Unfortunately it is also the national flag of Turkey,' Nabiha replied, frowning. 'The British will not allow it, but I think they may have problems.'

Nabiha was right. A few minutes later they passed a British officer trying to order the removal of similar Islamic banners which traditionally adorned the holy shrines of the local burial ground. Rose noticed one old man shaking his fist at him. Otherwise the people wore expressions of amused indifference which seemed to say, 'We know the Ingleezi are mad anyway. What does it matter?'

As they drove on, a column of soldiers went marching past, some Indians, some who looked more like Egyptians, a horse-drawn cannon at the back. Above the rumble of wheels and the thump of sandalled feet in the dust, the long drawn-out chant of the muezzin sounded from the tower by the mosque.

'They say special prayers for the war today,' Abdu told them. Over his shoulder, he screwed up his eyes and broke into a passable imitation of the muezzin. *'Ya Kawwi! Ya Aziz! Ahlak al Jarman wa ansur al Ingliz.'*

'O mighty and powerful One,' Nabiha translated for Rose's benefit. 'Destroy the Germans and give victory to the English.'

'What about the Turks?' Rose asked.

'No doubt the Mansab will make a sermon about the wickedness of those who side against the British, our great protectors. And then to follow there will be the usual prayers for the health of the Caliph, ruler of the Ottoman Empire.' She sighed. 'Religion is thicker than water. Is there not some English proverb like that?'

'Blood,' Rose said, half to herself.

Abdu let out the clutch with a loud clatter, seeing this as a suitable moment for intervention again.

'Al-atrak, the Turks, very bad people. Drink liquor, not like other Muslims.'

'But we are all believers in the Koran,' Nabiha said teasingly. 'We are bound for the same Paradise.'

Abdu smiled his jagged smile. 'Better to go to hell with the British than share Paradise with the Turks.'

Nabiha tapped him on the shoulder. 'Concentrate, Abdu. We have to pick up some stores from Cowasjee Dinshaw before they put up their shutters, remember.'

As they got out at Steamer Point, the heat and the flies descended again. Along the shabby arcade of shop-fronts Rose could see the usual memsahibs threading their way purposefully between the street beggars and the boat-boys, organizing their shopping operations from under their parasols.

'Rose! We're stocking up on everything.' It was Mrs Wilson calling out to her. She indicated the Somali coolie standing behind her, half-hidden by cardboard boxes. 'Who knows, with the Navy blockading the ports we may be all starving by the end of the month.' She rolled her eyes. 'Or raped in our beds by the Turks.' Catching sight of Nabiha, she flushed. 'How do you do, Mrs Fauzi. See you at the Club then, Rose,' she called as she hastened down the steps to the waiting trap.

Framed in the doorway of his emporium, little Mr Dinshaw folded his hands together and bowed in greeting. A gnome-like figure in white jacket and jodhpurs, with his black Parsee helmet that always reminded Rose of an inverted coal-scuttle, he began to bewail his lot as soon as they were inside.

'What is to happen to business? The go-downs are half-empty. No caravans can pass through while these Turkish barbarians are holding us to ransom out there.'

Gratefully, Rose and Nabiha gulped down the glasses of warm sherbet with which they had been presented.

'But they will soon meet their match,' he went on in his gnat-like voice. 'It is a lucky thing we have a fine garrison here, plenty of troops.' He turned to Rose. 'And a man like your husband to lead them.'

'My husband, yes.' She had a quick mental picture of Geoffrey, closing in on her at the top of the stairs, and felt a stab of panic. It was the thing she dreaded most, the possibility of finding herself alone with him again. Where was he now? Might he even be at the house when she got there?

'Chetwynd sahib is also number two Government officer, next to Sir Rawlinson.' Mr Dinshaw twinkled at her encouragingly. 'Maybe number one some day?'

Rubbing his hands, he trotted after Nabiha who was inspecting the stocks of food in the cavernous depths of the shop, dim and musky-smelling like the hold of a ship. Among the sacks of rice and flour, dried peppers and desiccated coconut, were shelves of silks and ribbons, tall jars of green and yellow oils and scents and next to these, tins of prickly-heat powder and Dr Collis Browne's Magnesium Mixture, and other indispensable items of British life abroad.

'Bandages?' suggested one of Mr Dinshaw's many sons. 'Many people are now buying first-aid kits. Or maybe you like new dress made?' He pointed to some faded cuttings pinned to the wall depicting turn-of-the-century memsahibs in trailing tea-gowns and feathered plumes. 'Plenty of parties now with this war?'

Rose managed a polite smile. 'Maybe in the cool season.'

Urgently she took Nabiha's arm. 'I must get back to the house. To see what is happening.'

Perhaps already there might be a message waiting for her from Hassan, she was thinking as they watched Abdu load up the supplies. Out on the *maidan*, throngs of natives were gathered around the statue of Queen Victoria where the latest news bulletins were posted up on the government notice-boards. Rose stared unseeingly out of the window of the car. The day of the Birthday Parade seemed a lifetime ago. Her mind was filled again with the memory of that moment of recognition as she and Hassan sat side by side. Even then, in the way his eyes had settled on hers, she had the sense of being claimed and at the same moment forewarned. Now she knew the real meaning of a line from Dante that had always haunted her. *'Nessun maggior dolore che recordasi del tempo felice, Nella misere . . .'* There is no greater pain than to recall happy times in a time of misery.

She turned away from the harsh glare of the isthmus and closed her eyes. As they neared the house Nabiha broke in on her thoughts. 'You're certain you won't change your mind and come home with me?'

'Quite certain, dear Nabiha.'

'Then you will be sure to come over tomorrow? We shall have news from Jehal by then.'

'I will come.'

The car turned into the drive. There was no *chokida* at the gate, no sign of servants in the compound.

'You want I should fetch somebody?' Abdu asked, carrying her baggage up the front steps.

'No, I shall be fine, thank you. Ayah will be somewhere inside.'

She waved reassuringly to Nabiha and the car drove away. But no Nur appeared as she went into the hallway. Out of habit, she lifted the telephone receiver, holding her breath. But the line was dead.

All at once she was overcome with a longing to lie down on her bed in darkness and blot out everything in sleep.

First, though, she went through the downstairs rooms to check for signs of Geoffrey's presence. There were none. It was as if the house had remained deserted from the day she left, except for a letter from home which someone had placed on the dusty surface of the desk.

Rose sat down wearily, hearing her mother's voice in her ear as she read. 'Your father and I are very worried about you, dear.' The writing was not quite as neat as usual, she noticed. Extra lines had been squeezed in around the edges of the page, no doubt to save paper. 'Geoffrey has his job to do, after all, but you are surely free to leave. Are most of the women and children not already evacuated? The Near East situation sounds dangerous now that Turkey has come into the war. I read in the papers that the Kaiser has turned Muslim and there are even rumours of marriages between the German Royal Family and the Caliph's! I would believe anything of these Boche, after their atrocities in Belgium . . .'

Rose read the rest of it in bed, propped up under the mosquito net. The last page had been added by her father. 'The casualty lists are bad . . . the Williams family at Hendre, the Lloyd-Joneses at the farm, Simpsons the chemists, all have lost boys in France . . . Labour problems are getting worse . . . girls signing up as land-workers now – your mother and her hospital committees . . .'

She imagined her father's dark bulk bent over the roll-top desk, the sound of rain on the window, the familiar smell of his pipe.

'Fortunately, the British in Aden will soon put a stop to enemy advances on that lifeline of Empire,' he ended. 'But all the same we would feel a great deal happier if you were back in this country till the whole affair is over. Hoping you will agree, Your loving father.' And then, 'Betty has asked me to enclose this.'

'This' was a picture postcard framed with roses and forget-me-nots, depicting a beautiful young woman waving goodbye to a handsome officer in khaki. 'All thinking about you,' Betty had written in her careful round hand. 'Please take care and watch out for those Turkish Terrors.'

Smiling to herself, Rose lay back and closed her eyes. The letter slipped to the floor. How unreal it all sounded. The messages and the people themselves seemed as remote as stars, tiny pinpoints of light left far behind as she travelled on, deeper and deeper into a world of her own. She fell asleep and instantly began to dream of Hassan. He was sitting outside a tent, writing to her on a flimsy piece of paper that kept blowing away. A sandstorm was coming up and the sky was darkening. She tried to read the crumpled scrap but it was indecipherable. Then her distress faded and she found herself drifting into a less troubled sleep, knowing that tomorrow there would be a message from him.

Next day there was indeed a letter waiting for her at Nabiha's, a neatly folded missive in the usual crested envelope. Apparently it had been brought from Jehal by one of the palace grooms just an hour earlier. It was mid-morning and Nabiha and Farid were sitting out on the terrace drinking coffee. As Rose tore open the envelope, they stood up tactfully and strolled into the garden. But after a minute, she called them back. Hassan's endearments, always lushly poetical, had sent the blood rushing to her face. Now she was in command of herself again.

'There are things he wants you to know. He says many of the tribes are defecting. The Turks have been joined by three thousand *mujahedin* of the Yarija and all the fighting strength of the Haushabi.' She frowned, concentrating on the next page. 'It seems the Turkish commander has promised to make the Haushabi sheikh the new Sultan of Jehal when they take the city.'

'That little cur,' she heard Farid say under his breath. 'And what of the British forces?'

Rose felt a wave of relief as she turned to the last lines. 'The Resident has promised four brigades with all the field guns necessary. They should be there in twenty-four hours.'

Nabiha clapped her hands. 'So it will all be over before we know.' She turned for the house. 'I must see about lunch.'

But Farid was buckling on his belt with its old-fashioned silver revolver. 'I must go. I promised Hassan I would ride back ahead of the British. He asked for his two best horses from the Aden palace – the *syce* and I will take them.' He drew her out to the courtyard. 'Your horse, Rose.'

Led by the groom, the beautiful chestnut mare was pacing to and fro, with Hassan's stallion following behind.

'Azziza!'

At the sound of Rose's voice, the mare turned her head with its long white blaze and gave a pleased snort of recognition. The thought of the two horses going into the battle zone was almost more than she could bear.

'I would ride with you . . .' she said to Farid in a low voice. Then she broke off, realizing how stupid she must sound.

Farid looked at her for a moment. Then he nodded and smiled.

'All will be well. We are in Allah's hands.'

He beckoned to Nabiha to take her inside into the cool of the drawing room. The smell of cooking wafted through from the kitchen quarters, but the thought of food made Rose feel physically sick. The two women sat in silence for a while, Rose's head on Nabiha's shoulder. They heard the clatter of hooves die away. A few minutes later there came the sound

206

of a motor in the drive. The bearer padded in softly and murmured in Nabiha's ear. With a look of surprise she turned to Rose.

'Were you expecting Lady Rawlinson to call for you?'

Confused, Rose shook her head. They both got up, but Eleanor was in the doorway before them.

'Dear Nabiha, I do apologize. Dear Rose.' She kissed them both with her usual warmth. 'I am so sorry to descend without warning but I heard you were back and I need to carry Rose off to the Sports Club.' Her eyes widened as she looked from one to the other. 'But your expedition? What thrills! How was it?'

'Lovely to start with,' Nabiha said guardedly. 'Then alas, not so peaceful.'

'But why the Sports Club?' Rose was even more bewildered. She noticed that Eleanor was dressed with untypical severity in an olive-green skirt and jacket, though the motoring veil tied over her topee added the usual touch of fluttering femininity.

Nabiha waved her towards one of the divans. 'Some coffee, Lady Rawlinson?'

'I'm afraid I'm late already, so I'd better say no. It's the WEC, you see,' she went on. 'The ladies' War Effort Committee. We meet every afternoon at the Club, those of us that are left. So I thought Rose should be with us as my number two.' There was an awkward pause. 'I would ask you to join us, Nabiha, but . . .' Her voice trailed away.

Nabiha laughed. 'But I am not allowed in, of course, unless it is Race Day. Please don't worry, Lady Rawlinson. I understand. Besides,' she added nonchalantly, 'it would not perhaps be very entertaining, this Committee?'

'Not in the least,' Eleanor agreed. 'Rather boring really. The army have set up their headquarters there, you see, getting ready for the relief expedition to Jehal. So there are troops camped everywhere.' She clapped a ringed hand over her mouth. 'Oh dear! Not secret information, I hope!'

Rose, making her departure, stole a look at Nabiha. 'I shouldn't think so.' They embraced in the doorway. 'You come to my house next,' Rose murmured. 'Nur has reappeared, so she will cook us something to eat.'

For some reason she felt her spirits rise as the Residency car took them along the sandy road to the Club. Perhaps it was because every mile brought her closer to the Jehal frontier and Hassan. The Club itself was on the way to the Sheikh Othman border post, and here and there they passed forlorn groups of tribespeople from up-country making their way towards Aden and the safety of the garrison.

'Poor little Jehal,' Eleanor murmured. She leaned closer and Rose caught the faint tang of peppermint on her breath to cover the first gin of the day. 'Do you remember that first visit? How sweet the Emir Hassan was to us – to you especially, I should say?' She glanced at her with a teasing expression.

'Of course I do,' Rose said faintly.

'I do hope there's no real trouble out there.' Eleanor used the word in the way the English always did, as a euphemism for bloodshed of any kind. 'Apparently if we move first, show the Turks we mean business, they may not come through to Jehal at all. That's what Harry says.' She peered out of the window at the first sight of the encampment. 'There he is now.'

In the distance Rose saw hundreds of tents completely encircling the Club buildings close by. At the end of the drive, a group of officers were gathered together in conference around Sir Harry.

'And there's Geoffrey – or should I say, Major Chetwynd, as he now is.' Eleanor lowered her voice. 'Are things going on better between you?'

Rose was staring at the tall figure of her husband, standing with his back to her, legs astride, clasping his stick behind him in a characteristic pose. She took a deep breath as the car drew up. 'I really haven't seen much of him. Being away and so on.'

In fact, it was her first encounter with her husband for more than a fortnight. What she hated most about it was the way he kissed her. Holding her hard by the shoulders he pressed a coarse-bristled mouth to her cheek. For the benefit of the onlookers there was a proprietary swagger about this embrace that made her blood rise. When she drew back she saw that his eyes were perfectly cold.

'So my intrepid wife is back from her travels?'

Rose nodded, forcing herself to smile.

'Lucky you got away when you did,' put in the Resident. He laid a hand on her arm affectionately. Underneath his white and scarlet helmet, his face was strangely drawn, Rose thought. 'From what we heard, the Turks were not far off.'

'And now they've followed you round from the west!' Major Beattie chaffed. 'It seems Mrs Chetwynd is the secret attraction as far as Ali Sayed Pasha is concerned.' The others laughed.

Eleanor's attention, meanwhile, had been caught by a series of winking lights that seemed to come out of nowhere through the haze of the far horizon.

'What's that?'

'Signal Corps. It's done with mirrors catching the sun,' said a tubby, jolly-looking officer Rose had not seen before. 'They send messages in Morse to the next outpost, and then we get the news back from our scouts in the desert. Enemy movements and so on.'

Turning to the Resident, Rose nerved herself to speak. 'I have just been with the Fauzis, Sir Harry.' I must not mention Hassan, she thought. 'They have news from the Sultan that some of the tribes have joined the Turks. They're already quite close to Jehal.'

'Yes, yes, we know all about that,' Geoffrey interrupted sharply.

But the Resident gave her a harassed smile. 'Thank you, Mrs Chetwynd. All information is useful. The situation is well taken care of, though. See for yourself.'

The men turned back to their maps and binoculars. Walking on with Eleanor, Rose realized for the first time the full scale of the transformation. Horses and soldiers milled about everywhere. What had once been the golf course was now covered with a sea of dirty white canvas and from it arose the steady tack-tack-tack of mallets on pegs. Out where the sleek horses had raced past the winning post on that long-ago afternoon, the dust swirled up from the marching feet of a detachment of infantry, exercising to the hoarse cries of the British NCOs.

Even as the two women stood watching, fresh contingents were arriving from the Aden road. Rose saw the red tarbushes of the gun-teams bobbing above their little grey mules, the heavy Maxims scoring the sand into ruts. To the banging of drums, a motley kaleidoscope of uniforms wound its way through the gates, bright turbans and embroidered waistcoats, brass helmets and sweating khaki, Arab *syces* in indigo rags were running behind with the transport donkeys. Black skins and brown mingled with the brick-red faces of the English soldiers.

'It's Empire really, isn't it?' Eleanor said with a touch of pride. 'Harry asked for everything he could get – Somalis, Sudanese, Gurkhas. The India Office was difficult as usual, of course. They always think Aden's just some kind of third-rate punishment station.' She smiled at Rose. 'But I think he made his point, don't you?'

Rose nodded, suddenly full of confidence. This was the army that was soon to be on its way to Hassan and his people. Eagerly she followed Eleanor past the stable block where the baggage camels jostled together, roaring and snorting, waiting to be fed and watered before the next stage of the journey. Piled on the ground around them was the usual medley of expedition equipment, from iron hip baths to canvas water buckets and crates of whisky.

Then suddenly, round the corner, all was peace and order. Memsahibs in hats looked down from the long verandah at the back of the Club where they had obviously been established for some time. Englishwomen are extraordinary, Rose thought. They somehow have this ability to enclose themselves behind invisible barriers and create their own little world, no matter what is going on around them. Here they were, amidst all these preparations for death and destruction, behaving as if they were in their own drawing rooms, or rather, as if they were amusing themselves at any of their regular afternoon gatherings on the Sports Club verandah, while their menfolk displayed their prowess on the golf course and the polo ground.

Miss Largesen, it was true, was industriously rolling bandages in one corner, assisted by Helen Dawson, the doctor's wife, and two or three ladies were sewing together. The other tables seemed to be occupied by the usual excitable games of mah-jongg.

Everyone stirred to greet the new arrivals. There were deferential smiles and a shifting of chairs for Lady Rawlinson, Rose observed, but a rather more wary welcome as far as she was concerned.

'So here is ze belle Mrs Chetwynd back from her explorations in ze wilds of Arabia!' declared Madame Ries, glancing up with needle poised. 'But in Aden we are so dull.' She held up the blue gauze she was stitching on to a pair of pith helmets. 'The officers from the Sudan swear by it to keep off sunstroke. Picturesque, *n'est-ce pas?*'

'I think I'd be better at the field dressings,' Rose said, smiling. She sat down by Mrs Dawson, whom she liked. 'Or is there anything else I can do?'

'You could start to learn bridge,' Mrs Wilson called out sternly from the mah-jongg corner. 'Such a disability not to play at a time like this.'

'After all, we must amuse ourselves in these dark days,' cried one of the younger wives, a pretty fair girl married to a shipping agent. 'We can't be left at Steamer Point on our own all day, so needs must follow the flag! At least I can play the piano.' She looked round with an arch smile. 'A farewell sing-song later on, perhaps? A little dance even?'

'Actually,' said Eleanor firmly, 'one thing we must do today is get one of the outbuildings set up as a field station. If there are any casualties on the expedition' – she hesitated – 'it's a long way back to the garrison hospital.' A silence fell. 'What is the water situation, by the way?'

'Not too bad,' Mrs Dawson replied. 'It's a bit of a strain on the wells, but the camels have been bringing in extra from Aden.'

Madame Ries brought out a cologne-scented handkerchief and fanned away some of the more persistent flies. 'A pity zey didn't dig ze latrine trenches a little further out. Especially now ze wind has changed.'

'The golf course will never be the same again,' sighed Mrs Wilson. 'Michael's furious.'

Rose felt caught in some kind of Alice-in-Wonderland dream. She wanted to shake them all until their silly hats fell off. 'When does the relief force move off?' she asked, forcing herself to sound calm.

'At first light tomorrow, I have heard,' said Miss Largesen. 'But it is still a big secret.'

210

'Perhaps if we give our officers tea, they'll tell us,' Eleanor suggested.

Everyone sprang up with alacrity. Bells were rung for boiling water. Caddies of Earl Grey and tins of home-made cakes were produced from special cupboards, and the procession made its way to that holy of holies, the Billiard Room, now apparently the Operations Centre.

It was stiflingly hot inside, even though every window was open. The overhead punkahs stirred up hazy drifts of smoke from pungently-scented Egyptian cigarettes. Perspiring faces looked up gratefully as Rose moved round the long table dispensing steaming cups.

'Manna from heaven, produced by angels,' cried one Hunter Pasha.

'This Aden thirst,' an older man rejoined. 'Even worse than Khartoum in a sandstorm.'

'Well it's hardly a white man's country, old chap. Miserable heap of dust that it is!'

'Surely there are the club servants to do this,' Rose heard Geoffrey protest to Eleanor as she sat pouring tea.

She laughed cheerfully. 'Seems they're enlisted to the colours.'

'Lazy devils. It's the Arab idea of punctuality that always gets my goat,' he confided. 'One time's as good as another to a Muslim, as long as he's wasting it.'

Eleanor was looking around the room. 'Where's Harry?'

'Got a bit of a headache, I'm afraid, Lady Rawlinson. Went down to the dispensary to get some aspirin.'

From across the table, Rose saw a look of anxiety pass over Eleanor's face. She was moving round to speak to her when someone nearby jumped up to take her hand.

'Martin Foster. You remember me, Mrs Chetwynd? From Perim?'

'Of course. Mr Foster.' For a brief moment, she was thrown back into the horror of that day, the dank smell of the lighthouse and Geoffrey's step on the stair. She saw the young man's spectacled face smiling nervously into hers. 'You were so kind,' she said. 'And what are you doing here?'

'Just part of the defence force, like everyone else.' He laughed, pushing his glasses up on his nose which was still peeling from sunburn, Rose noticed. 'I suppose it's my Arabic, actually. The powers-that-be seemed to think I might be useful when we get to Jehal.'

'Ah yes. Jehal.'

There was a brief pause. He had a way of looking at you, she thought, that was shy and penetrating at the same time. 'We leave at dawn,' he said.

'Then you'll be gone by the time I'm on duty again,' she went on.

'On duty?'

'The Ladies' Committee.' She laughed apologetically. 'It seems we'll be holding the fort here during the emergency.'

There was more she wanted to say, feeling he was someone she could trust. 'Give my best wishes to the Emir when you get there,' she began. But Eleanor was beckoning to her. She pressed his hand. 'And good luck tomorrow.'

Eleanor's expression was serious. 'I must get Harry home. It's one of his bouts of malaria, I'm afraid. But worse than usual. I don't know why.'

Rose was not sure what constituted a usual bout of malaria. But certainly the Resident looked a sick man as he got into the car with them. He sat back in the corner seat shivering violently, his face clenched.

'Had it before,' was all he said. 'A good night's sleep and I'll be in the saddle at dawn.'

'He still plans to ride out with them,' Eleanor murmured to Rose, under the noise of the engine. 'I've tried to persuade him that he won't be fit. Hopeless.' She shrugged.

'Will there not be motor transport going out?' Rose asked.

Sir Harry gave a grimace that was meant to be a smile. 'And get bogged down in the desert before we've even begun?' He closed his eyes and went on, half to himself. 'Anyway, if I am out of action for a day or two, Geoffrey Chetwynd's perfectly capable of getting the stunt off the ground.' He seemed to forget Rose was sitting next to him. 'Knows the ropes all right, even if he is a rum sort of chap.'

Eleanor's eyes caught Rose's. But neither of them spoke. Sir Harry's voice trailed away and he seemed to be sleeping, his chin on his chest.

'Don't worry,' Eleanor said, as they reached the Chetwynd house. 'It always looks worse than it is. A course of quinine works wonders.' She squeezed Rose's hand. 'Same time tomorrow then? You'll be here?'

'I'll be here.'

It was difficult to sleep that night. Nur's family had moved into the servants' quarters to keep her company, and hour after hour the lu-lu-luing of the women and the shouts and claps of the men rose up from around the fire in the compound. It was obvious that the local people knew what was afoot. The army was going into battle against the invaders. It was something to celebrate, something to make a good-luck sacrifice for.

Looking out from the bedroom verandah, Rose saw they had dragged one of the young goats from its pen. Two men held it fast, its head pulled back. A third man had a knife in his hand, and at the same moment that Rose leaned out, he made a swift thrust down across the animal's throat. The thin bleating stopped. There was silence for a second or two, then a roar of approval.

Rose saw the bright blood glitter in the sand. Turning away, she choked into her handkerchief. She had seen this thing done before. But tonight it was different.

She searched for the sleeping powders, remembering the last time she had taken them with Geoffrey outside the door, and the boy Saleh . . .

She made herself break off that train of thought. On an impulse she took two of the powders, and lay down in the dark, missing the string of prayer beads. Running them over between her fingers and murmuring Hassan's name to herself always seemed to bring him mysteriously close. Perhaps out there across the miles of desert, Hassan was speaking to her, the beads she had sent him held in his hands. Even now, he must be up in the palace tower, watching and waiting for the first sight of the British expedition at the balcony window where he had first reached out and touched her.

She turned on her side and fell asleep, facing Jehal.

❧ 11 ❧

THE sleeping powders always produced a sense of heaviness the next morning and Rose found she had overslept by two or three hours. Nur brought her tea and toast, and water for her bath. Afterwards she slipped on the linen skirt and pink striped blouse that had just come back from the wash. Fortunately the Residency car was late arriving. Then, to her dismay, she saw there were no passengers inside, neither Eleanor nor Sir Harry.

'I'm afraid it's worse than we thought,' ran the brief note in Eleanor's scrawl, handed her by the driver. 'Harry went into the garrison hospital last night and Doctor Jack says it's blackwater fever. I am with him here, so grateful if you could take a lead with the Committee today. Will be in touch again very soon.'

So Geoffrey was now in charge of the campaign. Worried though she was about Sir Harry, this was Rose's uppermost thought as they drove towards the Club. It was something that filled her with an alarm she did not care to analyse. From time to time the Indian driver in front shook his head and spoke gloomily of the condition of the Resident sahib. But Rose was staring out at the weather which was overcast, with the kind of wind that flicked the sand up into your face and left the grit between your teeth. For the troops on the march it was better than overhead sun, she thought.

Then when the Club came into view, she could not at first take in what she saw. What was extraordinary was that nothing had changed. Yesterday's picture was exactly the same. There were the lines of tents, the milling soldiery, the horses, the camels and the guns. Only one thing was different. Instead of the scenes of preparation everywhere, there was the unmistakeable sense of a lull, as if for some reason or other everything had ground to a halt.

Rose's head began to throb. What could have gone wrong? Why had the expedition been delayed in this way, allowing twelve precious hours to slip by?

Hurrying up the verandah steps, she saw the memsahibs deep in discussion over the remains of their tiffin. Among the dishes were spread the pages of the weekly English newspaper.

'What's happened?' she called. 'Why haven't the troops left?'

214

'A change of plan.' A worried-looking Miss Largesen came towards her. 'You've seen the news?'

'No.' Rose stopped by the nearest table to steady herself, looked down and saw a headline with a strange name. Gallipoli.

'Sit down, my dear. You look pale.' Mrs Dawson was pouring her a cup of coffee. 'Something to eat, perhaps?'

Rose shook her head, gulping the gritty black drink. The page was still dancing in front of her eyes.

'It's the Dardanelles,' Helen Dawson went on. 'It seems the British are being completely wiped out.' Her voice was incredulous. 'The Turks are just mowing them down.'

'The worst thing is they're firing on the hospital ships too. Shells, bullets, even German aircraft.' Miss Largesen, usually so resolute, looked close to tears. 'The Red Cross is like the red rag to the bull.' She blew her nose fiercely.

Rose forced herself to concentrate on the small print. 'Heavy casualties,' she read. 'Thousands of dead and dying lying out on the open beaches . . . the special courage of the Australians and New Zealanders in the face of disaster.'

'It's terrible,' she heard herself say mechanically. Her mouth was dry. To her shame, she found herself only thinking of Hassan. Was this what could happen in Jehal?

'They are beasts, these Turks,' Madame Ries broke in. 'They torture their prisoners too.'

'Barbarians,' said someone else.

As Rose struggled to make sense of it all, Miss Largesen's words came back to her.

'What is this change of plan then?' she asked.

'The Relief Expedition has been cancelled,' Miss Dawson replied. She turned away awkwardly. Rose looked at the other faces, saw relief on some, apprehension on others, embarrassment even.

'Your husband is in command, you see,' Mrs Wilson explained, as if to a child. 'Now that the Resident's been taken ill. The new plan is to let the Turks take Jehal and draw them on towards Aden. Then the British stop them in their tracks here at Sheikh Othman. Give them everything we've got!'

Rose's heart was beating so fast, it was hard to breathe. She felt very sick, the bitter coffee rising in her throat. She was aware of Helen Dawson's hand on her shoulder.

'Your husband has called us into the conference, so that he can outline the position to everyone. They're waiting for us now.'

Inside the long room, yesterday's atmosphere of expectancy had gone.

215

The table had been pushed to one side and chairs ranged in a semicircle while the officers stood chatting together in undertones.

Rose stood very still in the doorway, letting the other women go forward to sit down. She wanted to be as far away as possible from the man at the far end of the room who faced the gathering. He looked very spruce today, her husband, with his new haircut and freshly-pressed uniform. She watched him carefully as he placed his hands on the desk in front of him and leaned forward to speak.

'New developments demand military flexibility,' he was saying. 'From the setback in the Dardanelles, we now see the kind of enemy we're up against. There seems little point in taking on these Turks on their home ground, as it were, so close to the Yemen. With this new strategy we allow the Turks to occupy Jehal. After which pointless little victory they'll be raring to advance on Aden, thinking the British have gone to sleep perhaps.' He laughed. 'Instead, we meet head on here at Sheikh Othman with all the forces at our command, the garrison behind us and the guns of our warships all along the isthmus.'

'In other words,' put in Major Wilson from his seat alongside, 'Jehal is the bait, and the trap is set here at Sheikh Othman.'

'Exactly.' Geoffrey repositioned his swagger-stick on the desk and surveyed his audience. 'Any queries?'

'Does His Excellency know of this change of plan?' The questioner was Hunter Pasha, who still held a lunch-time glass in his hand.

'Hardly.' Geoffrey's tone was cold. 'I'm afraid the Resident's condition rules out any kind of discussion. But I'm perfectly certain that he would be the first to condemn any unnecessary waste of British lives – and native lives, of course.' He stared at Hunter Pasha, whose gaze returned to the polished toecaps of his boots.

Directly in front of her, a tall red-haired officer with the badges of the Seaforths on his jacket got up to speak.

'Surely, sir, shouldn't we be looking for a chance to get out there and avenge British pride as soon as possible? Give Johnny Turk a lesson he won't forget, while he's off his guard?' He looked around the room. 'The rest of the world will expect it of us, surely? Arabia and Mesopotamia are vital war fronts for the British.' He paused. 'And we won't want to seem to be shirking a matter of honour, will we?'

Rose saw Geoffrey's face stiffen. She knew this was her only chance. As if impelled by a force outside herself, she heard herself speaking in a voice that seemed to belong to someone else.

'On the question of honour, has not a treaty been signed between the Sultan of Jehal and the British Government? A treaty which faithfully

216

promises His Highness all military support in return for his loyalty to the British cause? Is that treaty now worthless?'

It was like throwing a stone into a lake. There was a startled silence, then the ripples spread from one side of the room to the other, as heads turned and papers rustled.

'I'm afraid this discussion is not open to civilians.' Geoffrey spoke thickly and she could see a muscle twitch in his cheek. 'Even my charming wife. So her observation is not a valid one.'

'On the contrary, sir, it seems to me that the point raised by Mrs Chetwynd is the only valid one.'

She had not noticed Martin Foster in the doorway. As he came forward to speak, his usually diffident manner dropped away.

'The whole idea of the British presence in Arabia is rooted in our good relations with the native rulers. The Sultan of Jehal is our oldest friend in the Protectorate. Unlike some of the others, he has made his allegiance clear. What will happen to our reputation if this treaty is dishonoured in this way, if we sit tight in our bolthole and let Jehal be overrun? What will the Empire think of us?'

Rose saw him swallow as he tried to control the passion of his appeal. He looked around at the faces in front of him, and then at Geoffrey.

'Surely it is not too late to revert to the original plan and start out for Jehal even now?'

'I'm afraid it is too late, Mr Foster.' Geoffrey was barely glancing at him. 'Though I must admire your concern for what is, after all, a handful of mud houses in the middle of the desert.' He smiled to himself. 'Also, I can assure you that the Sultan's family will be as thick as thieves with the Turks in no time at all. Brothers in Islam and all that.' Briskly he folded up his map. 'The fortifications are being set up, the guns got into position, and this is where we take our stand, here on British territory.'

On this rallying note, which aroused at least a few 'Hear, Hears!' he moved towards the door. As he paused, Rose heard him say in his drawling voice, 'I'm afraid this is no time for any of your Empire sentiment, Mr Foster. War is a profession, you see, unlike the Political Service, and people like you have to bow to the experts.'

Mrs Dawson came forward from the other women.

'What about the wives, Major Chetwynd?' Her manner was polite but cool. 'What do you want us to do?'

'I think you should all go back home,' he said dismissively. 'Except those of you with Red Cross training.' His eyes were on Rose. 'The rest of you will be simply in the way.'

Even before he had finished speaking, Rose had turned on her heel and was walking fast out on to the verandah. She knew if she stayed inside a minute longer she would faint. She was down the steps and halfway across the dusty little garden before Martin Foster caught up with her.

'Mrs Chetwynd! You mustn't upset yourself.'

He scanned her face to see if she was crying. In fact it was not grief that Rose felt, but an overpowering sense of outrage. She found she was trembling from head to foot.

'Our friends have been betrayed,' she burst out in a low voice. 'Hassan has been . . .' She stopped herself, then looked up at him pleadingly. 'Is there nothing we can do?'

'Nothing, I'm afraid.' He searched for something to reassure her. 'They may be able to make their own stand at Jehal after all. The Turks have nothing like the build-up here that they have in the Dardanelles.'

Rose spun round furiously. 'And what about the crack cavalry regiment, trained by the Germans in Damascus? What about the *mujahedin*, burning and plundering wherever they go? How will the Sultan's little army stand up to them, do you think, now we've deserted them?'

Mr Foster looked startled. 'I think you know more than we do.'

'I *care* more. Emir Hassan is our friend, my friend . . .'

Her voice broke and she covered her face with her hands, no longer even trying to conceal what she felt.

'I say, Mrs Chetwynd,' he said in a tone that was suddenly soft with concern. The morning clouds had disappeared. The sun was burning down on them now, sending runnels of sweat inside Rose's starched cotton blouse. The mingled odours of charcoal ironing and lily-of-the-valley cologne was something she would always associate with this awful day.

She felt his hand under her elbow. He was walking her towards the shade of the solitary gold-mohr tree that stood in the centre of the compound.

'You mustn't give way like this.' She found he had placed a handkerchief in her hand. When she looked up from mopping her eyes, she saw he was staring at her from behind his blue-tinted glasses with something like disbelief on his face. 'It doesn't help, you see.' He glanced back at the club-house, and the groups of soldiers outside the nearest tents. 'People are always watching. You have to think of yourself.'

Rose handed back the handkerchief.

'How far are the Turks from Jehal, do you think?'

'About one day's march.' He hesitated. 'Perhaps the Emir will come to some agreement with them, surrender terms.'

'Never!' She spoke the one word with all the force she could summon. The sun filtered through the canopy of red flowers like the glow of a furnace. In the distance, she saw the blink of the mirror signals again. 'A message,' she said quickly. 'At least we could send them a message. Warn them that there is no relief force on its way.'

He shook his head. 'And let the whole of the Turkish army know that too? That would make things even worse. It would put our own people here in danger too.'

She stepped back from him. 'So you'll do nothing to help? Even though you know something terribly wrong is happening – and others here feel it too?'

They stood in silence facing each other for a moment.

'Foster! You're needed,' someone called from the verandah.

He looked away. 'There's nothing we can do. We're under orders here, remember – your husband's orders.'

'But I am not,' she said under her breath.

He touched her arm. 'Won't you please come inside, Mrs Chetwynd, out of the heat?'

'Not yet.'

She turned from him sharply, almost running across the compound, anywhere to get away from the presence of the British. She had no plan, though for a moment she had thought she must set out for Jehal herself. But she knew at once that this was a fantasy. To make one's way on horseback across fifty miles of unmarked desert was something only an Arab could do, an Arab who was already familiar with that part of the country. But where would she find someone who would undertake such a thing?

Curious faces looked up at her as she found herself walking distractedly along the lines of tents, sharp-eyed Bedouins around their cooking fires, levy soldiers burnishing the new machine guns they called the 'Cacklers of Death'. Not one was known to her, though there were the usual nods and salutes as she passed. The camels were couched now, freed of their burdens, and further along some horses poked their heads out over the stable doors at the sound of her footsteps.

Automatically Rose put out her hand to stroke a velvety nose. Inside the *syces* were squatting to eat their rice in the cool dimness. The familiar grin of Nabiha's houseboy caught her eye.

'Yussuf!'

Without even thinking, she beckoned to him quickly.

'What are you doing here?' she asked him.

'My mistress tell me come help.' He swallowed the last of his rice. 'You want I should take message?'

'No, thank you, Yussuf.' Just for a moment she hesitated. 'A message for someone else,' she hurried on. 'You know the way to Jehal?'

'Of course, memsahib. Many times I go with master and mistress.'

'And you can ride?'

He nodded, laughing, as if the question was a ridiculous one.

'Then come with me.'

The stable at the end was empty. Seating herself on a sack of straw, Rose searched her bag frantically for pencil and paper. All she could find was the letter from Hassan. The back page was empty and across it she scribbled the first words that came into her mind.

'Hassan,' she wrote. 'You are in great danger. You and your father must leave at once. The Relief Expedition has been cancelled and the British now plan to let the Turks take Jehal, then stop them here at the border. I am terrified for your life – if they should take you hostage . . .' The words trailed away. What else could she say? She added only her name, folding the paper back into the envelope and re-addressing it to Hassan.

The boy was watching her intently, his eyes shining.

'You will hide this,' she told him.

He took it from her and thrust it between his shirt and his belt.

'And you will take it to the palace at Jehal and give it to the Emir. Only to the Emir. But Yussuf' – she gripped him by his thin shoulders – 'It is a dangerous journey. You have to find a good horse, for a start.'

'There are plenty,' he said carelessly.

'But to leave without being noticed?'

'I will say I go to the Fauzi house.'

'And then there may be enemy soldiers on the way, soldiers from the war.'

She could feel his muscles braced for action. He hardly glanced at the Marie Thérèse dollar she slipped into his hand.

'I am a Bedouin,' he said simply. 'We like war.'

She smiled at him. 'You will ride fast?'

'Always I ride fast.'

Standing very straight in front of her, the boy saluted her in the British fashion, and was gone.

After a moment, Rose walked out into the compound again, briskly, as if returning from some official mission of enquiry. From the verandah she saw Miss Largesen watching her with interest.

'I was just taking a look at the horses,' Rose told her. 'Poor things, they seem a bit underfed.'

'Unlike our precious officers.' Miss Largesen's face was scornful. 'I have just been round to the kitchens and it seems they've ordered a four-course dinner this evening. Windsor soup and Red Sea salmon to start with and port and melon to finish, plus two cases of Graves and one of

220

champagne.' She sniffed. 'All of a sudden you'd think the war was over instead of just beginning.'

Rose helped her to fold up some of the sheets she had brought with her from the mission hospital.

'You are staying on here then?'

'Of course. Myself and Helen Dawson. As permitted by your husband.' She looked up sharply. 'You want to stay with us? There is a spare camp bed on the upstairs verandah.'

'Yes, please do.' Mrs Dawson had appeared in the doorway, calm-looking as ever with her neat grey bun and gleaming spectacles. 'Lady Rawlinson was going to stay with us, I know, if she had been here.'

Rose felt sudden remorse. 'What news of Sir Harry?'

Miss Largesen shook her head. 'It's too soon yet for a turning point. But he is a fine strong man. We must hope and pray.'

She stumped across to the store cupboards with an armful of linen. When she was out of earshot, Helen Dawson put her hand on Rose's arm.

'You were very brave to speak out as you did just then. But it was rather unwise perhaps. Especially with your husband . . .' She bit her lip, looking back into the room. 'You know what some of the wives are like. Best to tread carefully for a while.'

'I understand. And thank you.'

Rose was aware of a new strength returning. She began to be filled with a sense of resolve. If there were to be charades, it was a game she was better at than the rest.

'I think I need to wash my face,' she said.

At the end of the verandah was the spiral staircase that led to the ladies' room. Halfway up she stopped, her hand gripped tight on the thin rail. A shadow had fallen in front of her. She looked up and saw Geoffrey standing at the top, legs astride, his hands in his pocket.

'How dare you confront me as you did just now,' he said softly. He passed his tongue between his lips as he stared down at her, as if contemplating some pleasure to come.

She took a deep breath and walked up the rest of the stairs. Only when she was in front of him did she say the word.

'Coward.'

She knew he would strike her. Even so, the force of the blow came as an insult to her senses. She recoiled instinctively, holding her face. 'Cowardly and stupid,' she went on in a rush, while she still had the courage. 'You have made the worst mistake of your life today. When Sir Harry hears . . .'

'Sir Harry!' He spat out the name. 'It's your beloved Emir you're so worried about. Why don't you ride out on your Arab steed to rescue him

221

then, make a complete fool of yourself, eh?' He thrust his face close to hers, his eyes bolting. 'Whatever you do – just one thing – you'd better keep out of my way! Go home and don't come back!'

'On the contrary, I'm staying.' With a quick movement, she drew past him. 'Mrs Dawson and Miss Largesen have asked me to do so. You need not worry. I shall certainly not be coming anywhere near you.'

She did not look back. Inside the ladies' room, she locked the door behind her and leaned against it for a moment, her eyes closed. Then she went over to the bowl of water on the marble slab, rolled up her sleeves and splashed her face, over and over again. Studying herself in the mirror, she saw the mark of Geoffrey's hand quite clearly across her left cheek. Carefully she rubbed a powder paper over it, until the red patch was almost covered. When she had combed up her hair, she stood quite still and pressed her hands together.

'Please God,' she said silently to her reflection, 'let Hassan get away safely.'

She slipped her fingers between the buttons of her shirt and touched the moon pendant hidden beneath.

Everything depended on Yussuf. As she went back downstairs she had a sudden clear picture of him, riding hard over the dusty tracks, his head bent against the wind. She turned into the main salon and saw that the memsahibs were now gathered around the card tables.

'Perhaps I can join you for that bridge lesson,' she suggested brightly. She read uncertainty for a moment on the faces turned towards her. Fans were fluttered. In Eleanor's absence, she now counted as first lady, Assistant Resident's wife no longer but the burra mem. But Mrs Wilson swiftly set the tone.

'I'm afraid all the tables are full at present,' she said in a disdainful little voice. What an ugly mouth she had, Rose thought. Just like a rat's, a rat in blue flowered voile.

'Another time then,' she replied sweetly. As she moved away, she heard a giggle, then a low buzz of gossiping voices. It was a relief to pass through on to the front verandah, until she saw that it had become a sort of Officers' Mess. Men in open-necked shirts sat sprawled on the low canvas chairs, spurred boots cocked up on the rails. Voices were raised and there were glasses and bottles everywhere as an aged bearer shuffled between the tables.

'No ice?' one declared indignantly. 'You expect the Guards to fight without ice?'

There was a burst of laughter. Rose could see no sign of Martin Foster. Quickly she slipped out through a side door. This corner of the verandah was used as a reading room, empty now, somewhere she could rest for an hour and try to get rid of the headache which seemed to beat time to all her thoughts relentlessly, like a metronome. Beside the long cane chair there was a pile of *Illustrated London News*. She glanced through one of them for a moment or two, but the pictures of the King and Queen inspecting wounded troops at Victoria Station only made her anxiety more unbearable. Closing her eyes, she found herself listening to snatches of male conversation drifting towards her from the next verandah.

'Nothing for a day or two anyway. Might even get in a spot of shooting.'

'Ripping sport up in the Hejaz, d'you know. Hundred and seventy grouse in one day and only seven guns.'

There was a pause, then something that alerted her again. 'Can't say I care for this fellow Chetwynd.'

'Nor I. Damned shame about Rawlinson. We'd have had a proper scrap at Jehal with him.'

'Mrs Chetwynd's all right though.' A chuckle followed this observation. 'A real dazzler, eh?'

'Mad about Arabs, I'm afraid, old chap.'

'Too bad.'

'Hi you, *syce*! Take the bridle off my horse and *dini* a drink of *moyah* . . .'

The conversation died away. Flushing furiously, Rose picked up a book from the table. It was Isabel Burton's *Inner Life of Syria*. In spite of herself, she became absorbed until an apologetic voice distracted her.

'So sorry. Didn't mean to disturb you.' And then, as she sat up in the chair, 'Won't you join us for tea?'

Martin Foster looked composed now, almost cheerful. He had changed into a white mess jacket, as had most of the other officers.

'You're feeling better?' he asked.

She nodded. 'A little.'

The glare of the day was draining away into sunset and on the ground in the compound the last stage of a game of polo was in progress.

'Would you do us the honour of handing out the prizes for us, Mrs Chetwynd?' the red-haired captain of the Seaforths called to her.

As she moved across to the seat drawn out for her, the sound of the Last Post bugle came floating over from the levy lines. The melancholy reverberations seemed to hold back for a moment the brief dusk of Arabia. Everyone stood to attention, watching the Union Jack come down in silence. A native orderly folded it up with reverent movements and handed it to the Colour Sergeant.

It was like the curtain coming down on a play, Rose always thought. In the past she had watched the ceremony with an enjoyable sense of emotion. Tonight she felt only shame.

The Captain was at her elbow. 'Ready then, dear lady?'

It seemed that the prize for the winning polo team was a large bottle of brandy. Rose handed it over with the appropriate kind of smile. Tea-time had given way to sundowners and a round of Abu Hameds was ordered. This, she discovered, was a lethal mixture much favoured at Cairo's Ghazira Club, consisting of equal quantities of gin, vermouth, lime juice and soda – 'with a good dash of angostura,' Lewis Pasha reminded them.

The memsahibs, who had emerged from the bridge room, swiftly grew merry. Tonight was to be Ladies' Night, a farewell to the wives before they returned to their homes at Steamer Point. Drinks were succeeded by a formal dinner – starched white tables crowded into the stifling heat of the dining room – and finally dancing to the accompaniment of an old upright piano.

'Just like the Waterloo Ball,' chaffed Major Wilson, leaning closer across the table. He was obviously preparing to ask her to partner him. Chattering voices closed in around her and her eyes were stinging with the haze of cigarette smoke. The whole long day had acquired a sense of nightmare unreality. She was not used to alcohol. In an effort to quell the rising tide of fear that she felt, she had drunk three glasses of wine. Now everything about her seemed to be happening with unbearable slowness. How could she get through the night without knowing what was happening to Hassan?

'Excuse me.'

Rose turned to find Martin Foster at her shoulder. Gratefully she accepted his invitation to dance. At least it was a chance to escape from the others.

'Where's your husband?' he asked as they threaded their way around the room. The boards beneath their feet were gritty with sand, mixed in with the sawdust strewn by the servants.

She lifted her chin. 'At the bar. Drinking with Major Beattie. He's been there all evening, thank God.'

One of the officers had produced a violin that was raggedly out of key. But the tune he was playing alongside the piano pierced through with sudden sweetness. 'Let the great big world keep turning . . .' Someone next to them was humming the words. It was one of those wartime songs that had the ability to catch at your heart for no reason at all. 'For I only know that I love you so, and that no one else will do . . .'

Rose felt Mr Foster's hand tighten on hers and his arm move closer around her. Suddenly the burden of what she had done was too much for her.

'I have to tell you . . .' she began, so quietly that he had to put his head close to hers to catch what she was saying.

'Sorry?'

'This afternoon – I sent a message to the Emir. I told him the change of plan, told him they must leave at once.'

She looked up at him, seeing his face freeze in disbelief.

'But how. . . ?'

'One of the Fauzi servants.'

'You wrote a note?'

Just for a second she faltered. 'It was the only way to be sure.'

He had drawn away from her so that he could look into her eyes. 'If anyone should find out . . .'

'How can they? No one else knows, only you. And you I trust.'

Something like pleasure struggled with the expression of dismay on his face. He missed his step for a moment, then with an effort continued to guide her in time to the music.

'Rose,' he said under his breath. It was the first time she had heard him use her name. 'You have done a most reckless thing. This is not a game, you know. It is war. People die.'

'Hassan could die,' she whispered fiercely.

He shook his head, staring at her. 'But to take things into your own hands like that.'

She stopped dancing. 'Better to leave it to fate? Leave him abandoned, and his father?' His arm was still around her, his hand on hers. Violently she twisted away from him. 'You are just like all the others. And I thought . . .'

A few eyes followed her as she moved swiftly through the dancing couples and out on to the back verandah. She reassured herself that most people were too busy enjoying themselves to notice anything odd. At the top of the stairs she fastened the screen door firmly behind her. At least he would not follow her up here with more reproaches and recriminations.

In the beds at the far end, Helen Dawson and Miss Largesen sat up anxiously. The oil lamp on the floor between them was turned down low, throwing grotesque shadows on the latticed partitions.

'Are you all right?' demanded Miss Largesen. 'You are out of breath.'

'Sorry. I suddenly realized how late it was. I was doing my social duty, you might say.' Nervously she went over to the bed in the corner and began to loosen her skirt.

'Sleep while you can,' Helen Dawson told her. Without her glasses, her hair loose on her shoulders, she looked strangely vulnerable, even frightened, Rose thought. 'There is a rumour that the Turks may be through sooner than expected. After all, there'll be little resistance at Jehal . . .'

Her voice trailed away.

'I'll put out the lamp, then,' said Miss Largesen.

Rose shivered, settling herself on the thin mattress. She drew the sheet up over her head. At least she could pretend to sleep.

Almost the last thing she heard was the clatter of traps outside as the memsahibs were taken safely home to Steamer Point. In the bar room below the last roisterers were slurring over the familiar drinking chorus of the Rifle Brigade:

> 'Jolly good song, jolly well sung,
> Jolly good comrades everyone!
> If you can beat it, you're welcome to try,
> But always remember, the singer is dry.'

Finally the voices died down. The wine had its effect on her and she must have drifted off. She was roused by Miss Largesen shaking her by the shoulders.

'The alarm's just sounded. Something's been sighted out there.'

Mrs Dawson was on her knees trying to relight the lamp. Struggling to fasten her clothes, Rose pushed past her to look out. Down below she saw the figures of soldiers running towards the line of trenches in front of the camp, where the gun positions were. Over the desert beyond, the first glimmer of dawn was breaking. From far away, somewhere out of sight, there came the crackle of rifle fire.

Now Rose was running too, leaving the women behind, running down the stairs and out across the compound. Someone called out to her to stop but she took no notice. As she came closer to the defence line, she could see the flash of the rifle-fire now, brilliant in the half-light. Directly ahead in the distance she could just make out the silhouettes of a body of men on horseback, flags flying behind them.

'Damned Turks!' she heard the officer in front of her exclaim. 'Stealing a march on us.'

All around her, lined behind the barricades of sandbags, men were loading their rifles. Others were pushing the field artillery into position as lanterns were rushed to and fro. There was the rattle of cartridges running into the carbine guns. Everyone seemed to be shouting at once.

Then again she saw the rifle fire flash upwards from the advancing party. At the same instant, something clicked in her brain.

'Don't you see?' she called out. 'They're not firing at us. They're firing to let us know they're coming! Firing into the air!'

'Get Mrs Cheywynd out of here!'

It was Major Beattie's voice from somewhere behind. Out of the mêlée, she saw Martin Foster running towards her.

'Firing into the air,' she repeated desperately. She seized hold of his arm, willing him to listen. 'The way they always do.'

She heard him take a quick breath.

'Oh God!' He sprang up looking towards the command post. 'Major Chetwynd! These are not the enemy! These are people from Jehal!'

The horsemen were closer now, galloping hard. Voices were shouting out in Arabic, something indistinguishable. Through the swirling dust, two figures in front were emerging. Sharper than anything else was the face of the leading horse, the long white blaze she knew so well. Above it, there was the glimmer of a green turban.

'Hassan!' she whispered.

Turning, she suddenly saw Geoffrey, just two yards away. He was standing on the barricade, the troops lined waiting on either side. His left arm was raised in the signal to take aim. In his other hand, he held his field pistol, cocked and steady, directed straight ahead at the approaching riders.

'No!' she cried, with all the strength she could muster.

There was a split-second pause before he dropped his arm, and the command rang out.

'Fire!'

PART THREE

Aidrus

❦ 1 ❧

'THE Emir was killed?'

The young woman's eyes were rounded in suspense as she leaned forward in her chair. She shifted the clipboard on her knee. Once again it seemed to Rose that there was something menacing about the neatly-sharpened pencil poised to record her answer. For a moment she was unable to continue. Something of the horror of that Aden dawn of thirty years ago had caught her fast again, locked her into the old familiar nightmare where no words would come.

'The Emir Hassan,' prompted the interviewer, a dark pretty girl called Jenny Patmore. 'He was killed?'

The question seemed to come from a long way away. With a great effort Rose turned her eyes from the window where she had seen, clearly printed against the blackness, the flash of gunfire and the falling body.

'No. Not Hassan,' she replied softly. 'It was his father they shot, the Sultan.'

'How terrible.' Rose watched the girl groping for the right words, sympathy struggling on her face with professional pleasure at the drama of the story. 'Did he die outright?'

'Not quite.' Rose hesitated. The next picture was always a confused one – the muffled figure lying on the table in the whitewashed stable room, blood soaking the brown cloak, Hassan's face rigid with shock in the glare of the lantern, then the door closed against her.

'The army doctor operated on him straight away, but it was useless. Apparently the bullet had gone in at the temple and penetrated through the jugular. Miss Largesen told me he was unconscious almost until the end. Then he opened his eyes and said, "In the name of Allah, give me water." He died as he drank.'

'You were not there?'

Rose looked down at her hands where the nail-brush had refused to remove the traces of soil from her morning session with the greenhouse geraniums.

'I'm afraid it was all too much for me.' She spoke with deliberate lightness. 'I fainted and had to be taken home.' She glanced up at the girl with a smile. 'Women did in those days, you know. Sink into a swoon like that. I wonder why they don't any more?'

But Jenny Patmore was impatient to return to the thread of the story. She brushed the fringe back from her forehead.

'A tragedy like that though, Lady Foster – there must have been a great scandal.' She broke off suddenly. 'Sorry! I've come to the end of my notepad, would you believe it?' She jumped to her feet. 'I've got another in the car. Do you mind hanging on? You're not tired?'

'No. Not at all.'

Rose watched with a touch of envy as the girl dashed out, plaid skirt flying behind her. She was in fact beginning to feel more than a little weary. She had been talking now for over an hour, with a short break for lunch, sifting through memories that had been packed away undisturbed in her mind since her marriage to Martin. She got up to put a log on the fire. When you were fifty, you could be caught off guard by the past. For a moment she felt a sense of disorientation that was almost like vertigo. Why on earth had she agreed to see this Miss Patmore in the first place? Even now she was not at all sure what it was about, only that a letter had come out of the blue from a government film organization inviting her to contribute to a new documentary series. The British Role in the Middle East – that was a 'working title', they said. Her experience of early days in Aden would give the right kind of historical perspective.

'All this stuff I've been telling you, Miss Patmore,' she said as the girl reappeared, pink-faced from the cold. 'It's not actually going to be incorporated into the film, is it?'

'No, no, Lady Foster. More for the record, as it were. Background and all that. And do please call me Jenny.' She threw off her jacket and moved to the fire to warm her hands, turning with the quick smile that had charmed Rose from the start. 'Besides, you've been so polite about everyone. I don't think you've given away any secrets.'

Rose went across to draw the curtains, unable for a moment to trust her expression. Perhaps it was the effort of keeping back the real truth of her life in Arabia that had made her feel so exhausted. As it was, she had simply recounted what might have been the impressions of any young colonial wife, the dinner parties, the excursions into the desert, friendships with the local ruler's family, visits to the harems and souks. Finally, there was the tragic episode of the death of the Sultan as the Turks invaded the protectorate.

'I was asking you about the various repercussions,' Jenny went on. Rose turned to find that clipboard and pencil were at the ready again.

'Your husband – your first husband – how was he affected?'

Rose sat down again and studied the fire.

'It was the end, of course,' she said in a flat voice. 'The end of his career. As you say, it was a great scandal. The Emir accused him publicly of the murder of his father. There was also the official charge of dereliction of duty. By withholding the reinforcements to Jehal he had countermanded Government orders, you see. The Resident was a sick man. But he sent word that my husband was dismissed his command the next day without even a court martial. Then the India Office discharged him from the service. It's all in the records. They were the terms demanded by the Emir. You know the Islamic code – an eye for an eye.'

She was looking at Jenny now, and saw the girl's glance dart up at her from her notebook.

'But it was not murder, surely, not a deliberate killing?'

Rose hesitated. 'My husband was a very strange man. I really don't think he was quite sane at the time. He hated the Emir . . .' She broke off. Jenny was no longer writing. 'But this is personal history, very personal. Not for your researches, of course.'

'Of course not. But I can't help being curious. Why did he hate the Emir?'

Rose had collected herself again. 'Some silly feud. I think secretly my husband hated all native people. Anyway, he sailed off to South Africa and I came home. Our divorce went through in 1918. I never saw him again. According to my solicitors he died in 1935.'

'And what of the Emir? He is still alive?'

At these words, Rose felt an almost physical sense of shock. The possibility of Hassan being dead had never entered her mind. Otherwise she would surely have known the moment . . .

'I imagine so. He's about my own age,' she said carefully. 'We've been out of touch for so very long. He followed his father as Sultan, of course.'

'You never went back to Aden?'

'Never.' She hurried on to safer ground. 'As you know, I remarried. Someone I'd met in Aden, Martin Foster. Strange, isn't it? We bumped into each other on a train coming from Cairo, towards the end of the war. Then of course, he went back into the Colonial Service and we lived all over the world: Africa, the West Indies, Gibraltar, ending up at Government House, Fiji.' The thought of Martin was calming somehow and she smiled. 'If only he was still alive, he'd be the one to tell you stories.'

'You've told quite a few yourself,' Jenny reminded her. 'I've read all your books. I love them.'

It was Rose's cue to go over to the shelves at the far end of the room. Jenny followed and stood beside her for a few minutes, politely turning pages that still exuded the dank smell of tropical climates. But Rose could tell that her mind was still on Arabia.

'Why did you never write about Aden?' she asked.

'I suppose because the experience was too painful – at the time, anyway.' On an impulse she added, 'Geoffrey was not the only one who left in disgrace, you see.'

'You mean the Emir gave away the secret?'

'The secret?' Once again, Rose felt that jump in all her senses.

'The note you sent to Jehal telling him to leave.'

'Oh, the note.' Rose drew breath, then frowned. 'Goodness, did I mention that? I'd forgotten. You are good at getting people to talk. But you'd better not use that bit because no one else ever knew. The Emir told no one.' She faltered for a moment. 'I may have been persona non grata as the wife of the Commanding Officer, but Hassan did not betray our friendship. He realized I had done it with the best intentions, and what happened was nobody's fault but my husband's.'

'It was brave of you, though. And you've never been back?' she repeated.

What penetrating eyes the girl had. Yet there was a warmth about them. It seemed to signal a purely personal rapport at work between the two of them.

But now she pulled down the secret blind that she had used to protect herself for so long.

'No, I never went back. That was the end of Aden.' She replaced the books. 'Why don't we have some tea? I'll go and find Betty.'

'And so you never saw the Emir again, Lady Foster?'

'Just once.' She spoke over her shoulder from the doorway. 'He came to London for a government conference – 1917, I think. Excuse me just a minute.'

In the kitchen was Betty, standing at the table buttering scones with that faintly irritable air that meant she had been left out of things for a little too long. Rose thought she looked suddenly old. Her shoulders were bent and the overhead light caught the grey in her sandy hair.

'Still asking questions then, is she?' She turned and scrutinized Rose sharply. 'Not upsetting you, is she?'

Rose put her hands over her face for a moment, then took them away and straightened the scarf at the neck of her cardigan.

'No, no, of course not. I'm just a bit tired, that's all.'

Betty clicked her tongue as she set out the cups on the silver tray. 'Dragging up all that silly old past again. Things that are best forgotten.' She put her hand on Rose's shoulder. 'Some things that only you and I know about.'

And Hassan, Rose said to herself. And Nabiha, of course. Abdullah, perhaps. But these were only the names of ghosts now, locked away in another time, another place. Sometimes she wondered if they had ever really existed. Or had it all been fantasy, a plot for a book she had constructed in her head and never written down?

'It's only the history stuff she wants to hear about,' she told Betty. 'Nothing personal. And she's an awfully sweet girl. Come and have a word when tea's ready.'

Back in the drawing room she found Jenny Patmore sitting on a stool by the fire, hunched over a photograph album. As Rose came in, she sprang up guiltily.

'I hope you don't mind. But you did say you'd put them out for me to see. I just couldn't wait.'

She had put on a pair of horn-rimmed glasses which made her look inquisitorial. Now she snatched them off as if she hated them.

'I should be the one with the spectacles,' Rose said. 'I keep pretending I don't really need them.'

'You probably don't. You're awfully young-looking, being so slim and everything.' She spoke directly, with no trace of flattery in her manner. She turned to the album. 'I recognized you straight away. You were really beautiful.'

Why did the past tense always hurt, Rose thought? It was ridiculous to mind any more. She remembered Sir David Trevelyan at the Colonial Institute reception. 'How does it feel to be always the prettiest woman in the room?' Dear David, who came back to her mind so regularly it was like being able to talk to him still.

'The camera will love you. There's no doubt about that.'

Jenny had put on her glasses again and was peering closely at the faded sepia snaps. 'You can see it even here. This must be the horse you were telling me about – Azziza? And this is the Emir Hassan?'

Rose took a fleeting glance at a young man in jodhpurs and turban. She reached across and turned the page quickly.

'There's the Raj in full swing, the kind of thing you were asking about. The garden party at the Residency, and that's a New Year's Eve Ball at the Club!' But something else was on her mind. 'What did you mean – the camera will love me?'

'Well, we do hope to get you on film at some stage, if that's all right? It will make a marvellous juxtaposition with these old pictures. I only wish I'd had the camera crew with me today.'

'I was just wondering about the cameras.' Betty had arrived with the tea tray, smiling excitedly. Obviously, previous reservations had been cast aside at the mention of filming. 'I'm a real film fan, I am. We don't have any cinema up here at Glynceiriog. But I never miss going when I'm at my sister's at Llangollen. Do you know many films stars, like Margaret Lockwood or Leslie Howard?' she asked.

'No romance in our films,' Jenny smiled. 'Just dull old current affairs.' She took the cup Betty had poured for her.

'These are Betty's scones,' Rose said, passing the plate. 'They're famous.'

'Thank you.' She looked up at her hesitantly. 'Actually, I haven't mentioned this yet in case it threw you before we did our interview. But we do have another plan. At least, the producer does. I know he very much hopes you might feel able to agree to it.'

'What plan might that be?' Out of the corner of her eye, Rose saw Betty perch herself on the chair by the door.

'Well, as I was telling you, our camera team will be spending a few days in Aden to cover the turn of events there. What we really need is for you to come with us, so that you can be our link person.'

'Link person?' Betty piped up, mystified.

But Jenny was scanning Rose's face, judging her reactions. 'You could describe the contrasts between old and new so well. There'd be a chance to talk to some of the Arabs who were there in your own day – the Sultan himself, if he's still around. It would put everything into perspective somehow – the heyday of the British in Arabia, and now the breakdown of the whole concept of Empire.'

Rose's reaction was one of confused disbelief.

'I – I couldn't possibly. I haven't the faintest idea of what's going on there now. I've no interest in politics at all.'

'We don't want a political lecture,' Jenny said patiently. 'It's the personal touch we need. And after all you're not exactly a nonentity. Your books have made you quite a name.'

'But that's different,' Rose protested. 'I've never done any filming in my life.' In fact, none of these objections were uppermost in her mind. Above all, she was thinking of Hassan. She had a picture of herself politely shaking hands with a middle-aged stranger, both of them stepping around the past as if it were a frozen lake where the ice might give way at any moment. She turned to Jenny apologetically.

'No. It's out of the question, I'm afraid.' She shook her head. 'I just wouldn't have the nerve.'

'And she hates flying – don't you?' Betty broke in. 'Remember when you came back from Kenya, how upset you were?' She got up quickly. 'I'll just get some hot water.'

Jenny's face was sympathetic. 'I know how you feel. I've sprung a bit of a surprise on you, after all.' She leaned forward impulsively. 'But I'd be

236

there with you. And the producer's very experienced, one of the best. I think you'd really enjoy it. You're that kind of person!'

Rose smiled in spite of herself. 'Not any more, I'm afraid.'

'I know it's lovely up here.' Jenny was looking around the lamplit room with its glowing Indian carpets, pottery from Africa on the shelves, the yellow walls hung with prints of Pacific Island plants and birds. 'But you must find it a bit quiet after all your travels – a bit lonely?'

The last word touched a nerve. For no sensible reason Rose felt tears threaten, the faintest prickle, somewhere just below the surface. She patted the girl's hand without replying.

'Well, you don't have to decide here and now. We're not flying out for another few weeks. Come to London. We'll talk again.'

Jenny was getting up to go, the album still in her hand. As she gave it back to Rose, a loose photograph in a crumpled tissue folder fell to the ground. She bent to pick it up, smoothing the paper back. But before she had time to study it properly, Rose had taken it from her.

'Sorry. That's something else.'

Her heart was hammering as she slipped it into the pocket of her cardigan. How on earth had it found its way down here among the albums?

'Of course, things are boiling up a bit in Aden at the moment,' Jenny was saying. 'Out in the Protectorate, that is. There's no danger inside the Colony. But I expect you've been reading about it?'

Rose forced herself to concentrate again. 'I don't see the papers much. I'm wrapped up in my novel at the moment – nineteenth-century Australia.'

'Well, I can certainly let you have all the Aden cuttings if you need them,' Jenny told her briskly. 'What we're concentrating on at the moment is the business of cutting through the Colonial Office red tape. The Governor of Aden is someone called Ferguson.'

A vague recollection slipped into Rose's mind of a chunky bulldog figure in safari jacket and rather long shorts. 'Of course, Jimmy Ferguson. He was in Uganda with us years ago. He's a bachelor, a bit of a dry stick, but not too bad.'

Jenny's face lit up. 'That's splendid! A personal contact always works wonders. No doubt he'll be asking you to stay at Government House while the rest of us doss down at some house of sin in the bazaar.'

'You're forgetting one thing,' Rose said sharply. 'At the moment I've no intention of going out there at all.'

'Sorry.' Jenny's tone was contrite. 'I do tend to get a bit carried away.' They were standing in the hall, Jenny tucking her fringe into a red

237

tam-o'-shanter, her eyes sparkling. 'But I do hope we can meet again, Lady Foster, whatever happens.'

'I'm sure we shall.'

Rose wrapped herself in her duffle-coat. 'I'll come with you to the gate with my torch.'

Outside it had begun to snow again. From the hillside above came the chuckling call of the owl, setting out on his nightly rounds.

At the end of the path Jenny turned back to look at the house, its low-slung roof set in the crook of the mountain. 'Such a marvellous place! How did you find it?'

'I've known it all my life. My family lived in the big house down there, across the stream. This used to be three up-and-downs for the quarrymen and so on. So I was always up here when I was little, playing with the children. They'd been empty for ages when we came back from abroad. It seemed the obvious thing to make our home here.'

She stopped to open the door of a shed from where a frantic barking had begun. A handsome cream labrador rushed out and plunged at her joyfully.

'Be careful driving,' Rose called as the girl got into her car. 'My daughter never stops grumbling about the track whenever she comes to see me. Thinks I'm mad living up here.'

Through the window Jenny laughed. 'I think you're a very lucky lady. See you in London. And thank you again.' With a wave she was gone, bumping away down the lane.

For a moment Rose stood quite still. With the white flakes falling around her, she felt like one of those tiny figures in an old-fashioned glass paperweight which has been turned upside-down and shaken. Yet the day had begun calmly enough with all the familiar rituals – Betty coming in to light the fire and bring up her coffee, work on the papers and books on her desk by the window, the smoke from the farm chimneys below rising up through the trees.

Now she stood hunched in her coat and hood, her thoughts whirling about her. To go back to Arabia. What a crazy idea! It would be like crossing a minefield with traps and pitfalls on every side, each one primed to blow up the safe, solid image of self she had so painfully constructed over the last three decades.

She started as the dog gave a yelp of impatience.

'All right. Come on then.'

As she walked home, she saw the lights go on down at the village hall. She reminded herself that she had to get her African slides ready for her talk to the Women's Institute next Tuesday. Further along, the last bus was trundling along from the town. As the sound of the engine died away up the pass, there was silence again. Or rather, the silence of Pentre-fawr that was always overlaid by the faint hum of the wind against the mountain, and the rustle of the stream at the bottom of the valley. All this Rose registered as usual. But it was as though she were suddenly a stranger, an outsider walking through to somewhere else.

Had the long-ago past really the power, once resurrected, to come between you and the real world like a ghost? The snow had stopped now. The white glimmer of it, laid across the darkness of the horizon, reminded Rose of a mirage, a thing she had not thought of for years. Damn the London people and their eager young researcher! As she got to the gate, she met Betty setting off for home, a figure of solid reality in her fur boots and old tweed coat.

'Don't you go and catch cold now, Miss Rose,' she scolded. 'Dawdling along like that. I've left your soup on the Aga.' There was a troubled look on her face as she moved closer in the light from the house.

'You won't go, Miss Rose, will you?' She spoke urgently, almost in a whisper. 'I know it would only make you unhappy. After putting the whole thing behind you, and with you only just getting over Sir Martin passing on . . .'

She broke off at the sound of the telephone through the French windows.

Rose squeezed her arm. 'Don't worry, Betty. We can have a good chat tomorrow. Anyway, I've already decided.'

She hurried inside. She was hoping for something to bring her back to normality again. Now, picking up the receiver, she suddenly thought of all those Aden calls, the handset hot and gritty in her hand, Hassan's voice at the other end.

'Yes?' she said, still trying to catch her breath.

'Mother,' came a clear, stern voice. 'You promised to ring me, remember?'

Rose closed her eyes. Why was it that this perfectly nice child of hers had inherited Martin's most maddening quality? Somehow she felt Mary's air of righteousness more keenly as she grew older. She looked like Martin too, with her high colouring and earnest spectacled gaze.

'Sorry, darling,' she said automatically.

'Busy scribbling away, I suppose?'

'No, no scribbling today. As a matter of fact,' Rose went on, deliberately casual, 'some journalist came to see me.'

'Oh really? About one of your books?'

'About a film.'

'Film? Goodness!' Mary sounded impressed and at the same time deeply suspicious.

'They want me to go out to Arabia.'

There was a shocked silence at the other end. Then, 'Mother. You must be joking. What on earth for?'

'To make a documentary about the British in Aden.'

'Aden!' Mary's Roedean vowels went up another notch in her indignation. 'You can't go there, for heaven's sake! Haven't you been reading the papers?'

'Not really.'

'Well it could be Palestine all over again. The Egyptians are arming the tribes. There are anti-British uprisings every other day. We're sending in the army from Cyprus.'

'Fighting's no new thing among the tribes,' Rose replied.

'Anyway, what do you know about Arabia, mother? All your books are about Africa.'

'It was before you were born,' Rose said quietly. 'I was there with my first husband.'

'You never talked about it,' Mary protested.

'No.'

'There's obviously no question of you actually going. It's far too dangerous. Michael says these wretched Arab League people should have been put down right at the start.'

Typical of Michael, Rose thought, smuggest of smug Wirral solicitors. He always talked about the new nationalist leaders of what he called 'British Spheres of Influence' as if they were dogs with rabies.

'Oh, I don't know,' she replied. 'I think it's time for change in the Middle East. The West have been trying to run their affairs for long enough.'

'Well, you just do as you please, of course.' Mary's tone changed to the defensive as she went on. 'I know you get a bit lonely up there on your own. I've been telling you for ages you should go on one of these cruise things. Or join the golf club at least.'

Rose had slipped off her boots and was standing barefoot on a damp patch of lino feeling rather cold at this far end of the house. Next to her, the dog whined impatiently. 'Must go now, dear. The fire will be going out.'

'Keep in touch,' Mary said sharply. 'Ring at the weekend.'

'I will. Love to Sophie – and Michael.'

Putting down the phone, Rose felt a wave of relief. In the kitchen she poured herself a rather too strong gin and tonic. Hope I'm not getting like Eleanor Rawlinson, she said to herself. She hadn't thought of her for years. Now she felt guilty for not going to see her more often, at what was politely called a nursing home, the year before she died.

Glass in hand, she climbed the narrow stairs to her bedroom. Switching on the lamp at the table by the window, she was aware of a mounting nervousness, as if she was bracing herself for some kind of test. There, stacked beside the typewriter, were the pages of the chapter she was working on. But all the time, she knew the real reason why she had come up here.

Like a sleepwalker, she turned away to the door which led to a small back room, full of disused bits of furniture and other belongings. For a moment she stood looking at the tall Victorian cupboard she had inherited from her mother. Then she pulled out a chair to stand on, and reached behind the top ledge for the key that was there. Dust showered down as she brought out a small suitcase, the leather top scratched and dented, the whole thing plastered with peeling labels. In the bleak light of the overhead bulb, some were still decipherable – SS *Medina*, the Seramis Hotel, Cairo, GWR Paddington to Bala.

A sheet of newspaper was needed so that she could lay it down on the camp bed in the corner. The little key was rusty. It was so long since she had used it. Even now, as she fiddled with slippery fingers to fit it into the lock, she felt the power of that old urge to look back and remember. At the start after leaving Aden it had been like a drug, this need to remind herself of Hassan and the reality of what had happened between them. It was an instinct she obeyed blindly, in secret. Many times after being in other places with other people, she would search out the little case with a thudding heart, fearful that it might have disappeared in her absence.

Then when she married again, she had felt ashamed. There was a shabby furtiveness about keeping something hidden from a husband for whom she cared so deeply. But still she could not destroy what she had kept. It would be like putting an end to some living thing. So she had let the suitcase lie unopened in a place where no one would see it. She never thought about it, had never needed to see it again, until this moment.

Now she could feel her heart tumbling around, just as it used to, as she lifted the lid. She had forgotten she had wrapped everything in the *chador*, her black silk purdah cloak. She unfolded it and caught her breath at the perfume of sandalwood. It was frail and musty now but it still had the ability, beyond anything else, to conjure up that other woman – a stranger to her now – that reckless, passionate girl of eighteen.

'Hassan,' she murmured. She pressed the gauzy stuff to her face, spreading it around her on the bed where she sat. Out of its folds rolled the silver necklace with the rubies and cornelians. Half-hidden beneath it was the little moon necklace on its chain.

The silver and the precious stones glowed as brilliant as ever. But it was strange how diminished and faded everything else looked now, pressed roses from Jehal, a picture of Hassan in his Emir's robes, spoilt by the English shoes and socks she had teased him about, not realizing till afterwards how she had hurt his pride. On the back he had written in Arabic, words that he said were too intimate to be put into English. It was tucked into the book of poetry belonging to Trevelyan. With her fingertip she picked out the grains of sand from the spine, the last trace of the sandstorm that day at the beach house perhaps. There were notes too, crumpled scraps secretly passed at parties or delivered at the house as the car went past to the palace at Jehal.

It was like an archaeological dig, Rose thought, each fragment revealing another layer in the relationship. And there at the back, in an old crested envelope, was the final clue, the last link with Arabia. The sight of her own handwriting could inflict a sense of misery even now. But it had to be read – memory was a deceitful guide. The reality of what had happened was here before her.

'Beloved Hassan,' she had written. 'I am with Nabiha. I still cannot believe the horror of what has happened with still no chance of a word between us. The worst thing for me is the knowledge that I set the tragedy of your father's death in motion by sending you the message to leave Jehal. I keep asking myself whether, if I had only told them what I had done, they would have been prepared for you and the mistake might never have been made. Or was it a mistake? Perhaps the deed would have been done anyway, by the madman who is my husband. You will know by now that he is leaving the country by the next ship. But I, my darling – what am I to do? The pledge between us cannot change surely. I will go anywhere, wait anywhere for you. But you must tell me. The agony of not knowing is too much to endure. Please send a message, or come yourself if you can. R.'

This letter had come back to her with Hassan's reply. She remembered vividly the sight of the green paper, the moment she had brought it out of the envelope, somehow knowing what it would mean.

'I am returning your letter as a token that there can no longer exist between us any kind of tie, not for the present at least. I accept this fate, even though my heart is destroyed by it. There is no alternative, Rose. Because of what has happened, we must become strangers again. Your husband killed my father. I should have put my dagger into his throat that day at Perim. It seems I am a fool as well as a coward. Now in the eyes of Islam, the shame is as much on you who carry his name as on him.

'In my heart I blame myself for everything that has happened. It is a punishment on me for forsaking the path of my inheritance and, the worst crime of all, for ignoring the laws of my religion. I allowed myself to fall in love with you, an infidel, one of a race who can never be anything but an enemy to us Arabs, in spite of all they say to the contrary. For myself, my

242

own life must be dedicated by way of recompense to the service of my people. It is in my power now to bind the tribes together. The war can be the way towards independence for the whole of Arabia. Believe me, Rose, I shall not stop loving you. But I shall not see you again. You must go back to your own country and make your life with your own people, marry again perhaps. The madness has left us both, you see. We must return to the real world again. I pray for you, and remember you. H.'

One more note was returned, this time without an answer.

'I beg of you, Hassan,' Rose had written. 'Let us meet, if only once. This is too cruel, for both of us.'

She picked up the dried flowers again, crushed them in the palm of her hand. She was crying now, not silently, but with long racking sobs that shook her whole body as she lay face down on the camp bed.

How long was it since she had wept like this – thirty years, perhaps? She had thought you had to be young to give way to such overpowering emotion. But it seemed she was wrong.

After a little while, she sat up slowly and felt in her pocket for the snapshot she had taken from Jenny when it dropped from the album. The suitcase was where it belonged.

She studied it for a moment, rubbing her eyes. The small figure in the centre was suddenly clear. A smiling baby boy with tousled black hair leaned forward to take his first steps across an English lawn. One hand was held by Hassan, the other by herself.

Idris, she said to herself. How was I able to let you go? But what else could I have done?

❦ 2 ❧

'WHAT else could I have done?'

The grey-haired woman sitting across the table shrugged her shoulders.

'You had no alternative. It was an impossible situation.'

Rose and Cynthia Nunan were lunching together at the Royal Empire Society. It was an annual ritual, faithfully observed. Half the time was spent bringing themselves up to date with their current news, the rest in revisiting familiar landmarks of their mutual past. They didn't discuss the future very much. There usually wasn't time.

Considering they had been talking hard since they first sat down, they had disposed of their prawn cocktails and grilled soles fairly rapidly. Both were hungry. Rose had travelled up from Wales that morning. Cynthia had driven in from Sevenoaks – 'appalling traffic and such awful drivers these days'. Now they were toying with some brie, having conscientiously refused pudding, still with enough of their favourite Pouilly Fuissé left in the bottle for a last glass each. 'But now here you are,' Cynthia went on, 'about to put yourself into another impossible situation, going back to the very place that brought you so much pain.'

'Not just pain,' Rose said, half to herself.

Cynthia was silent for a moment, staring out of the window. Then she turned back to her friend.

'Do you remember coming aboard that ship at Aden? You came to tell me you were not going home to England after all because you and the young Emir had fallen in love.'

'How could I forget?' Rose replied. 'It was the most important decision I had ever made.'

'Then you'll remember how I warned you that you were putting yourself in a position of great danger, risking everything you had made of your life. Well now here I am, in 1948, having to tell you exactly the same thing.'

'Dear Cynthia. I honestly think you're exaggerating. There's no fighting in Aden itself. And anyway, the film people take care of all the security side of things.'

'You know quite well that's not what I'm talking about.' Rose flinched,

244

and took another sip of her wine. There were times when Cynthia could sound positively severe. 'It's the emotional dangers I'm worried about, the whole idea of stirring up a relationship that's already ruined your life once . . .'

'Not quite.'

'Well, let's say you were lucky enough to come through it in the end. So why go looking for trouble again?'

She broke off as the waiter advanced on them to distribute the rest of the bottle between them.

'Is to your satisfaction, Lady Foster?' He twinkled at Rose, who knew him well.

'Very good, Giorgio. As always.'

Alone again, the two women leaned forward across their wine, surveying each other with the fond irritation of best friends who have long given up the idea of correcting each other's faults. Appearances were also immaterial. Rose, studying Cynthia, saw not so much the impending double chin and the patchy powder, but the snub-nosed smile of the lovely girl on the *Medina*, her straw boater tilted forward to shade her large brown eyes. Middle age was just a disguise, Rose thought. Talking close together like this, they were young once again, deeply frivolous and wildly serious in a way their present-day friends and family would hardly recognize. So much so that it was always a shock for Rose to glance across at the mirror on the opposite wall and see the figures of two sophisticated fifty-year-olds, one a little too fat, the other too thin, both clad in smart tweeds and obviously bent on an enjoyable day's shopping at Marshall and Snelgrove's. Cynthia's hair, Rose noted, had lately been cut to frame her face rather flatteringly. Perhaps she should adopt the same image rather than fastening up her wild auburn-streaked mop in a knot at the back of her head.

'What I can't understand,' Cynthia continued, 'is how you came to change your mind about going out there at all. When you spoke to me on the phone a couple of weeks ago you told me there was no question of it. Now here you are packed up and ready to go the day after tomorrow.'

'Not quite packed up. I've hardly any decent hot-weather clothes at all. Will you come shopping with me this afternoon – point me in the right direction?'

'Yes, if you answer my question.'

Rose gulped down the last of her wine. It was no good trying to pretend with Cynthia.

'The film people had a letter from the Colonial Secretariat giving details about key figures they should talk to for the programme. Among them was Hassan's name – His Highness Sir Hassan Ahmed Karim Bin

Seif, KBE, Sultan of Jehal. When I realized for a fact that he was still alive, I suddenly knew I had to see him again. Just once, if only to satisfy my curiosity. How has he aged? What has he done with his life? That kind of thing.'

She saw Cynthia still looking sceptical.

'I'm not planning any earth-shattering reunion,' she laughed. 'But it suddenly seemed ridiculous to try to avoid it. I know we had a stormy parting. We were both so terribly distressed that last time in Cairo we hardly knew what we were doing. Maybe this is the chance to heal the rift after all these years. You do see, don't you? The company have been so pressing. It all seems meant in a way.'

'That *kismet* thing all over again, darling?' Cynthia said in her dry way.

'Destiny was David Trevelyan's word. Dear David. What would I have done without him?' She looked around her, out through the double doors on to the marble landing. 'Do you know, it was in this place that I first met him. Geoffrey had brought me along to be vetted by the memsahibs. David was a breath of life in all that stuffiness. He gave me the idea of what Arabia could be like.'

'And look what happened.' Cynthia shook her head. 'You haven't written to Hassan, have you, for heaven's sake? Told him you're coming?'

'I have not.' Rose was indignant. 'If there is to be a meeting, let it just happen. Whenever I've tried to manipulate things it's been disastrous. I'm only going to be there for a fortnight anyway.' She sat up straight, briskly, adjusting her pearls. 'Besides I'll be working, remember. I think it will be fun, don't you? I might even start writing for films. And I have been feeling dull lately. Flat, you might say, getting into a rut, I suppose.'

Her friend eyed her speculatively. 'Yes, you have let yourself go a bit. You look somehow – not old, but sort of wound-down. Lost your old sparkle a bit. It's not surprising, really, after all those years of nursing Martin. Poor old Martin.'

The head waiter was at their side, looking down at them benevolently.

'Coffee in the drawing room, Lady Foster?'

'That would be lovely.'

'We need to put our feet up for half an hour if we're to do battle with the department stores,' Cynthia said as they made their way down to the next floor. Stepping out of the lift, they were confronted by a very wrinkled, very brown little man in an immaculate pinstripe suit, who sprang forward and took Rose by the hand.

'Lady Foster. Good to see you. You don't come up enough nowadays.' He planted a quick kiss on her cheek before disappearing into the lift. 'Let us know next time.'

Cynthia was watching with a quizzical smile.

'I see you still have your fans.'

'Hardly,' said Rose, who was nevertheless feeling fortified by the encounter. 'Old Lord Templemere was Martin's friend. He came out to Fiji on some Foreign Office swan when we were there. He's on the council here, like me.'

'Still the old Colonial hand then?' quipped Cynthia.

'Stop needling me, wretched creature!'

They were laughing as they settled themselves on a sofa by the window. The only other people in the room seemed to be fast asleep – a bishop with the *Daily Telegraph* over his chest and a very old lady crumpled up in a fur coat smelling of mothballs in an armchair just behind them. A gloomy-looking maid in black and white placed a tray of coffee in front of them and creaked out again through the green baize door.

'Cynthia,' Rose said in a low voice as they sipped their coffee. 'Would you do something for me?'

'What's that?'

'Remind me.'

Cynthia looked mystified. 'Remind you of what, dear girl?'

'Myself.'

'What on earth do you mean?'

'Well . . .' Rose hesitated then plunged on. 'One of the reasons I gave myself an extra day in London before we fly out was to make contact with the past again. That particular bit of the past I mean. Oddly enough, we've not talked about it for ages and it's got lost somehow. I was deter mined to make a new life for myself and it seems I succeeded rather too well.'

Cynthia put her hand on Rose's. 'Meeting Martin again just at that point was the best thing that could have happened. Now that was destiny, if ever there was such a thing.'

'But the gap I'm talking about. I've deliberately blotted it out over the years. If I do get it clear in my mind again it will somehow help when I see Hassan. If I see Hassan,' she corrected herself. 'So that things will sort of be joined up again.' She looked at Cynthia almost pleadingly. 'So talk to me about it again. You're the only person who can.'

'Well, I can only tell you how it seemed to me,' Cynthia said in a matter-of-fact way, pouring out more coffee. 'There are some moments I can never forget. Your telephone call first of all. You'd been back in this country for a month and I'd heard nothing apart from your letter telling me you were on your way home, and what had happened at the camp.' She sighed. 'That was a terrible letter, all blotched and scrawled. I could hardly bear to read it.'

'I remember I posted it at Port Said,' Rose put in. 'I was so wretched on

247

the boat. I didn't know it but I was two months' pregnant by the end of the journey, so that didn't help. I tried to take an overdose at one point – sleeping pills – but I was too sick to keep them down. Captain Strong was marvellous, the old man I met on the Perim trip. If it hadn't been for him I wouldn't have got a passage for months. He saw me through it all, bless him. Funny, the people you come across so casually who turn out to play such a vital part in one's life.' She accepted one of Cynthia's Turkish cigarettes.

'I know I shouldn't, but I can't resist the scent of them.'

Cynthia was staring out through the window, her eyes narrowed against a wisp of smoke. 'Strangely enough, you sounded quite calm on the telephone. I suppose it was the calm of desperation. You were ringing from your parents' house. Someone might have come into the room at any minute so you had to be quick. Then you said you'd discovered you were pregnant, three months. It had to be Hassan's child, even though you'd been told after your miscarriage that you'd never conceive again. But there was no doubt about it. A doctor in Liverpool had just confirmed it. And he'd refused point-blank to do an abortion. You said I was the only person you could turn to. I knew you were at the end of your tether.'

'You simply gave me instructions. Pack your things and come and stay, you said. You can have the baby here with me, then we'll decide what to do. My God, it was like a light at the end of the tunnel.'

'I'll never forget the sight of you when you arrived, though. Your face was like paper, huge eyes staring through – it was like meeting a stranger. You'd tried to hide your waistline in a hideous mustard-coloured jacket and skirt. You'd been crying so much, you couldn't cry any more. Then you had a sort of nervous breakdown. It went on for quite a while. Lucky Francis was at home. He knew what to give you, how to treat you.'

'It's strange the things that go through your mind at a time like that,' Rose said. 'I was certain that if I'd had a love affair with an Englishman, instead of Hassan, I would have tried to settle at home again with my parents, and pass off the baby as Geoffrey's. It's what lots of women have done, after all. But to try to conceal the fact that the baby's father was not a European, that was too much to hope for. I'd already come through a scandal in Arabia. I couldn't face another in Wales.'

'I've often wondered what you told your parents.'

'Can you imagine giving them the news that I was pregnant by one of the native rulers? It was bad enough letting them know I was getting divorced. No, they knew nothing about the baby. I said I was coming south to stay with friends, take on some war work. Betty guessed something was wrong, of course. That was how she came down to help, later on. But those letters I wrote home! Have you forgotten them?' Rose shook her head, feeling a kind of savage wonder at her ability to survive the trauma of it all. 'Every one of them was a lie, until I met Martin again.' She sighed. 'Now I ask myself how I did it.'

Cynthia leaned back against the cushions and looked at her reflectively. 'You're a much stronger person than you pretend you were, even at twenty. You were absolutely determined that Hassan should be told nothing. You made Francis and me swear that under no circumstances would we try to get in touch with him.'

For a moment, Rose felt the old pain touch her heart again.

'He had refused even to see me, remember, cut me off from his life completely. I made a vow I would never again ask him for anything. I was going to manage with the baby whatever happened. I knew there was no other way. I'd turned my back on Arabia for good. I couldn't even bear to read the Near East war news, Lawrence in the Hejaz and all that.'

'You wouldn't read anything,' Cynthia said. 'I can see you now, sitting up in your room, sewing away at baby clothes as if your life depended on it, hardly speaking to anyone. You liked music though. You'd listen to the gramophone up there, hour after hour.'

'Bach Partitas,' said Rose, suddenly remembering. 'So unlike me. But it was the kind of sound that somehow seemed to impose order on things. I needed that. No more soaring emotions. No more passion of any kind.'

'You had a phobia about meeting people. The only place you liked to go was a little corner of the beach, right up against the cliffs. It was always deserted, and being so close to the house you could walk there. You'd take an old Bedouin rug with you, and one of those Chinese parasols, and sit against the rocks with your sketchbook until the sun went down. Francis said it was the best therapy there was.'

Even as Cynthia was talking, Rose could feel again the touch of cool English sand against her skin. Ahead was the sparkling line of sea that could be any sea. The baby had first started moving on one of these days. The rippling sensation was part of the oceanic swell and sway, a dreamy state in which all practical thoughts were held at bay. For the sake of the child, she must try not to distress herself any more. The awful wound that had been inflicted on her would slowly heal. Already, the loss of Hassan was something she was learning to think of as a death, and there were plenty of those around in the black-bordered lists in the papers every day.

'The war was a help, I suppose, though it's an awful thing to say. Everything was confusion. So many young widows. I suppose my little problem was hardly noticed.' She was watching Cynthia's face trying to judge her reactions. 'Did I make an awful fuss about actually having the baby? It's somehow completely blurred in my mind.'

'Not surprisingly, you had quite a lot of anaesthetic. You were at home

249

of course, with us, and I was with you quite a lot. When things got tough, there was something you kept asking for. What was it?' Cynthia mused for a moment. 'Oh yes. One of those Muslim rosaries. I had to search your drawers for it. When I found it, you grabbed hold of it and held it tight in your hand right until the baby was born.'

Rose nodded. 'Afterwards I gave it to Nabiha to keep for him.'

'Anyway.' Cynthia caught up with her thoughts again. 'In the end, there he was, a marvellous-looking infant. He had a mop of black hair and eyes like a hawk and he yelled to high heaven. You could see straight away he was no English baby. Right from the start he had that olive-gold sort of colour, rather like those Italian paintings of the Holy Child.'

Rose couldn't help smiling. Cynthia always had a weakness for the cultural image.

'On a practical level though, what did you tell the nurse – and everyone else?'

'That you were the wife of an Egyptian diplomat, old friends of ours, and you'd come to England to have the baby because of the war. Just as well really. You mentioned Hassan's name quite a lot when you were going under. Nabiha was the other person you asked for.'

'Nabiha.' Rose spoke the name softly. 'Maybe I'll see her too in Aden. She must be around seventy now.'

'You could have stayed on with us, you know,' Cynthia told her. 'After you had the baby. We had our own two but the house was big enough for us all. You were absolutely set on making your own way though. Obstinate as usual.'

Rose touched her hand. 'I knew I had to break away. You'd both given me quite enough of your life. And then, Sir David coming up with the idea of a part-time job at Leighton House. Once I'd found someone to look after the baby in the afternoons, I felt sure I could make a go of it.'

'I didn't see the baby again until we were going abroad again. You remember you brought him to see us, the day before . . .'

'The day before Nabiha took him,' Rose said quickly. The process of stripping away time was revealing a tenderness beneath she had not imagined.

'You saw him again, though?'

'Three times – no, four.'

'And after that?'

'Nothing. I've told you before. I made a pact with Hassan that there should not even be letters. I was getting married. The next year I had Martin's baby. It wouldn't have been fair.'

'And now you're breaking that pact?' Cynthia's voice was gentle but the words stung.

'Hardly.' Rose turned away to look for her handbag. 'I've accepted a professional engagement that has nothing to do with Hassan or anyone else. I have to be free to live my life as I choose. Surely I've earned that, haven't I?'

'Of course you have.' Cynthia got up and held out her hand. 'Come on. It's time to buy clothes. Make you beautiful again, now you're going to be a star.'

Rose felt the sense of release between them as they emerged on to the street and hailed a taxi. For the next two hours they were engrossed by the present again. The major decision to be made was the choice between a chic spotted suit in navy and white or a plain black linen dress for cocktail parties. There was a yellow flowered cotton with a full New Look which Cynthia liked, and one of jade lawn which Rose preferred.

'And the matching stole is ideal,' she said. 'I still can't forget the horror that poor Mrs Anderson caused when she turned up at a mixed party in bare shoulders. Geoffrey said she'd done it deliberately to attract attention, but it was simply that no one had thought to tell her the rules of dress in a Muslim country. The other memsahibs were delighted, of course.'

Listening in, the elderly sales assistant forgot her aching feet as she held out a silky cream shirt for Rose to inspect in front of the mirror.

'Where are you staying, by the way?' demanded Cynthia, who was rattling her way through a rail of skirts.

'Government House. Didn't I tell you? The Governor's someone I know from Uganda. When he heard from the Government Film Unit that I was coming out, he wrote and asked me.'

'Home from home,' Cynthia teased.

'Not after my Welsh cottage,' Rose protested. 'Which reminds me, I will need one or two practical things if I'm going to be knocking around in jeeps and things. A bush jacket, or whatever they call it nowadays, a pair of slacks?'

In the end, Rose bought everything. It was so long since she'd been shopping for clothes, she felt extravagant. And yes, the shop would deliver to the Royal Empire Society tomorrow.

'At least I don't have to think about a topee this time,' she said to Cynthia going down in the lift. 'Remember Simon Artz at Port Said. The smell!'

They both pulled faces and went on laughing until they were out in the street.

Saying goodbye left a lump in Rose's throat. Cynthia's underlying concern stayed in her mind as she walked down towards Piccadilly. What if the whole idea was a terrible mistake? It was dusk now, the crowds jostling

251

homewards past the bright shop windows, and she was longing for tea. Did the Ritz still do the Earl Grey mix with Lapsang, and the tiny *petit fours* even in these dreary post-war times?

Without making any conscious decision, she found herself walking towards the tall grey building with its archway of lights over the entrance. Inside the long carpeted hall, she glimpsed the pink tables of the dining room, the shaded lamps and chattering groups, and felt immediately countrified and out of place. A waiter showed her to a table in the corner and took her order, politely but without wasting time. Sitting back in her chair, she was aware of feeling totally apart from the people around her. She knew the real reason why she had come here. Cynthia had taken her back to a certain point in her life. But this was where she had to pick up the thread again. At first she was not sure if the trick would work. Like a spool of old film, memory too could perish and disintegrate if it was not brought out and run through from time to time. But suddenly it was all too easy. She had only to look across to the doorway for the present to fall away as if it had never existed . . .

✣ 3 ✣

I⊤ is an afternoon in the autumn of 1916. It is my first visit to the Ritz and I am sitting at a large table in this same corner with Sir David Trevelyan. There is a file of papers in my lap and I am feeling nervous. I'm here to take notes at an informal meeting of delegates from something called the Arab Bureau. Apparently they have come to London to discuss a new strategy for the war in the Near East. Sir David spends more time doing this kind of liaison work for Government than he does at Leighton House.

It's hard to concentrate because my mind is on Idris. He's developed a bad cold which kept us both awake last night, and I seem to be catching it too. I can't smell the late yellow roses in the vase on the table. Then Janet was late in arriving to take over and had forgotten to bring a new tin of milk powder, so all was chaos, Idris wailing his head off in the midst of it. I say nothing of this to Sir David. He knows I have a baby to look after and that I am separated from my husband. Sometimes, remembering the letters I wrote him from Aden, I feel he guesses the truth. But he has a delicate sense of tact and knows very well it is a subject I would avoid at all costs.

A very old waiter comes up and tells him the party has arrived. Sir David asks for them to be shown to our table. I have a sudden premonition of some violent disruption about to take place in my life. I turn and see, coming through the door, two British officers and two Arabs, one in the flowing robes of Mecca, the other in plainer dress with the grey head-shawl of the northern states. All four are strangers to me. Sir David stands up to meet them.

And then, a few steps behind, as if giving himself a chance to study the company, I see Hassan. At least, I see someone whose image I still frame in my mind half a dozen times a day. I see the face I have carried with me for the last fifteen months, lodged in the most secret place in my heart, someone who holds the hidden spring to every impulse and experience that has made me the woman I now am. I see my lover and my enemy.

At that moment, Sir David takes me quickly by the arm and says in a low voice, 'You must promise not to faint or make a scene. Sultan Hassan wrote begging me to arrange a meeting with you while he was in London with the delegation. I thought this was the simplest way.'

Hassan is still behind the others. His eyes are on me, carefully

253

expressionless, as he walks across the room. He is wearing khaki, the usual army jodhpurs and boots, but with an Indian-style tunic buttoned to the neck, and the familiar green turban with its looped cockade. I am conscious of the effect of his startling looks on the people at the other tables.

All this while I am fighting panic. I can feel myself sweating under my blue serge dress – not one of my most flattering garments – as I deliberately organize my defences. Sir David is introducing me to the party. There is much shaking of hands and exchanging of greetings. Then Hassan stands before me, smiling politely. The clasp of his hand, his palm against mine, sets up a recoil in me I have to struggle to disguise.

'We know each other from Aden days,' he says.

His smile is as tense as a wire. He is thinner, with a scar on his cheek that was not there before.

None of the others seem particularly interested in who I am. The Arabs display graceful politeness to conceal their innate discomfort at the presence of a woman among men. The English officers accept the tea I pour with jolly brotherly grins of complicity at the strangeness of the situation.

'Your husband was in Government there?' asks one of them, in a perfunctory sort of way.

'Yes,' I reply and nothing more. It is obviously assumed I am a war widow. Getting out my notepad and pencil, I glance up and see Hassan looking at my wedding ring, the same silver ring he gave me at Zara. I need it for respectability's sake and to buy a new one would be an unnecessary expense. Sir David has placed him next to me. When the others are talking he says in a low voice, 'I have to see you alone. Please. I have only three days in London.'

'What a shame,' I hear myself say in my social voice. 'I have to go away to Wales this weekend.'

The older Englishman is growing restive. 'Perhaps we could turn to business then. We are seeing the War Office tomorrow. We should welcome your advice, Sir David.'

The conference that follows is a blessed diversion. My shorthand, mercifully, now comes automatically. Meanwhile I ask myself why he should want to see me now. Why has he broken the resolve that was made at such expense to us both? Has he somehow found out about the baby?

In between notes, I snatch glimpses of his face. There is talk of an Arab revolt, a phrase I remember from the past. It is something he obviously feels passionate about. He spreads out his hands as he speaks, his eyes darting from one to the other. The officers from Cairo are more restrained, pressing the dignitary from Mecca who is a relation of the

Sherif Hussein about the leadership of such an uprising. It would have to be well funded if it were to succeed in driving the Turks out of Central Arabia. The failure of the British at Jehal last year still rankled. But it could still be redeemed if only Government would instigate a new front into the Yemen.

'But will they?' Hassan shrugs his shoulders. 'The Aden Government seem to have lost all interest in the war. They are quite happy to let sleeping dogs lie, as long as the Turks keep out of Aden itself.'

The old Emir in the grey head-shawl raps on the table. This what they have come to tell the British. The Turks must be encircled. More arms must be sent, more money for the tribes.

Sir David says there is one sure way to win the support of all the Arabs. They must be promised their independence in return, not just from the Turks but from any foreign power, the British included.

Rose sees a bitter look pass over Hassan's face, an expression she remembers well. 'That is something I have been told before, Sir David.'

There is much mention of a young intelligence officer called Lawrence. It seems he is a brilliant maker of maps, a strategist, someone with a burning sympathy for the Arab cause. Only a few days ago he was at Jeddah with Sir Ronald Storrs, conferring with the Sherif. The chief task of the tribes would be to blow up the Turkish railway at Hejaz. Everything else would follow, Hassan declares.

So the talk goes on. Every now and then I find Hassan's eyes on me, willing me to meet them. But I will not. There is a pause for fresh tea. I look at my watch. It is my chance to escape.

'Would you forgive me, Sir David? I'm expected home at five.'

'Must you go?' His question has a special edge to it.

'I'm afraid so. I'm sorry.'

I have to leave quickly or I will lose my resolve. All that is required is an apologetic farewell to the circle around the table, a nod and a smile that includes Hassan with the rest, before I hurry out through the door.

Socially, there is no possibility of Hassan leaving with me. I have made it quite obvious that I cannot countenance any further contact. It is a small victory but I do not feel victorious. Instead I feel as if something has broken inside me. I am turning into Green Park now, half-running, past the strolling groups of people enjoying the last of the afternoon sun. I have to cross over the grass to reach the opposite gate. Through the fallen leaves, there is the rustle of footsteps behind me.

'Rose.'

It is Hassan's voice with that intimate urgent tone of the past. He catches me by the arm, drawing me to a standstill. I try to get back my breath but his face, close to mine, has a wildness about it that frightens me.

'How can you turn your back on me?'

'In the same way as you turned your back on me in Aden.' I fling out the words, trembling, moving backwards to put distance between us. Somehow it is the physical proximity that I fear the most.

'Can't you even listen to what I have to say?'

The tree behind us shields us to a certain extent from the curious gaze of passers-by. I suddenly see myself through their eyes, a rather dowdy young Englishwoman apparently being engaged against her will by a dark-skinned foreigner who looks like one of the Indian princes in his tunic and turban. As in Aden on the day of the races, I am intensely aware of his alien 'otherness' here in this London park with the English walking their dogs and the scarlet omnibuses threading the grey streets beyond the trees. Two nurses in Red Cross uniforms turn to look back with expressions of fascinated dismay. I begin to walk on towards the gates.

'Please leave me alone. How dare you try to intimidate me like this!'

'Rose, where are you going?'

'Home, of course.'

'Home.' He repeats it like a password. We are outside on the pavement now. With the same instinct for escape, I hail a passing cab. But before I can close the door, Hassan has followed me into it.

'Ebury Street,' I tell the driver faintly.

As the taxi swerves down Buckingham Palace Road, the driver points out the aerial guns pointing skywards from inside the walls.

'Our King's well protected, anyway,' he says over his shoulder. 'You with the Indian Army, sir?'

Hassan responds. It is not the place for private conversation. But as we draw up, he says in a low voice, 'I made a mistake. I want to explain, ask you to forgive me if you can.'

'I cannot.'

This is all I say. With frantic resolve, I jump from the cab, leaving him to search for the fare. My key is ready. The door is opened and closed behind me before he can reach it.

For a moment I lean on the other side and close my eyes, fighting to keep my nerve.

'Rose, please.'

His voice fades as I run up the stairs. So does the sound of the doorbell.

In the room at the top, Idris is in his cot. He has hauled himself up on his feet, clinging to the rails, making excited noises as he always does when he sees me. His eyes are huge and bright and he stretches out both arms for me to pick him up. In the kitchen Janet is putting on her coat. I press the money into her hand, desperate for her to go before I break down.

'He's been fed. All ready to sleep. Cold seems better too.'

'Thank you, Janet. That's fine.'

'Same time tomorrow then?'

'Bless you.'

Once she has gone, I sit down by the little gas fire, holding the baby close. The milky smell of him, the softness of his cheek against mine, make me feel weak. A shudder runs through me. Relief or anguish? Both perhaps.

My back is to the nursery door, which is open. The first moment I know that someone is there is when a shadow falls across the chair.

'Dear God!'

I turn to see Hassan standing quite still, his face frozen in disbelief. Of course. Janet would have found him still waiting on the doorstep and let him in without demur – as she went out.

Hassan's eyes are fixed on the child. Idris stares back at him, a mirror image of his father's expression. Hassan's face is working now. His hand goes to his heart, just like the hero in an operatic climax. The moment is totally unreal. I see him trying to speak but no words come. A loud piping cry from Idris breaks the silence. Then Hassan moves forward, clumsy with shock, holds out his arms.

'Give him to me.'

The note of command is not to be disobeyed. Every ounce of concentration is spent on a fierce scrutiny of the child's face. As he takes him in his arms, he smiles in huge disbelief. I see his eyes glisten with tears. Over the baby's head, he looks at me for the first time.

'He is ours,' he says simply. 'And you did not tell me.'

'How could I?' I heard my voice break. 'What could you have done?'

What happens next is broken into a dozen fragments with no proper sequence to hold them together. One minute I am standing alone, looking at Hassan and his son. The next, the three of us are pressed together, Hassan's arms encircling us so tightly I feel his heart pounding beneath his tunic.

Not surprisingly, Idris objects to this treatment and starts to howl. In one way or another, we are all of us crying and hugging each other. Finally I pull away and try to restore order by returning Idris to his cot and pulling the covers over him. After a little soothing, his eyes close as if exhausted by all this emotion.

There is another moment now when Hassan's arms are around me, still standing behind me, his head against mine. I turn out the lamp. It is dark in the next room too, except for the dying glow of the fire in the grate.

What we say to each other as we lie down on the rug in front of it makes no real sense. Everything is lost in the turmoil of release after so much misery and despair. Only afterwards, embraced face to face, I remember his words, spoken so quietly.

'Will you let me take him back, Rose? It's the only way, isn't it?'

❧ 4 ❧

Rose had known the question would come, right from the moment Hassan had taken the child in his arms. The Arab bond between father and son, the power of that pride of blood, was something that had been brought home to her only too painfully after the horror of the Sheikh Othman shooting. Since then it seemed there had been another tragedy, something that affected both his private and public life. His wife Miriam, the doll-like creature of the harem, married for fourteen months, could not conceive. After examination, the doctors had pronounced her barren. But all unknown he had this son. It was a miracle.

The words were tumbling out now as Hassan sat before Rose, crouched on his heels, holding both her hands, his eyes brilliant in the lamplight.

'Above everything, he is proof of our love, Rose. At the end of all the hardships and the separations, here he is! Here we are!'

At last Rose was able to speak. 'And now I am to be separated from my son. Me, his mother,' she whispered fiercely. Her whole being was in revolt at the idea. 'To give him up now. After all I've been through with him! How can you even think of it?'

'Foolish woman.' He stroked her hair tenderly. 'Who spoke of separation?'

Slowly and carefully now, he outlined a plan. It was something like the plan they had made together at Zara when he had put the silver ring on her finger. She would leave England and live in Cairo. He would buy her a house there. Every few months or so, he would come with the child for a long stay. There would be shorter visits too, whenever he could manage to get away. It was perfectly acceptable in Islamic eyes for a man of his status to keep a second wife in another place. No one need ever know who she was. Cairo was a big city, far too busy with its own affairs to care about the private life of a tribal ruler from the Aden protectorate.

But Rose's mind was on the small boy in his cot in the next room.

'And what about Idris? How would you explain him to your family? He would live with you in Jehal?'

'Of course. Fortunately he has more of my colouring than yours. To adopt a child from another branch of the family is good Muslim custom.

259

He will be introduced as the son of one of our dozens of cousins from other parts of Arabia, an orphan. And if anyone guesses the truth, that he is mine by another woman, that also is custom and would not be discussed in polite society. He even has a good Muslim name. What made you think of Aidrus, my darling?'

'Idris,' she corrected with a smile. 'It's a Welsh name too. I thought it would combine the two races.' Something of her incurable romanticism stirred again. She looked at him dreamily. 'So one day he might become the next Sultan of Jehal?'

'God willing. You have given me a son who is already a young Emir.'

'And your wife, the beautiful Miriam,' Rose went on, trying to keep an edge of bitterness out of her voice. 'She would be a good stepmother to him?'

'It will change her life to have a child to look after. She has a sweet nature and the last year has been hard for her.'

'What about the war in Arabia? There could be dangers.'

'What about London?' Hassan countered. 'The times are dangerous everywhere.' He looked around the shabby room, at Rose's pale face. 'And what kind of life can you give him here, a woman alone and a son with no known father?'

Rose got up and went to the window, drawing the thin curtains more tightly against the darkened city. Her mind was in confusion. It was true that she had been at the end of her tether more than once in recent weeks. The Nunans were going abroad again and she had no one else to turn to. Sometimes the responsibility of bringing up Idris on her own, struggling for financial independence in a man's world, seemed too much to face. War widows and orphans had every public sympathy. But how could you explain a half-caste child to inquisitive neighbours and friends? People sniffed at scandal so quickly, she discovered. It was like a scent you carried with you without even knowing it. The lie of the Egyptian diplomat father would soon wear thin. And how could it ever be fair to the boy himself?

Even now, though, she could not be sure. Hassan had been given back to her. The strain of the past was erased and their love was wonderfully alive again. Cairo might be the only solution. And yet, here in England, it all seemed so bizarre.

'I don't know, Hassan. I must have time to think. The journey to Aden, for instance. Who would look after him? It's hardly a father's task for so young a child.'

'There is something else,' he said, coming over and taking her in his arms again. 'Or rather someone else. Nabiha.'

'Nabiha?' she asked, startled. 'I haven't heard from her since I left

260

Aden. I didn't write. I felt I couldn't without telling her the truth of the situation.'

'She will understand that. The point is, Nabiha is coming to London next week. Farid Fauzi is joining our delegation and bringing her with him for a visit.' He held her chin and looked at her closely. 'You will take Idris to her? Then she will take him back to Aden with her. It will be hard – even harder if you wait until he's any older. Remember from now on our lives are joined again anyway. In just a few months we shall all be together.'

It seemed to Rose that once more, fate had arranged things for her. Hearing Nabiha was to be in London – that was the deciding factor.

Yet taking Idris to the hotel where she was staying, on that cold late evening in 1916, she had suddenly felt sick with fear. It was his first ride in a taxi and, woken from his sleep, he had chirped and chortled all the way, waving his arms in his new blue woollen coat. Look at him closely, she was saying to herself. In six months' time, he will have changed again. The silky fringe of black hair will be thick, perhaps curly. Kept indoors by the women away from the sun, he may have lost his dark rose cheeks, the smooth olive skin paling to ivory. He will be starting to talk, but they will be Arabic words.

'You must be good. Good boy, Idris,' she told him in mock severity, wiping the dribble from the deeply-cleft lower lip that was so like Hassan's. All the time she was trying to control the choking that rose in her throat. Think of it sensibly, she reasoned. He is not going away to strangers. He is going to his father, the man you love, to live among a people you love. The time spent away from him will fly past. You will still be the mother of his heart. And there will be marvellous reunions.

These were the things Nabiha told her too in the chintzy hotel bedroom with a cot arranged in the corner. The emotion of the meeting between the two women swept them along, and Rose's misgivings vanished. As usual, Nabiha was swift and practical in everything. Her own children were now in their teens, but babies were second nature to her, she told Rose. Feeding and sleeping matters were dealt with in minutes and as Nabiha held him against her shoulder talking, Rose could see Idris settling himself comfortably against this warm, scented stranger.

Her eyes searched the eyes of her friend.

'At this age, he's too young to fret for you,' Nabiha said, answering the unspoken question. 'He'll sleep and eat and feel secure – and look around at the world. It's best to go quickly now,' she added gently.

'There's so much to tell you,' Rose said. 'So much I want you to know.'

'I shall be coming to Cairo to see you. Time enough then, dear Rose. All that matters is you and Hassan have found each other again, and you have the child to hold you together,' Nabiha replied.

'I have.' She turned back to her son. On an impulse she took the amber beads she wore on her wrist and slipped them around his neck. 'To protect from evil,' she said, in the Arabic phrase.

Nabiha smiled. 'What evil?' she asked.

'This war – this awful war. Idris was conceived at the start of it, and still it goes on. If anything should happen to him on the way to Aden . . .'

'We are all in God's hand,' Nabiha said firmly. 'Now go.' She held out the drowsy child.

Rose kissed him quickly on the top of the head. Then she embraced Nabiha and fled.

✤ 5 ✤

THE tea on her table at the Ritz had long grown cold. Behind her, the waiter was discreetly waiting to clear away. In a dream, Rose paid her bill and hurried back to Northumberland Avenue.

Once again the evening news placards on the street corners told of bloodshed in the Middle East, as they had done thirty years ago. The repercussions of the British withdrawal from Palestine seemed endless. She was feeling nervous now, not at the possibility of danger, but at the prospect of appearing knowledgeable in front of the cameras. It was something she must discuss with Jenny Patmore and the producer at their meeting. How much of an expert on recent events was she supposed to be? Or were they looking for a series of purely personal encounters? She had conscientiously studied the file of press cuttings and reports sent her by the research department. Aden itself was usually relegated to a paragraph or two, something about the need to keep a firm control over the Colony in the face of political disruption everywhere else in the Middle East.

All too easily Rose could imagine Hassan's frustration. In her mind she saw the young man of 1916, fervently expounding the cause of Arab unity to the British advisers in London. Her time-travels of the last few hours had brought up fragments of the past which overlapped and over-shadowed the reality of the present. She and Hassan were the links that held the fragments together. Meeting again was the only way of making a continuity of it all. And yet that meeting might be destined never to happen. For reasons of his own, Hassan himself might come to the decision that it was not to be, just as he had done thirty years ago.

'In'Shallah,' she said to herself out of old habit, as she turned up the steps of the Royal Empire Society headquarters. 'Let fate decide.'

'You look tired,' said Jenny Patmore. She had been waiting for Rose in the foyer, and now got up from her chair to greet her.

'Sorry I'm a bit late. It's been quite a day,' Rose told her. 'I'm certainly glad to see you.'

It was true. Rose felt a warm attachment to the young woman, even though they had only spoken on the telephone since their meeting in Wales. The handshake they began turned into a hug. Jenny drew back, inspecting her protectively.

'I don't want to worry you, but something's happened.'

'The expedition's off?' Rose was surprised at the dismay she felt.

'No. We still fly out the day after tomorrow. But we've just had news confirmed of an invasion by the Yemeni Army across the Protectorate border. Some of the local people have had to flee their homes. A small group of them have decided to seek exile in England.'

'In England?' Rose was puzzled. 'They must be Arabs with money.'

'I've forgotten the name of the place. The bulletin said they had relations here in London.'

Rose's tiredness had suddenly gone. She was at once immersed in the drama of what was happening out there.

'Let's go up to the drawing room to talk. We can have drinks up there.'

'I'll just leave a message at the desk for Mike.'

'Mike?'

'Mike Farrow. The producer.'

For some reason Rose was feeling apprehensive about this encounter. Nor was there much chance to ask Jenny about the kind of person he was. No sooner had they settled themselves at a table when Rose saw a dark stocky man in a grey suit come in through the door and look around the room with an assertive air.

'There he is now.'

Standing up, Jenny beckoned him over.

'Don't mind his manner,' she said quickly. 'He's quite a softie when you get to know him. And he does make marvellous films.'

His briskness was intimidating, Rose had to admit. The handshake was short and sharp. From behind his glasses he seemed to be assessing her coldly.

'Lady Foster. I'm not expected to address you like that for the next fortnight, am I?'

'Of course not.' Rose felt affronted. 'I'd like to be Rose to everyone, right from the start.'

'Don't worry. You will be.' He laughed abruptly. Rubbing his jaw along the line of dark stubble, he glanced at Jenny. There was an edge of sexual appraisal to that look which Rose found distasteful, but Jenny seemed used to ignoring it. 'We're a pretty rough lot on the production side. The crew won't be used to the ways of memsahibs, I'm afraid.'

'Oh dear. It looks as though you've got me in the wrong slot, Mr Farrow,' Rose said. 'Is that how you're going to project me, as some Colonial die-hard? If so, I shall resist you every inch of the way.'

Her directness seemed to ease the tension slightly.

'Sorry. Just a joke. And I'm Mike, by the way. I'm only glad you can do the film with us, as I told you on the phone. You're all set for the flight?'

'I am.' She watched him take off his glasses and polish them carefully. She sensed at once that no real rapport could exist between them, the kind of connection she had with her publisher or agent. This was a different breed altogether. In the meantime, she was impatient to learn more about the crisis on the Aden borders.

'Jenny tells me there's been some kind of invasion out there?'

He shrugged his shoulders. 'Not much more than a minor skirmish I shouldn't think. But it's sent a few of the local bigwigs scuttling for safety, I gather. Back to dear old Mother England, as usual. Could be just the start of the real thing, of course.' He tilted back the last half of the whisky that had arrived with the gin-and-tonics and reached for his briefcase. 'Point is, there's this little troop of refugees arriving in London tomorrow and I think we should cover it for the programme. It'd make a good opening shot or two, their trust in the old Empire while extremists of their own race are destroying their whole life.'

'Do you know what part of the Protectorate they attacked?' From Rose's point of view it was a vital question, but Farrow was obviously not interested.

'I wouldn't be able to pronounce it anyway. And I don't think it matters to the great British public. It's the simple human story we want, you talking to them in front of the camera as they arrive. How's your Arabic these days?'

'Not up to much, I'm afraid. But there's bound to be someone speaking English. There always is.'

'A typical Empire-builder's point of view, if I may say so.' He watched her, waiting for her to take the bait.

'Just an accurate one, that's all,' she said lightly. She suddenly felt sure of herself, and young again. 'So where do we meet tomorrow?'

'Don't worry,' Jenny put in reassuringly. 'It's Victoria Station. But I'll come here to collect you.'

'You've got enough to think about. I'll meet you there. It'll be the boat train?'

'That's right. Three o'clock,' Farrow told her. 'No need to prepare any questions. Except to try to find out what's actually going on in Aden, apart from what the papers tell us, which is pretty vague.'

'Talking about papers,' Jenny said, as they prepared to leave. 'I've found a couple of cuttings that might amuse you, snippets from the past.' She gave Rose one of her private smiles. 'Both from the same year, actually. 1919.'

Rose was in her room in her dressing gown when she opened the envelope and unfolded two yellowing slips of newspaper. The first thing that met her eye was a picture, a photograph of Hassan as she remembered him. He seemed to be standing to attention in his ceremonial robes with a group of British dignitaries. At his side was a small boy. Rose's heart jumped. It looked uncannily like someone else, somewhere else. Of course. The picture of Hassan taken at the London Coronation of 1902, the one she had seen at the palace at Jehal on the day of the picnic.

The cutting was from the *Daily Telegraph* and underneath there was a caption. 'Among the Eastern potentates taking the salute on the Imperial Dais at yesterday's Victory Parade was His Highness Sir Hassan Bin Seif, Sultan of Jehal in the South Arabian Protectorate. Much amusement was aroused by the presence alongside his father of the three-year-old Emir Aidrus, dressed identically in tribal turban and cloak with a miniature sword in his sash.'

Where was I then, was Rose's instant thought. How could Hassan bring the boy to London and I know nothing about it? She looked again at the date – 20 July, 1919. Of course. As if in confirmation, the second cutting slipped out from underneath. It was a short paragraph from the social columns which Rose recognized at once.

'The marriage took place quietly on 10 May at St Peter's Church, Belgravia, of Mr Martin Foster and Mrs Rose Chetwynd. The couple leave shortly for the New Hebrides in the South Pacific where Mr Foster takes up an appointment as Assistant Colonial Secretary.'

Rose lay down and switched off the light. But she was not sleepy. The spartan mattress and high ironwork frame had the familiar feel of Public Works beds in tropical outposts, and were no doubt considered equally appropriate for Colonial Service officials on leave. Her thoughts revolved around the cuttings. It was somehow part of the curious pattern of things that these two reminders of the past should come together. Always in her own mind, her separation from her son was inextricably bound up with her second marriage. Even her accidental meeting with Martin Foster again was a result of the way she had left Hassan and Idris that morning at Cairo Station in the February of 1919.

'Can't I help?'

These, characteristically, had been the first words she had heard from the young Englishman in uniform sitting in the corner of the compartment. She had her back to him, had only half-glimpsed him as she boarded the train. Pushing her suitcase on to the piled-up rack above her head, she had no wish to be confronted by anyone at that moment.

'Please don't bother.'

It was more difficult than she had thought and she leaned her head against the partition to get back her breath. Then as the train lurched into motion, she felt everything begin to sway around her. The next moment the man was on his feet pushing the baggage into place for her. Sinking into the corner seat, she dropped her head forward into her hands. She was unprepared for the intensity of the wave of misery that came over her. She sat there motionless, struggling to contain it, her face hidden.

'It is appallingly hot,' said the English voice again. 'Everywhere is crowded too. Not a porter to be had.'

Only when she looked up did they recognize one another.

'Good Lord! Is it really Mrs Chetwynd? Rose Chetwynd?'

'I'm sorry. I had no idea . . .'

There began the usual tangle of explanations, but he broke off to search in his pocket.

'I always seem to be finding you a handkerchief.' He indicated her cheek. 'Bit of a smudge. Soot everywhere on these trains.'

To cover the awkwardness, he went on talking as Rose brought out a mirror and dabbed at her face. 'I've just finished a spell with the Camel Corps at Gaza. That was my war. Quite an exciting one. Just had a week's leave in Cairo and now I'm on my way home.' He broke off again and leaned forward to take the handkerchief back. 'I say – are you all right?'

'I'm not, actually,' she heard herself say. 'I'm afraid I've been crying.' She grimaced. 'As usual.'

He was smiling a little now, but with that expression of concern she well remembered. She saw he had grown better-looking. The beaky schoolboy features had broadened out and his colouring was now brown, rather than pink, something which emphasized the intense hazel brightness of his eyes. He also seemed to have done away with his glasses.

'Why this time?' he prompted.

'I've just said goodbye to my son.' She paused, staring out of the window, giving herself time to swallow back fresh tears. 'I don't think I shall see him again. Not for a while anyway.'

'You have a son?' He looked startled.

'Not Geoffrey's. Hassan's. The Emir, you remember.'

It was out before she could restrain herself. They had been speaking in undertones. But even if they had been carrying on a normal conversation, no one would have paid them the slightest attention. Every corner of the long compartment was crammed with soldiers and their own section reverberated to the accents of the English Beys and

267

Bimbashis setting off home on leave. It was rather like a boys' school train at the end of term, Rose thought, as the chatter and laughter rose above the rattle of the train. Kitbags and bundles were piled everywhere, topped by helmet boxes, sword-cases and canvas water bottles. Servants had spread blankets over the hard leather seats of the box-like constructions the Egyptian railways called sleeping cars. Canvas blinds had been pulled down against the glare of the sun. But this only served to make the atmosphere even more turgid. And nothing would keep back the dust, thick coffee-coloured clouds that seeped in through every crevice as the train rolled on through the parched Egyptian fields.

Martin was bending to unfasten his haversack, partly perhaps to conceal his shock at what she had told him. He produced an old field thermos and poured out what looked like lime juice. Amazingly it was still cool. As she sipped some, Rose felt revived.

'It's a long journey,' Martin said. 'Tell me what happened. If you feel you can, that is,' he added with his usual diffidence.

'Where to start?' she asked.

'Well, you got back to England safely, I suppose. I saw you off on Captain Strong's old bucket, you remember. It must be three years ago. You asked me out of the blue if I could get you a passage urgently. It was the only thing I could think of. You never wrote though, afterwards.'

She saw the reproach on his face fade as she began to talk. Instead, something like pity replaced it as she told her story, swiftly and as honestly as she could. She was surprised at the ease she felt in telling him, something she had done with no one else, now the Nunans had gone. When she came to the last part, the words rushed out almost violently.

'Cairo was a mistake, the whole idea of it. I pretended at first it was going to work. It was wonderful to be with Hassan of course that first time, and with my little boy. You can imagine the reunion. We all stayed at the Continental. I remember how luxurious it seemed after England even though the war was still on – dinner on the terrace under those huge Egyptian stars, camel rides to the Pyramids, little Idris perched in front in a ridiculous red fez Hassan had bought him from the souk. I felt a bit conspicuous, of course, not being one of the English parties. But I suppose I was too wrapped up in happiness to notice. Hassan had taken a suite for us. We were quite a self-contained little family.'

'And now you've all been together again?'

She nodded, biting her lip. 'This time I was supposed to stay on in Cairo, settle down there. Hassan had bought a flat for me, quite near the centre. I don't think I've ever felt so out of place anywhere in my life.'

'You've always been so at home in the Arab world, though,' he said.

'But don't you see?' Rose went on with fresh vehemence. 'This wasn't my Arabia. There's no escaping the British presence in Cairo. You can't get away as you could in Aden. Army everywhere, army wives, army parties. The Egyptians themselves are a race apart, anyway. And what was I supposed to be? A Sultan's mistress without even the companionship of the harem. I tell you, do you know what I felt like when I was there on my own? Like one of those Edwardian kept women with a house in St John's Wood. What's that old song – a bird in a gilded cage?'

'At least it was gilded?' Martin suggested, trying to joke.

'Hardly. It overlooked one of those courtyards, and the noise was incredible – singing, quarrelling, shouting, beggars and hawkers everywhere. Alongside the luxury of the rich there was such poverty in Cairo. The heat was something different from Aden too. Even at night the air was always dead, you could hardly breathe. I existed on what little sleep I could snatch just before dawn. Driving out at night, you'd envy those figures wrapped in their *galabeahs*, sleeping on the pavements.'

'But wasn't it all different once the Emir was there, and your little boy?' She saw an intense curiosity sharpen his face. It seemed more important than ever to tell him the truth.

'There were good moments together, of course. But you can't really live on four weeks, twice a year, can you?' She looked down at her hands in her lap, at the silver ring she was twisting around her finger. 'Besides . . .' She hesitated, then went on. 'I began to feel – how can I describe it? – somehow distanced from both of them. Their life seemed to be somewhere else. Idris is so lively now, talking all the time, more in Arabic than English of course. Everything he told me was about what he did in Jehal with his father. And his mother.'

'But you . . .'

'He calls Miriam his mother – Hassan's wife. Naturally he was too young to remember who I was when I first saw him again. We thought it best not to confuse him. And then there would be the problem of what he told the family back in Jehal. So I was a sort of auntie. Pretty Lady he called me.' She turned away, her face momentarily out of control. 'You can imagine the terrible difficulty of all that, for me.'

'And Hassan – your relationship with him?' he pressed gently. 'Has that changed too?'

She paused. Somewhere a shutter came down between them. 'What we have together we shall always keep, I think. It doesn't change, does it, the first time you fall in love? But we can't live it through in everyday life. It's something apart, you see. And separating each time becomes more difficult. So we quarrel, cause each other pain.' She met his eyes again. 'When the time comes for them to go, it seems so wrong that I can't go with them. I have the strangest feeling of homesickness for Aden. It's become so strong, it's not to be endured. So this time, I . . .' Her voice dried up again.

'This time?'

'I told Hassan to sell the flat. It was a sudden instinct that I had taken the wrong road. In Cairo we could only end up making each other unhappy. There are other places, of course, as Hassan keeps telling me. Beirut or the Mediterranean – he likes Italy. I don't know, Martin. Things seem to be falling apart. Perhaps it was too much to hope that it would ever work.'

She broke off, pretending to look for something in her handbag. He leaned across quickly and placed his hand on hers.

'I'm sorry. I've tired you. Don't talk any more. Close your eyes and rest for a while. Then we'll try and find ourselves some food.'

The rest of the journey passed in a strange haze. There were changes of train, the night ferry to Dover, and then Victoria Station in the dawn light, bleak and grey. Stepping out, Rose felt exhausted and dishevelled. Yet there was a curious new lifting of the spirit. Something had happened on the journey between Martin Foster and herself. It was as if she had been thrown a lifeline of some kind. Now, as the time came to go their different ways, it was clear to her that he wanted to see her again. There was a protective quality about him that she found infinitely reassuring. She had not realized then that he was in love with her, had been perhaps since that day at Perim, nor how much she was to come to depend on him.

Three months later, her divorce papers came through and he asked her to marry him. He had just been given a Colonial Service appointment in the Pacific. For Rose it was the chance to make a clean break with the past, with Hassan, with Idris, with Arabia, with everything that had enthralled and racked her for the past six years. She told herself she had had enough of both ecstasy and pain. Conventional uncomplicated happiness was what she was in search of. With Martin it was what she found.

Always afterwards, the moment that opened the door on this new life for her was not the wedding itself, nor even their arrival in the South Seas, but the end of that journey from Cairo. Standing together at Victoria Station in the bitter cold, he had asked her if he could call on her as soon as he had found rooms in London. Then, as they parted, he had suddenly leaned close to her and kissed her on the cheek. Turning back, she saw him staring after her, his face still flushed, a hand raised in salute of some pact between them.

❧ 6 ❧

NOT surprisingly sleep that night on her spartan bed was coloured by dreams. Rose was still thinking of Martin next morning as she set off for her assignment with the film unit. All these years later, she still retained a fondness for Victoria Station. Making her way through the echoing stone entrance halls under the familiar clock, she remembered the sense of firm ground she had felt there at Martin's side, of coming home to reality after the chimeras of the past. She had to remind herself sharply of the very different situation she was now about to confront. For the little party arriving from Arabia, this place was the beginning of exile.

She looked among the crowds in the concourse as she threaded her way towards the arrival boards.

'You've seen the papers, I suppose?' said a voice behind her.

Startled, she turned to find Mike Farrow at her heels, a different figure today in corduroy jacket and scarf. Behind him were bunched a tribe of young men armed with cameras, microphones and lights. They were not introduced but simply nodded at her, looking harassed.

Caught off guard, she repeated, 'The papers?' Then, collecting herself, 'I did look at the *Manchester Guardian* first thing. I couldn't find anything about Aden.'

'The *Guardian*,' Farrow snorted. 'This is where you have to look for news.' He unfolded the *Daily Express* from under his arm. Rose caught a glimpse of a couple of headlines on a small side column: 'Fighting Escalates On Aden Borders. RAF Strafe Yemeni Forces Near Zara.'

'Zara.' She said the name out loud in disbelief. A picture clicked in her mind of ochre-coloured houses, a room at the top of a winding staircase where she had slept with Hassan, peaches growing on the wall outside. It was the obvious point for an invasion, as the Turks had discovered in 1915.

'You know the place?' Farrow's expression was almost wolfish in its eagerness.

'The place and the people. It's part of Jehal, the furthest corner, up in the mountains.' As she spoke, her mind was running ahead. She was thinking not just of Hassan but of the Fauzis, Nabiha and Farid. It was their tribal land up there, a place where friends and relations went for

272

the hot season, including members of the Sultan's family. She looked around quickly. 'Where's Jenny?'

'Over by the barrier. We'd better get there too. The train's due in at any minute.'

Even as they got to the gate they could see the curl of smoke at the far end of the line. Other people were crowding past now on to the platform. The hiss and grind of the engine was deafening. Carriages clattered to a standstill and Rose felt sudden panic. What happened next? Then Jenny was at her side, clipboard under her arm.

'Don't worry. I'll explain when we see them. We only need a few words. It's mostly pictures on this one.'

'But for God's sake ask them the right questions,' Farrow snapped in her ear. 'What are the British doing to help? What are the political implications? Is it the beginning of the end?'

Rose had a sudden urge to laugh. She tried to imagine weary refugees having time to think about such finer points, let alone the ability to express themselves in English.

Then, with a shock, she saw getting out of a compartment a figure that instantly turned a key in her mind. She knew him, yet she did not know him. He was elderly, an old man in fact, stoutish with a shock of white hair. But that bearing, that commanding air, could only belong to one person.

Without hesitation, she was darting through the crush. Behind her, she heard someone ask about her ticket, and Farrow's voice intervening. All her concentration was fixed on the man ahead. He was wearing an old-fashioned English suit that had seen better days. Around him clustered a group of veiled women. The sight of the black purdah cloaks made her catch her breath. It brought back the past with a physical jolt, so that when the man turned towards her the name flew from her lips before she could stop to think.

'Abdullah! It is Abdullah, isn't it?'

But the face that looked back at her was so puzzled, she almost lost her nerve.

'I'm sorry,' the man said. 'I think we are strangers.' The voice was the same too, guttural and rapid. The face was puffy with age but the huge liquorice-coloured eyes had all the old animation.

'I'm Rose, Rose Chetwynd. Don't you remember, at Jehal? It's a long time, more than thirty years ago.'

All the while, his expression was slowly breaking up, changing from blank incomprehension to disbelief, then pure delight.

'Rose! Ingleezi Rose!'

He rolled out the name on a crescendo. The next minute she was engulfed in a huge embrace, rich with the scents of tobacco and some spicy cologne. Then he stepped back and looked at her again.

'*Wallahi!* But you do not grow older. Except you are too thin.' His face quivered with emotion. 'And you have not forgotten your old friends.' He indicated the women behind him, who had gathered some children around them, and two younger men, wearing shabby jackets over their tribal dress, who also appeared. 'You are here to greet us in our time of trouble.'

Rose felt an instant pang of guilt. Absurdly she was putting out her hand to the women, but they drew back like frightened birds, sheltering behind Abdullah.

'Of course I want to do anything I can to help. But in fact, Abdullah, I knew nothing of all this until yesterday. I'm here with these other people, you see.'

She looked over her shoulder to see Jenny coming to the rescue. They were from the film company, she explained. They wanted to let the British people know what was happening in Arabia. Rose was here as an old friend of the Aden Arabs. If he could say a few words to her about the situation. . .

Abdullah needed no prompting.

'It is the beginning of the end for the British,' he pronounced. 'The handing over of Palestine to the Jews was a tragedy. Now the Arab nationalists are arming the tribes in the Yemen, training them to infiltrate the Aden Protectorate and then the Colony. The British can never win that kind of warfare, even with bombs.' He turned to the people behind him. 'And these are the ones caught in the middle, just a few of them with enough money to get out. They want to settle in England while there is still time. Others will follow.'

'Can Government in Aden do nothing to stop it?' Rose asked.

'Government!' Abdullah shrugged his shoulders. 'They should arm the tribal rulers so they could fight their own battles against the Yemenis as they've always done! They should fight the Palestinian propaganda about the wicked imperialists, make some progress towards self-government for Aden. There are many moderate leaders who need to be heard – the Sultan of Jehal, for instance, your friend and my friend. Sending in the RAF is not the answer. It only causes more problems.'

'What is your own reason for coming to London?'

'I must see people at the Colonial Office. These sheikhs from two of the other border territories are with me to try to explain to your ministers how to avoid tragedy in South Arabia.'

At this point, he bowed briskly and clapped his hands in Mike Farrow's direction. 'May we go now, sir? We have friends waiting for us at Marble Arch. You know Marble Arch?' he asked Rose.

'Of course. You have an address?'

'There is a flat. We can talk there. You must stay with us.' He spread out his arms. 'There is room for everyone.'

'I think we should come along too,' Farrow told Rose in an undertone. 'Take some more film.'

Rose shook her head, surprised at her own firmness. 'I'm sorry. This is private.'

'I do not like that man,' Abdullah said to her in the taxi. 'What are you doing with these people?'

It was the moment to take the plunge. 'I am going with them to Aden. Tomorrow.'

'To Aden?' He looked at her with dismay. 'After so long?'

There were others in the taxi with them, the two sheikhs sitting silent and incongruous on the tip-up seats opposite, their eyes on Rose.

'Is there still danger?' she asked warily.

'Different kinds of danger. You must take care not to travel outside the colony without security. And then . . .' he hesitated. 'You will see so much change.'

'Sultan Hassan,' she put in, unable to hold back the question any longer. 'He is well?'

Abdullah answered with the same formality. 'He is in good health, praise be. Pressed by Government as usual, and besieged by these threats of a takeover by the Yemen. It is a pity you will not see him now the frontier has been closed.'

It was a blow she could not contemplate yet. And his son? she wanted to ask, but dared not trust herself. 'What of dear Nabiha and Farid? I so want to see them too.'

'Farid died five years ago. He was an old man,' Abdullah said in the matter-of-fact Arab way. 'Nabiha is still alive, but sick. She has cancer, they say, a cancer of the eye. It has made her blind, alas.'

'Oh no!' It struck at Rose's heart. She could not bear to think of that lustrous kohl-encircled gaze of Nabiha's wiped out for ever.

'She has people looking after her. She will be very happy if you can visit and talk.'

'Of course.'

'Now there are others who will want to talk to you. Look, we are here already.'

The next few minutes went by in the jumbled, unlikely way of a dream. There was a tall block, a tiled entranceway that smelled of poverty, a tiny lift that jolted its way to the top floor as if it would never get there. A passageway with names scrawled on the walls led to an anonymous door at the end of a row of half a dozen others. Outside stood six empty milk bottles.

'They are all here then,' Abdullah said, pressing the bell. As the door opened, the faint sound of Arabic music became a flood. A very fat, very old black woman stood there in a flowered overall, shaking with laughter.

'You remember Ayesha, from Zara? Nabiha sent her to look after us. Wherever our people go, she goes too.'

Still laughing and shaking her head, the old lady crouched to kiss Rose's knee. A pretty woman, unveiled, in a long red shift, appeared and drew them in, talking in Arabic all the time. From the bedrooms along the landing came more music, loud chatter from a group of teenage girls with long plaits. At the end, the door to the sitting room was also open. A middle-aged man stood up to greet them from the table where he was writing. For a wild moment, Rose thought it was Hassan. There was a likeness in the high cheekbones and the wide mouth. But then she realized he must be several years younger.

'Did you not meet Omar when you were in Jehal?' Abdullah asked, as they shook hands.

'I'm afraid I don't remember,' Rose stumbled, disoriented by the different currents of activity contained in the little flat. Who were they all, and what were they doing here? In the corner of the room, a news report from the BBC World Service was coming from an old wireless set, giving news of Arab casualties in Palestine. Every now and then the telephone rang in another corner, but no one seemed to take any notice of it.

'I should have remembered,' Omar responded gallantly. 'But I was away at school at the time. I am the Sultan's younger brother.'

'And when he was at home he was too busy writing verse and playing the *oudh* to talk to visitors,' Abdullah chaffed.

Dimly now, Rose remembered Hassan telling her about the young poet in the family. Looking around her she saw touches of an Arabian encampment in this bleak little working-class setting. There were framed texts from the Koran on the wall, brightly-coloured rugs embroidered with pictures of Mecca on either side of a window that looked out over the sprawling grey rooftops of West London. On the sideboard a family photograph of Farid and Nabiha caught her eye, with a young boy in *futah* and sandals who could only be Hassan.

'How long have you been here?' she asked Omar. It was the only way she could frame her amazement. 'Why did you come?'

'I came six months ago. Hassan sent me to make some kind of base here for any relations who had to leave suddenly. When the British handed over Palestine, we thought there would be an uprising against Government there and then. As you can imagine, a Sultan's family are never exactly popular in a revolution.'

'Now it is starting in earnest,' Abdullah put in. 'But little by little, through the back door, through Yemen.'

Rose felt guilt overtaking her afresh. All this time, her friends had been setting themselves up in a new country, her country, and she had known nothing about it.

'Perhaps things will be back to normal soon,' Rose said with more conviction than she felt. 'You may not be here for long.'

Abdullah's face was grim. 'Things will have to get a lot worse first. Blood will be shed. The British will be replaced by political extremists and they will put an end to us if we return.'

From the kitchen where the women had gathered, there was the clatter of pans and high-pitched voices. Cooking smells emerged that summoned up the past with startling power. Ginger and cumin were in them, the richness of almond chicken, and in the background Turkish coffee simmering.

A hand touched hers. There was a whispered command from one of the girls.

'Miriam. She wants to see you.'

'Miriam?' Rose turned to Abdullah, totally confused.

'Hassan's wife. She was with us at the station.' He looked at her quizzically. 'She recognized you from Jehal. Your visit to the ladies at the palace, remember?'

Rose's mouth went dry. It was the last thing she was expecting. 'My Arabic,' she stammered. 'I've almost forgotten every word.'

'You will be surprised,' he replied. 'Her English is not at all bad. You'll see.'

Rose found her hands clammy with tension as she knocked on the bedroom door. It was the kind of feeling she had not had since she was young. When she went in, she realized that the woman lying on the bed was equally nervous. She had taken off her *chador* and propped herself up against several brightly-coloured satin cushions. Instead of the tiny heart-shaped face she remembered so vividly, Rose saw an elderly woman, weary and overweight. There were dark circles under her eyes and the eyelids were puffy with crying. Remembering the doll-like creature who had drawn her, laughing, into the dance at Jehal, Rose found herself wanting to cry. Only the hands were the same, soft and small, with the painted mitten patterns and henna-stained palms of the harem. She held them out now to Rose, trembling a little. Rose took them in hers. They both smiled.

'Rose,' she whispered tentatively.

Rose nodded. 'You have had a bad time?'

'Bad times. Firing everywhere. From the roof we see the sparks of the guns flying every night. Yemen guns. We think we will be killed. The new house Hassan built there up in the mountains is all burned down when the British drop bombs. He say best we come straight away here.' She pulled up the coverlet and Rose smelt the familiar scents of sandalwood and jasmine. 'Look.' She waved her hand around the room. 'There is time to bring nothing. Just family things. And these.' She held out her hand to show the glitter of a diamond and an emerald, pointing with childish pride to a ring shaped like an aeroplane. 'Is modern fashion. Hassan buy it from Beirut.'

For no sensible reason, Rose felt a twinge of the jealousy of youth. Then it was gone. The two women studied one another with a kind of tenderness.

'Not much talk,' Miriam said. 'I forget the English. But Hassan made me learn, because of the baby.'

Rose sat stiffly, her hands tight on the chair beneath her.

'What baby?'

'Your baby.' Miriam was smiling again now. 'Yours and Hassan's.'

Rose stared back, trying to grapple with the enormity of what she was hearing.

'I don't understand . . .' she began.

'Rose,' Miriam said, almost playfully. 'We are not young now. No more secrets. I have no children. But you give a son. Your son.' There was a pause that was almost unbearable.

'You knew?' Rose asked finally.

Miriam brushed the question aside. 'I knew. Women know. Men think they clever. But we are best.' She put her head on one side, her dark eyes intent. 'He look like you I think, little bit.'

Rose swallowed. 'Was he a good son?'

Miriam's expression was both sad and angry.

'Good baby, bad man. He leave us long time ago. He want war, want fighting, in Egypt, in Palestine, in Yemen. He never come back.'

'I'm sorry.'

'Is not your fault.' She searched for words. 'Hassan too is wild one. You remember this?'

'I remember.'

'But Hassan is good husband. And your husband? Nabiha tell me you marry again.'

'He was good too.' Rose's throat closed. She found she could say no more.

Then Miriam took her hand again and drew her close. Gracefully she leaned forward and kissed her cheek. 'So when I see you today I wish to say thank you, Rose. Thank you for the baby. Thank you for Aidrus.'

❦ 7 ❦

RETURNING to Aden was an image that had been in Rose's mind continuously over the past few weeks. She had visualized it so vividly, that first glimpse of the desert again, the tawny sweep of the Empty Quarter stretching away beyond the granite passes of the mountains. In a way she was fearful of a place where she had touched such extremes of joy and despair. Even now her dreams were still branded with those events, ritual scenarios that obstinately refused to be overlaid by any of the experiences of later life. But there would surely be the sense of coming home again too, as the aircraft swung over the southern tip of the Arabian peninsula.

The curious thing was, when the moment came, she felt none of these things. Instead, she found herself staring blankly out of the cabin window at what looked like a schoolroom relief map of papier-mâché ranges and yellow sand. Perim lighthouse was a plasticine blob in a blue mirror sea on which the ships crawled past like insects, making for the straits of Aden.

'Bab-el-Mandeb,' she said to herself. 'Gate of Tears.'

But it seemed to mean nothing. It was as if some local anaesthetic had been applied to the spot where the source of emotion must lie. Instead she found herself making mechanical lists in her head about hand baggage, passport and currency.

'Getting ready to mop up a few tears?' Farrow called to her in an attempt at jocularity from across the aisle. 'The return of the native and all that.'

'That's right,' Rose replied, simply because it was the easiest thing to say.

She met Jenny's glance in the seat next to her. She had a feeling the girl understood that things were not quite so simple. There was a mystery about human responses that defied analysis. Perhaps it had gone forever, Rose thought, the intense passion I once felt for this country, the sense of being where I was meant to be, enfolded into a landscape and a people so effortlessly I seemed to shed my old superficial self and somehow discover my natural element. Perhaps, after all, it was because I was in love. And that can certainly never happen again, she told herself. So I must learn to do without the rose-coloured spectacles. See Arabia through plain glass.

Especially as I'm supposed to be observing the current scene as some kind of journalist.

The plane was coming down to land now, tilting over a totally unfamiliar layout of white suburban houses surrounded by tarmac. The airport was new too, of course, looking very much like any of the other colonial airports she had been through over the last twenty years except there was no surrounding jungle, only the glitter of crushed sand under the wheels and the salt-white flats on either side.

'Looks as if someone's expecting us,' said Farrow over her shoulder as they emerged on to the steps. 'Or expecting you, perhaps I should say.'

He nodded towards the glossy black Daimler parked alongside the runway with a chauffeur at the wheel. A tall fair young man in tropical khaki who could only be an ADC strode over.

'Lady Foster? I'm Jeremy Carlton.' He greeted her with a crisp salute. 'H.E. sent me to welcome you. He's waiting for you at GH. Got tied up in a meeting with Leg. Co.'

This all-too-familiar code language was somehow reassuring.

'His Excellency's at Government House – he's been at a meeting of the Legislative Council,' she translated for Farrow and the others, feeling like an interpreter of some native tribe.

Introductions followed, and with a ceremonial flourish the ADC produced half-a-dozen crested envelopes out of his pocket. 'Sir James hopes you'll be able to attend a cocktail party this evening. Don't bother about formalities, though. Just Red Sea kit.'

Seeing Farrow's mystified expression, Rose translated again. 'Black trousers, cummerbund, white shirt, no tie.'

'It's a reception for Lord Simpson actually, some VIP from the FO,' Jeremy Carlton went on. 'You might be interested in getting him for your feature.'

'Perhaps,' Farrow said ungraciously. 'Can we get out of this appalling sun? I imagine there's a taxi to be had somewhere to take us to the hotel?'

'Waiting outside the Customs and Passport Offices. And now if you'll excuse us. Check-in formalities are waived for Lady Foster as a guest of the Governor.'

'Must try it sometime,' Farrow called after them.

'His assistant's very nice.' Rose's tone was apologetic as Carlton followed her into the car. 'The girl, Jenny Patmore.'

'She certainly needs to be,' said the young man, smoothing back his shiny blond locks. 'He seems a bit of a smart-alec to me.'

'Oh, these film types,' Rose said smoothly. She was well used to dealing with ruffled ADCs. 'They're not noted for their diplomacy, I'm afraid.'

'Well, he'd better watch his step with H.E. Sir James doesn't suffer fools gladly.' He smiled at her with sudden charm. 'But you know him, of course, Lady Foster?'

'From old Uganda days.'

'And this is your first time in Arabia?'

It was the inevitable question. Rose had already decided how to deal with it.

'I was here briefly, a long long time ago. It was my husband's first posting.'

It was the truth. Martin had come out from England as a young District Officer to Perim. It also avoided the need for any mention of Geoffrey Chetwynd. Not that the name would mean anything to a newcomer like Carlton, or most other people nowadays, but it was best to be on the safe side.

She had been glancing out of the car window as they drove along, talking. Suddenly, she broke off mid-sentence and stared ahead. Her heart was hammering.

'Where exactly are we?'

'Sheikh Othman. Quite near the frontier to the Protectorate.' He pointed to a cluster of shabby wooden buildings rising out of the dunes, a flag or two fluttering here and there. 'That's the famous Aden Sports Club.'

'I know,' she said in a low voice. She hesitated. 'Can we stop for a minute?'

'Of course.' Politely he tried to mask his surprise as he tapped the driver on the shoulder. 'It was here in your day then?'

She nodded. 'It was – quite a landmark.'

The car had drawn into the side of the road under a flamboyant tree. The shade had a reddish glow to it as the light filtered through a canopy of flame-coloured flowers. Perhaps it was the same tree where she and Martin had stood talking in the dusty little compound that fateful morning.

She turned to Carlton. 'May I get out? Just a quick look.'

'Better put your hat on. The glare out there's terrific.'

'I've got my sunglasses.'

As she slipped them on, walking a few paces away, she remembered the dark glasses Nabiha had handed her, driving back from the Races. Now as then she was grateful for the mask they offered. She was aware that, just briefly, something had happened. It was the kind of awakening she had been waiting for and it was painful, so painful.

It was the place itself that had pulled the switch. It was here, more than anywhere else, that the crucial, unalterable scenes had been enacted. Revolving through her mind, she saw again Hassan fall from his horse as

Geoffrey raised his whip, saw his eyes meet hers across the crowded clubroom at the news of the outbreak of war, saw the cloaked figure in a green turban galloping out of the half-light towards the flash of gunfire.

She took a deep breath to steady herself. Standing just behind her, Jeremy Carlton took it for a gasp of admiration.

'Terrific view of the desert, isn't it? The state of Jehal is just beyond the horizon. There to the other side is Aden itself, Steamer Point and the harbour.' He pointed across the haze of the isthmus. High up, a solitary hawk was wheeling and calling. 'They say they're planning to build a huge oil refinery out there in the next few years. There'll be a whole new European settlement.'

Shading her eyes, Rose was looking away behind her. 'We lived somewhere over there, close to the oasis and the gardens. It was an old Arab house, rather beautiful really.'

'Must be the Air Vice-Marshal's place. I expect they'll ask you over while you're here.' He looked at his watch. 'Better be getting on though. H.E. likes his swim before lunch. I think he was hoping you might join him.'

'Lovely.'

The rest of the drive gave her a chance to compose herself again. She tried to concentrated on what she was seeing, jumbled impressions of old and new, concrete housing blocks ('mostly RAF'), the dhow-yards by the waterside ('Noah built the ark there, they say'), the Italianate balconies of the Crescent Hotel, and the peeling arcades of the shopping front. How many more Europeans there seemed to be among the Arab crowds, especially females, pink and peeling in the sleeveless dresses that had always been taboo for the memsahibs of the past, making an even more grotesque contrast with the black shrouded figures of the women in purdah. Weary passengers off the ships milled about the chalked-up boards – 'Come see! Best Fashions Lucky Tailor'; 'Duty-Free Perfumes Don't Miss Bargains'. Once again she caught the familiar whiff of spices from the back-street cafés, felt the hot leather of the car seat burn through the thin material of her dress as the perspiration slid down her back. The gritty touch of sand dust was part of the air you breathed. For a moment, she remembered the way all these things had been inseparable from the state of violent excitement she had lived in, caught on the razor-edge of ecstasy and despair.

Then it was gone, like a light turning off. She was back again, trapped in her sensible fifty-year-old self. The road ahead was winding towards the heights of Colonial protocol. There was the clock tower that had always reminded her of Big Ben. There was the long green-painted verandah of the Union Club, and the imposing stone front of the Chief Justice's residence. Government House at the summit was a surprise though, a Hollywood-style edifice with its white colonnades and Moorish arches swathed in livid-pink bougainvillea. The tribal guards at the gates stood to attention and slapped their rifles in salute as the car rolled through. Rose found herself smiling at the thin dark faces framed in red turbans, as if they were people she knew.

'This is a change,' she said to Jeremy Carlton as they drew up. 'The old place was a shambles, more like a barracks than a house.'

'Wait till you see the pool.'

Indian servants in starched white tunics were on the steps to take charge of the luggage. Inside, Rose found herself immersed in coolness and the embalmed kind of elegance peculiar to all Government Houses – part Oriental palace, part five-star Edwardian seaside hotel. There were the curious juxtaposed scents of mansion polish and tropical flowers, huge old-fashioned Harrods suites, highly-varnished portraits of the King and Queen, potted palms in brass pots burnished to a military sheen. The deep respectful silence was broken only by the creaking whirr of the huge ceiling fans and the padding of bare feet on tiled floors as the bearers moved about their duties.

Following the ADC, Rose found herself out on a long terrace at the back of the house. At the far end she glimpsed turquoise water, striped awnings, and a chunky, reddish figure in navy blue trunks coming forward to welcome her. Sir James took her by both hands, then changed his mind and wrapped her in a bear-like hug.

'Rose! Marvellous to see you again. Apologies for the state of undress and all that.'

'It's marvellous to be here, Jimmy. Terribly sweet of you to have me.'

It was the straightforward blustery sort of greeting that she needed at that moment.

'You look in good form.' He was beaming at her with undisguised delight, rubbing his moustache, grey eyes screwed up shyly under bushy grey eyebrows. 'Well now. Drink first or dip first?'

'Both together, please. Just like Africa. But I'll have to change, won't I?'

'No need to hang on for lunch, Jeremy,' she heard him say to the ADC as she went in to be shown to her room. 'I've told Ahmed to bring us a cold buffet so we can relax, have a bit of a chat on our own.'

The chat was pleasantly predictable, covering the whereabouts of various Colonial Service friends, Rose's life since Martin's death, and the books she had written.

'Read 'em all, dear girl. Didn't fork out for them I'm afraid, but the library out here's pretty good. Just the kind of thing I mean to get down to myself one day, when I've got the time.'

There was the faintest breeze under the awning as they sat drinking coffee in the long planters' chairs that were certainly a relic from the old Government House. Ferguson had put on a rugby-striped towelling gown, and Rose had one of her old Fiji sarongs wrapped round her neat black swimsuit. She felt in control of herself now, even detached. It was the moment, she judged, to bring the talk round to the political situation. At the back of her mind, puzzling her ever since she arrived, had been the whole business of the border crisis. To read the newspapers in England, you would imagine a colony on the edge of a bloodbath, she told him. And there was the matter of the Zara refugees. As she described their arrival at Victoria, she saw again the little encampment in the top-floor flat up the Edgware Road, heard Miriam's recounting in broken English how they had fled from the burning house.

'So what on earth's going on up there, Jimmy?'

'Ah yes. Well. A bit of an awkward incident really. You see, it's been British policy for years now to give the border villages a bit of air-strafing whenever the tribes need keeping in order. Pretty harmless exercise on the whole. Sometimes the RAF drop notes first and no one suffers a scratch.'

'Go on,' Rose said.

'Then just a week ago we had this report that the Yemeni Crown Prince had launched a full-scale military offensive against us. Apparently he'd taken over a fort as his base, just ten miles our side of the border. Unfortunately, when the RAF went in, they mistook our Sultan's house for the fort. Right next door to each other! d'you see. Did a fair bit of damage, I gather, but we'll be compensating them, of course. Sent the Yemenis packing, anyway.'

'Some of the Sultan's family too, it seems,' Rose said dryly.

'Yes, well. I don't know why Sir Hassan simply didn't bring them all down to Jehal or even into Aden itself. He's got plenty of places for them. Perhaps he wants to keep his wives separate – he's bound to have more than one.' He gave one of his barking laughs. 'Or perhaps he's got money salted away in London. Never quite know how the Arab mind works. Or maybe he knows about something blowing up there, that we don't.'

'The Palestine business can hardly have helped the cause of British popularity. Being turned out of your own country to make way for Jewish settlers must seem like an act of pure betrayal to any Arab, however hard the politicians try to explain it away.'

Ferguson nodded glumly. 'Even Egypt's turned against us now. They say Farouk's actually inciting the terrorists against us. As usual, the poor old British soldier pays the price. And the Colonial administrators in God-forsaken places like this, of course.' He mopped his forehead with his towel. Rose saw a look of resolve come over his face. 'Still, it is the only foothold of British power left to us in this part of the world, now India's gone. We must do our best to keep it in good order.'

Rose took a deep breath. 'And where exactly does Sultan Hassan stand in all this?'

'In the middle, as usual,' Ferguson said shortly. 'Walking a bit of a tightrope, really. On the one hand he puts forward all these high-flown, old-fashioned ideas on democracy and progress, the kind of thing he learned from his tutors. On the other, he's trying to move his people out of the Middle Ages, mostly against their will, with only a few years to do it in. And then there's the handful of young revolutionaries, half-educated student types, who can't wait to spill British blood to get what they want. So he certainly has his hands full.'

There was a pause which Rose pushed herself to break. 'Are you in fairly close touch with him? How do you get on with him?'

'Oh, he's a nice enough chap. Charming manners and all that. Middle-aged now, of course, like the rest of us, though he still has all these mixed-up idealistic causes at heart. Arabia for the Arabs and so on. But he's basically not anti-British, wouldn't fall for all this Commie propaganda, I shouldn't think.' He yawned, scratching his stubbled head. 'No, that's more his son's line of country, I'm afraid.'

'Who's that?' she asked casually.

'The Emir Aidrus. A real troublemaker, I hear. Fortunately he's been out of the country since he grew up, studying the politics of revolution, you might say, anywhere in the Middle East where there's any kind of an uprising going on. Now, rumour has it, he has his eye on Aden, hand in glove with the Yemen. The Sultan claims he washed his hands of him years ago, opposed to everything his father stands for. But can you believe it? After all, blood's thicker than water. That's why we can never put our total trust in him. You can't really put your money on someone with a son who's a traitor, can you?'

Rose could think of nothing to say. She was tingling in every nerve, trying to absorb the shock of what she had just been told. At the same time it was as if a key had turned in some lock at the back of her mind. She was aware of Ferguson staring at her.

'Are you all right, Rose? You look rather pale all of a sudden.' He leaned forward, concerned. 'You should really go in for a siesta.'

'I was thinking. What an awful situation for his father.'

'Yes, I suppose so.' He was still looking at her, but with an expression of dawning comprehension. 'Of course, you remember Sultan Hassan from your own days. Under unfortunate circumstances, to put it mildly. Martin did tell me something about Geoffrey Chetwynd,' he went on awkwardly. 'The tragedy of the shooting and so on.'

But not about my part in the scandal, Rose thought to herself. Martin would never have betrayed that confidence to anyone, she'd swear to that.

'Martin should have got this job, you know,' he said suddenly. 'Arabia was where he should have ended, not Fiji. But rumour had it that the old fogeys at the Colonial Office couldn't back him because he'd married Chetwynd's widow. After all, Chetwynd blotted his copybook here in no uncertain fashion. Blotted it in blood, you might say.'

Rose flinched. Jimmy Ferguson was not renowned for his tact.

'Must have been pretty awful for you, Rose,' he went on, trying to make amends. 'Of course, you were extremely young. Not much more than a schoolgirl.'

She forced a smile. 'That's all right, Jimmy. It was another life. But it reminds me. When your nice young ADC asked me if I'd been here before I'm afraid I told him a white lie. I said I'd been here with my husband ages ago but I didn't specify which husband. I mean . . .' She stumbled for a second. 'I mean, what's the point of raking up old history? Especially when I'm supposed to be here as an observer with impeccable credentials.'

She was relieved to see the Governor take this as lightly as she had tried to make it sound. He simply winked at her conspiratorially, then got up and drew her to her feet.

'My dear girl, rely on me. My lips are sealed. Besides, who would there be these days to make the connection? Only the Sultan himself, and he's holed up at Jehal for the duration.' He chuckled, still holding her hand. 'Just as well, perhaps. He might not be all that pleased to see you again. Might put a price on your head,' he teased. 'Doesn't a wife share the husband's guilt in Islamic law? Even though it was an accident,' he added hastily.

'It was no accident,' Rose said in a low voice. She saw a look of bafflement on his face. 'But please – let's not talk about it any more.'

She felt an appalling weariness all of a sudden. The web of deception was still producing fresh threads to entangle her. Perhaps Cynthia had been right and the whole visit was a terrible mistake.

'Sorry. Of course not. No need for you to go back to the past anyway,' he went on cheerily. 'Not the way you're looking today, and the name you've made for yourself. By the way, the conversation we've just been having about the state of the nation.' He glanced at her shrewdly. 'I take it that was a run-through for the real thing?'

'If that's all right with you.'

'Tell them six o'clock, then. We'll fit it in before the party. Now go and have your sleep.'

'Dear Jimmy. Thank you.'

Not surprisingly, Rose found she could not really sleep. In her mind, over and over again, she was piecing together a portrait of Aidrus, put together from the fragments of her conversations and what Jimmy Ferguson had just told her. None of it matched up with her own mental snapshot of a tiny boy in a red fez, enormous eyes brimming with tears as she wrenched herself away from him at Cairo station. His life is nothing to do with mine, she told herself, any more than Hassan's has been. It is a mere accident of fate that I have heard anything of him at all. And yet there was that tiny thread of heartache that still pulled at her. Perhaps it is his mixed blood that has made him a rebel, she thought. He was a wilful baby, she remembered. There had been violent tantrums, even when he was very small. And then she stopped herself. These were absurd mother's thoughts, belonging to someone else. Instead, she made herself concentrate on the task ahead, worrying that the interview session would be a disaster for one reason or another.

In fact, it all went more smoothly than she had dared hope. By arriving fifteen minutes early, Mike Farrow had managed to get pictures of His Excellency engaged in his afternoon game of croquet on the Government House lawn – the only lawn in the Colony – with Rose as his opponent. As they reached the final hoop they were interrupted by the evening ceremony of the lowering of the flag. Mallet in hand, Sir James stood rigidly to attention as, up on the parapets, a lone sentry sounded the Last Post on his bugle, and in the distance beyond, a blood-red sun slipped down between sea and sky.

'A good one, that,' the Governor remarked, tapping the winning ball through. He considered himself an expert on tropical sunsets and awarded them marks for performance. 'Did you get the famous green flash, just as the light hits the horizon?'

'We did, sir. It was splendid.' Farrow had obviously decided to be on his best behaviour. 'And now if you and Lady Foster could settle yourselves on the verandah our cameraman can get some shots while you're talking. A touch of imperial afterglow in the background perhaps.'

'Well done, Rose,' Jenny Patmore murmured to her after the interview. 'Sir James certainly eats out of your hand, doesn't he?'

'Looking at you out of the corner of his eye was quite an encourage-ment, too,' Rose said, for the young woman had put on a New Look red-flowered dress, almost ankle-length like her own, which perfectly set off her dark colouring.

'Good stuff.' Mike Farrow raised his glass at her. They were standing together as the first guests arrived for the party. 'And the croquet worked beautifully. Drake and his bowls kind of thing, with an Arabian Armada looming in the background!'

'What's that about Drake?' A pale young man with a shock of red hair had detached himself from a nearby group. 'Do tell me, how on earth does he come into the story? I thought you were compiling one of those earnest reports of the drab and dreary world of the late 1940s. How the waves of post-war unrest are affecting the British bastions of Empire, those spheres of influence in the Middle East now crumbling before the Communist threat.'

His impersonation of an American newscaster made Rose laugh. His normal voice was faintly Welsh and he introduced himself as Goronwy Evans of the British Council. With his Red Sea kit he was wearing a cummerbund of flowered brocade. She saw Farrow fix a disparaging gaze on this item of clothing before replying.

'Just a metaphor,' he snapped. 'Working on documentaries doesn't preclude the creative touch, you know.'

'Obviously not, with a brilliant writer like Rose Foster on the team.' Evans turned to her with genuine enthusiasm. 'We have all your books in the Council library. They're immensely popular you know. I like the *Pacific Diary* best. How does our Arabian outpost strike you by comparison?'

'A bit like a South Sea island in a way,' Rose said. 'I mean, the isolation of the European community. Their life seems to be totally cut off from the rest of the peninsula. I suppose it always has been.' She heard her voice trail away.

'Ah yes, our little expatriate circle.' Evans turned to look round the room with a roll of his eyes. 'Our excellent Governor you know, of course. Decent fellow, not much imagination. Have you noticed the way he's always jingling an enormous bunch of keys in his trouser pocket? Desk keys, despatch-box keys – I do believe he thinks he has the key to the Colony itself tucked away somewhere on his ring. A private property the British can open or close at will, keep for themselves for as long as they want.' He flashed her his enfant-terrible grin. 'And do please quote me if you like.'

Next to them, Jenny was quick to respond. 'Perhaps we could fix a chat and a film session sometime? The impact of Western culture on the Islamic world and so on.'

He shook his head. 'I think I'm more useful incognito, don't you, running through the cast list? The owl-like gent over there in the incredibly shabby dinner jacket. That's our eccentric Chief Justice, goes into court in his swimming trunks, under his robes of course. The tall grey-haired one with a cigarette holder is the Colonial Secretary, famous

289

polo-player and breeder of Arab thoroughbreds, breaker of female hearts in his spare time. Then there's our latter-day Lawrence of Arabia, the little chap with the beard. He's the Political Agent for the Protectorate, writes Arabic poetry and plays the *oudh* like a native. These are our characters. The rest are a pretty dull lot – contract people, the ex-Indian Army lot, Captain this and Major that, and a few oil-company officials and their wives who still think they're living in Surbiton.'

'And the local inhabitants – do they get a look in at something like this?' Rose was remembering the haughty sheikhs and the dusty tribesmen of the Race Day enclosure.

Evans nodded to a watchful circle of middle-aged Arabs in suits, conspicuous by the large glasses of orangeade they were sipping. 'Just the tame ones. The editor of the English-language weekly, the headmaster of the school for the sons of chiefs, a rich coffee merchant or two. That kind of thing. All the interesting ones are persona non grata. And of course there's the fascinating Sultan Hassan, tucked away in Jehal, alas. His son was quite a famous black sheep before leaving for the wilder shores of insurrection. I used to hear him holding forth when he was still a student, at meetings of something called the Sons of the South Liberation League. Till Government closed it down, of course.'

'Now you've got a liberation movement with a vengeance,' Farrow suggested. 'Moving in through the back door.' Rose saw him glance at her, wondering why she had fallen silent.

'Something rather more violent, I'm afraid. But there's still time to damp it down, encourage the moderates instead. If only the Colonial Office would move with the times. Can you imagine – the people of Aden don't even know what an election is!' He broke off. 'Anyway, here's H.E. About to lead you in the direction of the horse's mouth, I imagine.'

'He's in my study. He's agreed to be filmed and he has a statement to make.' The Governor sounded flustered.

'I'm sorry?' Farrow asked, bemused.

'Lord Simpson. No interview, though. Says the situation's too delicate.'

Farrow shrugged his shoulders at Rose. 'Might as well give it a go, I suppose.'

Rose was experiencing a depressing sense of flatness. It was the usual game of charades. Had she come all this way for such a tame experience? She felt her hackles rise at the very sight of his lordship, fattish and smooth-faced, seated behind a large mahogany desk with his papers before him, in the attitude of Royalty about to make a Christmas broadcast. She took the chair opposite, smiling mechanically, while

Farrow conferred with the cameraman and sound recordist. Jenny sat down by the door.

'Film afterwards, please,' the Minister pronounced. 'And mind no questions, Lady Foster.' He wagged his finger at her. 'Not even from such a charming interviewer as yourself.'

There was silence while he put on his spectacles and cleared his throat.

'With regard to the current unrest on the borders of South Arabia, His Majesty's Government wish it to be known that they will continue to repel the Yemen invaders and put down insurrections by local dissidents with all available land and air forces. The recent petition by Arab leaders for moves towards limited self-government has been rejected. The importance of Aden, both strategically and economically within the Commonwealth, is such that HMG cannot foresee the possibility of any relaxation of their responsibilities for the Colony.'

Rose watched him as he laid down the paper with a satisfied air. She looked down in her lap at a note Jenny had slipped her earlier on.

'This protest to Britain that has just been registered by the Yemenis at the United Nations Assembly, Lord Simpson . . .'

But she got no further. He held up an imperious hand. 'Lady Foster. Off the record, we must be prepared for many such moves. It is all part of Soviet policy to undermine British power in the Middle East. But I don't think it need trouble us,' he went on expansively. 'We do have a very special relationship with the Arabs, after all. T. E. Lawrence and so on.'

'The Arab Revolt,' Rose said sharply. 'It was quite useful to us, wasn't it, when they had to put down the Turks? The trouble was, we've never somehow managed to keep our side of the bargain, have we?'

Surprised, Lord Simpson stuck out his lower lip as he stared back at her. 'I'm afraid this isn't a history lesson, Lady Foster. I can only say that we always treat our loyal Arab rulers with absolute fairness. Under our treaty conditions, however, we do have perfect freedom to depose or deport any who betray the trust we have put in them in times of emergency.'

Rose felt a sudden spark of fury, an old fury that went back to a stifling morning of 1915, and a room full of khaki-clad Englishmen. He's just a bully, she thought. Geoffrey taught me to recognize the type.

'Someone like the Sultan of Jehal should be quite an authority on betrayal, Lord Simpson. His father was shot and killed by the British and his people left to the mercy of the Turks. Our famous Treaty of Friendship wasn't much help to them then.'

She stopped and swallowed. She was startled to see Lord Simpson's expression change.

'You seem to be exceptionally well-informed on all this,' he murmured. He leaned forward across the desk, almost amorously.

'We've all done a great deal of research, Lord Simpson,' Jenny put in quickly from the back of the room. Farrow was occupied in checking the sound recording.

At the same movement, a servant arrived with a tray. In the opposite doorway, the Governor had appeared.

'Time for a drink, I should think.'

In a few seconds the atmosphere had been defused. But inwardly Rose was chiding herself for letting her emotions run away with her. It could be dangerous. At the same time she was aware that her anger had somehow titillated the Minister.

'To your health, Lady Foster.' He raised his glass to her. 'Indignation suits you, if I may say so.'

Unbelievably, beneath the desk, she felt a large foot nudge against hers.

'What a shame we're not to be a fellow guests here at GH during my stay.' The foot was placed firmly over hers. 'I'm afraid I'm putting up at the Air Vice-Marshal's. Unless Sir James relents, of course.'

Rose looked across at Jimmy Ferguson. She knew him well enough to realize that his expressionless face concealed intense irritation. As she stood up, he shepherded her towards the door.

'I'm afraid we're running behind schedule rather,' he told the others. 'We have to be at the Union Club at nine, I promised faithfully.'

'Sorry about that,' he said when they had left the room. 'Springing the Club on you out of the blue. But I thought you'd had just about enough of old Simpson one way and another.'

'Especially another,' Rose replied.

'He's well known for it, I'm afraid. Especially when he's had his regulation three White Ladies.' Catching Rose's look, he burst out laughing. 'His favourite cocktail. Can't stand the stuff myself. Smells like a tart's dressing-table.'

'But honestly,' Rose protested. 'At his age.'

Ferguson jingled his keys. 'I'm afraid one is just as susceptible to a pretty woman at sixty as at twenty.' He glanced up at her under his eyebrows. 'And you are very pretty, Rose. Always were.'

'Jimmy. That's very sweet.' Taken aback, she laid a hand on his arm. 'But what's this Club affair?' she went on quickly. 'Do I have to change?'

He looked at her in her full-skirted yellow dress. 'I'd never forgive you if you did. As a matter of fact, it's their annual fancy-dress, St George's Night, believe it or not. I'm exempted as guest of honour, so therefore you are, thank God. We get a buffet supper if you're hungry. And don't worry about Simpson,' he added. 'He's off to the Air Vice-Marshal's. What about your producer and that nice little Jenny and the rest of the crew?'

'They're taking a look at the local night-life. Not for me!'

292

St George's Night at the Club, Fancy Dress, Buffet Supper, Rose said to herself as she went upstairs for her stole and bag. Nothing had changed. She saw clearly the invitation card that Geoffrey had brought home soon after their arrival in Aden. They had been asked to join Major Beattie's party, all of them dressed ridiculously for a tableau entitled The Village Wedding. Geoffrey was the vicar, going to great lengths to borrow his costume from the army chaplain, not finding it funny at all. For herself, she remembered concocting some kind of scarlet cassock and white ruff to go as a choirboy. At that time, she had met Hassan only once, at the Birthday Parade, had spoken to no other Arabs at all, apart from servants. Certainly none would be permitted as guests at the all-white Union Club, not even the Sultan and his family.

This evening, it was exactly the same. As the Daimler drew up at the Club, the only Arabs to be seen were those clustered around the entrance to stare at the spectacle of the sahibs and memsahibs so curiously garbed. Hassan had told her once that the local people believed that the St George's evening was some kind of religious festival, and the clothes the English wore represented various tribal ancestors and holy men. But it was hard to read the dark faces pressed to the trellis screens that fenced off the compound from the street. The sight of the Governor seemed to impose solemnity on the occasion. Some stood to attention as he strode through the door and Rose was conscious of suppressed whispers at the sight of a woman at his side.

Now they were mounting the wide wooden staircase that creaked at every step, the banister rails worn to a sheen by a hundred years of sweating pink palms. She glanced at the baize notice-boards on the wall. As ever, there was a list of new members, those with subscriptions owing, the times of mail day. Entries were still open for next week's regatta and on Sunday there was to be a concert of classical gramophone records in the library.

At the top of the stairs, the mingled fumes of alcohol, cigarette smoke and scented close-packed bodies met you like a solid wall, so that you had to stand quite still for a minute, adjusting to the heat and the noise of the place. The whole of the long verandah was jammed with tables, and the floorboards shook under the feet of the dancers inside. It was something Rose recognized at once, that sense of feverish enjoyment, the way people drank too much, laughed too much, anything to blot out the gruelling tedium of everyday life and the strange emptiness of the surrounding deserts, whiling away their sentence until the next leave home.

'Your table's over here, Your Excellency.'

A nervous Club official disguised as Charlie Chaplin led them through. People around them got to their feet. New arrivals were always avidly

293

scrutinized, but walking in with the Governor, the ADC behind them, Rose felt herself the object of particular curiosity. It was absurd, but she experienced exactly the same nervous lurch of the stomach as she had at eighteen. The only difference was that she had since acquired the art of appearing composed whatever her inward feelings. It was especially useful when you were being introduced, as now, to a circle of strangers dressed as the court of the Emperor Nero. Nero himself was the managing director of British Petroleum, it seemed. Under the vine leaves and the togas, she recognized the Colonial Secretary and the Chief Justice with various assorted concubines and slave girls who spoke with the unmistakeable accents of the British Raj.

'Just a flying visit, Lady Foster?'

'I'm afraid so.'

'Going to put us in the movies, I gather?'

'Sort of.'

'Glorious Technicolor?'

'Hardly.'

Oysters and tall glasses of Black Velvet were being served, another St George's ritual. The Governor was being courted at the head of the table. Meanwhile, fellow guests on either side had reverted to more important topics.

'Surprised to hear the old CJ didn't get his K in the honours.'

'Marjorie's got this amazing cure for prickly heat – something to do with boracic soda.'

'Apparently they were seen together quite openly at the RAF pool after church.'

'The Arabs just don't make good servants. I told her you've got to try for an Indian or a Somali.'

Rose looked out at the lights of the ships in the harbour below. It had always been like this at the Club, the suffocating feeling of not belonging, the secret urge to be away out there, somewhere in the mysterious otherness of Arabia that lay so close, and yet so tantalizingly shut off. Now it was worse because of Hassan. Try as she might, she could not erase the thought – that beyond the harbour, beyond the isthmus, lay the frontier and Jehal. Did he know she was here? Might there be a message for her at Government House? Could she herself not make any kind of approach, even a telephone call?

You must stop this, she told herself. It's humiliating. You're living in the past even to imagine such things.

Ferguson leaned across to her. 'Here comes the Air Vice-Marshal. Minus his lordship, you'll be pleased to hear.'

Right from the start, there was something about Teddy Hall and his wife Mary that touched a chord in her mind. But it was too faint to be identified. Besides, she had met so many similar couples abroad, he grey-haired and urbane, she a rather brassy blonde, plumpish, with that relentless vivacity some women acquire in middle age.

The oysters had given way to the ritual European food, so distasteful for religious reasons to the servants who had prepared it – dry-as-dust sausage rolls, ham vol-au-vents and bacon angels-on-horseback. The champagne was good, though, contributed by the French Consul. Three glasses were consumed in rapid succession by Mary Hall, who seemed keen to strike up a friendship. So did her husband.

'Lord Simpson was very impressed with your conversation,' he told her. 'Your knowledge of the country in particular.'

'That's very kind. But I'm sure there's a lot we need to see for ourselves, if we're to get an up-to-date picture of what's happening here.'

'Difficult time to get around with these border troubles,' he went on. 'Still, perhaps we could bend a few rules and fly you up-country a bit. After all, we need to put it on record perhaps that we're not some kind of Luftwaffe outfit, exterminating the tribes at random.'

'I know my producer would be most grateful,' Rose said. 'And it would be tremendously rewarding from my own point of view, of course.'

'I'll see what can be done then. Might even come along for the ride myself. You too, Sir James?'

'Not diplomatic, I'm afraid,' Ferguson replied. He stood up and executed a schoolboy bow. 'Meanwhile, I haven't yet danced with my guest.'

Inside, the little Italian band on the dais were playing a samba, arousing some latent Latin American enthusiasm in Rose's partner.

'Do you know, I'm rather enjoying myself.' He hummed through his teeth, more or less in time with the beat, as he hopped and bounded around her. 'Thanks to you.'

He squeezed her hand hard. Then, remembering appearances, he glanced amiably around at the other dancers. 'Got to judge the best group in a minute or two. What do you think? The 1920 Flappers or the St Trinian's gang?'

'For sheer topicality it'd be hard to beat our lot,' Rose said acidly. 'Nero fiddling while Rome burns.'

She saw his face fall. 'Rome being Aden.'

'Sorry. Let's not talk politics. No one else has mentioned the subject all evening.'

'Except the Air Vice-Marshal. He seems only too happy to provide you with a conducted tour of the troubles. As long as he gets his picture in the newsreel, of course.'

'Film,' she corrected automatically. 'We shan't be much longer, shall we?' She had a sudden picture in her mind of a note waiting for her at Government House, a green crested envelope on the silver salver in the hall.

'As soon as I've presented the prizes, we can be on our way. About ten minutes. You must be exhausted.'

The music had come to an end.

'Is the ladies' still hidden away behind the Billiard Room?' she asked him.

He laughed. 'How on earth would I know?'

But it was, of course, the same hot shuttered room with what appeared to be the same two Somali ayahs sitting in the corner, one knitting, the other weaving garlands of jasmine. They looked up and smiled at her, offering her towels, and water from the brass jug on the marble table to wash her hands.

Rose surveyed herself in the long mirror on the wall, thankful for a moment's peace. But then the door opened and she saw Mary Hall behind her, staring at her with wide eyes.

'I still can't believe it.'

Rose turned round. 'Believe what?'

'That it's little Rose Chetwynd. The Lady Foster thing misled me, no Christian name. And yet I had this feeling we'd met somewhere. Rose Chetwynd,' she repeated, shaking her head, her voice slightly slurred.

Just to hear that name made Rose feel sick. But it was not so much the shock of being discovered. It was being thrust back into that other self by someone she didn't even know, or even remember. There was something sinister about it, threatening even.

'Were you in Aden then?' She forced lightness into her manner. 'All those years ago?'

'You'd never remember me. You were far too wrapped up in your own affairs.' It was said laughingly, but there was a sting to the last word that Rose found painful. 'And of course I wasn't in your social strata then. Teddy was working for a shipping firm. He went into the Air Force later on in the war. That was the year after that scare with the Turks, after that awful business with your poor husband . . .' She broke off, flustered. Rose saw sweat breaking out under the face powder.

'After the shooting of the Sultan,' she said coldly.

'That evening at the camp,' Mary Hall went rushing on. 'I was the one who played the piano – "Let the great big world keep turning" – remember? It was quite a party. Only you never cared for that sort of thing, did you? Always wanted to be off with your Arab friends. One Arab friend in particular, if I remember rightly.'

She was peering beadily at Rose out of the corner of her eye as she applied her lipstick. Then, with an impatient gesture, she snapped her compact shut.

'Oh come on, Rose! We all make mistakes in our youth and you broke just about every rule in the book. Still, you were just a slip of a girl, totally naïve. Everyone knew you were having the love affair of a lifetime and half the women in the colony envied you for it.' There was a gloating look in her face as she leaned closer. For the first time Rose realized she had been drinking whisky along with the champagne. 'Come on, tell me,' she breathed. 'I've always wanted to know. Was he the most marvellous lover, your Emir? The Sheikh of Araby and Rudolph Valentino rolled into one?'

This time the wave of nausea Rose felt was almost unbearable. Even the scent of jasmine, always so sharp and pure in her mind, was tainted now by this horrible moment. She shrank away, leaning against the table.

One of the ayahs touched her shoulder lightly.

'Memsahib is sick?'

'No, thank you. I'll be fine.'

She took the damp towel and pressed it to her forehead. Mary Hall was still staring at her, but this time with a vaguely disappointed expression.

'Sorry, darling. I hadn't realized. I've had a few over the eight as well.' She struggled with a zip for a moment. 'We'd better be getting back to the table or we'll be in hot water with H.E. Time for a gossip next week, perhaps. You're staying for a few days?'

'I – I'm not too sure.'

With an effort, she steeled herself to walk up the stairs with Mary Hall's hand on her arm.

'The funny thing is,' the woman went on, 'I'd never have recognized you. But then that old bearer jogged our memory. He's always talking to Teddy about the good old days in Aden, and all the young sahibs he worked for. Then he pointed to you on the dance floor and said, "There is someone I remember. That is Mrs Chetwynd. Wife of Chetwynd Sahib." I tell you, it gave me the shock of my life. Teddy was shattered. He was quite a pal of Geoffrey's, you know. Thought the whole business of booting him out was appalling. I'm afraid he rather put the blame on you for being a naughty girl. We must hurry, though. It's time for the toast to St George.'

A servant standing in the hallway proffered a tray of drinks. Mary Hall took a whisky, Rose a glass of red wine. She needed something to steady her nerves for the last few minutes.

As they went upstairs, Mary Hall continued to talk. Rose wished she could close her ears. And just because one of the bearers chanced to recognize her, after all that time. It seemed extraordinary.

'Which one was it?' she asked. 'Where is he?'

They had reached the large landing half-way up.

'Over there.' Mary Hall indicated an old man in a white turban who was polishing glasses, half-hidden by a screen. 'Oh dear. He's seen us.' She moved on. 'I'll leave you to it.'

It was right somehow that Rose should find herself standing alone in a shadowy corner of the staircase as Ram Prasad came towards her. She knew it was him the moment he emerged. That squat spider-like way of moving hadn't changed since the days when he spied on her telephone calls from behind the verandah door. He was slower now, of course, and badly bent, the flat face wrinkled and blotched with age. But when he came to a halt a few feet in front of her, the black protuberant eyes stared up at her with just the same gleam of malevolence that had so intimidated her all those years ago.

'Memsahib.' He spoke so softly, it was almost a whisper. 'You remember me?'

Rose stood her ground, though the impulse to back away was overpowering. She was determined to show no sign of emotion.

'Yes, Ram Prasad. I remember you.'

'Chetwynd Sahib. He is dead?'

'Yes, he is dead.'

Suddenly he darted his head forward like a snake and hissed, 'You killed him.'

She bit her lip to stop it trembling. 'He died in South Africa, ten years ago.'

'No, memsahib.' He was half-smiling, his mouth curled back to reveal betel-stained gums. 'You killed him, memsahib. You killed his good name. My master was destroyed by you, his wife.'

Rose began to back away, groping for the banister rail behind her.

'And now you come back.' His voice rose higher, thin and reedy. 'So that I, Ram Prasad, can repay what you did to Chetwynd Sahib.'

While he was speaking, she watched the fat hand with the bitten-down nails reach out to the table beside him. On it there was an oil-lamp burning, a relic of the Club's early days, with its ornate Kashmiri shade of coloured crystal. As he snatched it up and held it in front of her, there was a split second when she was unable to move. Then, slowly it seemed, she flung herself away to one side.

At the same moment there was the crash of splintered glass. She saw the flame dart forward at her feet. All around was the stench of petrol and she was aware of two servants running down towards them. One of them was stamping out the smouldering mess on the floor, the other had hold of

298

Ram Prasad. A third man, close behind, gently supported her where she stood, leaning against the banisters.

'You are all right, memsahib?'

'Yes, yes,' she replied shakily. 'I think so.'

'This fellow is crazy. He should not be allowed in this place.'

He handed her the towel he was carrying. For the first time Rose noticed a wetness on her face and down the front of her bodice. For an awful moment she thought it was oil from the lamp. Then she saw the empty glass still clutched in her hand, and realized it was wine.

She looked up at Ram Prasad, still facing her a few feet away. His arms were pinned behind him, but he made no attempt to struggle. As they pulled him away, his eyes were fixed on the red stain spreading across the yellow cotton of the dress.

Once again she heard that thin cracked whisper.

'Before you leave Aden, it will be blood.'

❧ 8 ❧

THERE was one thing for which Rose was grateful. The actual incident went almost unnoticed. At the time the other guests were crowded together on the top verandah drinking a toast to St George proposed by the Governor. Even when one of the bearers hurriedly drew the ADC aside, those nearby had no idea that anything was wrong.

For Rose herself, the enormity of what had just happened was only brought home to her by the expression on Jeremy Carlton's face.

'What on earth. . . ?' he began as he surveyed the scene, the servants mopping up the debris, Rose sitting on a chair in the alcove sipping the brandy they had brought her. He made an effort to recover himself.

'The man who did this? Where is he?'

'The police guard have taken him, sahib.'

He bent over Rose. 'Are you hurt?'

'No. But I would like to go back to the house.'

'Here. I'll take you down. H.E.'s just leaving anyway.'

Sitting in the back of the car, Rose found herself starting to shiver violently as Jimmy Ferguson climbed in beside her. The arm he put round her was surprisingly comforting.

'I can hardly believe it. What an appalling thing! Damn lucky you were not seriously injured, or even killed.' He raised his voice to Carlton, sitting in front. 'The fellow's unbalanced. I've noticed him before. Just last week I told them he should be put away. Well, he certainly will be now. Our Judge will see to that.'

He turned back to Rose and made little patting motions against her shoulder. 'But why on earth should he go for you? Did he say anything?'

'Not really.' Lying was so much easier than trying to embark on the truth. She tried to laugh. 'Perhaps he just didn't like the look of me.'

'And you were so enjoying the evening. Spoilt your pretty dress too, I'm afraid. I hope you'll allow me to make compensation. As your host, it's the least I can do.'

'Honestly, Jimmy, it's no problem. It'll clean.'

She drew away a little as the car drew up at Government House. Only a few lights showed in the windows. Inside, the darkened rooms were empty and still. Jeremy Carlton took his leave of them as they stood

300

together in the hall. Silently the Indian butler appeared, waiting for his orders.

Ferguson glanced towards Rose. There was an awkward moment.

'I'm sure you could do with a nightcap.' He indicated the verandah where bright moonlight slanted in, gleaming on white cane chairs and low tables. 'Lovely night. Just the thing for sitting out with a lonesome bachelor.'

He sounded hearty, but the expression on his face was almost pleading. Rose hated herself as she shook her head.

'To tell the truth, Jimmy, I'm absolutely done in. Besides, I must get out of this dress.'

'Of course. Sorry. I almost forgot.' He straightened his shoulders. 'Up you go, then. See you in the morning.'

As she moved towards the stairs, the salver on the table caught her eye. 'No messages, Vijay?'

'No messages, memsahib.'

It was true she was exhausted. But she knew there was no question of simply falling asleep, not for hours anyway. The whole episode went on revolving through her mind, from start to finish then back again. Reason told her that Ram Prasad could do her no further harm, physically at least. But now there was no escaping from the past. Mary Hall would see to that too. The visit had been poisoned irretrievably, it seemed. A sense of failure pressed down on her like a migraine.

It was illogical, she knew, but a word from Hassan could have broken the spell. Such a thing was obviously not forthcoming. All she could do was steel herself to get through the next three days as painlessly as possible, if only to fulfil her obligations to Mike and Jenny. At least the promised plane trip over the interior would be a distraction. As a writer, she would make the most of that material, she told herself, falling asleep in spite of everything.

But she did not sleep for long. A discreet tapping at the door roused her at what seemed to be still the middle of the night. In fact, her watch said half past six and she could see streaks of sunlight through the blinds. With another tap an elderly servant came in with a tray of tea.

She turned away, blinking. 'Never mind the tea,' she told him drowsily. 'I need to sleep on for a while.'

'Sorry, memsahib,' he whispered. 'But someone is here.'

'Someone for me? At this hour?'

He had moved across to the French windows and was deftly drawing up the blinds.

'Waiting outside, memsahib.'

Curiosity overcame laziness. Perhaps Mike or Jenny needed her urgently. Throwing back the mosquito net, she reached for her dressing gown and went out onto the balcony. In the driveway below was a young man on horseback, an Arab, with another horse on a leading rein beside him. He turned his head to scan the front of the house and she stepped back quickly into the room again.

'Who is it?' she asked the bearer, wanting to shake him for being so mysterious. 'What does he want?'

For answer, he pointed to a folded note on the tray, which he had put down on a side table. Rose snatched it up and felt something run through her like a spark along a wire. Only one person used that green paper. There was no need to look at the signature. She sat down on the bed because her legs were suddenly shaking.

'Why are you keeping me waiting?' he had scribbled in pencil in the familiar, sloping schoolboy hand. 'There are only two times to ride in Arabia, the hour before sunset and the hour after dawn. Or have you forgotten?'

She looked up to see the bearer studying her with polite curiosity. The room looked just as it did a minute ago but inside her head everything was changing shape faster than she could follow.

'Could you tell the *syce* I'll be ready in ten minutes?'

He nodded, still bemused.

'Oh, and let His Excellency know I've gone riding with friends, would you?'

It took more than ten minutes, of course, to shower and dress, pulling on a pair of cotton trousers and an old navy blue shirt, rummaging in her cases for her boots. There was no time for make-up, just the flick of kohl around the eyes, something she still did every day of her life, after Ayesha had shown her how in Zara. A smudge of oil against the sun, her hair fastened up in a hasty knot, and she was slipping down the stairs, her bag over her shoulder, with the furtive joy of a runaway schoolgirl.

'Hassan.'

She repeated the name to herself like a code word, not stopping to analyse this delight, only touching the note in her pocket to prove to herself that it was still there.

Outside the house, the young man was waiting, just as she had seen him. He saluted her with the independent air of the Bedouin servant, tilting his turban over his tangled locks as he grinned round at her.

'*Kef halek.*'

'*Kef halek.*'

His horse was a nondescript grey, hers a sleek chestnut creature, so like Azziza it was uncanny.

He said something that seemed to mean the mare was nice and quiet as he brought her up to the steps for Rose to mount.

'Good,' Rose said in English. 'It's a year or two since I've ridden, I'm afraid,' she told him as they set off down the drive at a brisk trot. 'The Sultan,' she went on. 'Where is he?'

He shrugged his shoulders apologetically and spread his hands. 'No Ingliz.'

But she had no real need to ask. She knew exactly where they were going, even though the way there was unfamiliar. It was still so early that there were few people about. Outside the Union Club two porters were sweeping out the entrance and stacking up empty beer crates. For a sickening moment the scene with Ram Prasad flashed through her mind again. But already it was fading, irrelevant as some grotesque charade in the calm light of morning. From the little minaret of the fisherman's mosque at the bottom of the hill, the first call to prayer came floating out. Elation rose up inside her as if in response to that summons, powerful and mysterious. She was about to see Hassan again. There in front of them was the coast road and beyond it the sea, silver-coloured in the low-lying sun.

'Sultan,' said the *syce*.

He pointed towards the familiar rocky bluff at the end of the bay. In the distance she could make out a solitary figure on horseback, a man in jodhpurs and a white shirt who sat very straight and still in the saddle, watching them approach. For a moment, he looked exactly like the Hassan of thirty years ago and she felt her heart turn over as it always had done. Then, screwing up her eyes against the sun, she saw the glint of grey hair.

'Who is this stranger?' she asked herself. She fought down panic, gripping the reins more tightly. As they came closer, he raised his hand in greeting. She raised hers in response, slowing the mare down to a walk. It was as if she could will the moment not to move on, holding it fast like a picture in a frame. Instinctively she knew Hassan was willing the same thing. But the silence had to be broken.

'Good morning, Lady Foster.'

'Good morning, Your Highness.'

Rose had thought that when their eyes met, that would be the moment of release, the moment of knowing everything. But she found him studying her face with such intentness that she had to look away to contain her emotion.

He held out his hand to her. It was a formal English handshake. Both of them were acutely aware of the servant watching them from a few paces away. Briefly she felt his fingers tighten around hers before she drew away. He had not really changed, she thought. Maybe it was because beneath the surface she was looking at the young Hassan. The slanting angle of the cheekbone and jaw was looser now. The wide, sensual mouth was compressed at the corners by deep lines, making him look harsh and sad. But the extraordinary eyes were as brilliant as ever. He was suddenly laughing at her as he rubbed his cropped head.

'Why have I gone grey?' he demanded. 'While you are still the colour of your youth?'

Now she was able to laugh too. 'Not quite,' she protested.

'Yes, you are still a youthful woman.' There was a pause after this announcement. 'Even after so long. You know how long it is?'

'I know.'

There were a hundred things she wanted to say, but even to begin seemed quite impossible. The important questions remained somewhere below the surface. Do we still belong to each other? Or was it all youthful bravado, a stage of our lives that is now meaningless?

That earlier electrical charge of happiness had drained away. An awful shyness had descended on them. She sat stiffly in the saddle, staring out at the desert, trying not to care too much. Hassan glanced at the *syce*.

'Go on ahead,' she heard him say in Arabic.

'Ahead?' she asked him, as the young man rode off. 'Where is that?'

'The frontier post.'

'But the border is closed,' she said quickly.

'Not to me,' he replied with some hauteur. 'Not to my guests.'

'Are we riding all the way to Jehal, then?' she went on, half-joking.

'There will be a car waiting.'

They had begun to walk the horses along the beach, she slightly behind. He looked at her over his shoulder without smiling.

'You do not refuse my invitation, I hope?'

'I – I thought it was just an early morning ride. I'm staying with the Governor. I have to spend the day with my colleagues from London. The Air Vice-Marshal has arranged something . . .' Her voice faltered.

Abruptly he wheeled his horse round in its tracks. With a gesture she remembered well, he swept his hand palm down from left to right. 'These things,' he said angrily. 'Are they so important to you? You and I – do we not deserve a small piece of time together – we two, who were everything to each other?'

His face was quivering, his eyes fastened on hers. Then with a thrust of his heels, he jerked the horse around again and broke away into a canter. But when she caught up with him, he still would not look at her.

'Do I mean nothing to you then?' He flung the words at her as she rode alongside. 'You do not even let me know you are coming to Aden. I have to hear from Government House.'

'Please slow down,' she said shakily. 'How can we talk like this?'

Sulkily he reined in his horse to walk again but said nothing, still staring ahead.

'Can't you see?' she went on. 'I didn't want to force a meeting on you. I felt you might not wish to see me again. Might not wish it at all.'

'Might not wish it!' he mocked. 'You take it all so lightly then? Yet you still wear that.' He pointed to the silver ring. She had transferred it to her right hand the day of her engagement to Martin. 'Even though you ran away from me at Cairo. Even though you threw away the life I had planned so carefully for us.'

'I had to,' she said in a low voice. 'It would have been half a life. Less than half. I wrote to you to explain. I wrote again about Martin.' They had come to a standstill again and sat facing one another.

'Writing! What is writing?' he retorted. 'You who said we belonged to each other, body and soul.'

'You who sent me away in the first place,' she whispered bitterly.

'But I came for you, didn't I? Came to England to fetch you away with our son. But it was not enough for you, was it? You had to turn to someone else in the end.' He bent his head. 'As for my own life.' He placed a hand over his eyes, as if all at once he was immensely weary. 'Everything I have worked for is breaking up around me. It seems I am a person who must always be betrayed. Even by those I most love.'

Rose could bear it no longer.

'You must stop!' she cried passionately. 'You must stop accusing me! How do you know what I am feeling? How do you know the things I've reproached myself for, over and over again, all these years?'

There was silence as they stared at each other, appalled at their power to inflict such pain on one another, now as then. With a sudden savage movement, he swung himself off his horse and walked up to her.

'Get down,' he said, taking hold of her reins. She saw entreaty on his face as he looked up at her. 'Rose,' he said. 'Oh, Rose.'

It was the first time he had spoken her name. To hear it again, with that hoarse, caressing inflection of his, moved her like nothing else. But she was angry still, and more than a little frightened.

'Why must I get down?' she asked, looking away.

He bent his head and lightly, ceremoniously, kissed her knee.

'Because I want to embrace you.'

Before she could move, he reached up and took her by the waist. Tense with misery, she felt herself resist, but he was too strong for her. With an awkward movement, she took her feet from the stirrups and half-fell against him. He held her fast, his arms wound around her, and she clung to him like a child.

'You're shaking so,' he whispered.

He stroked her hair and looked into her face. They kissed each other with tender gravity, and then again, more slowly.

'There,' he said. 'Isn't that better?'

She nodded, not trusting herself to speak, holding his hand against her cheek. The horses, meanwhile, had begun to stroll in search of the grass that grew in tufts at the edge of the dunes. With a curse, Hassan broke away in pursuit. She watched him tether them to an old thorn tree and saw how happiness gave him the look of a young man again. He came back to her and took her by the hand.

'We shall walk, just for a few minutes. Along the edge of the sea. It's something I always imagined us doing, the kind of thing we were never really free to do.'

He put his arm around her, pulling her close, so that their footprints merged in the wet sand.

'Poor Hassan and Rose,' she said gently. 'The star-crossed lovers. Always the obstacles ahead, always the barriers in our path. Never a proper future like other couples.'

'Except now, perhaps?' He stopped and looked at her.

'Now?' she echoed, taken by surprise.

'It is something we must talk about.'

'Not now, not yet.' She laid a finger across his mouth. 'Dear Hassan! Still so impatient. But today . . .' She took a deep breath, as if inhaling pure happiness. 'Today, let's just be free.'

He kissed her hand. 'There is one thing though. Nabiha. I told her you were in Aden. You would like to see her?'

'Nabiha!' How could she have forgotten? 'But I *must* see her, of course. Can we go now, on our way? The house is quite near here, isn't it?'

'That's what I thought.'

Back on their horses, Rose told him of the arrival of the contingent from Zara at Victoria Station, of meeting Abdullah again, of talking to Miriam.

'Your wife,' she reminded him, half-teasing. 'Don't forget Miriam. I may be a widow. But you are still a married man, are you not?'

'Rose, you know perfectly well that an Islamic marriage is totally different from yours in the West.' He spoke with more than a touch of exasperation. 'Ours was an arranged match. We made the best of it. But – how can I put it? – it does not cause us unhappiness to be apart. Miriam was determined to leave. She is a very nervous woman. It was a bad experience up in Zara and there will be worse. She is better with her people in London. I am in touch, of course . . .'

She cut him short. 'We talked about Idris, Hassan.'

'Aidrus!' He frowned.

'Hassan, I couldn't believe it. She told me she knew. She guessed whose child he was right from the start. And she didn't mind. She was happy to have him.'

'He was my child as well as yours,' Hassan said abruptly. There was a closed expression on his face Rose could not penetrate. 'It is all too long ago,' he went on. 'So much has happened since. You would not understand.'

'But you must tell me.'

They rode on without speaking for a moment, walking the horses. It was quite hot now and the only sounds were the creak of saddles, the jingle of harness, the soft regular plod of hooves in the sand.

'Let us say my son came to hate me, or rather to hate everything I represented. And then he broke my heart.' She heard him sigh. 'He went away. He was still very young. He had made friends in the Yemen, in Cairo, in Beirut – violent men, fanatical men. I have not seen him or heard from him since.'

'How long ago was that?'

He shrugged. 'Does it matter? Seven, eight years ago.'

A barrier had come up between them. It was the old one of East and West, and Rose knew it well. She would struggle against a blow of fate, or at least try to analyse it rationally. Hassan would simply accept it and turn away with that ingrained resignation that sometimes maddened her.

'You don't want to talk about him?'

'Please, Rose. He has gone from my life as he went from yours all that time ago. God has written it. We must accept. Besides, why do we make ourselves miserable, today of all days?'

They were coming to the track that led off from the beach to the oasis. 'Look.' He touched her arm gently, pointed to some low concrete buildings in the distance, where the light flashed on corrugated roofs. 'Do you remember what was over there?'

Rose felt her throat contract. 'The beach house. Our beach house. What have they done to it?' she demanded indignantly.

Hassan laughed. 'Was it some kind of national monument then? To be preserved for ever? I hate to tell you, but it's now a Ministry of Defence headquarters. A sign of the times, I'm afraid. This is where they train the British soldiers for desert warfare, poor fellows.'

They rode faster now and soon ahead of them Rose saw the familiar ochre-coloured front of Nabiha's house rising out of the trees. Just as clearly, she conjured up pictures of Nabiha in her elegant silks at the Races, in her old blue travelling robe at Zara and, most vivid of all, Nabiha in the chintz bedroom at Brown's Hotel, holding Idris against her shoulder, her handsome, haughty features suddenly soft with concern. Be prepared, Rose told herself. She is twenty years older than me and she has been very sick. Even so, she was shocked at the sight of the woman who waited for them at the gates. At first she took the stooping figure in a black purdah cloak to be one of the servants. But Hassan held up his hand warningly. 'She is almost blind,' he told Rose quickly as helped her to dismount. 'She wears the veil now to shade her eyes from the light. She finds it more comfortable than dark glasses.'

Rose was stricken. It seemed the cruelest of ironies that Nabiha, who had so daringly rejected purdah, should now have to return to it as a refuge. But before she could reply, Nabiha was standing before her. She was leaning on a silver-topped cane, her head cocked eagerly to one side.

'I know it is Rose,' she said. 'There is only one person in the world to whom Hassan speaks in that particular voice.'

In all the past forty-eight hours, it was the first time Rose had cried. But now she could not prevent tears springing as the two of them embraced. She tried to catch back her breath, but it was no use.

'Why not cry, Rose?' Nabiha murmured comfortingly, patting her shoulders. 'It is something women must do at a time like this. So many years gone by, so many things to remember.' She took her by the hand in the way she had always done. 'Come. We must go and sit down inside. With the blinds drawn I can take off my veil and be carefree.'

In the dimness of the drawing room, Hassan left them together for a few minutes. A servant brought tall glasses of iced lime juice and soda and Rose drank gratefully. Sitting opposite her, with her back to the half-light from the long shuttered windows, Nabiha still held her by the hand, patting it softly from time to time. The face she had uncovered was not so much lined as faded, like parchment. but somehow the light had gone out of it, now that the lustrous black of the eyes had turned to a glassy gray, unfocused and opaque. The change was chilling, as if a ghost looked out at you. But then she leaned forward eagerly to talk, that bubbling musical stream of words that Rose remembered so well, and she was transformed into Nabiha again.

'Imagine, Rose!' she said, bracelets tinkling as she wove her hands to and fro. 'To me, your face is just the faintest of blurs. So I cannot see if you are still beautiful. Is that not kind of fate?'

'Very kind.'

Nabiha reached out and touched her hair. 'It is still the colour of amber?'

'Sort of.' Rose was smiling, in command of herself again. 'Not as bright as yours, though.'

'Ah! I have made the journey to Mecca since you saw me last.' She fondled the thick reddish plait that lay beneath her spangled shawl. 'So now I may dye it with henna to show the world I am a holy woman.' She lowered her voice. 'And Hassan? He is still the most handsome man?'

'I think he is.'

'It is a miracle you have come back, Rose. I sometimes thought it might happen. You two . . .' she shook her head fondly. 'You two can never escape each other. It is the story of the two grains of sand, remember?'

'The sandstorm blew them apart. And when the wind died down, they found themselves on a different shore but together again, side by side.'

A look of sadness came over her face. 'But Aidrus, that little boy. Who could have foreseen?' She stopped herself, then bent closer to Rose. 'Hassan will not speak of him. He has tried to blot him out of his life. But I did not think this possible.'

'What do you mean?'

'I think that things are pulling them together, things we cannot yet see. There will come a time when they must confront each other. I cannot say more.' She laid her hand with its square-cut emerald ring across her breast. 'It is what I feel here.'

She turned her head. She had heard Hassan's steps before Rose did.

'And so now we are both widows,' she was saying as he came into the room. 'You are lonely, Rose?'

'I live on my own but I am not really lonely. I have my books and my garden, and my friends of course. I have a daughter not far away.'

'Why do you not live with them?'

Rose smiled. 'It is not our custom. Besides, I like my own house. It's so peaceful up in the mountains in Wales, like Zara.'

'Like Zara was.' Hassan was standing behind her. She was painfully aware of his exclusion from the life she was describing. There were no corresponding pictures in his mind of the house wrapped in snow with the river below. Perhaps he felt it too, for there was a sharpness in his tone, as he went on. 'You wanted to use the telephone? It's in the hall.'

'Oh yes. Thank you.'

In the doorway she said to him, 'When the film people hear I am going to Jehal, they will want to come too.'

He thought for a moment, then gave a nod. 'Very well. If you wish it. But not until tomorrow.' He touched her cheek. 'Tell them ten o'clock at the frontier. I will send an escort.'

She could tell Mike was pleased from the tone of his voice.

'And the Air Vice-Marshal's offered us a flight over the Yemen border later in the week. I met him last night.'

'Even better.' He paused. 'You're with friends today, I take it.'

309

'If that's all right.'

'Okay. I'll do the souk then – dissident carpet sellers and all that. Jenny can take notes. Till tomorrow then.'

The conversation with the Governor was not so easy, though the relief in his voice was unmistakeable.

'I was worried about you, especially after last night. All the bearer could tell me was that one of the Sultan's servants had brought a horse round for you.' Then, with a note of forced jollity, 'His Highness hasn't abducted you, has he?'

'Actually, Jimmy, the message was to say that Nabiha Fauzi wanted to see me. She's an old friend and she's been very ill, so it was difficult to refuse.'

She ran her finger along the dusting of sand beneath the phone, remembering those morning calls of Hassan's. Now he was standing close beside her and she could think of nothing else, only the need to be with him.

'So you'll be back for lunch,' Ferguson was saying.

'Well as a matter of fact, the Sultan is here at Nabiha's and he's invited me to make a trip to the palace.'

'At Jehal?' There was a pause. 'Most unwise. It's in the danger zone, you know. You're out of our hands, I'm afraid, once you cross the frontier.'

'Oh, I think I can rely on his protection, don't you?' she said easily. 'And he's arranged for the rest of the team to join us. So it's quite an opportunity, isn't it?'

'Be it on your own head, then,' he said in a cold voice. 'If you're determined to be the intrepid reporter. Which reminds me, your flight with the Air Vice-Marshal's off, I'm afraid. He rang and had a word with me. Seems he's got cold feet about the idea. Wouldn't say much, just something about you being a "security risk". God knows why. Waffling on about "past connections", whatever that means. Anyway, I have to go now. Leg. Co. meeting. Keep in touch, though,' he added.

'I will, and thank you for being so understanding.'

There was another pause. 'Be careful,' he said as he put down the phone.

She turned round to find Hassan watching her, leaning against the wall with folded arms.

'Why are you smiling?' she asked him.

'Just that I see a new Rose. Rose the journalist, Rose the famous writer. Perhaps you are a Mata Hari too, on a secret mission to spy on me for your precious Government.'

Rose laughed. There was an unmistakeable touch of jealousy in his manner, something she remembered from the past.

'Who have you been talking to, Rose?' came Nabiha's voice, slightly querulous. 'Lunch is waiting.'

'It's my work,' Rose told her, going in quickly to sit beside her. Trays of delicious cold food had been placed on low tables in front of the divans, stuffed aubergines and prawns, and bamyia figs. 'That's why I'm here at all, you see.'

She began to eat and saw that Hassan was as hungry as she was.

'What are you writing about us?' Nabiha wanted to know. 'I hope you will say how we want the British to stay. How we must not be deserted and left to the mercy of the young riff-raff who want to run the country for themselves.'

Rose looked across at Hassan. He raised his eyebrows as if to say, 'This is the other side of the coin, you see. This is the split I am trying to tell you about.'

'I expect that will all come into the story,' Rose reassured her.

'In Aden itself, everything is peaceful,' Nabiha went on. 'Why do you not stay here with me? It is where your heart is, surely? Here I am, alone in this great place. You can live here and write your books. And be with Hassan too.' She nodded, smiling. 'This is his house too, whenever he needs it. He knows that.'

'Oh, Nabiha,' she said, laying her head on her friend's shoulder. 'Why are you still so kind to me?' She saw Hassan looking at her intently. 'Perhaps I could stay for a bit, anyway. Not go back to England straight away.'

'In'Shallah, in'Shallah. It is in your hand. The two grains of sand, remember?'

'I remember.' Rose saw that she was suddenly looking exhausted. 'But we have to go.'

'And Rose,' Nabiha whispered, as she kissed her goodbye, 'don't let it all slip away this time. Hold on to what fate has given you back. It will not come again.'

9

'NABIHA loves us dearly,' Hassan said, as they rode away. 'But she does not understand what is happening in this country. She is living in the past.'

'Perhaps she's lucky. When she was talking about me staying on in that house with her . . .' She reached out for Hassan's hand and they looked at one another. 'I had this picture of how it might have been, or rather could never be. A sort of dream life, cut off from the outside world, nothing changing, like the palace of the Sleeping Beauty with Nabiha as fairy godmother . . .'

'And would I have to cut my way through the brambles every time I came to wake you with a kiss?'

They were in the roadway now and they drew apart as a party of Bedouin came past, driving their laden camels into Aden market. Dust swirled up behind them and fragments of their loud chattering voices followed Rose and Hassan as they rode on.

'Their life doesn't change. If you're a nomad, you just keep moving on, taking your own world with you.' There was a note of envy in Hassan's voice. 'For the rest of us, though, I look ahead and see nothing but unrest, hatred and violence. Not just here in Aden, but everywhere in the Middle East. It is the legacy of history. Who knows who the survivors will be?'

Rose was looking ahead. Through the palm trees she had seen a flat rooftop, a glimpse of white walls with green shutters. The sight struck her like a blow. She had almost forgotten.

'We pass your old house this way,' Hassan was saying. 'Do you mind?'

She swallowed hard and gave her horse a little kick. 'Not if you are with me.'

'The Air Vice-Marshal lives there now. A stupid man, dreadful couple.'

'I know.'

'If someone sees us, there'll be talk, of course.'

'There always was.'

'Even worse, they might invite us in.' He smiled at her conspiratorially. 'If we go past at a gallop, though?'

Rose nodded. They had almost reached the end of the drive. Hassan's horse leaped on ahead, but hers was slow to follow. The gate stood open.

The thick shrubs and the overhanging jasmine had all been cut away and there was a clear view of the house.

Some unimaginable impulse made her pull hard on the reins. For one brief moment she needed to confront the place that had haunted her for so long, dreaming and awake. The horse beneath her shuddered, rearing its head as it came to a standstill. Rose was trembling too. Sand flies darted and whined about her hands and face. But she remained quite still, half-hidden by a tall acacia tree, staring out of the shadows towards the steps that led up to the porch.

In that instant, Geoffrey stood there, facing her, in the doorway. The image was so real, she could smell the whisky on his breath and the sour tang of his sweat. Fear had a smell too. Even now she could catch the sickening whiff of it. She closed her eyes, then opening them again saw herself look out from the upstairs balcony, dreading the moment when he turned into the drive in the rattling army gharry. On the flat roof above, there was the pagoda with its painted trelliswork where a night-lamp would throw huge shadows on the canvas screens.

She wanted to move away, move away fast. But, caught in the past, she and the horse seemed to be turned to stone. Then she heard Hassan's voice.

'Rose! What are you doing? Come on!'

Simultaneously other voices broke in on her. From the direction of the ground-floor verandah, she heard the unmistakeable tones of English women, upraised with that shrill memsahibs' edge and punctuated by laughter. An immediate picture came into her mind of Mary Hall and her friends gathered for their morning session of mah-jongg, the cigarette smoke and the gossip, the cups of iced coffee on the polished mahogany side tables, the Constable prints on the walls to remind them of home. No doubt their hostess had been regaling them with a description of her encounter with Lady Foster, alias Rose Chetwynd. At any moment they might appear, making their farewells.

'Is something wrong?' Hassan was at her side, taking hold of the horse's bridle. 'Are you unwell?'

At his touch, they moved on. A guard in tribal uniform had appeared from the *chokida*'s hut beneath the trees. He stood watching them as they rode away, obviously puzzled.

'I'm sorry,' Rose said breathlessly. She was still trembling and her forehead was wet with perspiration as if she had just come out of a fever. 'It was the house. Stupid of me.' She turned to Hassan. 'I haven't thought of Geoffrey for so long. Then all at once, he was there. I'm sorry,' she said again.

'Poor Rose.' He rode close alongside protectively, brushing against her. 'I should have thought.'

'The past never really goes away, does it?' she said quietly. 'Just last night . . .' She broke off, biting her lip.

'What happened?' He glanced at her, disturbed.

'Something silly, really. You remember that awful bearer of Geoffrey's, the one who got the boys for him? The one who hated me so much?'

Hassan had stopped and was staring at her. 'Go on.'

'Well, he was there at the Club. He recognized me and all of a sudden he just – just went for me. It was all right,' she went on quickly, seeing Hassan's expression. 'No harm done. He's mad anyway, apparently. He's safely under lock and key now. But it was something he said that was worse, a kind of threat.'

'He threatened you?' Hassan's face was suddenly wild with rage. 'And you only tell me now?'

'Darling, it's all over now. And it was nothing he was going to do to me. More like something that was going to happen anyway.' She laughed, trying to make light of it. 'A dire prophecy, like the witches in *Macbeth*.'

He looked so comically puzzled by this, she laughed again. She was going on to tell him about the Air Vice-Marshal's wife, then stopped herself. What was the point? Besides, they had reached the frontier post, and the two Jehal soldiers on duty were saluting gravely. The young *syce* was waiting for them too. As they dismounted, he took the horses off on a leading rein with his own while Rose and Hassan got into the car that was parked alongside, in the shade.

'Do you remember the old Sedanca?' she said.

'It lasted us for years. But I think the Chevrolet goes better over the desert.'

'Still the same green. Still the same flag on the bonnet.'

'Of course.'

The chauffeur's back was very close. But they were content now not to talk, simply to sit close to one another, their hands linked under the brightly striped dust-sheet that lay across their knees. Rose was remembering all those other journeys to Jehal, the car ploughing across the sandy furrows like a boat against the tide. Village houses and oasis plantations were magically conjured up out of the expanse of desert as the miles fell behind. Not far from the old township, Hassan became restless, drumming his fingers against the upholstery, turning to look out from one side to the other.

'You will find changes at Jehal,' he said suddenly. 'It's best to tell you before we get there.'

'Tell me then.'

314

'A great many of the palace people have run away. Just a few days ago I had what you might call a visit from the revolutionaries. They'd infiltrated from the Yemen. They're the ones who are causing all the trouble up on the border.'

'Who are they exactly?'

'They call themselves the Sons of the New Islam – Palestinian refugees, Egyptian intellectuals, Yemeni mercenaries – anyone with a grievance against the old order, against the British in particular. They preach a rather lethal cocktail of *Das Kapital* and the Koran. Unfortunately they've acquired arms and money. So they're good at persuading the tribes to defect. When they made their swoop down here, they mostly just frightened people away. As you know I have no army of my own, and it wasn't that kind of attack. More like a demonstration of intent.'

'You were here at the time?'

He shook his head. 'Alas, no. Otherwise they wouldn't have dared. As it was, they simply took the place by surprise. Then when they'd finished they left again as quickly as they'd come.'

Rose was staring out at the narrow streets and alleys. It was the bazaar quarter, normally thronged with people. But today the place was strangely quiet, with closed shutters and only a few passers-by who lounged on the corners with a sullen, intimidated air.

'But what did they actually do?' she asked.

'You'll see. I think it was meant to show me the writing on the wall. Literally.' He pointed to the front of the palace as it came into view. On either side of the tall iron gates, the walls had been daubed with slogans in scarlet paint. Rose leaned forward with an exclamation of disbelief.

'They're the usual things,' he went on. 'Power to the People. Death to the British Infidels. Oh, and something a bit differet – Sultan Hassan Puppet of the Imperialists.'

Two guards in shabby khaki saluted the car as it approached. The gates swung open and they drove through into the courtyard. Getting out behind Hassan and looking around her, Rose could not believe where she was. In her mind there was a clear picture of the place as it used to be, a rich mosaic of overlapping beds of flowers, white oleander and crimson bougainvillea, tall shrub roses and the golden lilies in Persian pots that had been the pride of the Jehal gardeners. Now it was a desert, scattered with the remnants of torn-up plants and broken tiles. The central fountain had been totally smashed. Only a rusty trickle ran out over the paving stones where a small boy in ragged shorts was disconsolately raking up the debris.

315

'Can it ever be the same again?' Rose murmured. She felt suddenly sick with apprehension.

Hassan was silent. Following him on to the lawns, she caught her breath. In the centre of the grass a huge fire had been burning, and amongst the ashes there were the remains of what looked like pictures. She stirred the charred canvas with her foot. Hassan's face stared up at her from under the broken glass and she moved back, shaken.

'Your portrait.'

He nodded. 'They burned all the pictures, right back to my early ancestors. To make a human likeness is against Koranic law, they say. I believe this was just brute vandalism.'

He turned on his heel. 'I told the servants to have it all cleared up before I returned. But of course, there are no servants. Except for one or two of the faithful.' His voice softened. An old man in a white tunic had come stooping down the steps and now greeted them both in turn with a shaky salaam.

'You remember Abdul,' Hassan said to Rose. 'He was only a gardener in your day. Now he looks after us all, eh, old man?'

Abdul's face wrinkled up into a grin. '*Salaam walaikum.*'

'*Salaam, Abdul.*'

Shuffling ahead, the old man led the way inside through to the main salon. The heavy English furniture was still in place but there was a forlorn look about every room. Curtains hung soiled and torn and the walls were stripped bare. Rose looked in vain for the silver swords and the great curved daggers that used to hang along the corridors. Strangest of all was to see bare floorboards with only the occasional Bedouin rug for covering.

'The carpets,' Hassan said in a low voice. 'That is the saddest thing. You remember the great Persians and Afghans, very old and faded but still so beautiful, every one with a story of the past in the patterns. Abdul wept when he told me. It seems they didn't just take them as loot, they actually cut them up into pieces with knives. Divided them into strips so that there was one for each man.' He bent his head away from her. 'It is the age of the barbarians, Rose.'

Rose was examining a broken window. 'And this?'

'That's the work of the other barbarians. The next morning the British sent in an army contingent, to protect my property, they said. They were showing the flag by way of discouraging future assaults. It was only a two-day exercise, but this part of the garden outside was turned into a football pitch.'

At this point the old man drew him aside and they exchanged a few words. Hassan turned back to her.

'Rose, I must see some people. There's a deputation from my state council and I need to talk with them.'

'Of course.'

'So Abdul will show you to one of the guest rooms, part of our modern improvements.' He smiled grimly. 'I don't think my visitors were interested in that part of the palace. Abdul will bring you some tea and you can rest for a bit.'

As he left, he touched her elbow. 'Don't forget to dream.'

It was one of the little phrases they used between themselves. Rose had forgotten it but now she thought of all the times it had passed between them before long journeys of separation, after stolen meetings at the beach house and chance encounters at official receptions. She lay down on the brand-new bedspread with its Marshall and Snelgrove price label still intact and closed her eyes. She did not care for this anonymous suite with its chintz-covered chairs and pastel bathroom. But it was cool and quiet and when she woke she discovered she had slept for almost two hours.

A tap on the door revealed Abdul with towels on his arm.

'Bath?' he suggested.

'Thank you.'

'Then Sultan say take you to the water gardens.'

Even though she would have to get back into the clothes she was wearing, at least she could get rid of the dust and sweat of the day's travel. Perhaps tomorrow she could borrow a shirt of Hassan's.

As for the water gardens, that remained a mystery. Then, walking with Abdul across the terrace at the back of the palace, she realized they were following the path through the date plantation. It was the place where she and Eleanor Rawlinson had been entertained by the young Emir and his father to a picnic lunch, complete with family silver and the Jehal brass band playing 'The Blue Danube'.

By now the sun had gone down. At the end of the path, the last golden streamers of light fell across an overgrown lawn that had once been the tennis court. Here Abdul left her, pointing towards the old summerhouse at the far end. Framed in the doorway sat Hassan, cross-legged on a rug. He was wearing his turban now and some kind of loose tunic and trousers. He looked to Rose almost exactly like his father, just as she remembered him, playing his board game in the dappled shade, waiting for his guests to arrive.

And she, Rose. How did she look to Hassan, she wondered as she made her way across the grass? She was suddenly nervous at the strangeness of it all, this dream-like sense of time repeating itself.

As if in response, he called out to her.

317

'Stand still for a moment, Rose.'

She obeyed, smiling back at him. 'What is it?'

'Nothing,' he said as she came on towards him. 'Just that you could have been that girl all over again. The strange young English woman with the bright green eyes that always seemed to demand an answer.'

'An answer to what?' She sat down close to him. He handed her a glass of mango juice from the tray beside him.

'The question we were both asking ourselves. Do you feel what I feel?'

'You were on the path ahead of me and you turned to look back at me. That was the first moment, wasn't it?'

'That we knew we were in love? No, I think I knew it when I rescued you at Port Said, you and that adventurous friend of yours. What was her name?'

'Cynthia. And then there was the Birthday Parade, sitting next to you.'

They had done this before, many times, counting the steps along the way together. Every now and then one of them said, 'We were crazy,' or 'We were so brave, you know.'

'And we still are?' Hassan asked.

'It seems so.'

A sudden clap broke through the stillness. Startled, they both looked up. A wood dove flew out of the mango trees above their heads.

'There were always pigeons,' Rose said dreamily.

'Pigeon-shoots too, in the old days. And the games of polo and the tennis parties with the English guests. All gone.' He sighed, looking across to where the remains of a tennis net hung like a huge cobweb from the broken posts. 'It's partly my fault, I suppose. Perhaps I've been spending too much time in Aden. There have been so many meetings with Government lately, conferences with the various Arab organizations, all trying to thrash out some sort of compromise. Not very successfully, I'm afraid.'

His voice dropped. For a moment Rose caught an expression of bitter regret on his face. She saw him struggle to hide it.

'It was different for my father,' he went on. 'He simply lived the quiet life on his estates, like one of your country squires.'

'You still shoot, though?' She pointed to a row of battered bull's-eye boards hanging in the bushes nearby. 'Target practice, anyway.'

'Not me. The Sons of New Islam, getting their aim in for the next uprising. I told you they were well equipped. They actually had the nerve to leave a cache of Russian rifles hidden away in the cellars.' He swore softly under his breath, then reached out and stroked back her hair. 'But you don't want to hear any more of all this.'

Rose said nothing. Once again she had the feeling he was holding something back from her, unwilling to change the mood of the evening. Dusk was falling now, so swiftly you could almost see the particles of darkness sifting down around them out of the fading sky. They stirred as a lantern came slowly towards them.

'Here's Abdul to tell us dinner is ready.'

Hand in hand they followed the old man down a narrow side path. 'He said water gardens,' Rose murmured to Hassan. 'Is there really water here, from the oasis?'

'From the pipes,' he corrected her. 'You remember that mad Russian engineer who was busy constructing a water supply to the palace? It was my father's pride and joy. Well, it appears there was some to spare so they put up a fountain and a waterfall on the way. Not surprisingly that didn't last long. But the name still sticks. Sounds grand, doesn't it? In fact' – he waved towards the clearing ahead – 'it's just the same old picnic place. I know you like picnics. All you English do.'

A circle of lamps stood on the ground, casting a yellow glow on the darkness of the surrounding shrubberies. White jasmine flowers shone out like tiny stars, loosing waves of perfume into the warm air. In the centre stood a long table, covered in a white damask cloth. It was laid for two, with a small gilt chair at either end. A crystal bowl of tiny pink Jehal roses had been placed in the centre, flanked by silver candelabra. The air was so still the flames from the candles barely flickered. Another more acrid scent rose up from the mosquito coils standing in the saucers beneath the chairs and sending up wisps of slow-burning smoke.

'Abdul thinks of everything,' Hassan said, as they both sat down. 'The mosquitoes here can be quite bad in the early evening, especially when they scent fresh English blood.'

Rose was still spellbound by the setting. Everything glowed inside that magical circle and she could feel her whole self glowing too.

'It's beautiful, Hassan. You're a genie of some kind.'

He bowed towards her with a flourish.

'Eat,' he commanded, indicating the array of dishes now being laid out by Abdul and the two young boys. Saffron rice with cashew nuts and okra, nuggets of lamb glazed with honey, tiny roasted quails on a bed of grapes. In the background, Rose could see a fat black woman in a long red shift, outlined against the embers of the charcoal brazier, as she slapped down pancake bread on to the hot stone.

'She's a relation of Ayesha from Zara?'

Hassan nodded. 'Her daughter.'

'Tell her I saw her mother in London. She sends her love.'

He put down his skewer of lamb and beckoned to the woman. She came over and unselfconsciously squatted beside him, her face shining with pleasure and the heat of the fire as he relayed Rose's report to her. Then she waddled over to kiss Rose's hand and the exclamations and questions continued, until she remembered to rescue the bread from burning.

Halfway through the meal, Hassan sprang to his feet.

'There's no brass band any more. But you may prefer this.'

On a trestle table behind him was an old-fashioned wind-up gramophone. He put on a pair of glasses to study the stack of records alongside – a gesture which caught Rose unawares. It seemed so incongruous, like part of a disguise, that she found herself smiling.

'Does he make you laugh then, this old slave?' Hassan demanded. He had put on a Louis Armstrong recording of 'St James Infirmary Blues', and was leaning back in his chair again, smiling back at her lazily. 'I like him so much. He reminds me of one of the old servants, who used to sing to us when we were children.'

'Was it a good childhood?'

'A very good childhood, although my father had me beaten regularly, especially when I hadn't learned my Koran.'

But they had talked too much of the past, he said. Now as they drank their coffee he wanted to know about her life in Wales. Had she mourned her husband greatly? Had he been kind to her? A good lover? And so, inevitably, the way led back again to their own past, and the parting at Cairo station.

'Did I really make you so unhappy?' he asked her. 'So unhappy you had to end it all there and then, and find a nice Englishman instead?'

Rose watched the candlelight play over the curving Oriental planes of his face. He had taken off his glasses, and those long heavy-lidded eyes were studying her intently.

'It's just that I had so little of you. It wasn't enough . . .'

She broke off, feeling herself blush. 'Look at us,' she went on in a low voice. 'Sitting here so elegantly, at either end of the table, waited on hand and foot. It's hardly the place for confidences.'

'So. It is time to go inside. You want more coffee?'

She shook her head. Leaving the servants to their own meal around the fire, he picked up one of the lamps and led the way out of the clearing. On the path he put his arm lightly around her as they walked towards the palace. Neither of them spoke until they came to the steps that led on to the terrace at the back of the house. Rose looked up at the top-floor balcony, screened with trelliswork, and experienced a shock of recognition.

'The harem quarters. The women still live there?'

'No one is there now. They have all gone away.'

Rose was standing at the entrance, her hand on the bell-rope with the old iron ring at the end of it. Something about the place still stirred her imagination. She shivered.

'I came here that day with Lady Rawlinson. I was very nervous, very excited. I didn't know what to expect.'

Hassan did not reply, but with one hand pushed the door open. Out of the shadows the wide old stairway could be seen. She went up slowly, ahead of Hassan, the lamplight throwing long shadows on the carved banister rail and the dark red walls. At the top there was still the same little gate to keep the children in, where a small boy with jam on his face had peered out to watch the two strange English ladies arriving.

Carefully she put her hand on the latch, heard the answering creak as it opened before her and she found herself in the long salon. The shutters were closed. The heavily-scented air hung warm and undisturbed. Incense was in it, and sandalwood and half-a-dozen musky French perfumes of the kind beloved by Arab women. It was as if they were all still there, hidden behind the long silk curtains and the fretted screens, waiting only for the sound of the flutes and the drums to bring them out for the dance. In a place that was never silent, the stillness was unnerving. Rose remembered especially the sound of twittering voices she had first heard as she glanced up from the terrace with Eleanor Rawlinson, wondering if the creeper-clad lattices had concealed some kind of aviary. Now she stood in the centre of what looked like a deserted ballroom, peering around at the old-fashioned plush sofas that lined the walls, the low mosaic tables alongside for the tiny coffee-cups and the tall glasses of lime juice in their silver holders.

'Nothing has changed.' She was whispering, like an intruder.

'The rebels didn't touch this place,' Hassan said, behind her. 'No good Muslim would dare to defile a harem, and these people are religious fanatics. But the women didn't wait to find out. They made off for Aden with the children and servants in the middle of the night, and they'll stay there until things die down a bit.'

'And will they?' Rose asked. 'Die down, I mean.'

'This time, yes. But next time . . .' He shrugged. 'Who knows?'

He put the lantern down next to one of the couches and they sat facing each other, like polite visitors.

'This is where I first met Nabiha,' Rose said. 'And here I sat next to your mother, trying to think of the right things to say.'

Very gently he touched her hand. 'Does it seem so unreal, us being together again like this?'

Rose paused for a moment, staring down at his hand on hers.

'No. Somehow the opposite. The real part of my life has always been you.' She hesitated again, searching for words. 'How to explain? It's as if there have always been these two streams, forking away in different directions, one in the open, the other underground. The open one is my everyday self that has gone about its normal business for the last thirty years, packing and unpacking in different houses, looking after my family, making sensible conversation with my friends, loving my husband in a quiet comfortable sort of way.

'And then,' she went on, turning to look at Hassan, 'there is the other self, the secret, hidden me that feeds on everything we have ever done or said together. That is where the real core of my life has always seemed to be. Everything that's true or vital seems to belong there, locked in the dark, but circling through me, giving me life in a way.' She placed his hand over her heart, feeling the warmth of it through her shirt. 'It's the self that belongs to you, Hassan. You created it, you see. We each of us were what the other made us, I suppose.' She bent her head, suddenly overcome. 'Goodness, what a long speech. Sorry.'

He put his hand under her chin, forcing her to meet his eyes again.

'What you are saying is that you love me. You always have and you still do.'

'Yes,' she said meekly.

'As I love you?'

'Yes.'

'Good.' He brought her face to his and kissed her, not searchingly as on the beach, but with a swift sureness that seemed to seal a pact. 'But Rose, this underground stream of ours.' He said it almost teasingly. 'Is it not out in the open air at last? There's nothing left to divide us, or to keep secret any more.'

She was puzzled. 'It's not so simple, Hassan. We still have to live in different worlds.'

He got up and began to walk up and down. He had taken off his shoes and she watched him pad over the carpets with that long graceful stride of his, turning on his heel to come back to her as if he were in some kind of cage.

'Now we must be practical.' He darted a look at her as he spoke. 'I have not been quite honest with you over my circumstances. Nor with Nabiha, either.'

'What is it?' She felt suddenly torn with apprehension, as if, once again, something was to take him from her there and then.

'The cache of arms I told you about. It was discovered by the British and I was accused of collusion. They seem to think I'm secretly plotting some kind of combined coup with the militants. I think it was the last straw as far as the Colonial Office are concerned. They need a scapegoat and I'm the ideal victim. Even the fact that I've offered to mediate between the rebels and Government is regarded as highly suspect. "A foot in both camps," is how they put it. "Nationalist sympathies" is another useful phrase. As if any true Arab could not have hopes for nationhood as opposed to some alien Colonial regime.'

As she listened, the Governor's words came back to her. 'How can you trust a man whose son is a traitor.'

'But that's ridiculous,' she said lamely.

He sighed. 'Rose, you don't understand. The British have never trusted me. Now is their chance to replace me with a nice tame Sultan who'll do exactly what they want. As it happens I have a cousin who's perfect for the job – a really stupid man who only thinks of horse-breeding and can't wait to get his hands on my estate.'

Rose was appalled. 'Can Government do that? What will happen?'

'They have the ultimate power. After all, Jehal state is part of the Protectorate, subject to Government edict. So on grounds of conspiracy, first they depose me, and then they deport me, in as polite and gentlemanly a fashion as possible, of course. It's the traditional method of dealing with uncooperative rulers. The point us, I hear from my contacts that it's to be put into operation very soon. Within the next few weeks, possibly.'

By now, she was totally bewildered. 'But Hassan, what will you do?'

'Go into exile, like so many others. In a way, I've been expecting it. I think I lost heart some time ago.'

How had he kept these charged emotions concealed from her until now, she wondered? Just as swiftly though, his expression changed again. With a new air of elation he came over to where she sat and crouched at her side, taking hold of her hands.

'But Rose, this is the extraordinary thing! Just as I am facing this calamity, out of the blue you come back to me. I may not be as strictly religious as these fanatics up on the border but there is one saying of the Prophet's I have to believe with all my heart. It is written that Allah is merciful. While he takes away with one hand, he gives with the other.' He stared at her with the wide, brilliant eyes of a twenty-year-old. 'This gift is you. And this time I'm keeping it.'

She couldn't help smiling. 'So am I to be wife number two? I know you're allowed four, but maybe you'll be content with just Miriam and myself.'

He frowned. 'You always joke about this thing. It is very English, very irritating. Please be serious.'

She pressed her thumb between his eyebrows. 'Don't be cross. I am serious. I know we'd be happy together, but where? What about Miriam? What about my own commitments in Wales?'

Even as she spoke she had a picture of him in the crowded little flat in the Edgware Road, staring out at the smoky London streets. Even more strange, she saw him walking down the muddy lane to the farm in Burberry and boots, on his way to collect the milk from a bemused Davy Evans.

'It's quite simple,' Hassan broke in eagerly. 'For a few months each year, you go back to Wales and I go back to Miriam.'

'And then? Not Cairo again?'

He took her by the shoulders and shook her with mock exasperation.

'Do you think I am still the same provincial young man? My frontiers have extended a little in the last thirty years. You remember me telling you, even then, how much I loved Italy?'

'I do remember,' she protested, trying to wriggle from his grip.

'Well, last year, a merchant friend of mine from Alexandria told me he was selling a place in Positano. Not a grand villa. Just a small house, overlooking the bay. He thought I should buy it. He said he could see trouble coming in the Middle East, just as I could. So I bought it. It was all the capital I had left, after setting up the family in London. But at least it is my own. What do you say, Rose?' He looked at her questioningly. 'Romantic, you must admit, that view over the Mediterranean. Even though it's not the Arabian Nights palace you always wanted.'

'I never wanted . . .' Rose expostulated, before she realized he was teasing her. He leaned over her, putting his hand across her mouth, pressing her down against the cushions. As he drew the length of her body against his own, all her uncertainties flew away. Gently he took his hand away to kiss her.

'Wherever we are is home,' she said in a whisper. She turned her head, looking around at the long shadowy room so full of memories. 'Can we go to bed now? A proper bed?'

He broke out laughing, then stopped and quickly put his finger to his lips.

'Hush! I thought I heard someone.'

Both lay rigid, listening. Rose could feel his heart hammering against her own. Then they heard a voice calling up faintly from outside, Abdul's voice.

'Sultan sahib. Is that you up there?'

'He's seen the light. Perhaps he thinks there may be intruders again.' Raising his voice, he called back.

'Yes, Abdul. It's me. Is anything wrong?'

'Message come for you, Highness.'

'Damn.' He hesitated. 'I'd better go down. You wait here.' He looked down at her. 'Just as you are. I shall be straight back.'

He took the lamp with him. Closing her eyes against the darkness, Rose was suddenly afraid, aware of how fragile their happiness was. She had a sense of powerful forces conspiring against them. She turned on her side and shivered. Threat was in the very air around her, though the shape and direction of it was impossible to define.

Hassan was only away for a few mintues. When he came back, she reached out for him, clinging tight.

'You're trembling,' he said. 'You must be feeling guilty, Lady Foster.'

But she recognized the forced lightness of his voice.

'What is it, Hassan?' She searched his face in the lamplight. His eyelids were lowered and he seemed absorbed in tracing the thin silver chain round her throat, with its moon pendant hanging below.

'Nothing. One of those notes.'

'What notes?'

'Anonymous. Unpleasant. I've destroyed it.'

But the feeling of foreboding would not go away.

'Hassan, please.'

'No more questions.' He pulled her to her feet. She heard the quick intake of his breath, as he pressed her to him. 'We have better things to think about. Here and now is all that matters.'

He picked up the lantern again. Taking her by the hand, he led her down the room. Long mirrors lined the walls and as they went by, Rose caught the glimmer of their reflections moving side by side, like ghosts.

Then the mirrors ended. Hassan was holding back the heavy curtain for her to pass through into the inner rooms. It fell behind them. On the other side, there were no ghosts, only warm flesh and blood, darkness and each other.

❧ 10 ❧

AT first, standing together on the balcony next morning, they thought it was the sound of an oncoming storm. It was the time of year for the *khamsin*, the seasonal wind that gusted in from the Empty Quarter, driving sheets of hot sand like smoke across the parched landscapes for days on end. The sky had a leaden stillness about it, and from somewhere to the east there came a low, rumbling vibration, faint at first, then steadily growing louder.

Hassan leaned forward intently.

'That's not a thunderstorm. It's a plane. Can you see it?'

Both scanned the clouds lying low on the horizon.

'There!' Rose pointed to a glint of grey above the palm trees. 'It's coming from Aden. RAF maybe?'

'Too small. Looks more like a private plane.'

'Do you often get them over this way?'

He shook his head. They both felt a rising unease. They were prepared for the arrival of Mike Farrow and the others by car from the frontier soon after ten. But it was little more than eight and they had only just finished breakfast, which had been laid out by Abdul in the dining room behind. This time alone together was even more precious, now there were so many things to be decided. Besides, last night still hung about them, holding back the outside world. Coming together again, discovering they were still the same two people beneath all the changes the world had inflicted on them, had been an experience of such intensity it made everything else seem quite unreal.

'It's like being in a state of shock,' Hassan had said.

'Or convalescing,' Rose suggested, stretching out to feel the delicious weakness, almost forgotten, of the aftermath of long love-making. Lying together at dawn in that dusty scented bedroom, stealing out to walk in the gardens, it had seemed to Rose that they had fallen in love all over again. They would stare at each other unspeaking, then break out into disconnected sentences, struggle against tears suddenly, then laugh out loud for no reason, and all the time they had to reach out and touch one another quickly, tenderly, as if the delight of each other's presence was still something not quite to be believed. It was very hard to move away

326

from each other, out of touch. When they went back to their separate rooms, their thoughts went on entangling, meshing together with the old closeness.

'Look, we have come through,' Rose said, half to herself. They had bathed and changed, Hassan into an old beach-coat while she had found for herself a loose cotton robe from the harem, faded turquoise with white embroidered crescent moons at the neck. Now they were standing together in that corner of the balcony where Hassan had first reached out to take her hand, the evening after the picnic.

'We have come through,' she murmured again.

'More poetry?'

'Whitman or Lawrence. I can't remember which. But it keeps running through my mind. It's true, isn't it?'

'It's true.'

He laced his fingers in hers. The brown gloss of that supple Oriental hand against her cold-looking English skin was something that had always fascinated her. Half fearfully, she looked up at the face so close to hers in the morning light and saw marks of age she had not noticed before. The faint dark pouches beneath his eyes and the slackening skin of the jawline caused her a pang of sadness that was physical. All at once he seemed to her unbearably vulnerable. And yet there was a curious fellow-feeling about this sadness, as she thought of the changes in herself, the start of a new line here, another grey hair there, all the tiny inexorable prints of time passing.

'Are you a religious man, Hassan?'

He did not answer at first but went on steadily looking into her eyes.

'I go to the mosque. I say my prayers,' he replied slowly. 'And I shall love you till the day I die. That is my religion.'

The sound of the plane made them look away. It was louder now as it whirred and circled towards them like some threatening insect. Then it disappeared behind the greenery of the oasis. After a minute, the engines died away.

Hassan went to the door.

'I'd better tell Ali to take the car over.'

Inside the dining room, Rose poured herself another cup of coffee. She was suddenly tense with apprehension. When Hassan came back, she read the same thing in his face.

'I expect it's Farrow and the crew.' She touched his arm reassuringly. 'Some change of plan.'

'We'd better get dressed, whoever it is.' He forced a smile. 'Otherwise your reputation will be in question yet again, Lady Foster.'

As she passed him to go to her room, he took her by the waist almost roughly.

'Remember, Rose, whatever happens today, we have plans to make. Urgent plans if we're to get away next week.'

'How can I forget?' She put her hand against his cheek. 'In the meantime, I need to borrow a clean shirt. A nice one, please, as we have visitors.'

Changing in her room, she thought of what he had told her last night. He wanted to be abroad when the official summons came from Government House requiring him to relinquish his title. It would at least be more dignified, he explained, to be out of the country by choice rather than to be sent out by the British. Besides, the situation was worsening daily and he now feared for her safety if she stayed on indefinitely. They must seize the chance and leave for Italy as soon as possible. Could she? Would she?

Of course she had agreed. Instead of returning to London with the others, she would stay on with Nabiha for just a few days. Government House was now out of the question. Then she would fly out to Rome where Hassan would meet her, and together they would drive down to his house at Positano.

That was where Rose's mind stopped. Wales, family, house, Betty, all these things had to be thought through separately, later on. But first must come Italy and the chance to be alone, without pressures or intruders, a chance to begin their life together. Above all, they had to prove that such a future was real and not just a mirage or a romantic dream.

As for today, there were her professional obligations to be honoured and then she would be free. It was an immense relief to find Mike and Jenny waiting for her when she went downstairs, sitting with Hassan amongst the pre-war Harrods furniture in the main salon.

'I knew it was you in the plane,' she cried. She seized Jenny in a grateful hug. 'I told Sultan Hassan you must have decided to fly here from Aden instead of driving out. But where did you get the plane? You know the RAF turned us down, I suppose,' she bubbled on. 'No trip to the mountains after all, I'm afraid.'

Then she saw Hassan's face and stopped. Mike Farrow was on his feet, pulling a map out of his pocket to show her.

'Actually, Rose, that is just where we're going. Up to Zara.'

'Zara?' Rose echoed, startled.

'We were just explaining to His Highness that there's been an unexpected development,' Jenny put in. Her face was alert with excitement, her long fringe pushed back into a yellow headscarf. 'Rather a scoop from our point of view. A message came to us at the hotel last night from the rebel leader. He wants us to fly up to their headquarters to interview him so that he can explain to us what the campaign is all about.

Things are perfectly quiet at the moment, apparently,' she added. 'But it seems he heard there was a film unit from London and he wanted the chance to put his case, I suppose.'

'Where's our cameraman?' Rose asked.

'Down with dysentery, alas, and the sound chap,' Farrow replied. 'But I'll do what I can with stills.'

'I see.' Rose paused uncertainly. 'What about Government permission? We'll never get it, you know.'

'That's okay. We're acting independently,' Farrow said.

Suddenly irritated by his jaunty air, the very way he was smoothing out a crease in his explorer's safari jacket and matching trousers, Rose said sharply, 'In fact, it's inside Sultan Hassan's territory. You know that, I suppose?'

There was a pause. 'I hadn't realized that, I'm afraid.' Farrow looked across at Hassan, glasses glinting.

'Mine in name only,' Hassan said. 'It's part of a Colonial Protectorate, so the British have the final word there. But I must ask you first about your plane. How did you come by that?'

'Hired it from that French millionaire chap, the one who runs all the export companies. Our pilot is French too. Maurice Devereux. Seems pretty experienced in this kind of flying. Knows the country and all that.'

'More important,' Hassan broke in, 'does Lady Foster have to make this trip with you?'

'Certainly she does.' Farrow had recovered his confidence, glancing at Rose in some surprise. 'My pictures aren't much use without her copy – all her famous purple pieces about the perilous outposts of Empire,' he added with an attempt at lightness.

'In that case I suggest I accompany the expedition.' Hassan spoke in a low level voice, but there was no mistaking the urgency behind it. 'Lady Foster is an old friend of mine and as my guest her safety is my responsibility. Also' – he smiled at Jenny – 'the safety of any English-woman venturing into such a risky situation.'

'That's very kind of you, Your Highness.' Rose saw that the effect of Hassan's charm on the opposite sex was as strong as ever, and as unselfconscious. Caught off guard, Jenny was blushing. 'But we do have a problem here.' She hesitated, glancing uneasily at Farrow.

'Out of the question I'm afraid, sir. The one stipulation made by the commander at Zara was that no Arab should accompany us. Sultan Hassan, in particular. He'd obviously heard Rose was visiting Jehal.'

Rose saw Hassan's mouth tighten. She knew he was having difficulty controlling his temper.

'May I ask the name of this so-called commander? No doubt some Yemeni mercenary or other, a runaway from the Egyptian Army perhaps?'

Jenny was unfolding a piece of paper from her pocket. 'I'm afraid my Arabic's very limited. I jotted it down phonetically from the man who brought the message. 'Idris,' she began, and stopped.

Hassan had taken the paper in his hand. He bent his head to study it, almost unwillingly, as if it was something he did not wish to believe.

'Aidrus Bin Seif,' he repeated carefully.

When he looked up, it was on Rose that his gaze rested. His face had become rigid, an expressionless mask. Only his eyes burned through, holding hers. Rose stared back at him, her heart thudding. She heard Farrow speak as if from another room.

'You look shocked, sir. Do you know this man?'

There was silence for a moment, everyone looking at Hassan.

'Yes, I know him.' He crumpled the piece of paper in his hand and dropped it to the floor. 'He is my son.'

'Your son?' Farrow's voice rose in disbelief. He cleared his throat. It was a development that had taken him out of his depth. 'And you didn't know anything . . .'

Hassan interrupted him. 'I know nothing of my son. I have nothing to do with him. We parted as enemies years ago. He told me his one aim in life was to rid Arabia of Western invaders by any means possible. It seems that's just what he's doing, inside his own country.'

'According to the message, he's ordered a ceasefire.' Farrow was searching for some way of lessening the tension. 'I have the feeling he wants to make overtures to Government, perhaps to come to some kind of terms with them.'

'But evidently not with his father,' Hassan said in an undertone.

'I'm so sorry,' Jenny murmured. 'It must be a terrible blow. Hearing about it like this. His involvement in the uprisings, I mean.'

She looked to Rose for help. But Rose was powerless. She had not moved since Hassan had spoken the name, and now she still stood gripping the carved mahogany frame of the sofa in front of her. If she let go, she might faint, she felt. No words would come. No words could come until she had fought down the turmoil inside her. This was her son too, and no one must know it. She looked towards Hassan with mute appeal and saw him rally himself.

'The situation is intolerable,' he told Farrow. 'I really must protest at any of you becoming entangled in this kind of political ploy.' He paused. 'Lady Foster especially.'

Farrow glanced at his watch. 'That's our job, I'm afraid. This kind of opportunity's something we simply can't ignore.'

330

Rose knew she must speak now. Quite clearly she saw what she had to do.

'Mike's right. Of course we have to go.' She turned to Hassan. 'Don't worry, Your Highness. We'll be fine. After all, it's only a there-and-back mission. Isn't that right, Mike?'

'Absolutely. Just a couple of hours at the camp and we'll be on our way down again. But we'll have to hurry, we're losing time already. The pilot wanted to take off again right away.'

'Then I must just collect my things. Shan't be a minute.'

It was her only chance for a last word with Hassan. To her intense relief he followed her into the hall.

'Rose, what are you doing? How can you possibly go?'

She turned to face him. 'You knew something was wrong. The note that came last night. It was from Aidrus, wasn't it?'

'It wasn't signed. But there was something about the writing.'

'What did it say?'

He threw up his hands. 'I don't remember exactly. Something about time running out, a sort of threat. If you want to live, you must leave at once. That kind of thing.'

'Perhaps he was trying to warn you.'

'That kind of man doesn't stop to warn.' He caught her wrist. 'You will have to come face to face with him. Do you realize that?'

'Our son.' She looked at him pleadingly. 'Is he such a monster, then?'

He stared at her in dismay. 'You want to see him?'

'Wouldn't any mother? Do you think I have no feelings at all?'

She began to run up the stairs ahead of him. She did not look back but heard him following at her heels. Inside the bedroom, he took her by the arms with a grip so hard that it hurt.

'These feelings of yours. You'll be able to hide them, you think? In front of strangers, dangerous strangers? Do you really imagine it will be possible to meet and talk and give no sign at all of your real relationship?'

'Isn't it something I've been doing all my life, hiding what I feel?' Her eyes filled with angry tears. 'I should be pretty good at it by now. Or hadn't you noticed?'

She tried to push him away, her hands shaking. With a groan he folded her against him.

'Rose, darling Rose. It's just that I'm fearful for you.' He stroked back her hair. 'The strain on you will be so very great. Is it really what you want?'

She swallowed, fighting for self-control. 'What else can I do? To refuse would only involve more pretence, saying I'm ill, or I'm frightened, all these excuses.' For a moment, she sat down on the bed, holding his hand.

'Aren't you the one who always taught me to go where fate leads? If a thing is destined, it is destined, and there is no point in trying to change it. That's what you believe, isn't it?'

He shook his head. 'You were always good at arguments. Much better than me.'

'Besides, it's such a little thing, Hassan.' She was on her feet again, dabbing at her face in the mirror, pushing the few things on the dressing-table back into her bag. 'I'll be back in just a few hours. Perhaps you could go over to see Nabiha, tell her our plans.'

He sat with his head in his hands. 'I should be with you. But if I come, it will be like touching off a fuse with those people.'

She came over to him again and put her hand on his shoulder. 'I could take a message from you, if you told me what to say to him.'

He turned away. 'No message. It would be best to make no mention of me at all.'

'That might be difficult. He knows I've been on a visit to Jehal.'

'You'll manage. You always do. Now you must go, quickly.'

He got up and they stood looking at each other. Everything seemed to be happening so fast.

'Are you all right?' he whispered.

'Yes, I'm all right.'

Once again they held tightly to each other. All their other kisses and embraces, last night's and the very first one of more than thirty years ago, seemed to be compressed into this moment. Rose gave herself up to it, blotting out everything else from her mind. It seemed to be the precious sum of everything she was, this love of theirs, and she knew it then as at no other moment in her life.

They drew apart and stood back studying each other.

'Be careful,' he said.

'And you.'

She had to hurry now. The others were already outside the palace waiting for her. Hassan watched them go from the steps, but she felt no need to look back as the others did. She held his face in her mind, close to hers, heard him say her name in her ear as the car took them away.

'What an extraordinary thing!' Mike's voice broke in from the front. 'This chap Aidrus being the Sultan's son.'

'It's quite well-known in Aden,' Rose said shortly. 'But it was obviously painful for him that he should reappear in this particular way.'

'Even more painful to be told he wants no contact with his father.'

Rose nodded, grateful as usual for the girl's sensitivity.

'So where's this plane of ours?' She peered out as the oasis greenery came into view.

332

'It's only a little twin-engine thing.' Farrow pointed to the clearing behind the trees, and Rose saw something in the distance that looked like a boy's toy aircraft, cheerfully painted red and white. 'That's to distinguish it from any military aircraft. But it's a racy little thing and dependable, Maurice the pilot tells me. He's been up and down the Red Sea in it for the past ten years, so he's pretty experienced.'

Face to face with Maurice Devereux on the runway, Rose felt less reassured. He was one of those heavy, saturnine Frenchmen, badly shaven, with eyes that looked away from you as he shook hands. There were forecasts of storms coming in from Jeddah, he told them. Visibility was already poor, so he must insist they made their visit as short as possible. As he turned to climb back into the cockpit, Rose caught a whiff of whisky and grimaced.

'Not nervous of low flying, I hope.' Farrow was settling himself in the front seat of the tiny compartment with his camera equipment spread out around him.

Rose and Jenny buckled themselves in behind. The roar of the engines starting up drowned Jenny's voice, but leaning towards her, Rose heard her say, 'Your maid, Betty. I remember her saying you weren't too keen, that day I came to see you in Wales.'

'Oh, Betty!' The instant picture of a small sturdy figure in boots and headscarf was something to hold on to as the plane lurched upwards. 'I think she was trying to make sure I didn't come. She thought it would be a mistake.'

'And has it been?' Jenny asked, looking round at her.

Rose knew it was not idle politeness that prompted the question. Jenny had become a friend and her concern was real. Which was why she must be particularly careful about what she said, and how she said it.

'Certainly not,' she replied crisply. 'I'm enjoying every minute of it. More important, I'm very enthusiastic about our material. I really think we came at the right time. You can feel it's a watershed, can't you, for the British as well as the Arabs?'

'What about Sultan Hassan? Has the friendship survived in spite of what happened to his father? No more recriminations?'

'No, nothing like that, thank goodness. It's such a long time ago. Such a lot has happened since. He's a very remarkable man, of course.' She paused. There was a pleasure in talking about him, she found, even in such general terms. 'I think I've got some very good stories, just hearing about his own life, and the way thing have changed.'

'Mike got some splendid pictures. He's immensely photogenic, of course.' With youthful awkwardness, she tried to temper her obvious

333

admiration – 'for a middle-aged man, that is. That was when we were waiting for you.'

She studied Rose more closely, brown eyes narrowed thoughtfully.

'It was extraordinary. When you first came into the room, you looked somehow radiant, just like those early snapshots. You were a young woman again.' She frowned. 'And then, just a few minutes later, you seemed to change. All at once, you were terribly on edge. Your face actually aged. You don't mind my mentioning it, do you? Only I was worried.' Impulsively she reached out to put her hand on Rose's. 'Was it the thought of confronting the Mountain Wolf in his lair?' She laughed. 'That's what they call him, apparently, this rebel commander.'

'The Arabs are great ones for nicknames,' Rose said.

'Anyway, at least there's two of us,' Jenny went on. 'Englishwomen, I mean. We can keep the flag flying between us. And I've jotted down a few background points for you, when it comes to the interview.'

'What are you two girls gossiping about back there?' Mike called irritably over his shoulder. He had his camera pressed to the tiny window, clicking away every few minutes. 'If you look down here you'll see some of the most spectacular scenery in the world.'

It was true. Through the clouds, the grey volcanic ranges of the interior reared upwards in jagged peaks that almost seemed to touch the wings of the plane. In between, far beneath, she glimpsed lion-coloured patches of desert, tiny villages, a narrow river that wound its way through the *wadi* as in a landscape painting from the Renaissance. She could clearly see the mountain road she had travelled along with Nabiha, trekking in carefree gypsy style on the way up, riding back in panic a few days later, making for Aden in Hassan's wake.

'I made this journey on horseback,' she told them. 'Part of the way at least. The Turks had invaded from the Yemen, just after the start of the First World War.' She stopped. How could you begin to describe it, as it had happened?

'Good Lord,' said Mike in a perfunctory voice. 'History repeating itself in a way.'

But Jenny Patmore understood. Rose could see her staring out of the window, trying to imagine it.

'This must be Zara, then?'

Rose leaned across, saw below them a postage-stamp view of a mountaintop crowned with stone fortifications and thought, as she had done the first time, of the Welsh castles of childhood holidays. Village houses clustered around the slopes and then, when the ground levelled out in the distance, she saw something different. They were flying low now. On the edge of the plateau she could just pick out a jumble of fallen boulders, a broken archway. Of course. It was the ruined palace where she had ridden out with Hassan, where they had slept under a full moon. She closed her eyes and heard again the crash of the Turkish guns from the cliffs behind, as they struggled to saddle the mules in that awful dawn.

The memory merged into the sudden roar of engines, stuttering now as the plane banked steeply. Rose caught sight of a clearing that looked like a primitive landing strip. Twice the pilot circled over it, retreating each time as the wind pressures buffeted them off course.

'Third time lucky,' he called back to them over the racket.

Once more the plane tilted at a crazy angle and then came down quite fast. The ground flew up to meet them and then they were jolting over the broken chippings. Brakes screeched and they came to a standstill. With a groan, Jenny released her grip on Rose's arm.

The pilot was scrambling from his seat.

'See what I mean,' he growled. Rose saw him wipe the sweat from his eyes as he ushered them down the tiny gangway in front of him. 'It's this damn sandstorm, getting nearer all the time. So only an hour on the ground or we'll be in trouble.'

'You'd better stick with us, anyway,' Mike told him. 'No point in you hanging around here.'

Climbing down, Rose found her legs were shaking. She looked around and recognized nothing. The greenery she remembered, the fields of barley and the fig trees, had all been swept away. The whole place had been turned into a military garrison. Soldiers in rag-tag uniforms gathered around tents and lorries to watch the plane arrive. Every mud-walled building had its screen of sandbags. Even the air smelled different. The lemony crispness that always greeted one at this kind of altitude was tainted by something strange. Gunpowder, was it? Or charred wood? Or a mixture of both? Whatever it was, Rose found it disturbing.

All the time, she was searching the faces of the reception party who walked them down the runway. Two were guards of some kind in camouflage khaki. Others seemed to be local hangers-on, wearing the tribal kilts and shawls of the mountains and armed with daggers and bandoliers. At the front was a plump young man in a shabby cream suit who looked Egyptian. He could be Aidrus, Rose thought. She held her leather bag tightly under her arm as if to steady the beating of her heart.

'Colonel Aidrus is waiting for you at the fort,' the young man said. 'I am Masad, his private secretary.' He shook hands with Farrow and the pilot, nodded without smiling at the two women. 'There is a jeep.'

His English was good, but he did not want to talk. As he drove fast along the stony track, his gaze was concentrated on the steep slopes falling away on either side. The village houses were left behind, some showing damage from recent shelling. Did the old Fauzi house still stand, Rose wondered, with its walled garden and its pool? Round the bend appeared the fortified building they had seen from the air. It had an even more forbidding air at close quarters, with its crenellated turrets and loophole windows.

'Do you remember this place?' Jenny whispered as they got out.

'Only from a distance. I never came here.'

More soldiers were squatting around the entrance, eyeing them with tense expressions as they climbed the steps. The immense old door had been bleached by time to the texture of driftwood. A clammy wind was blowing, with the sting of sand in its tail. Rose shivered. This was an Arabia she had not known before.

The young man in the cream suit pulled at the long rope with its iron ring. After a moment they heard the rasp of bolts.

'Please follow,' he said, leading the way inside. There was no sign of the person who had unbolted the door. The place seemed empty. Bare flagged floors gave way to linoleum with an incongruously cheerful pattern of red flowers. Rose caught a glimpse of tin trunks piled up in corners, rifles hanging from a row of wooden pegs like schoolboy belongings. There was an air of makeshift living about the place. No woman came here, Rose thought. Somewhere above them a crackling wireless was broadcasting a news bulletin from Cairo.

At the end of the passageway they came to a large room containing a few items of decrepit Western furniture: some upright chairs, a kitchen table, a cabinet ranged with tins of American soft drinks. The young man withdrew, leaving the four of them standing together in the middle. There was an uneasy silence which no one liked to break. Fainter now, they could still hear the voice of the Egyptian newsreader. I must sit down, Rose thought, before the dizziness begins.

All at once the door on the other side was opened, revealing a thin young man in a dark green uniform and a scarlet headcloth. He did not move forward but simply stood there, hands clasped behind his back, legs slightly astride, as he looked quickly over the group.

'Good morning. I am Colonel Aidrus,' he said in clipped English. 'It was good of you to come.'

He strode towards them, hand outstretched. Rose was the furthest away and she had a moment to study him as he greeted each in turn. The face was remarkable, pale in colouring, with fine narrow features, the jawline framed in a very short black beard, the eyes brilliant and intense under long heavy lids. The full mouth was so like Hassan's it was absurd. Rose registered all these things with the split-second clarity of a flashlight photograph. She had a strange sensation of detachment, as if this encounter was happening to someone else.

It was only when he stood before her, smiling directly at her, that everything changed. His eyes, she saw, were not black or brown but curiously olive-coloured, flecked with gold. That green is mine, she thought. I remember it when he was born. He shook her hand and the touch of his palm against hers felt so intimate, so familiar, that she trembled. A picture of the tiny boy whose hand had clasped hers as he took his first unsteady steps flashed into her mind. She stepped back quickly.

Aidrus had obviously noticed nothing. Or did he look at her with some brief quickening of interest, this middle-aged woman journalist sent out from London to sum up the politics of South Arabia in a few brief sentences?

'Lady Foster, I believe?' he said, with an edge of irony in his voice.

'Rose Foster, Colonel,' she replied. 'That is my name as a writer. It's how I like to be known.'

He nodded and turned back to the others. 'I think your work has very great influence. It tries to bring the real world to the British people. It is how would you say, something radical.' He laughed. 'Like myself.'

'May I?' Farrow stepped forward to focus the lens of his camera.

'Of course.'

Almost unconsciously, Aidrus tilted his chin sideways as he went on talking. The red cloth wound low over his forehead and knotted at the back set off his profile to fine effect. He is vain, Rose thought. That is one of the clues. Vain but insecure, and also under great strain. She noted the restlessness of his hands, the air of tightly-strung energy he exuded, as strong as the tang of cologne.

'I know our time is short.' He was looking at the pilot. 'Bad weather is predicted.' He led them towards the door. 'Perhaps we can talk as we eat. You must be in need of a drink too. No alcohol, I'm afraid,' he said, lowering his voice as they went into the next room. 'I do take the odd whisky. But the Mullah here would not be pleased to hear that.'

He indicated the elderly Arab, already seated at the far end of the long chequered cloth which had been set out on the floor for a meal. He did not get up as Aidrus presented them to him but merely mumbled a response in Arabic as if it was beneath his dignity to disturb himself further.

'The Mullah is the spiritual leader of the border tribes in these parts,' Aidrus told them. 'He is also very close to the King.'

'The King?' asked Farrow.

'The King of Yemen,' Aidrus replied, surprised. 'You British always behave as if that country didn't exist.' He waved his arm towards the mountains that were just visible through the narrow windows. 'But there it is, just ten miles away, the oldest and most powerful kingdom in the

Middle East. It is our heartland. We in South Arabia are all Yemenis. What you call Aden is British-occupied South Yemen. Some day, quite soon, it will be one again. That is what you must understand.'

He was speaking excitedly now, his voice at a higher pitch. A reddish patch stood out on either cheekbone. Then he stopped himself.

'I beg pardon – I am forgetting my manners as host.'

Rose was glad when she was placed at a little distance from the Mullah, with two of the tribal elders between them. She had disliked him at first glance. Now she was aware too of the wave of hostility he directed against the European guests. The long white robe he was wearing, and the embroidered white skullcap, only emphasized the grossness of his features. The nose was hooked and heavy, the tiny eyes embedded in puffy folds of flesh flickered from side to side restlessly.

Aidrus, however, sitting opposite, was watching her narrowly as she brought out the notepad and pencil from her bag.

'Would you forgive me?' She spoke with a confidence that was entirely assumed. Making notes, she decided, might help to steady her nerves. 'But I need to get down what you have just said and time is short.'

'As you please. But do not go hungry.'

Dishes of rice and curried goat, extremely tough, were being circulated. At her side Jenny was looking uncertainly round for cutlery.

'Just dip in with your fingers, the right hand not the left,' Rose told her under her breath.

'So you know the Arab ways,' Aidrus remarked, still watching her. 'I thought your husband served in Africa?'

She looked up, trying to conceal her dismay. 'You have also been doing some research on me, Colonel,' she said lightly. 'What else do you know?'

'Only that you are the widow of a high-ranking Colonial Officer. Otherwise, why would you be a guest at Government House? But your Arabian connections,' he went on. 'You also lived in the Middle East?'

'Rose was actually in Aden at one time, weren't you?' Farrow put in. 'When your husband was in Government here.'

What was the point in denying it, Rose thought. As far as Farrow was concerned, her Aden links were a vital part of her credentials.

'Didn't you travel up to Zara too, you were telling us?' he pressed her.

Rose nodded. At least there was the satisfaction of seeing a startled flicker pass over the Mullah's face. She had known from the start he understood English perfectly well.

'It was only for a short while,' she said quickly. 'And it was so long ago, the period of the First World War. Before your time,' she added, half-glancing at Aidrus. Somehow she could not bring herself to meet his eyes directly.

'Before yours too, I should have thought,' he said gallantly.

'You're very kind.'

Aidrus turned to the Mullah who had intervened in Arabic.

'He wants to know where you stayed in Zara?'

'At the Fauzi house,' Rose said. 'They were friends of ours.'

'Ah, the Fauzis.' The expression on Aidrus's face had changed. There was a ruthless edge that she had not seen before. 'The moneymakers, betraying their own people to run with the imperialists. Like their friend Sultan Hassan. I suppose you knew him too? Or was it the old man in those days, the one shot by the British for his pains?'

'I met them both,' Rose said faintly.

'You know Sultan Hassan is my father?'

To Rose's relief he looked round at the others as he made his announcement.

'Never mind,' he went on, without waiting for their reactions. 'It is of no consequence. He will not be at Jehal for much longer. There will be no hereditary rulers under our regime.'

He paused, glancing across at Rose with raised eyebrows, as if awaiting further questions. Mike and Jenny were looking at her too. With a struggle she collected her thoughts.

'What made you a rebel in the first place, Colonel Aidrus?'

He hesitated for a moment. 'My upbringing, I suppose. I saw how my family had been humbled by the British, made to play the imperial game by a system of alternating threats and bribes. And at every crisis they were betrayed. The British always betray their friends.'

'And yet there's supposed to be some kind of natural affinity between the British and the Arabs. Even if it is a love-hate relationship, something seems to draw them together. Wouldn't you agree?' Rose had not consciously framed this question. But now she searched his face as if the answer to it was vital to her.

He threw her a look of scorn. 'That's a fairy story the British have invented for their own convenience. Lawrence of Arabia, Gertrude Bell and all that romantic rubbish about kindred souls. I look for the practical evidence of that concern for the Bedouin and what do I find?' He spread out his hands. 'Here in Aden, show me the roads they have made, the hospitals they have built, the schools they have set up for our children!' He smiled bitterly. 'I see only a port that is crammed with shipping to line the pockets of the business tycoons. I see a military base ready to strike out at anyone who threatens British power in the Middle East. And then there's the Colonial administration to make it all legal and above-board, though none of the inhabitants of the place have ever been given the chance to vote for representatives of their own.' He shook his head. 'What a disgrace for a once-proud race like ours to be fooled like this.'

As he was talking, Rose found herself torn by two quite different emotions. In another half-hour or so she would be on her way back to Hassan, a thought which filled her with longing and impatience. Yet at the same time she was gripped by the need to come as close as possible to this extraordinary stranger who was her son. She would probably never see him again. It was an encounter designed entirely by fate, like some arabesque pattern that had come full circle. As Hassan had guessed, it was perhaps one she had secretly wanted all along. Giving up your baby for adoption was no rare thing. She had told herself so many times. Did all such mothers secretly feel the need to see that child once more, to know how life had treated it? Was there otherwise a gap in their lives that could never be mended?

She studied the thin, intense face of the young man opposite, who looked little more than a student as he harangued them. She did not know whether she loved or hated him, remembering what he had done to Hassan. She only knew how deeply disturbed she was, even as she told herself she could not afford such emotions.

A silence had fallen. Outside, the low whistle of the wind was rising against the walls. In another part of the house, a door slammed. The room was growing dark. The other Arabs had been talking together in low voices, but now they too stopped. She realized there was a new emotion she was trying to pin down in herself, and it was fear.

'We must go,' Maurice said. 'We cannot leave take-off any longer.'

As they got to their feet she knew there was one more question she had to ask.

'Does it have to be by bloodshed? For Aden, I mean. Is there no other way?'

His eyes were not on her, but on the Mullah's behind her.

'The British took us by force. We shall expel them by force. That is what I have been training my army for – Syrians, Yemenis, Egyptians, Palestinians. We are well-equipped. The Russians are giving us plenty of weapons. And in Aden itself there is also a well-established terrorist network. So all is set in motion for war, yes. Unless . . .'

'Unless?' Rose pressed him.

'Unless the British will agree to a withdrawal. If we are given a firm date for independence, we're prepared to hold our fire. Then we can start getting our plans for a peaceful takeover into operation. We have set out our terms. It is up to Government to make the choice.'

'What are the terms?' Farrow asked. He was putting away his camera.

Rose watched Aidrus bring out a folded brown envelope from his pocket. To her surprise, he handed it to Farrow.

'It is all down here.'

Farrow looked bewildered. 'For our report, you mean?'

Aidrus straightened his shoulders, standing almost at attention.

'I am requesting that you deliver this document to the Governor.' His voice had a new staccato ring to it. 'In person. Immediately you land.'

'I don't understand,' Farrow said coldly. He looked down at the envelope in his hand.

With a quick movement, Jenny came forward between the two men. Indignation had given her confidence. 'Is that the real reason for asking us up here?' she demanded. 'Just to act as a diplomatic messenger service?'

'Please,' Maurice intervened. He had begun to sweat again, Rose noticed. 'If I don't get the plane off the ground in the next five minutes, there will be no landing anywhere.'

'Your pilot is right.' Aidrus led them towards the door which stood open on to the passageway beyond. 'The jeep is already waiting.'

'Let's hurry,' Rose said in a low voice to Farrow. She was overwhelmed by a desire to be out of this house and on her way back to reality and Hassan. Automatically she turned back to Aidrus. 'Thank you for the interview. I wish there was more time to talk.'

He was smiling faintly. 'There will be more time to talk. If you wish it.'

As he spoke, an extraordinary thing happened. Farrow, Jenny and Maurice had already gone through the door. Rose was about to follow but Aidrus brought down his arm so that her way was barred. Her sharp intake of breath made the others turn.

'What's going on?' Farrow asked. His face was suddenly white. 'Can't you see we're leaving?'

'*You* are leaving,' Aidrus said. 'But Lady Foster will be staying with us for a little longer.'

Rose stepped back. She was aware that the men in the room had moved closer behind her. She turned swiftly and saw that only the Mullah remained seated. His head was lifted now and he was staring at her with something like triumph on his face. She turned back to Aidrus.

'How much longer?'

'Until we receive an answer to our demands. The right kind of answer. I have given them a deadline of noon tomorrow.'

Farrow and the others stood helplessly in the passageway. Two soldiers, their hands on their rifles, had moved forward on either side of the door.

'This is unbelievable.' Farrow's tone was blustering. 'Are you seriously taking Lady Foster hostage?'

341

'Let us say she is a guest of the Sons of the New Islam,' Aidrus said smoothly.

'And you really believe this is the way to get what you want?'

'To make Government take us seriously, yes. We believe so. It is something new for us. But there will be a great deal more hostage-taking in years to come, believe me.'

'You realize the RAF will be sending up a rescue mission within hours,' Maurice told him. 'The kind of mission that will raze your camp to the ground.'

'Poor Lady Foster,' Aidrus replied. 'With so many casualties, she would not stand much chance of survival, I think. And we were planning to take such good care of her, give her the best of treatment as her hosts.'

Jenny stepped forward between the two soldiers. Rose saw she was biting her lip to stop her face from trembling.

'I will stay too.'

Aidrus shook his head with a look of mock regret. 'I'm afraid that is not possible. It will only complicate the issue. Besides, there is no need. We are civilized people. She will be provided with a female companion and quarters of her own.'

'But why are you keeping her?' Jenny burst out.

'How would you put it? A guarantee of good behaviour from the British? Something like that.' His tone changed abruptly as he spoke to the pilot. 'And now I must insist you leave. At once.'

He signalled to one of the soldiers. A rifle was prodded against the pilot's shoulder.

'There's nothing we can do,' Rose heard him say to Farrow in French. 'At least if we get back to Aden . . .' He left the sentence unfinished.

'You'd better go,' Rose spoke briskly. The hint of fear she had felt earlier was now an overpowering reality, but she would not show it. 'I'll be back tomorrow. Tell Jimmy Ferguson I'll be looking out for the plane.'

'This is terrible.' Farrow reached out to take her hand, but the guard stepped between them. 'If you harm her . . .' he flung at Aidrus, as they were led away.

Halfway down the passage, Jenny turned with a despairing look at Rose. She had a long cardigan over her shoulders, Rose noticed. On an impulse, she called out, 'Your cardigan, Jenny. May I have it? The night will be cold.'

She looked at Aidrus. He nodded brusquely. Running down the long flagged floor, she took it from the girl who had begun to cry.

'Stop it.' Rose embraced her urgently. 'Listen,' she said in her ear. 'Sultan Hassan. You must let him know what's happened, straight away. Tell him everything, everything.'

She was pulled back by one of the soldiers. Shaking off his hand, she stood to watch them go. There was little dignity about the departure of the little group as they were hustled out through the front entrance. She was crying herself, now that they were out of sight. All at once, she felt an appalling loneliness.

'And now,' said the voice of Aidrus behind her, 'perhaps we can continue our talk, Lady Foster.'

❧ 11 ❧

SHE turned and saw the group in the passageway blur. Close by, there was a rough wooden bench pushed back against the wall. She bent over and sat down, her head bent in her hands, her eyes closed. When she opened them, Aidrus was standing in front of her.

'You are ill?'

With an effort, she got to her feet again.

'You said I was to have my own quarters. Please take me to them. I need to rest.'

'Very well.'

In the doorway, the white-robed figure of the Mullah had appeared. He stood quite still, watching them. Even at a distance Rose could feel the dark force of his presence. Aidrus went quickly over and spoke to him, them crouched before him to kiss his hand and his knee. As he came back to her, Rose was struck by the look of concentrated fervour on his face. He hardly glanced at her.

'Come with me,' he said, leading the way through the front entrance. One of the guards sprang forward, but Aidrus waved him aside.

'I will drive.'

Halfway down the steps, she stumbled slightly, catching her heel on a broken stone. He gripped her arm, whether it was to restrain or to steady her it was hard to tell. At the contact, Rose felt a shock run through her. Did he feel it too? They came to the armoured car that stood in the drive. He opened the door for her, again without a look or a word.

'Where are you taking me?' she asked fearfully, as he climbed into the seat next to her.

'Somewhere you already know.'

He drove with reckless energy, clashing the gears as they rattled down the track. Glancing down at his hands on the wheel, Rose saw a wedding ring. Carelessly twisted round his wrist was a string of amber beads.

Rose's mouth went dry. She was remembering Hassan's beads, the ones she had put in the hand of her baby at Brown's Hotel. But why should it be the same ones, she told herself? Every Muslim has his string of prayer beads and more often that not, it is made of amber.

She sat holding herself very straight, as close to the window as possible.

Somehow, this enclosed promixity was almost unbearable. Ahead she could see the village, when he suddenly braked to a standstill. Flinging open the door, he sprang to the ground, then stood there, staring into the distance.

Rose did not dare to speak. She leaned forward, trying to follow his gaze. The wind was still rising and the horizon was overhung by a sulphurous pall of dust.

'The plane,' he snapped at her. 'It should be taking off now. Or are you not very concerned?'

Long minutes seemed to pass while he continued to scan the line of rocks beyond which lay the airstrip. In front of her, on the dashboard, she noticed the prayer beads, lying where he had dropped them. She nerved herself to pick them up and examine them. She caught her breath. Only one string of beads could have Hassan's seal. It was engraved on the gold pendant beneath the tassel. She heard Aidrus exclaim and she dropped it like a thief. Very faintly, there came the sound of a plane's engines.

'There it is!'

He pointed up to the fleck of white which rose against the clouds like a leaf in the wind. As he turned to Rose, his eyes were brilliant above the scarlet headshawl that had blown back against his face.

'*Alham d'Illah*,' he said, gasping, as he flung himself back into his seat.

Rose sat with her hands clenched in her lap. The sight of the beads had set up a whole train of emotions which she was now struggling to contain.

'Why are you not pleased?' he demanded, frowning. 'Don't you want the letter to get through? The quicker Government make their bargain with us, the quicker you will be free.'

Just for a moment, her self-control snapped.

'Bargain!' she whispered fiercely. 'Do you think the British go in for bargaining like some of your merchants in the souk, haggling over the price of a carpet?'

In a flash, his hand came out to strike her. But he held back, his face contorted with anger.

'You insult me. I think you should be more careful! Just because I am treating you with courtesy does not alter the fact that you are a prisoner. Remember that! A woman should know better how to keep quiet.' He glanced at the silk scarf across her knees, and snatched it up. 'Here. Cover your head at least, now you are in a Muslim country.'

'But I am not a Muslim woman.'

'No, you are not. And yet . . .'

He had drawn back into his seat. His anger had subsided and he was frowning at her with Hassan's frown that had already marked a single cleft between his eyebrows.

'And yet I think you are not quite an Englishwoman either. There is something different, something that puzzles me. When I spoke of the British, for instance, and the way we have been treated by them, I felt you were sympathetic. You said nothing and yet I saw from your eyes that you understood.'

'I understand how strongly the Arabs feel about foreigners running their country,' Rose said. Her voice was deliberately light. She even tried to smile. 'Perhaps it's because I'm Welsh.'

'Ah yes, Welsh.' But his eyes were still searching hers with a baffled expression. 'There is another thing. Or rather, two different things that contradict each other. From the moment we met, you were on your guard with me.' He hesitated. 'Not as the others were, because they were in the rebel camp, confronting the Mountain Wolf.' He laughed, showing very white teeth. 'No, not that. But something personal, as if I was a threat to you in some way. And yet, how you stare and study me.' He shook his head. 'That is the contradiction. There is something familiar between us, as if we have met before. I feel it, but cannot put my finger on it.'

Now she could tell him, Rose thought. But what would be the repercussions? And what of her pledge to Hassan? He might be the real victim of the truth. She knew nothing of how an Arab mind would react to such a revelation, especially with a man as unstable as Aidrus. Besides, what would she gain from it, apart from that one moment of overpowering emotional release? She had only to be patient and rescue would come, though how and when she could not yet visualize in any detail.

A sudden gust of wind shook the car. With an impatient movement, Aidrus started up the engine. The moment had gone.

'We should just make it before the storm comes,' he said.

Already in the distance, long curtains of dust were billowing up from the desert. On the outskirts of the village people were putting up shutters and driving their animals into the compounds. They passed a large house where the front walls were broken and blackened by fire.

'The Sultan's family were staying here. But the women took fright and left,' he said carelessly. 'That was before I arrived.'

'Where is your wife?' Rose asked.

'The other side of the camp. The women's quarters are there.' His face softened briefly. 'She is expecting a baby in two months. A son, God willing.'

It caught her unprepared. She turned away, lest he should see how moved she was. His son, her grandson. She took a deep breath and stared out at the narrow streets. All at once, she knew where they were going.

'The old Fauzi place?'

He nodded, pulling up outside the tall narrow house with its courtyard door.

'Now we call it the Tower of Freedom. We use the rooftop as our observation post. We have our briefings here. It is the command base. There are many rooms, perhaps you remember?'

'I remember.'

A young woman had appeared at the entrance, dressed in black trousers and jacket, a black scarf tied under her chin.

'I hand you over to Jamila now. She is from Palestine. She will take care of you.'

The girl had opened the door, without smiling, and Rose got out with a feeling of trepidation.

'I will visit you again in the morning,' Aidrus went on. 'We will wait together.'

'Wait?'

'For the plane with the Government reply.' He raised his eyebrows in a mocking way. 'Perhaps the Governor himself will bring it, as he is such a friend of yours.'

As he was turning away he remembered something else. 'Tonight is the start of Ramadan. Tomorrow we fast, so tonight we feast. I hope we do not keep you awake.' The wind was whipping into their faces, as he looked up at the darkening sky. 'And let us pray for clear weather by morning.'

The first wave of the storm broke on them as Jamila bolted the outer gate. With the sand swirling around them they ran, heads down, into the house.

'You will be in the room at the top. The women in these parts always keep to the upper storeys.'

'I know.' Rose was looking up at the twisting staircase, with its worn stone steps and walls of crumbling plaster. The memory of past happiness went flooding through her, like a light going on. 'I have been here before.'

'When?' The girl's voice was sharp. She had a rounded flattish face, the skin badly pockmarked. The small black eyes studied Rose coldly.

'Many years ago.'

'Sightseeing.' She spat out the word as if she was naming a crime. 'The British like sightseeing, pretending to live like the Bedouin. So very picturesque, are they not?'

She spoke the pedantic English of someone more used to writing it. Rose felt there was little chance of establishing any kind of rapport with her, but she would try.

'Are you a student?' she asked, as she followed her up the stairs.

'I was a student. Now I am a soldier.' Turning at the top she reached inside her shirt and brought out a small revolver. Her eyes were on Rose's face, watching her reaction. 'My family were all killed by the Israelis in the May War. I got away with the other refugees. Did you know there were eight hundred thousand of us?' She paused, pushing the gun back into her belt. 'The army taught me to use this, also automatic weapons. I am very skilled at it now,' she added, with a touch of schoolgirl pride.

She brought out a key from the bunch at her waist and bent to open the door. Brusquely she motioned Rose inside.

'I must report to council. There is a lamp. There is a bathroom. The door will be locked. Food will come later.'

For a moment she brought her face close to Rose's. There was cardamom on her breath from the seeds she had been chewing.

'Are you frightened?'

'A little,' Rose said, knowing it was what she wanted to hear.

She gave a quick smile. The door banged behind her and with a strange sense of release Rose heard the key turn, heard Jamila's footsteps fading down the stairs. More than anything else she wanted to be alone. Gratefully she sank to the ground and sat cross-legged and motionless, her arms clasped tightly around her knees so that she might stop shaking.

With hungry eyes, she stared around at the room she thought of as hers. No, not hers, theirs. How strange it was, strange but somehow fated, that she should be brought here. The shutters were closed, rattling violently on their hinges as the wind pounded against them. A storm lantern in the corner threw just enough light for her to see that everything she remembered had gone, the fantastical canopied bed where she and Hassan had made love in the early morning, the carved chest at the foot, the lacquered table and the Turkish rugs. Now all was bare except for a straw mat, and a couple of mattresses piled into the corner. The faces of Arab leaders unknown to her stared out from the torn posters and newspaper cuttings pinned to the walls. Strangely, on one of the shelves, there were a few unmistakeably feminine objects, an empty scent bottle, a comb, a tin of cheap talcum. It seemed the kind of place where women would be brought from time to time in secret.

Rose felt suddenly sick. She picked up the lantern and went into the bathroom. There was a strong smell of urine. The hole in the floor had been replaced by the kind of thunderbox the memsahibs of Aden used to complain about so bitterly. But it was something, at least. There was water, too, a whole jugful, an enamel bowl and a small piece of soap, and left behind on a hook on the door a towel that looked fairly clean.

She felt she must get out of her clothes. Everything she wore, from the skin upwards, was sticky with sweat and dust. She searched again, this time in the bedroom, and found a thin bedspread of printed Indian cotton folded under a pillow. Swiftly she undressed and washed, then wound this round her like a sarong. Weary though she was, she rinsed out her clothes in the bowl of water with the last scrap of soap. If she hung them against the shutters, the wind would dry them, and the sand would shake out afterwards. When she had done this, she lay down exhausted and fell asleep with the howl of the storm in her ears.

Please God let it pass, she said to herself, or the plane will not get through.

She was woken by a change in the sound, almost like a change of key. She had turned the lamp down low, but in the draught through the room it had guttered out. Sitting up, she listened intently. The wind seemed to have died away. Yet there was still a throbbing vibration in the distance, and moving closer.

She sprang up and fastened the wrap around her, feeling her way to the window. As she tugged open the shutters, a brilliant white flash illuminated the room. Did lightning follow a sandstorm? It was a split-second thought before the low rolling sound shattered into an explosion.

The shutter flew back in her hand. The whole house shook beneath her. Through the window she saw the landscape lit by flames. The planes were drawing closer. There was another thud, another violent eruption of smoke and flame.

Automatically, she flung herself on to the floor, her arms over her head. Crouching there, she counted three more explosions. Each one seemed louder than the last. In between she listened to the hammering of her heart, heard herself say Hassan's name, over and over again.

Then they stopped. The sound of the planes receded. But instead of silence, there was the crackle of fire and above it the sound of voices, women screaming, men shouting, the slowly accelerating roar of an angry crowd.

Rose sat against the wall. She was weak with shock, unable to believe that Government's response had simply been to launch one of their bombing raids. Or was it some independent show of strength by the RAF that the administration had been too late to prevent? The house seemed to have been spared, the rest of the village too perhaps, and the planes had concentrated on the camp. Whatever the motive, she feared the worst. She sat, numb and unable to move, waiting for what seemed hours for the door to be flung open.

When it was, it was almost a relief after the suspense of waiting. Even so, she could not suppress an exclamation of dismay. Jamila had unlocked the door. But it was the Mullah who stood there framed in the entrance, looking down at her. Over his white robe he had on a long coat of black lamb and the lower part of his face was wrapped in a black scarf. The soldier behind him brought forward a lamp, crouching low, so that the flickering flame threw huge shadows around the little room. Without speaking, the priest came forward towards her. He was leaning on a gold-tipped cane, breathing heavily. His mouth hung slightly open and Rose saw his tongue work to and fro between the glint of gold teeth. All the time, the small, close-set eyes never left her face. They seemed to be burrowing into her mind like maggots. Not for the first time in her life she was aware of the spirit of pure evil, and the limitless possibilities it allowed.

Suddenly, with a grunt, he bent down heavily, seizing her by the arm. Still without a word, he dragged her to her feet. Rose felt his strength, the furious strength of an old man, as he pulled her towards the side door that she knew led on to the roof. He motioned with his head for the girl to unlock it. The next moment she found herself outside, being pushed towards the parapet. Once more she heard the babble of angry voices.

For the first time he spoke to her. 'Look down. Look down.'

She obeyed, glimpsing a sea of swarming faces packed into the narrow street. Something like a collective sigh went up from them as they saw her, a sound more terrifying than any raised voice.

'They know it is because of you.' He spoke in good English, low and rasping at the back of his throat. 'Because of the Christian woman, the planes are sent by Government to drop their bombs on us. Three people killed, maybe more wounded.'

His hand tightened on her arm. As he pushed her harder against the stone, she saw his eyes travel over her bare shoulders.

'You know our law, Nazarene. A life for a life. What shall I do with you?' He gesticulated to the crowd, raising his voice. 'Shall I push you over to them?'

The crowd were chanting now. One man called out harshly above the others, a slogan of some kind.

'He is right,' the Mullah said softly. 'Punishment comes first. That is the proper way.'

Turning back, he dropped his grip on her arm, so that she almost fell into the room. In the corner, Jamila stood watching with a faint smile. Rose shrank back against the wall as two more guards came in with ropes in their hands. In her mind she had decided that if she kept perfectly still, made herself small and limp, like a rag doll, it would be easier for her. One of the soldiers, an older man with a round pleasant face, smiled at her apologetically as they tied up her feet, and then her hands. In this way, she was left sitting against the wall, her legs stretched out before her.

The Mullah stood looking down at her, picking his teeth. From deep inside her, a spark of fury rose.

'This is stupid,' she said, trying to make her voice as calm as possible.

'Tomorrow the Government people will come with their reply to your demands. They will make their deal and then they will take me away. Wasn't that the plan?'

'That plan is finished. The British have made a bad mistake. Now you will be killed, and they will be shamed before the world.'

'But you have to wait until noon. That was the agreement made by the Colonel. Surely he is in command of the operation.'

Even as she spoke, she knew she had made a mistake. He turned on her in a fury.

'No one comes before me. Do you not understand that our law comes from Allah and I am the keeper of that law?'

Rose tried to moisten the dryness of her lips.

'Nevertheless, I would like to see Colonel Aidrus.'

The old man thrust his face close to hers.

'When Aidrus comes, he comes with the firing squad. Now he is with his wife. When your friends from Aden bomb the camp, there is burning in the women's quarters. She is caught with the others. She suffers.' His eyes glistened with hatred, fixed on hers. 'You know how to suffer, how to burn?'

'I – I'm sorry for her,' Rose faltered.

'We can make fire too,' he went on, still crouched over her. 'We have irons. You know this custom?'

Rose knew about branding. Amongst the Bedouin it was used sometimes as a primitive medical treatment, sometimes as punishment, depending on the instruments used. She felt her whole body flinch. Was it possible or was it just a sadistic turn of the screw in the terror campaign?

'I think you forget you are on British territory here. You will be dealt with as criminals under our law when . . .'

'When what?' he retorted mockingly. 'What can the British do now? If they bomb again, the United Nations will stop them. If they send soldiers they will not last a day in the wilderness, fighting against the tribes. Besides,' he raised his eyebrows, 'the Yemen is only ten miles away. Would you rather the King decides what to do with you?'

He snapped his fingers at one of the guards. 'Show her,' he was saying in Arabic. 'This man is a Yemeni,' he went on, turning back to Rose. 'He has something you may like to see.'

With an eager grin, the soldier pulled out a crumpled package from his pocket and handed it to the old man. From it he drew out a series of photographs and laid them on the floor before her.

'This is our law,' he said. 'These men were traitors against Government. This is what happens in Sana.'

The pictures were bad and the light was poor, but Rose had a glimpse

351

of a scene that was grotesque in its horror – two severed heads on stakes, two decapitated bodies on the ground alongside, a ring of spectators in a crowded marketplace. The soldiers were watching her closely. One of them was laughing behind his hand in a way that reminded her of the peddlers of pornographic pictures at Port Said. The other had brought out a dagger from his belt. With a swift movement he touched her chin with the blade, then made a circular movement with it inches away from her face. This time they both laughed. Rose closed her eyes. She felt her insides wrenched by a spasm over which she had no control.

'Please,' she heard herself say to Jamila.

She felt her ankles and wrists roughly untied. The girl gave her a push. With head averted she stumbled into the bathroom.

She did not know how long she lay curled up on the stone floor. She only prayed it would be long enough for her to muster the courage to face what lay ahead. It was the Mullah himself she dreaded most, that brutal will of his she knew she could not breach, however hard she might try. But when the girl came to fetch her back, the room was empty.

'In the morning,' she said, 'they will take you away.'

She picked up the rope. When she had retied Rose's wrists, she paused.

'There is no need to tie my ankles again.' Rose was ashamed of her pleading tone. 'Surely you don't think I'm going to run away.'

Jamila shrugged her shoulders, dropping the other piece of rope. She indicated with her foot the straw mat in the corner. Obediently Rose lay down. She was shivering violently. Even inside the house, the temperature had plummeted as it always did at night in these parts.

'No mattress?' she murmured, clenching her teeth. 'No blanket?'

'I thought the English liked the cold.' Rose tried to draw away as Jamila bent down and pinched the skin on her shoulder. '*Ya, miskin!*' she whispered contemptuously. 'Why do you Western women try to be so thin? If you took on flesh as we do you wouldn't be shaking so.'

'Could I have my clothes back, at least?' She looked longingly at Jenny's cardigan still hanging from the shutters with her other things.

With a flaunting gesture, Jamila pulled them down and threw them on the floor, just out of reach.

'You may dress in the morning, before the men come.' She laughed. 'English women like to bare their bodies, don't they? Why are you suddenly so modest, Lady Rose Foster?'

It was the sound of her name, rolled off the girl's tongue so insolently, that goaded her beyond endurance.

'Your accent is very bad, I'm afraid,' she drawled. 'You really should not try to pronounce an English name.'

The girl kicked out at her violently. The blow struck Rose in the small

352

of the back. The sharp pain of it made her cry out before she could stop herself.

Jamila stared down at her with folded arms, her pudgy face impassive again. Incongruously, Rose was reminded of a bully at her boarding school called Selina, an older girl whom she had hated and feared more than any other human being. For a moment the thought made her smile.

'You are more cheerful then? Are you hungry, Lady Foster?'

'A little.'

'Thirsty?'

'More thirsty than hungry.'

'Then you will enjoy watching me eat and drink. It is what we Muslims do in the nights of Ramadan, preparing ourselves for our fast next day. But for a Nazarene like yourself, there are no such laws.' She shook her head. 'That is the trouble with being a race of infidels and atheists.'

She went to the door and brought in a tray covered with small dishes. Rose could close her eyes but she could not blot out the smell of spiced rice and meat, and coffee brewed with ginger.

She swallowed hard and turned on her side. She must think only of Hassan now, Hassan who alone would understand the Arab reaction to the raid of retribution, who would go to any lengths to get her back to safety. And then there was Aidrus. Whatever happened, she knew he would come to the house as he had said he would. At all costs she must hang on here in this little room, until that moment.

Every hour she woke with a start, thinking it must be dawn. Her watch was with her clothes and she had lost track of time completely. She had discovered that by rolling on to her stomach she could partly cover herself with the mat. On the other side of the room she was aware of Jamila, half-sleeping, half-watching, the storm lantern guttering in the shadows around her makeshift bed in the corner. In between, there were dreams, feverish, fragmented things conjuring up a mirage of happiness that was always just out of reach. Sometimes she was searching for Hassan's face at one of those Residency parties of her youth. Sometimes she was running through wrecked and deserted streets in Cairo or Port Said, trying to warn him of disaster. Once they were lying in each other's arms in hiding in the old beach house, both weeping with such an unbearable sense of loss that she woke half-choking with unshed tears.

Struggling to turn on her side, she looked up and saw the face of Aidrus, like a blurred reflection of the young Hassan of her dreams. The shock of it caught her off guard. She tried to sit upright against the wall but the cramp in her arms made movement difficult.

'English bitch,' she heard him say.

The savagery of his voice frightened her. Staring up at him in the faint light of early morning she saw that he was no longer the Aidrus of yesterday. He was breathing hard and he had a haggard, driven look. His skin was only a little darker than the streaks of grey ash across his cheeks. His clothes were torn and patched with blood. All this she took in at a glance, but it was his eyes that held her, wild and accusing, the eyes of a madman.

'Bitch,' he said again in a low, shaking voice. She saw the knuckles of his hands whiten, held stiffly against his sides. 'You knew that raid was coming, didn't you? You told the girl to describe to them exactly where the camp was, didn't you, to let them know to go ahead and bomb us?'

Rose was dazed. 'Which girl?'

'The English girl, Jenny. That was what you were whispering to her, wasn't it, just as they were leaving?'

'I did no such thing,' she said indignantly. 'Why should I? I only wish it had never happened. Your wife . . .'

His face was rigid now. 'My wife is alive. My son is dead. The baby was lost.'

This time Rose could find no words. The burning tightness rose up in her throat again. She could feel only despair, knowing what was to come.

'The Mullah has decreed your execution. You are in our hands. Because of these deaths, you too must die.'

She looked for some expression on his face and found none.

'But the reply from Government – you gave them until noon to respond.'

He walked across to the window, then turned to face her again.

'They have already responded. A message was sent from Aden to the wireless station above the *wadi*. It came at dawn. Government refuse all our demands. They are sending a civilian plane at midday. The pilot only will be on board, unarmed. If you are returned safely, they will forego retaliation. There will be no more raids on condition our forces withdraw from Protectorate territory within the week.' He was still standing very straight and stiff. 'That is the message.'

'And your response?' she asked, already knowing it in her heart.

'You will be sent back on the plane as requested.' He paused and cleared his throat. 'Rather, your body will be sent back on the plane. That is our answer to the British. Council proclaimed this just five minutes ago.'

'How? When?' Rose felt the absurdity of these questions but they were automatic. She suddenly felt quite removed from the scene.

He frowned. 'Why do you ask these things? Surely it is better not to know. Unless you are very brave indeed.'

Then, as he had done yesterday, he examined her with that curious, baffled look. For a moment, she felt like a human being, not just a cipher in a game. It made her frightened again, with all her senses alive to the horror and absurdity of what was happening to her.

'I am not brave at all. But I have to know.'

'Four men are in the firing squad. Outside in the courtyard, half an hour from now, you will be blindfolded.' He hesitated. 'I have given orders that the crowd will not be let in.'

He motioned to Jamila who had been standing in the doorway, rapt and motionless.

'Get her dressed,' he said. 'Quickly.'

❧ 12 ❧

IN the bathroom, she was shaking so much it seemed an impossible task to pull on the clothes that were scornfully held out to her by Jamila. But she struggled to do it, rather than be touched by the girl. Someone had left a broken mirror hanging behind the door. She had not noticed it before. Now she caught sight of the splintered face in the glass and recoiled. It was as if the bullets had already found their mark.

All at once, terror gave way to fury. The act of death in itself was unimaginable. The split-second agony, the blackness afterwards, these were abstract images. But the idea of her life coming to an end this morning in some squalid outpost in the mountains of South Arabia suddenly struck her as an outrage. Less than a hundred miles away, Hassan was waiting for her. A whole new life was about to open up for them.

Every nerve in her body quickened. She would fight for her life with the only weapon she had. As she pulled on her boots, she was conscious of precious moments slipping away. The weakness of hunger had faded. Only her mouth was now so dry, her lips so cracked, it was hard to speak. While Jamila's back was turned, she dipped her hand into the bowl of water, but it had been emptied, or almost. Swiftly she cupped the last few drops into her mouth, before the girl took hold of her again. Please God, let Aidrus still be there, she said to herself as she was pushed back into the room. The sight of him standing in the doorway, talking to one of the soldiers, filled her with a wild hope that was almost euphoric.

'Colonel Aidrus.'

Her voice sounded faint. He looked at her over his shoulder.

'I have one request,' she went on. She was forcing him to meet her eyes. 'That I may speak to you alone.'

'It is of no use,' he said curtly. 'Everything is settled.'

'But I must speak to you,' she went on. 'At once. In private.'

She saw her determination take him by surprise. He shrugged his shoulders and brought out an Egyptian cigarette from the case in his pocket.

'Just for a moment then. Time is going by.'

'I know,' Rose said quietly.

356

He nodded to the others. With a sulky air, Jamila followed the guards outside.

Aidrus moved across to the centre of the room and faced her, smoking. She could see that beneath the façade he was intensely strung up.

'For a prisoner facing death, you are very insolent in your demands, Lady Foster.'

Rose went over to him and stood very close. He was five or six inches taller than she was and she had to lift her face to look at him. She wanted to touch him, but she knew she must not, yet.

'Your son is dead, Aidrus,' she said. 'Would you see your mother killed also?'

To finally speak these words cost her every effort she was capable of making. She found it difficult to breathe. Her voice dropped away. She saw him bend his head towards her. His face was blank.

'What do you say?'

'Your mother, Aidrus. Even the most committed terrorist would not send his own mother to be executed.'

She waited. He looked bewildered, then irritated.

'So where is my mother? What lies are you telling me now?'

Nerves stretched to breaking point, she reached out and took his hand between hers.

'Here is your mother, Aidrus.'

With a violent movement of distaste, he snatched back his hand. In the other, the cigarette still burned. He dropped it to the floor and ground it out under his heel.

'You're mad. Your mind has given way. It's the death sentence. Some people crack up like this.'

For a moment, she saw something like pity working in his face, and curiosity. 'Why should you imagine something so strange?' he went on. 'That I am your son. Do you think it will save you?'

'It is the truth,' she replied steadily. 'You are my son.'

This time he lost patience.

'I've had enough of this,' he said angrily. 'I don't have to listen to such filth. That my father would so much as look at a Nazarene women like you, let alone . . .' He broke off and turned away. 'There is a limit, even to madness. I shall get the guards to take you down to the cells. You can wait there.'

As he moved towards the door, Rose felt all control stripped away from her. With a cry, she pushed past him and fell on her knees in front of him.

'Please, Aidrus. Can't you at least listen to me?'

Wildly, she reached up and grasped his hand, holding fast to it as if it was the only safety-line left to her before she fell into nothingness. Every rational thought had gone from her. She only knew she had to keep him with her, just long enough to make him believe her. As she clung to him, her fingers touched the prayer-beads, knotted around his wrist.

'Your beads, Aidrus. Look at them.'

'What have they to do with anything?'

'Beneath the tassel, there is a seal. Look at them.'

In spite of himself, he glanced down at his wrist.

'Yes, there is a seal, I know. I don't have to look.'

'On it there is engraved the name and crest of Sultan Hassan.'

He looked startled for a moment. She could see him trying to reason this away.

'So. It is sometimes the custom. You know about such things.'

'Aidrus, I know it because your father gave me the beads before you were born. When you were a baby, I gave them back to you. Before your father took you away.'

She had begun to cry now, her face in her hands. It seemed so hopeless, too strange a story to begin to make sense to him. With an exclamation, he pulled her to her feet. He was examining her intently, hungrily even.

'You are saying my father had an affair with you, made you pregnant and I was the result? And the only proof for this story is a string of beads?'

Rose looked past him at the bare little room.

'You were conceived in this room,' she said, half to herself. 'When I came up on that expedition with Nabiha Fauzi, it was really to be here with Hassan.' She caught sight of her bag lying on the floor in the corner. 'There is something else.'

As she darted towards it and snatched it up, there was a rapping at the door. One of the soldiers called out on the other side. Aidrus moved to open it.

'Wait,' she whispered. 'Please wait.'

But in her haste, she could not find the zip to the inside pocket. She saw him watching her. Something was holding them together now, something that cut them both off from what was happening outside the room.

There was another pounding on the door. Still staring at her, Aidrus called back in Arabic to the man on the other side.

'It is not yet time. Go down and wait.'

She had found what she was looking for. He held out his hand and she put into it the small photograph wrapped in tissue paper. At the same moment, she felt the last remnant of strength drain out of her. Wearily she sat down on the mattress and leaned her head against the wall, watching him as he took the picture to the window to study it.

'It was taken in England in 1917.' Speaking was a huge effort, but she must summon up the will to go on, however disjointedly. 'You were born

358

the year before, in London. Hassan came over for a conference. We were – reunited.' The word sounded so pompous and unreal. She cancelled it out of her mind. 'We were together again,' she went on. 'It was the day you started to learn to walk.'

There was a long silence. Aidrus still bent his head over the picture.

'It is my father. It is you.' He was speaking slowly, under his breath. 'And the child?'

'Look at the back. Hassan wrote on it later.'

He turned it over as if in a dream.

'It is in Arabic. It says' – he paused – 'It says, "Hassan, Rose, Aidrus. Allah protect and keep us." '

For the first time, he was looking directly across at her as if seeing her for the first time. His expression was one of simple astonishment. For a second everything seemed to stop.

'It is true then.' It was more of a statement than a question. She could sense his mind turning furiously, trying to get some kind of grip on the situation, and for the first time she felt sorry for him.

'I had not meant to tell you, ever. It was our secret, Hassan's and mine. It must be a blow, I suppose. Hassan's wife,' she went on tentatively. 'You always believed Miriam was your mother? Was there no talk of you having been adopted, the child of someone else in the family?'

She saw him shake his head, groping for words.

'There was some gossip about some cousin of my father's. I can't remember. Children pay no attention.'

'Oh, Aidrus, Aidrus.' All her defences fell away. She leaned forward, holding out her arms to him. 'You were such a marvellous child. It was so hard for me to let you go.'

He came towards her gravely, the snapshot held out in his hand. Then he seemed to crumple up in front of her. For a moment she thought he was going to put his head in her lap. But he remained crouched on his knees, his face in his arms.

'Why has God done this thing to me?' she heard him murmur to himself. He said it again, petulantly, like a child, rocking himself to and fro.

Very gently she put her hand to the crisp black hair that curled on the nape of his neck. But at her touch he drew back like an animal alerted to danger. He sat back on his heels in front of her, his eyes very bright. She could see him struggling to control himself, as if trying to hold back another very different reaction that lay at some deeper level of consciousness.

'Did you love my father?'

'I loved him with all my heart. I still do,' she said softly. 'We were very young when it happened, remember. Very young and very reckless. It was the great miracle of our lives, and the great tragedy too.'

'You met when you came to Aden. You were beautiful, I think.' He looked at her almost accusingly. 'You were married already?'

'My marriage was a prison. Hassan opened the door for me even though we were only together for so short a time – before and after.' She hesitated, seeing in her mind's eye the small boy in the red fez. 'Do you remember Cairo?'

He bit his lip and frowned, like a child trying to remember a lesson. 'There was a hotel with big rooms. Camel rides. And yes, an English woman was there sometimes with us. Very faintly there is a picture.' She waited, holding her breath. But he shook his head. 'I remember my father being very angry. We went back to Aden and I had to give my presents to the children of the slaves, our servants at the palace.'

Outside there was the sound of booted feet on the stairs, the clattering of rifles. He shook himself like a man waking from a dream and looked at her, appalled.

'What am I to do?'

She saw sweat break out on his forehead. Then suddenly he seemed to take command again. He was on his feet, looking at his watch.

'There may not be time. The plane is due in an hour. The soldiers are already in the courtyard.' His eyes held hers. There was anguish on his face. Very quickly he took her hand and pressed it hard. 'You must trust me. Wait and trust.'

Then he was gone, locking the door behind him. She sat quite still, straining to listen. He seemed to be giving an order to the guards. She could sense a drop in the tension. There was a murmured conversation and laughter, as voices and footsteps faded away.

I have to be ready, she told herself, for what she did not know. But the thought of action summoned up the adrenalin in her system. Her trousers and shirt felt comfortingly clean and dry, even though the sand that clung to them prickled against her skin. With an effort at normality she got up and pulled on Jenny's cardigan and tied back her hair under her scarf.

I suppose I should write a note, she thought vaguely, just in case. But who would find it? Who would deliver it? A wave of desolation swept through her. Hassan, she said, in some inmost voice. I have tried my best. I have done what I could to save my life and come back to you. Please forgive me for telling Aidrus. It seemed the only chance.

From the street below, the sounds of the crowd drew her back to reality. She must keep away from the window, out of sight. She sat down on the mattress, her bag on her shoulder. By her foot she saw the cigarette Aidrus had crushed out. The scent of it still lingered in the fetid air. I have

360

seen my son, she told herself. I have been close to him, touched his life again, if only for a moment. She felt her heart contract. Something deep inside her was satisfied. It was the painful satisfaction of a birth. Some circuit had been completed, even if her life should come to an end.

She had found her watch in her bag. It was a quarter to noon. The voices of the people outside seemed to be moving away. Out of the quiet came floating the call of the muezzin, summoning the faithful to prayer, the special prayers of the first day of Ramadan.

Without warning, she heard the key turn in the lock. Once more, panic ran through her. But it was Aidrus, his face tense.

'Here.' He held out what looked like a black purdah shawl. 'You know the *chador*? Cover yourself!'

She threw it over her shoulders. With rapid movements, he helped to secure the folds around her head and face.

'What's happening?' she asked him.

'I'll tell you as we drive. Do you remember the garden at the back of the house, the gate on to the side street?'

She nodded.

'There's a jeep outside. I'll be waiting.'

He led the way to the stairs. She paused at the top, disorientated for a moment.

'Don't worry. The house is empty. But hurry,' he told her in the same harsh undertone.

From then onwards, everything seemed to gather speed. There was the arched doorway at the bottom, the flagged path beyond, the overgrown pool and the stone steps leading down to the gate, all just as she remembered them, familiar fragments of the past now horribly distorted by fear. She flew by them like a ghost. The black veil over her face reduced everything to a sinister shadow-play.

At the gate, she struggled with the latch and felt someone on the other side of the wall unfasten it. Aidrus was there, taking her by the arm, helping her into the parked jeep. Slamming the door behind him, he started up the engine. Two or three women in a nearby doorway looked up briefly and away again. Then she was aware of the narrow streets of the village falling away behind them as he drove fast towards the outskirts of the settlement. She glimpsed the smouldering fortifications of the camp, tents and sandbags scattered in disarray. But strangely the scene was deserted.

'They are all in the mosque. The Mullah is leading the prayers.' He narrowed his eyes, staring into the sun. 'All we have to hope is that the plane is on time.'

'I don't understand. What has happened? What did you tell them?'

He glanced at her sideways, his mouth twisted in a bitter smile. 'Don't be misled with thinking I made some heroic plea for your life. That would only arouse instant suspicion. Besides, it would be quite hopeless. No, I lied, of course.' He leaned forward over the wheel, negotiating the potholes in the track. 'I said I'd received a second wireless signal from Aden cancelling today's mission. The plane would be arriving tomorrow instead. I was not questioned. No one thought it odd.'

'So the firing squad . . .' She found it difficult to string the right words together.

'The shooting is postponed until dawn tomorrow.' Again, he looked at her with that wry grimace. 'The Mullah has a taste for cruelty, as I expect you've observed. Now he can look forward to a more prolonged visit to your room, with a couple of soldiers to assist perhaps, and the faithful Jamila, of course.'

Rose felt nausea at the back of her throat. She had a sudden longing to breathe fresh air. But as she began to tug at the shawl beneath her chin, Aidrus put out a warning hand.

'For God's sake, don't take off the purdah. In that you could be any one of the army wives, going back to the women's quarters. But if anyone saw you without it . . .'

He left the sentence unfinished. Rose felt the quick touch of his hand on hers, as if to reassure her. It was the only sign of affection he had made since leaving the house. Once again, he seemed to be deliberately widening the gap between them. There was no time for emotion now.

'The plane,' she said. 'When it comes, surely it will be seen? Not everyone is at prayers?'

He shook his head. 'The landing strip is a good mile away from the camp, and further from the village. You will have two minutes to get on board before anyone can reach you.'

'And what about you? You will be in danger then, once they realize what's happened?'

'I'll survive,' he said grimly. 'I'm used to getting myself out of trouble.'

He pointed ahead. 'We're nearly there. You see that dugout in the rocks? We'll wait there. It's as near as I can get you without being seen. When the plane comes down, you'll have to make the last bit on your own.'

'I can run quite fast.'

He wrenched down the brake and brought the jeep to a standstill behind a thorn bush.

'Get down now and keep close to me.'

She was breathless as she followed him behind the shelter of the rocks.

'It's this stupid thing.' She began unwinding the black cocoon. 'Now this has to come off or I'll never make it to the runway. Besides, the people on board won't be able to recognize me.'

'There will be no people on board,' Aidrus said sharply. 'Only the pilot, and he will be unarmed, a civilian. This is the deal the British have set up.'

They were close to one another now, crouched down among the boulders looking out at the runway some fifty yards away. As he spoke, he rummaged in his pockets and brought out something wrapped in a cloth.

'Here, I almost forgot. You have not eaten since yesterday.'

She opened it to find a piece of the local bread with goat's cheese. Somehow this offering touched her more than anything else.

'And you?' she said, offering him a portion.

'It is Ramadan,' he replied severely. 'I must wait until sunset.'

He held out a leather bottle from his belt.

'The water in the well was full of sand, but it's better than nothing.'

'You're very kind.'

She gulped it awkwardly, partly because she was so thirsty, partly because she hated to drink when he could not.

'It is my duty.'

They fell silent, both searching the sky for a sight of the plane. It was very hot, with the sun striking off the surface of the rocks and only a few tiny pockets of shade.

'When you are back in Aden,' he said stiffly. 'You will be with my father? You will stay with him this time?'

'I will stay with him, but not in Aden.' She realized this was something she needed to tell him. 'He is leaving Jehal, abdicating as Sultan. It seems the British plan to depose him anyway.'

She could see from his face how startled he was.

'So he has offended his masters, has he?'

'He has never accepted them as his masters, Aidrus. Don't you see? He wants the same things as you do for the Arab world.'

'But he is not willing to fight for them.'

Rose felt despair. 'What good is fighting?'

'That is all that is left for us. You will see. It is the only way to rid ourselves of the British.'

'And so you will go on fighting, Arab against Jew, Syrians against Saudis, Persians against Iraqis. It will be the same old story.'

'Yes, as long as we allow ourselves to be manipulated by the West. But my dream is that we shall be free of America and the rest of you. And we shall have the money, oil money. You'll see.'

He broke off and looked at his watch, cursing softly.

'The plane is late. In five minutes, they will be out of the mosque. And here we are sitting talking politics.'

'What else can we do except sit and wait?'

She saw amusement in his glance.

'The fatalistic approach. It's something you have caught from us. I noticed it yesterday.' He sighed. 'So many things are now explained.' He spread out his hands and studied them. 'This skin of mine, always so pale. But I never imagined there was European blood.'

'Your militant friends would not approve, perhaps?'

She said it lightly, without thinking, anything to relieve the tension. She had forgotten he still had the photograph in his pocket. Before she could stop him, he brought it out, tore it across and across again until it fell to the ground in fragments. He turned on her savagely. She saw his hands were shaking.

'They cannot know. No one can ever know. Unless you tell them. Or my father.'

'Can't you trust me?' she said, taken aback. She put her hand on his sleeve. The arm beneath it felt painfully thin, like a schoolboy's. 'No one *will* ever know. It is something that belongs to Hassan and myself alone.'

He bent his head. The red flush had crept along the edge of his cheekbone again and he rubbed at his beard impatiently.

'You I trust. But him . . .'

'Why do you hate him so? You are his only son and you have hurt him so badly.'

'Did I say I hated him?' He looked up at her quickly. 'It was not I who took the soldiers into Jehal, you know. I did not lead that attack on the palace.'

'Who was it then?'

'The girl, Jamila. She has a special mission against the rulers, especially those who are in treaty with the British. She would kill without thought for the sake of her beliefs.'

'Why do you link yourself with such people? The Mullah especially. They are evil people, Aidrus, fanatics, a breed apart.'

He shrugged. 'Every revolution needs its extremists to give it impetus. The ends justify the means, don't you think? It's too late now.'

'If Government are willing to talk to you, it's not too late,' she said urgently. 'You could try for a compromise at least!'

'Government!' He shifted forward on to his haunches, his face glistening. 'Even now they have tricked us. There is no plane. And now we are trapped.'

But Rose held up her hand. She had caught sight of a glint of white against the blue.

'There it is.'

'All thanks to God.'

Together they watched the little plane descending over the cliff side, making towards the runway. The droning vibrations seemed to fill the whole plateau.

'The engines. Keep them down, keep them down,' she heard Aidrus say under his breath.

There was the grating sound of the wheels on the chippings as the plane touched down at the far end. Clouds of dust billowed out behind it. Aidrus looked quickly over his shoulder at the camp, and the village in the distance. Almost before the plane was at a standstill, Rose heard his voice in her ear.

'Now run, run as hard as you can.' As she got to her feet, she felt something pressed into her hand. 'The prayer-beads – for my father. Now go. And good luck.'

She took a deep breath and began to run. Straight ahead of her, less than fifty yards away, she saw the pilot's head appear at the cockpit opening. As she got close, stumbling on the loose stones, she recognized Maurice Devereux.

'Are you all right?' she heard him call.

'Yes, but there's no time,' she shouted back. 'We have to take off straight away.'

Her heart was pumping violently. She was not sure whether he had heard her. The engines had died away but the propellers were still whirring and clattering around. All her attention was focused on the cabin door at the back, now less than twenty yards away, and alarmingly high off the ground.

As if in answer to her prayers, the panel slid back and a boarding ladder was dropped over the side. A man stood in the open doorway. Then everything blew away in her mind, as she recognized Hassan.

'Keep inside!' she cried. 'Don't get out.'

Joy and terror seemed to almost strangle her. As in a nightmare, her voice had lost its carrying power. Without heeding her, he was down the steps and running towards her.

'Rose!'

Panting, she flung herself against him. 'They were going to shoot me. Aidrus got me away. Over there.' She pointed behind her. 'Now we must go, quickly.'

'Wait, just for a moment.'

Hassan was staring across the glittering stretch of the runway to the man who stood watching them from the rocks.

'Aidrus.' She heard him say the name under his breath as she tugged at his arm.

'We have no time. They will have seen the plane.'

But Hassan was only half listening. Helplessly, she watched him raise his hand in a salute of what? – recognition, gratitude, reconciliation? Very slowly, it seemed to her, Aidrus raised his hand in reply. Motionless, father and son stood facing each other, locked in some private moment in time.

A vicious crackling cut through the stillness. Away to the left Rose caught sight of a figure in black scrambling down across the track that led from the camp. She knew at once that it was Jamila and that she was armed with an automatic rifle. At the same moment she saw Aidrus fall to the ground.

The cry he gave at the moment of death was drowned in the next round of bullets. At the bottom of the steps Hassan seemed to falter and half-turn, clinging to the rail. Standing just above him, Rose watched frozen in disbelief as a scarlet patch sprang out across the front of his jacket. He looked at her, his face screwed up in astonishment.

She reached down to take his hands, then cried out at the dead weight of him. In the distance behind soldiers had appeared, running hard on the heels of the girl.

'Maurice! For God's sake!'

But he was already at her side, hoisting the limp body over his shoulder and into the plane. Together they got him on to the nearest seat. To her horror, she saw his head fall back, his eyes closed. She fell on her knees beside him and tugged at his jacket, her hand pressed against the blood-soaked shirt beneath. She heard herself begin a pointless kind of pleading.

'Oh no! Oh please no!'

Maurice pulled her away.

'Let me see.'

He bent down over Hassan. There was the ripping of cotton and Rose caught a glimpse of gaping flesh, obscured by a fresh gush of blood.

'It's too near the heart.' The Frenchman's face was shocked as he got to his feet. 'The pulse is very slow. I think he's going.'

'But there must be something . . .'

'There's a first-aid box in the rack. You can try to stop the bleeding. But I can tell you it's no use.'

They both heard a succession of bullets spatter against the side of the plane.

'I've got to get this thing off the ground or we'll all be finished.' He scrambled into the cockpit. 'The man should never have come, but he forced me to bring him,' he told her over his shoulder. 'He was like a madman.'

The engines stammered into life again, cutting out the gunfire and the babble of voices that seemed about to engulf them. Then the wheels were grinding over the runway, leaving them behind as the little plane lurched into the air.

Rose was not looking out. She had found lint and disinfectant and with clumsy hands she was tying the rough dressing down with strips of the torn shirt, cursing her total ignorance of such things. But the blood was seeping through relentlessly. His face was ash-coloured, his mouth drawn back at the corners. Every breath seemed a struggle. More than anything else, she prayed for him to open his eyes, if only for a second. But he seemed already to have gone away from her.

'How long will it take?' she called frantically. 'To get him to a doctor, any doctor, anywhere?'

The nearest is at Dar Saad, the Mission hospital,' he shouted back. 'Even that's too far. An hour at least.' He shook his head. 'He'll never make it.'

'But we have to try, Maurice.'

'Of course we try. There is a clearing near the oasis. Unless the drifts from the sandstorm have blocked it.' He shrugged. 'It's right on the edge of the desert.'

He turned back to the controls. 'Did you try him with the brandy?' he asked her.

'I couldn't get it into his mouth. I was frightened of choking him.'

Wordlessly he held out his hand. She passed the flask to him with a sinking heart, watching him tip it to his lips.

A low groan came from Hassan, but still he had not stirred. Very carefully she slipped into the seat alongside him so that his head rested on her lap. Looking down, she saw patches of his blood across the front of her shirt. Something came back to her, something she could not quite pin down. Then she remembered. Ram Prasad stood in front of her, the lamp upraised in his hand. There was splintered glass at her feet, the stain of red wine across her dress.

'Next time it will be blood.'

She heard the thin demented voice in her ear again, and shivered. The warmth of Hassan's body next to hers seemed the most precious thing in the world. Now she imagined that warmth was slowly ebbing away. She put her hand round his wrist and felt only a feeble flutter. At his feet was a blanket she had found. She pulled it over him so that the wound was hidden. Nothing else could be done.

She lay back in the seat. Despair was so total, she could not even weep. They were still half an hour away from Dar Saad. Through the tiny window she saw the mountain ranges of the interior dip behind them and the gleaming salt-coloured sweep of the Empty Quarter begin. They were flying low and the shadow of the plane's wings floated soundlessly over the dunes, like one of the hawks she had watched so often with Hassan. Somewhere down there was the beach house, the headland where the horses met and the road to Jehal. But that was all gone now, receding into the nothingness of the past. Arabia itself was disappearing, never to be seen again, and with it was going her whole life, slipping away like sand through a glass.

Hassan's face was turned to one side. She studied every familiar slanting line of eyelid, cheekbone and jaw. A thread of crimson was beginning to trickle from the corner of his mouth. Carefully she wiped it away. The beauty of the man was pathetic now, like that of a mortally wounded animal. Yet only two days ago, making love together, they had believed themselves invulnerable, arrogant in their joy.

Don't leave me, Hassan, she begged. Please don't leave me now. She felt herself summoning up all her will-power in her effort to penetrate that silent mask.

'Nearly there.'

Maurice's voice broke from in front.

'How is he?'

'Not good,' she managed to say.

She heard him swear as the plane swerved and juddered too close to the trees. The sand was banked up high, obscuring the approach. He seemed to be losing control.

'Try again,' she heard him grunt.

The plane rose sharply and circled twice. This time they dropped down fast. Automatically Rose leaned over Hassan, her arms tightening round him to cradle him against the impact of landing. But miraculously the sand muffled the wheels, flying up on either side in a thick curtain of dust. She could see ragged palm trees, the tin roof of the Mission, an ancient jeep parked in the full glare of the sun with a few figures standing nearby.

Now I have to face something else, she told herself, people coming to take him away, the agony of waiting alone for the end. It is inevitable, she thought. I have to let go. There will be things to be done of which I know nothing. His family will claim him and I will leave Aden, going away again as if I had never been back.

The plane had come to a standstill. Two hospital orderlies in dirty khaki had come inside. For a moment she held on to Hassan's hand, as she sat without moving. Almost without thinking she brought out the prayer-beads from her pocket and knotted them round his wrist. She saw the

Arabs glance at her curiously. Then they were lifting him out and Maurice was standing over her.

'I'd better go with them, explain to the doctor. It's my responsibility, you understand. There may not be room in the jeep,' he went on awkwardly.

She nodded. 'I understand. I'll follow you. It's only a few yards.'

She stood at the top of the steps, watching as they hurried the rough stretcher into the back of the jeep. Now he had gone from her she could not believe that the figure wrapped in the red blanket was really Hassan. Surely he was still with her, close to her.

The jeep drove away, bouncing across the sandy tracks. She climbed down stiffly. Out of nowhere, it seemed, a swarm of children was running towards the plane. Chattering and gesticulating, they clung to her like flies as she started to walk towards the buildings under the trees. A few village huts emerged, a flock of sheep browsing among the patches of green. Some women in black shawls stood watching her in amazement. Rose forced herself to return the customary greetings.

'*Salaam walaikum.*'

'*Ma'salaam.*'

'Hospital, hospital!' chanted the children. A small girl took her by the hand and led her towards the mud-walled compound. There was an archway at the entrance with a painted sign in Arabic and English. As she walked up the path, she saw Maurice coming towards her. His face was haggard.

'The doctor's with him.' He paused. 'At least he's not in pain.' She saw him look away over her shoulder towards the plane and realized he was desperate to get back to what was left of the brandy. 'There's really no point in our staying, Lady Foster. And I must get back to Aden to make my report.'

'I'll wait,' she said. On an impulse, she shook his hand. 'And thank you.'

As she walked on past the scraggy oleander bushes towards the open doorway, she realized she knew this place. More than once, a hundred years ago it seemed, she had driven out here in the cool of early morning with Eleanor Rawlinson to join the other memsahibs in their charity routine of distributing free milk powder to the village mothers. She remembered the elation of those expeditions. It was a private elation, the time of her first meetings with Hassan, and everything she did seemed fresh and magical.

Inside, all looked unchanged, the bare tiled floor, the ochre plasterwork, the mingled smell of sand and sweat and disinfectant. A row of women, squatting against the walls with their babies in their laps, could

369

have been the same women. The little nun in white who came forward to meet her was part of the same memory. In an instant of unbearable clarity Rose saw herself again, the eager girl of 1914 in a striped morning-dress and the shady straw hat that always pinched her scalp and gave her a headache.

Her head was throbbing now and she found it hard to concentrate on what the nun was saying to her. She was a girl still in her teens, a dark-faced Goanese with huge concerned brown eyes and a voice so soft it was only a whisper.

'Lady Foster, please come in and rest,' she said in her correct Mission English. 'It has been a terrible time for you.'

Rose let herself be led into the anteroom where a green blind hung against the sun.

'I will bring you some tea.'

She sank down in one of the shabby wicker chairs. 'Please,' she said as the girl moved away. 'The Sultan? What is happening to him?'

'Doctor Mackenzie will come and see you very soon. You must rest now and not be upset.'

Rose sat with her head in her hands. How can I not sense that moment, she kept asking herself, the moment of his death?

The tea, when it came, was very hot and very sweet, thick with condensed milk like the tea of thirty years ago. Rose took one sip and could drink no more. I am the key to this whole pattern of tragedy, she suddenly thought. I am the catalyst, now as then. If I had not come back to Arabia, this terrible thing would not have happened to Hassan. Aidrus, my son, would still be alive. And I would never have known how it was possible to inflict such mortal damage on oneself, simply by reopening the past.

For what seemed like an hour she sat without moving, almost without thinking. Footsteps outside went to and fro. The voices of the women rose and fell. Babies cried. Just tell me, she said to herself. Then at least I can begin that journey into darkness, the journey through the rest of my life alone.

When the curtain over the door was pulled aside, she was prepared. A tall elderly man, who looked very tired, came in. She registered the bloodstains on his white coat, Hassan's blood.

'Lady Foster?'

She nodded but found she could not stand up. She was searching his face but it remained expressionless.

'Your friend, the Sultan,' he went on in his slow Scottish voice. He shook his head. 'I can't believe it myself.'

Still she was silent, staring up at him. He put his hand on her shoulder.
'He's going to live.'